CHAINS OF DESTINY

THE PAX HUMANA SAGA
BOOK TWO

CHAINS
OF
DESTINY

NICK WEBB

www.nickwebbwrites.com

Summary: In 2678, Captain Jacob Mercer and the USS Phoenix must find a way to repair their damaged engines before Admiral Trajan can find them. On the planet Destiny, they soon learn uncomfortable truths about their hero, Admiral Pritchard, and discover that the Empire's plans may not stop at the destruction of the Resistance.

Text set in Garamond

Designed by Nick Webb

Cover art by Tom Edwards

http://tomedwardsdmuga.blogspot.co.uk

ISBN: 1796754374

ISBN-13: 978-1796754377

Printed in the United Sates of America

For Jenny, L., and C.

CHAPTER ONE

"Anya, what the hell are you doing!"

Lieutenant Anya Grace smirked at the comm speaker, even though she knew the voice shouting through it couldn't see her. "Keep your pants on, Captain. Stand by."

She wove her fighter through the cloud of shrapnel, debris, and Imperial bogeys as she aimed her bow straight at the heart of the NPQR *Sphinx*. After only three days of respite in orbit around the red dwarf star Laland 21185, the Imperial Centurion-class capital ship shifted into orbit just two klicks off the *USS Phoenix*'s stern and immediately opened fire. It was as if they knew exactly where they were: their exact orbital speed, inclination, orientation … everything.

"Lieutenant, I hope you're planning something unbelievably spectacular, because from this end you look like you're about to kill yourself and Nivens. You may have only been the Wing Commander for three days, but you're not exactly replaceable," Jake's voice replied, with the slight whine that told Anya he was supremely annoyed at her. Exactly how she liked it.

1

"Just watch, sir. You'll be so happy that you'll give me another ride on the Mercer Express when I get back." She smiled at her own play on words. *Heh—express.* He probably didn't even pick up on her insult.

"I'll do worse than that, Lieutenant," he said.

You promise? she thought. "Yeah, I bet you'll give me a nice dressing-down, as usual. Look, stop thinking about my glorious flat boobs and get ready to train your fire on my handiwork."

Looking back she saw she'd picked up a tail—two enemy fighters were in hot pursuit, matching her moves and pelting her with gunfire. She wove, using conventional thrusters to swerve around one of railgun turrets of the *Sphinx* at such a tight angle it threw her down into the seat at over five g's, but the maneuver brought one of the fighters directly into their sights.

"Fire, Nivens!" she yelled, but the streaks of red light shot out from the bow moments too late. She spun to look at him. "What the hell?!"

His face was a pasty white. "Hey, you've got to warn me before you pull a five g turn—you can't expect me to get a good lock after a stunt like that." His lips were pursed as in a valiant effort to keep his lunch down.

"Fine. Here we go again." She pulled at the controls and flipped them 180 degrees around an ion beam cannon protruding off the surface of the *Sphinx*'s gray hull. "There. Go!"

He squeezed the trigger and one of the tailing fighters exploded in a cloud of debris.

"Quadri, get this other one off my tail, would ya?" Anya shouted into her headset.

"Sure thing, Spitfire." The other space jocks on the *Phoenix* had given her a new callsign, and, while she put on a front of annoyed disapproval of the name, she kind of liked it. Quadri's fighter peeled off his previous target and blasted through the one tailing Anya, and she swung the bird around to aim back at the *Sphinx*. Dozens of streams of high-velocity railgun bursts leapt out of the Imperial ship at the *Phoenix*, and the *Phoenix* answered with bursts of its own, laying down a defensive screen against the worst of it and firing bright blue shimmering beams of ion cannon fire at the Imperial capital ship. Dozens of fighters swarmed around the two ships, though Anya knew they were dreadfully outnumbered. Again.

She couldn't shake the image of the piles of dead bodies in the makeshift morgue by sickbay where six of her fellow pilots had found a new home. A memorial had been planned for that day, but the surprise arrival of the *Sphinx* had tamped down those plans.

"Ok, Nivens. Here we go. Hold on to your ass."

He frowned dryly. "Consider it clenched."

She aimed right at a particular section of the ship, a section she was nearly sure contained the crews responsible for loading the nuclear warheads. *Three, two, one,* she counted to herself: at the last second she used the gravitic controls to reorient ninety degrees and fly parallel to the hull, which now streamed past her viewport just inches away. With the press of a button she initiated a short-range gravitic shift …

… and reappeared just meters away, on the same trajectory. She looked behind her, and smiled. In her wake, a cloud of debris streamed out from the *Sphinx*, and she knew her tactic had worked.

"It's all yours, Mercer. Do you think you can hit that small a target?"

After a moment of silence on the other end, Jacob Mercer's voice asked her, in awe, "Did you just blow a hole in the nuclear torpedo section? That thing has armor over two meters thick!"

"They're a funny thing, these gravitic fields. Even funnier when you're moving this fast relative to another nearby surface."

"Anya, forget everything I ever said about you. You're a genius!" he burst out, followed by, "Po, fire!"

One of the railgun turrets on the *Phoenix* swiveled and began firing a stream of slugs, which slammed into the two holes Anya left behind. Explosions leapt out from the now widening scars, and Anya saw Nivens fist pump the air out of the corner of her eye. He grinned at her.

"I wonder if they saw that coming," he said.

"Ensign, they never see me coming," she said without even a grin as she pulled on the controls to point at another incoming fighter. "Though I suppose it's us now, not just me. You still good with being my gunner, or do I make you piss your flight suit?"

"No ma'am." He squeezed off a round, piercing another fighter with a barrage of high-caliber fire and sending it crashing into the *Sphinx*'s hull.

"Good. You need a callsign, you know. I'm thinking Babyface."

"Please no," he said, firing off another few rounds at a stray fighter, which flew wide.

She veered away from an incoming fighter. "Or how about

4

Pencilholder? At least until you can pull it out of those clenched cheeks of yours. Come on, lighten up," she smacked his shoulder.

"Quadri's voice sounded over their headsets. "Hey Spitfire, I got a tail. Help me out here."

"On it, dickhead."

"What the hell? That's not my callsign!"

"Yeah, I know. Peel off to your right in two seconds.... Now!" Quadri's fighter turned wide to the right, followed by the Imperial fighter, which swung into the red streams shooting out from Nivens's forward gun.

"Thanks, Nivens," said Quadri from the headsets.

Anya pointed out the window, "Lieutenant Short, watch those bogeys on your flank." She gunned the engine to accelerate towards the beleaguered fighter.

Two short bursts from Nivens blasted them to oblivion. "Thanks, Spitfire. We owe you one."

"*Another* one," she replied.

Jake Mercer's voice pierced through the background chatter of pilots and gunners and the flurry of battle. "P-two, P-four, and P-eight, concentrate your fire on the starboard rail-turrets. We're going to knock the sucker out with a quantum field disrupter torpedo. Everyone else, cover them."

"You heard him, Nivens, lets go hunt ourselves a rail-turret," she said, swinging the bow around to point back at the *Sphinx*, still sparkling with railgun fire.

Nivens turned to her. "Sir, if we just opened up a hole in their nuclear section, can't we just do it again near a more sensitive system? Like, right next to some power conduits or something?"

She bit her lip before gunning the engine and swerving past some friendly fighters. "Brilliant, Pencilholder." The hull of the *Sphinx* loomed up closer, and Anya dodged some incoming fire from an ion beam turret. She pointed to an area on the hull. "Is that what I think it is?"

Niven's glanced down, checked his console, and nodded. "Yeah, that'll do."

"Right." The fighter plunged down towards the hull, and accelerated. "Preparing gravitic shift...." Anya gripped the controls tight in her white-clenched fists. The hull zoomed past just a meter away, the details washed away in a blur. "Now!" She thumbed the gravitic shift button....

And the universe spun wildly.

"Dammit!" Anya's head pulled hard to the side as the fighter spun uncontrollably and the angular momentum threw her against the seat restraints.

"Wha—what happened?" said Nivens through gritted teeth,

Slowly, the fighter's spin slowed, and when she could get her bearings Anya saw that they were several klicks away from the *Sphinx*. She scanned her board, examining some new readings that had appeared in the last minute. "They're generating some kind of wonky gravitic field. It's projecting just beyond their hull, probably to prevent us from doing exactly what we were trying to do."

The comm crackled on. "Anya, what the hell was that?"

"Check your gravitic readout, Captain," she said.

A momentary silence. "Looks like they were ready for you that time. Just get back over there and suppress their fire— we've got to get this torpedo outta here," said Jake.

"So, looks like the Empire is learning?" deadpanned Nivens.

"I'm as shocked as you are. Come on," Anya glanced out the viewport. "Our boys need us against those turrets."

CHAPTER TWO

Admiral Trajan strode onto the bridge like a black storm cloud descending on an unsuspecting town. His face stern and impassive, he motioned to tactical. "Report."

"Sir! The *Sphinx* shifted to Laland 21185 just moments ago. They should be engaging the Rebels now." Captain Titus glowered at his console. He'd been trying to direct the repairs of the forward section since the rogue Resistance ship had shifted suddenly away not three days ago, but the gravitic field wake left by the *Phoenix* had torn an even larger hole in its stead. Even if the *Caligula* were to dock at the Earth shipyards, repairs would take weeks. That was news Admiral Trajan would not be happy to hear, to say the least.

"Captain, prepare several gravitic pods. I have messages I want transmitted as soon as possible." The Admiral stared at him with his one gleaming eye. The gaping eye socket seemed like a perfect metaphor for the Admiral's soul—empty, scarred, and with an eye single to accomplishing his mission from Emperor Maximilian: Defeat the Earth Resistance at all costs.

Admiral Trajan handed Titus a data pad. "Here. See that

no one sees them other than yourself. And even that is inadvisable." The single eye flashed him a knowing glance accompanied by the barest hint of a sly smile, and Titus immediately understood the reference to the late Chief Engineer. Titus knew all too well that Trajan intended to leave no paper trail, no trace, no proof of his mission. As Trajan explained it to him, if the Senate were to ever find out, it would rock the Empire to its core—the faith of the people in the Emperor's commitment to abide by his own laws would be shaken irreparably.

"Very well, sir," said Captain Titus.

"And how are the repairs going?" Trajan looked down at the command console, studying the reports streaming by.

"Hull repair crews say they'll need at least three days to seal the breaches, at least temporarily. To repair them fully will require several weeks in space-dock."

"Gravitics?"

"Should be operational by the end of tomorrow."

Trajan glowered at the console. "I want it before then, Captain. Use whatever means at your disposal to motivate your engineering crew. The next stage of our plan requires it."

"Sir? The next stage?"

"Of course. You thought the destruction of the Resistance was the only goal? It was but the first step. The prelude to The Plan."

Titus shifted uncomfortably on his feet. Next step? Just how long would the Admiral be staying on board? "What about Mercer? And the *Phoenix*? And the *Heron*?"

"Yes, yes. We will deal with them. They are but two ships. Pawns, no more, in the grand scheme of things. Our vision lies higher, Captain."

Somehow, Captain Titus knew that the "higher vision" would not be forthcoming from the Admiral anytime soon. The man had a habit of playing his cards so closely to his chest that Titus had to wonder if even the Admiral kept his hand straight.

"Very well, sir. I'll encourage the new Chief Engineer to work faster. I'll redirect repair crews to engineering if that is all right with you?"

"It is, Captain. Gravitics is our number one priority right now. Everything else can wait. Even the hull, if necessary."

Trajan stood up straight from the command console and glanced around the bridge, nodding with approval at the cleanup job the repair crews had done. After the *Phoenix* shifted away, the resulting gravitic wake had sent such a jolt through the ship that several ceiling plates and deck girders had collapsed onto the bridge floor and multiple console panels had erupted in sparks from the electrical surges. Luckily, no one was killed, but the destruction maimed several junior bridge officers.

"And Captain, a word?" Trajan caught his eye and motioned towards the door that led to the hallway containing the ready room, now converted to the Admiral's makeshift quarters. Titus's heart sunk as he followed the man in the black Admiral's uniform with gold epaulettes dancing on his shoulders as he walked.

When the door to the ready room opened, Trajan pointed his finger in the air, indicating to the computer to perform some predefined function, and instantly the room was alive with the stark, rustic sound of two slow, mournful fiddles. One played against the other, forming a not quite harmonious counterpoint as it clashed with unholy intervals—not like the usual harmonies used in the music Titus preferred and certainly not the harmonies used in the state religion. He frowned with vague disapproval.

"New Frontier music, Captain. I've actually grown quite fond of it. It's what happened when you combine people of an eastern aesthetic with western folk instruments on the plains of some treacherous new world." Trajan sat at the desk and began fingering the console.

Captain Titus cleared his throat and stood at ease next to the desk, hands folded patiently behind his back. "I should mention, sir, that the final casualty report stands at 140 dead, ninety-two missing—most of those are marines from the two boarding parties sent to the *Phoenix*—and sixty-five still in serious or critical condition in sickbay."

"Thank you, Captain. Most unfortunate," Trajan said distractedly, not glancing up from the screen and only showing a passing interest. "Now, here is what I wanted to show you." He pressed one more button and the viewscreen on the wall danced to life with the scenes of the battle from earlier in the day.

"I've been studying the sensor readouts from the events of three days ago, Captain, and if I'm not mistaken they confirm my suspicions as well as the suspicions of Central Intelligence. Watch this," he said, pointing up to the screen.

Titus watched a close-up shot of the central portion of the *Caligula*, its railgun turrets unleashing a torrent of fire at the *Phoenix*. After a few moments, in the blink of an eye, a fighter appeared out of nowhere and immediately fired a torpedo out of its bow, which impacted with the hull of the *Caligula*, generating a secondary explosion that Titus guessed was the gravitic drive cutting out. A moment later the fighter disappeared.

Titus blinked in surprise. "Is this even possible?"

"It appears so, Captain. The CERN scientists have been holding out on the Empire, it seems. We shall have to pay them a visit."

"But if this is true, the implications for fighter tactics and engagement … the manual just got turned on its head, sir."

Trajan glanced at him askance, a shadow of annoyance passing over his brow. "Yes, I'm sure the bureaucrats in the fleet administration building will have a veritable manual writing heyday with this. But I'm more interested in two things. How will the Rebels use this against us, and how can we get our hands on the same technology."

"There's the *Roc*, sir. She's still got a full contingent of fighters on board. We can transfer them over here."

"Already done, Captain. They will be arriving within the hour. See that the fighter bay has room to receive them. We may have to transfer some of our fighters over to the other ships."

"Yes, sir." Titus turned to leave, but hesitated. "Will that be all, sir?"

"For now, yes. I have a few other ideas, but I will reveal them to you when they've matured a bit more," Trajan breathed deeply through his nose, his nostrils flaring. "We are on the cusp of greatness, Captain. Something our civilization has not achieved in 600 years. Not since the utopia following the Robot Wars has our race found such peace and prosperity.

You know, those blissful few decades in the twenty-first century? But those were destroyed by an unthankful few, and the Emperor and I will do everything in our power to attain order and peace again."

Titus strode towards the door, but Trajan's voice stopped him in his tracks. "Captain, you are of course welcome to read all those communications. Many of them concern the regular maintenance of the ship. Forgive me for taking the liberty of scheduling a refuel at the Praesidium, I had no wish to intrude on your responsibilities."

"It's no problem at all, sir. But thank you all the same." Titus wasn't sure whether to breath a sigh of relief, or to be even more worried, as clearly the Admiral was thinking about Titus reading those messages.

"I'm glad you understand." He maintained his steely gaze, his face inscrutable. "For the record, unless I expressly forbid, feel free to read them. In fact, I encourage it. If the unthinkable were to happen and I were to die during one of these missions, I would much prefer that you were to step in to fulfill my mission than anyone else, so you had better be familiar with the plans."

Titus hesitated. "Thank you, sir. I'm honored you would think that about me." And yet, now that he thought about it, he was sure he wanted to know nothing of Trajan's plans. Too much knowledge of the plans hadn't proved very agreeable to the health of the former Chief Engineer.

"Good. Very good," Trajan nodded, and turned to face the console screen. "So you are aware, many of these messages are for mercenaries scattered throughout the known worlds for whom Central Intelligence has given me contact information.

We will cast a wide net, Captain, one that our quarry will not be able to evade."

"And you hope that the mercenaries will cooperate with us? They are our sworn enemies, after all, the reason for the Pax Humana's existence."

Trajan turned back to his console. "I don't hope it, I know it. We will make it so that to cooperate will be to their advantage. At least temporarily, and temporary strategy is all these people think about. They have no long-term plans. No aspirations. Just the day to day work of pirating the shipping lanes for the next day's meal and to acquire prostitutes, slaves, and whatever other contraband they can get their hands on." He pressed a few buttons on the display, speaking almost absentmindedly. "And besides, the pirates were only part of the reason for the Pax Humana." He glanced back up at him. "But that is a story for another day, perhaps. I assure you, Captain, the pirates will do exactly what we want."

"But can we trust them, sir? They may take whatever payment we offer, but I hardly think they'll deliver such a valuable commodity as a capital ship like the *Phoenix*."

Trajan shook his head. "Trust them? No, I do not trust them. But my plan does not involve trust. When dealing with the underbelly of humanity, Captain, you must appeal to their worst natures. Their base, envious, lustful, gluttonous natures. To do otherwise would lead to feeling betrayed when they eventually act according to their natural state. I have no plans for receiving any type of payment or delivery from them, and yet they will serve our purposes all the same."

As vague as ever. For all the Admiral's bluster about including Titus in his plans, the Captain knew he never would.

It was not the Admiral's style. He was a lone wolf—but no, that was the wrong imagery. He was the eccentric, brilliant tactician, who by his nature could trust no one to understand him, his methods, or his plans. "Very well, sir."

Trajan closed his eye, and held a finger up at the music, which had struck a particularly dissonant chord. "Such dissonance. Many praise it. Calling it beautiful and different and acceptable." He opened an eye and stared at Titus. "I call it madness. Deviation."

A silence hung in the air with that last word. Titus wondered if he was free to leave.

"Dismissed, Captain."

The doleful, plaintive duo of fiddles followed him out of the room, and as it shut he breathed a sigh of relief. Ever since the former Chief Engineer had met his end in that room, Titus absolutely detested going in. Somehow, he knew that even when Trajan left, if he left, he would have to convert the room into another use and repurpose the adjacent conference room as his ready room. He couldn't bear the thought of sitting at the desk, staring at the dried outline that still stained the deckplate. He knew the maintenance crew would be able to remove all hint of the blood, but they could never cleanse the image from his memory.

CHAPTER THREE

Po cleared her throat. "Captain, we've only got fourteen of those things. You sure you want to waste one on the *Sphinx*? I think we can take her out without one."

Jake glanced up from his command console and eyed his XO. She looked tired. Incredibly so. Dark rims lined her dark eyes, and he resolved to order her to bed as soon as the current crisis was over. If they could only live through it, of course. "I know we can, Megan, but somehow I don't think the rest of the fleet is far behind. We need some breathing room before they get here to give us time to shift away."

The bridge was a flurry of activity, the officers manning the tactical octagon yelling out targets and coordinates to each other, the damage control supervisors punching furiously at their consoles, trying to stay ahead of the damage caused by the incoming fire thundering down on the *Phoenix*'s pockmarked hull. She was still limping along, severely damaged from the events of three days ago, and hadn't even had time to fully patch the gaping scars in the forward section left by the collision with the *Caligula*.

"And risking our necks to blow up the *Sphinx* will give us breathing room? Come on, Jake, let's just choose some coordinates and get the hell out of here."

Jake turned back to the front viewscreen. He'd been feeling irritable ever since the Imperial capital ship shifted into orbit, throwing off plans for the memorial honoring the fallen crew members, and Po's disagreeing with him in front of the rest of the bridge crew wasn't helping matters. He bit back a stern reply. Not that it would have mattered. Megan Po was the last person on Earth he felt he could be stern with. She would be like a mother if she wasn't one of his best friends.

"Thank you, Commander. Let's just get that torpedo loaded," he said, not taking his eyes off the viewscreen, which flashed the scenes of the unfolding space battle. The massive Imperial capital ship was starting to turn on its axis, moving its bow and port side towards the *Phoenix*, as the fighter squadron's efforts at destroying the railgun turrets was starting to yield fruit.

"Look. They're turning. Now virtually all their guns are pointed at us. Their ship is in far better shape than ours, Captain. We might stand a chance, but it's not going to be pretty. Let's just get the hell out of here."

Dammit. She was right. But he wasn't about to admit it in front of the bridge crew. Not yet. They weren't ready to see him as the inexperienced hothead he knew he was. They needed to see him as someone who took decisive action—someone who would always put his ship and crew first. He couldn't be seen as someone who was always being challenged by his senior staff.

"Thank you, Commander. Continue loading the quantum

field torpedo. Ensign?" He called out to Ensign Roshenko, who manned the helm. "Begin calculations for the Natrium system. Make sure we can make the direct shift—I don't want any pit stops along the way where the Imperials could ambush us."

"Beginning calculations now, sir," said the thin young brown-haired woman.

"Thank you, Ensign Roshenko. Ensign Ayala?" He stood and walked over to the bleached-white haired woman sitting at the tactical octagon. Intricate tattoos of trees, leaves, and twigs branched out from her neck onto the lower regions of her face, and dozens of rings pierced her eyebrows and ears.

"Sir?" she glanced up from her console. For some reason, Jake liked looking at her. She was attractive, sure—not overwhelmingly so, but the aura she exuded somehow calmed him. Her world had been destroyed over one hundred years ago when Corsica first started conquering its neighbors to form the Corsican Empire, or, the new Roman Empire, as it often styled itself. Belen rebelled, and as punishment the Imperial fleet leveled the surface with thousands of high-yield nuclear warheads. The bastards. Just one would have taught the lesson. Thousands was genocide.

They'd wanted to make an example. A demonstration of their power and resolve. And to let every world within the Empire know what happened to those who rebelled.

It worked.

Very few worlds ever rebelled after that, at least, not on the scale of Belen. Not that he was familiar with, anyway.

Except Earth. Old Earth, as the Corsicans called it. Perhaps that was why Jake felt a sort of kinship with Ayala, that maybe her presence on his bridge offered some sort of supernatural protection against the Imperials. It was true that the survivors of Belen held an almost mythical status throughout the Thousand Worlds. They were looked up to as sages. Almost like prophets. Rockstars at a minimum.

"Ensign," he began, leaning over her console. "I need you to scan the area around the star. Is there anything in orbit there?"

Ayala pressed a few buttons while replying, "Captain, we did a full scan of the area around the sun and the nearest four planets shortly after we arrived. Surely there couldn't be anything new—"

"I know, Ensign. Just humor me. Maybe look at all wavelengths this time, rather than just visible and radio."

"Any in particular?"

He had no idea what he was looking for. But the *Sphinx* had found them somehow, and Jake wanted to find out how. "I don't know. Ultraviolet? Terahertz? Microwave? You're the sensor genius, not me, Ensign," he said with a wink, and instantly scolded himself for it. He'd been trying to reign in his usual overly-friendly behavior towards women, now that he was commanding a ship half-full of them.

"Hardly, sir. I'm a weapons officer by training. I'm just filling in because—" she broke off, and Jake finished her sentence in his head.

Because the sensor officer was in the morgue. Cold and blue.

Keep the morale up. "I know, Ensign, I know. Just humor me. That's an order," he added, winking again—dammit! He straightened his back, nodded once at Ayala, and turned to his

XO.

Po caught his eye. "What are you looking for, Jake?"

"Something that will tell us how the Imperials found us."

A high-pitched beep sounded out from Po's console, stealing her attention away from the Captain. As she read the message, her eyes closed, and her lips moved, as if uttering a silent prayer.

"What was it?" Jake stepped towards her. To steady her in case she collapsed, which, combining her extreme fatigue with the whatever awful news she just read, might happen at any time.

"We just lost fighter P-five. Lieutenant Short and Ensign Pierce." She stared at him dangerously, as if daring him to continue the battle with the *Sphinx*.

He looked to the floor. Dammit, he hated running. If he had his druthers they'd plot a course to Corsica and let loose all they had at the Imperial capital. The quantum field disruptor torpedoes were far more potent than a simple nuclear warhead. Nukes had a blast radius and an explosive rating measured in kilotons or megatons. QFD torpedoes didn't stop—as such there was no absolute rating. They disrupted the quantum field, disrupting the wave functions of any electrons the field touched, propagating outward until broken up by an asymmetry such as a mountain or a body of water.

They could be as weak as a kiloton, or as strong as a few hundred gigatons, depending on the environment they were dropped on. After Jake finally learned all the details from Alessandro during that morning's chess game he understood why the Los Alamos program, code-named the Bronx project, was so secretive. He doubted that even Admiral Trajan knew anything about it.

Po was right. They couldn't afford to lose even one more fighter pilot. They'd lost six during the battle of the Nine, as it had come to be called in the days since, and with only twenty to begin with, they were down by almost half.

"Pull them back," he said, and without skipping a beat Megan Po was on the comm telling the fighters to hightail it back to the *Phoenix*, and then alerted the flight deck crew to ready the bay.

"Ben, cover their withdrawal," he said to his friend at the head of the tactical octagon. Jake noticed the man had hardly said a word during the entire battle, except quiet instructions to his crew.

"Aye sir, laying down a cover screen. Lieutenant, redirect fire from the *Sphinx* and set up a moving point defense after the final fighter." Ben's hands were almost a blur on his console, directing and coordinating the work of the crew beneath him.

"Ensign Roshenko. What's our status on those calculations?"

"Ready, sir," the young Ensign squeaked, before clearing her throat and intentionally lowering her voice. "Waiting on your command."

"Excellent." He turned to the communications station and pointed at the young Ensign he'd pulled up from Sciences to man the empty post. Falstaff? Tyler Falstaff? Sounded right— he went for it. "Ensign Falstaff, send word to Bernoulli in engineering that we're about to shift." The young man tapped a few buttons to carry out the order, suggesting to Jake that he got the name right. He looked up at the viewscreen covering the front of the room. "All hands, prepare for gravitic shift."

Ben's voice shouted out. His tone suggested something he hadn't expected. "Sir, I'm reading multiple new contacts."

"Imperial?" He knew it. The rest of the fleet, hot on the tail of the *Sphinx*. Without waiting for the answer he turned back to the helmsman. "Ensign, prepare to shift on my mark. Po? Those fighters in yet?"

"Not yet, sir. Another thirty seconds should do it."

Jake glanced at his console. "Who's left?"

She looked up, with a face that Jake could read as "he's not going to like this."

"Lieutenant Grace."

CHAPTER FOUR

"Captain Titus, sir?" Ensign Evans, the light-haired officer at the long-range communications station, looked up at the man pacing the bridge. Titus turned and approached to look over the man's shoulder.

"What is it, Ensign?"

"The *Sphinx* has just sent us a gravitic pod, sir. They've engaged the *Phoenix* and predict capture within the hour."

Titus slapped the man on the back. "Very good. I'll inform the Admiral." Titus swallowed. This was information Trajan would prefer to hear in person rather than over the comm— Titus had grown accustomed to the Admiral's idiosyncrasies, and this was one of them—important news was to be delivered face to face. He exited through the rear door of the bridge and walked down the long, curved hallway to the ready room and pressed the entrance request button.

A moment later, the Admiral's voice blared through the speaker. "Come in, Captain." The wail of the two fiddles he'd heard previously joined the Admiral's voice through the comm, and Titus said a silent prayer of thanks to Minerva that at least the man wasn't listening to the heavy metal screeching from a few days ago.

"You have news for me, Captain? I hope so, because I have news for you," said Admiral Trajan as Titus stepped through the door.

"Oh?" Titus looked at the man hunched over his console, intently reading some message.

"I've just received word from our long range communications of the arrival of a certain gravitic pod I've been waiting for. But, you first. Tell me what you have for me."

Titus swore softly at Ensign Evans under his breath—he'd just told the man not two minutes ago that he'd tell the Admiral himself.

"We've received word from the *Sphinx*, sir. They've engaged the *Phoenix*, and predict victory is imminent. I recommend we join them soon to assist in the boarding."

"Excellent news, Captain, and right in time, too." He leaned back in his chair and closed his eye, as if deep in thought. He held up a hand, as if conducting the music, which still droned on dolefully in the background. "The Petulant Minors. Have you heard them?"

"Sir?" Titus did a double take. He'd just delivered what he thought was arrestingly important news, and the other man was still listening to music.

"The music, Captain. It is a husband and wife team who call themselves The Petulant Minors. Their product really is quite good, after you've listened to it for five hours like I have. Gritty, yet soulful, and oddly delicate for such a forbidding environment it originates from. They live on a frontier world in the Empire—the planet Tiberius, I believe. Terraforming has

24

proceeded slower there than on most worlds, and life is difficult for the sparse inhabitants. They mine iridium. This music is quite popular on worlds like theirs."

He paused, drinking in the sawing tones playing against each other, the two fiddles dancing and pausing, striking harmonies before shifting to sudden dissonances and holding them, stubbornly, as if daring the listener to turn the music off.

"Terraforming is slow on Tiberius because the native cyanobacteria has not had time to produce enough oxygen for the settlers' needs, and all attempts to increase the production rates have failed. As such, all the settlers walk around with oxygen masks. Imagine that, Captain, living your life with tubes stuck up your nostrils."

Titus nodded. "Must be rather inconvenient." His nose twitched.

"Indeed." Trajan opened his eye and waved a hand at his screen readout. "I've been in contact with an array of individuals of ill repute. Pirates, mercenaries, smugglers—I've cultivated a variety of less savory contacts during my time as head of special operations for the Imperial fleet. And wouldn't you know it, the group that I've been expecting a reply from has indeed sent a message back to me, inquiring about our terms for their cooperation."

Titus raised an eyebrow. Perhaps Ensign Evans had not betrayed him after all.

Trajan continued, seeming to read his mind, "I ordered the long range communications crew to alert only me in the event of a response from one of these groups. I hope you don't mind, Captain," he glanced up at Titus with a look that told the Captain he had better not mind.

"Of course not, sir."

Trajan's gaze pierced Titus's, and he wanted desperately to look away, but instead focused on the one, live, unblinking eye next to the crater that leered at him in his peripheral vision.

"Good. It turns out that this particular pirate group has had run-ins with us before, and is seeking to make amends, perhaps to avert justice from us in the future. It won't, of course, but I think we can avail ourselves of the offer to help. And besides, their base is on a world we'll need to pay a visit to shortly." Trajan indicated the star map sprawled over the viewscreen on the wall.

"Oh? Which world is that?" Titus peered at the map, trying to recognize some of the stars.

"Destiny," said Trajan, tapping a few buttons and zooming in on a large blueish star. The system's technical data appeared next to it. "The Destiny system is home to one of our finest research institutions, Captain. Dr. Felix Stone directs it for us. The Imperial Cybernetic Institute. They answer only to the Emperor," he said, glancing up, "and me, of course. Top secret, compartmentalization level ten."

Titus moved closer to the map to read the technical data. The main planet looked forbidding. Average temperature of forty celsius. High winds. Mostly dust. Why in the Empire would anyone put an advanced technology center on a planet like that? "You say we have business there, Admiral?"

Trajan nodded. "Yes. To check up on the progress of Doctor Stone. For all his brilliance he is rather erratic. And depraved, if the stories are true. They say he likes to watch things bleed. Gives him a rise. But details like that don't concern me. What I'm interested in is if he's made any breakthroughs recently in his research. The Plan depends on it."

The Plan? Titus opened his mouth to inquire further, but Trajan was already standing up.

"Captain, I came to realize something the other day. I was thinking about our old friend, Admiral Pritchard. The Rebels still adore him. They idolize him. He's a legend. A cult figure, almost. And every day that he is not demonstrably dead is another day that gives the Rebels hope."

"But sir, isn't he dead?" Titus had seen the intel reports himself, and knew the likelihood was high.

"Possibly. But there is the uncertainty, and the possibility that he might be alive gives the Rebels hope. Something else to fight for. It reminds me of Old Earth history. During the Battle of Beijing in the Robot Wars of the twenty-first century, the last holdouts of the Communist army refused to capitulate for nearly a year after the fall of the regime, all because they thought the media reports of the death of the Communist leader were enemy propaganda. Even when contacted by highly placed officials in the government—the head of the army, even—the men refused to stand down, believing the appeals for cease-fire were a Western Robot ploy."

Trajan continued his walk around his desk, swiping the top of it with his finger and then examining the digit as if looking for dust. He nodded approvingly.

He continued, "They didn't give up because they believed they were right. They believed they could still win, and they believed that there was someone out there beyond the city who could still swoop in to save them at the last minute. All of those things were absolutely false, and yet they believed."

Trajan turned to face Titus. "The Old Earth Rebellion is the same. They are hoping for Pritchard's miraculous return—it's as if they think he's hiding away in some corner of the galaxy secretly building a fleet that will fly in and sweep the Empire off the Earth and chase us back to Corsica."

Titus hemmed. "And so you think that by letting the pirates kill Mercer and his companions, the mythos surrounding Pritchard will be damaged somehow?"

Trajan stopped pacing and fixed his eye on Titus. "Captain, please. I'm disappointed. You really have no idea what we're doing, do you?"

Titus shifted uncomfortably. "Well, I thought that if the remaining Rebels on Earth see that it only took a few pirates to destroy the *Phoenix*, that they might reconsider their view of the Pax Humana, and would reconsider their refusal to believe that the November family killed Pritchard and destroyed the *Fury* last year."

"Close, Captain. And yes, those are all worthy goals. I commend you." Trajan nodded at him. "But no, my main goal is to prevent the creation of another Pritchard. The Rebels don't need any more myths to idolize. No, Captain, the pirates are not going to destroy Mercer and the *Phoenix*, they are going to enslave them. They will be kept alive and well, and we will ensure video is taken of their enslavement and broadcast over all the news networks on Earth. The Rebels will see the man that would have been their hero in chains. Demeaned, demoralized, and dehumanized before their very eyes. The Rebels will see what happens when good people betray the principles of the Empire and succumb to the chaos of the pirates. And that, Captain, will help kill the Rebellion."

"Very well, sir."

Trajan continued his pace around the desk console, circling it and Titus, almost as if a vulture coming in for a kill. The Captain had half a mind to run from the room and steal a shuttle, fly it to Earth and find some mountain refuge where he could escape the Admiral's madness, but Trajan continued. "We don't kill causes by removing the leaders, Captain. We don't snuff out ideas by killing their followers. We kill causes by attacking the cause itself. The people of Earth need to see what happens to those who reject the Pax Humana. I know you'd prefer to send our entire fleet right now to the Laland system and destroy the *Phoenix* in short order, but if we do that, then another Pritchard will arise. Another Mercer. And after we kill that one, another will follow. An endless bloodbath."

Titus was surprised. He wouldn't have thought the possibility of a bloodbath on Earth would cause the Admiral to so much as bat an eyelash.

"And besides," Trajan sat back down and turned his back to him. "Once the people of Old Earth have seen the futility in fighting against the Pax Humana, then they will be prepared for The Plan. And Captain," he continued, sensing Titus's impending question, "you need not worry. I will tell you all about The Plan when we begin its implementation. But for now, focus on Mercer. And the *Heron*, wherever it may be. Dismissed."

Captain Titus saluted, and spun around to make a hasty retreat. As he made his way to the bridge and to Ensign Evans at the long-range communications station, he considered ordering the man to let him know whenever he had news to pass directly to the Admiral, but then he thought better of it. Admiral Trajan valued his game of private strategy and subterfuge, and would not look kindly on Titus's attempt to act as intermediary.

He sighed, and handed the pad to the waiting Ensign. Bit by bit, he felt his authority aboard his own ship slipping away from him.

CHAPTER FIVE

Ben caught his eye. "Captain, they're not Imperials. But there's a lot of them. And they're closing in fast on the *Sphinx*."

"Are they jamming us? Why can't we hear Anya?" he demanded.

"Unknown. Can't get a source on the jamming signal." Ben looked down at his console and pressed a few keys. "Captain, the new ships are firing on the *Sphinx*. I'm counting twenty-one vessels, ranging in size from a light carrier down to a handful of corsairs and mini-frigates." A hint of a smile pulled at his cheeks, the first Jake had seen on him all day. "And they're beating the shit out of her, sir."

Jake nodded, turning to smile at the screen. "Best news I've heard all day. Ben, redirect fire back at the *Sphinx*. Let's not let them have all the fun."

"Woohoo!" Came Anya's voice over the comm. "You seeing this, bridge? Hold on, we're gonna go help out. Can't let them have all the fun!"

He watched the battle unfold as the *Sphinx*, starting to drift out of control, lurched with multiple explosions. Yet she still put up a stiff resistance, redirecting fire towards the small armada of frigates and freighters that now swarmed around her, pelting her with a barrage of torpedoes, ion beam cannon bursts, and railgun fire.

And then, in the blink of an eye, it was over.

"They're gone, sir. The Sphinx has shifted away," Ben said, with as broad a smile as he ever let slip past his stalwart veneer.

Jake turned around with a grin wrapped across his face. Glancing at the tactical octagon, he gave a thumbs up, and the entire station of officers cheered, beating the air with exuberant fists—even Ensign Ayala, which to Jake looked a little out of place, like a Buddhist monk at a heavy metal concert.

"Sir, perhaps it's a bit premature for celebrations?" Ben said, still scowling at his console display. He put a hand through his perfectly gelled, sensible hair. "This is damned peculiar, Jake."

The clapping died down and Jake walked over to the tactical octagon and peered over Ben's shoulder. "What's going on?"

"The ships. They're moving towards us, but not all of them, and not all to the same spot. It's like they're flanking us —some of them went back past our stern, others below and yet others above." He glanced up at his friend. "It's like they're flanking us to keep us from moving. Don't they know we can shift away at a moment's notice?"

"Are they charging weapons?"

"Negative. We've got no indication of hostile—"

Ensign Falstaff interrupted. "Sir, they're hailing us. They're requesting visual," he said with a curt nod, his longish brown hair swishing slightly.

Jake raised an eyebrow. The custom in space was to communicate with audio only, a custom started by the Belenites, in fact, in the first few decades of exile from their destroyed homeworld. Somehow, it had caught on among most of the Thousand Worlds—Jake supposed out of solidarity.

"Put it on screen, Ensign."

In place of the red giant star and the smattering of freighters and cruisers appeared a man straight out of the novels Jake liked to read as a kid. A cowboy hat covered the man's stringy hair, scars stretched across the gaunt, weathered face, and a sly smile pulled at his sunburned lips.

"Imperial Cruiser! I am Captain Volaski." Jake noticed a thick Eastern European accent, possibly Russian. "If I may ask, why were you firing on your fellow ship?"

Jake approached the center of the bridge and stood next to his chair—he'd still not gotten used to thinking of it as his. In his mind, the chair was still reserved for Captain Watson, even though he knew that was silly.

"Captain Volaski, I'm Captain Mercer of the *USS Phoenix*, formerly the *NPQR Phoenix* of the Imperial fleet. I'm happy to say that we've commandeered our vessel from the Imperials and impressed it into service of the Earth Resistance Fleet, hence the battle you so fortuitously stumbled upon. If I may ask, sir, what is your business in this system?"

Captain Volaski maintained the tight-lipped, sly smile. Jake wondered if the expression was simply a permanent feature of the man's sun-beaten face, or if there was something more sinister in the man's thoughts.

"Business, Mercer, no more. My brethren and I regularly

patrol the less populated stars of this sector for, er, let's just say business opportunities." The last word rolled off his tongue, thick with the Russian accent, as if he were a salesman in an infomercial back in some seedy bar in San Bernardino.

Jake rolled his eyes. "So you're a pirate, then." It wasn't a question. In Jake's mind, the one benefit of the Pax Humana enforced by the Empire was the suppression of the roving bands of pirates, both of the organized variety and the lone wolves that roamed the settled parts of the galaxy like hungry hunting packs.

The sly smile lessened a bit. "We prefer the term trade syndicate, Captain Mercer. I assure you, our activities are entirely legitimate. We provide security to caravans of goods and raw materials and ensure their safe arrival at their destinations, as well as trading in various items that the Empire frowns upon."

"So, you're smugglers too," said Jake.

Captain Volaski let out a slow sigh. "If you want to call it that, then fine. When I saw you firing on that ship, Captain, I didn't think you were particularly the law-abiding type. Especially not arbitrary and cruel Imperial laws."

Jake cleared his throat. The man was right—they *did* spring the *Phoenix* out of a tight spot, after all. "My apologies, Captain Volaski, I did not mean to offend. We are happy you're here." Jake tried to sound genuine. In reality, he didn't trust pirates in the slightest. They were the lowest form of life in the galaxy— the Thousand Worlds were settled and built by men and women of grit and gumption, while the pirates merely leached the spoils. Travel in the galaxy was a dangerous thing indeed before the Empire showed up.

"I understand your concern, Captain Mercer." Volaski seemed to read his thoughts. "There are hordes of ships out here that you would do well to blast out of the sky. The shipping lanes, at least when the Imperials aren't looking, are a wretched hive of villainy and piracy. I echo your sentiments: we are glad we found you here. I'm not sure we could have taken out that heavy cruiser on our own."

Most definitely not, thought Jake. It would have taken twice as many smaller ships to take out the *Sphinx*, probably more when one considers all the fighters the cruiser could hold.

The man pulled his cowboy hat a little lower over his hair and glanced out of view of the camera, and nodded once before turning back. "So, Captain, where are you headed? As a ship on the run from the Empire, I assume you'll have need of supplies? Might I ask, how is your stock of provisions? Can we assist you in any way?"

"We have plenty of food and water, thank you. And if we don't get into a railgun battle with an Imperial cruiser every other day we should be fine on munitions," he lied. In fact, over the past hour they had run dangerously low on railgun slugs. But Volaski did not need to know that.

"Indeed. Very good. Do you have a destination in mind?

Jake shifted uncomfortably. "Our itinerary is our own. I hope you understand."

Volaski nodded. "I do. I assure you that you've got nothing to fear from us. We're on the same side now, Mercer. Very well, if we can be of no more assistance to you, I think we'll be going about our business."

Jake suddenly remembered his conversation with

Alessandro during the morning's game of chess. If they were to have any tactical advantage over the Imperials they would need the full capabilities of their next generation gravitic drive restored, and at the moment the thing was scaled down to the abilities of a regular one, only far more inefficient due to the non-optimal gravitic field configuration Alessandro had put it in.

The only way to get it back up to its full potential was to completely rebuild the substrate of the crystal matrix, and that meant a whole shitload of neodymium. 99.999 percent pure.

Jake turned away from Volaski, then paused, and glanced back up, "Unless you might know of any sources of rare earth metals. We've found ourselves in need of some raw material. Nothing urgent, but it's just one more thing on the grocery list, so to speak."

Volaski's sly smile opened up into a full-fledged grin. This one far less vaguely-sinister looking. This one spoke to Jake of one thing and one thing only.

Profit.

"Well you're in luck, Mercer. I know of a source of rare earths that likes to keep his dealings discrete. In the Filmore Sector, just a couple dozen light years away towards Arcturus, which is doubly good for you as it is in the exact opposite direction of Imperial space. It's just outside the official border, in fact." The man couldn't help but rub his hands together, and his cowboy hat bobbed up and down as he nodded enthusiastically.

"Thank you, Captain Volaski. Give me a few minutes to consult with my staff to see if it's not too far out of our way."

"Ok. Don't be a stranger. Volaski out."

Jake turned to look at Ben and Po who stood erect at their stations.

"I don't like it," said Ben right as the screen shut off.

Not surprising. Ben was the cautious, almost paranoid one, perhaps having to do with socializing so much with the gun and prepper crowds back on Earth. He smiled wryly. Perhaps they all should have hung out with the prepper crowds more— if there was ever a time to be prepared for a breakdown of society, it was probably then, as the Empire would likely respond to the Battle of the Nine with ruthless brutality. Earth was still in a whole lot of danger, in spite of their spectacular escape.

"Me neither, but it's tempting, to be sure," said Megan Po, holding an elbow with one hand and adjusting her neat bun with the other. "The pirate groups are sworn enemies of the Empire, so in a way it makes sense for us to work together, but we're playing with fire, Jake. We have no idea who these people are or what their motivations might be."

"I think I have an idea about their motivation," Jake said, remembering the man's enthusiastic smile at the mention of commerce. "But I agree, we can't trust them, even after their chasing off the *Sphinx*. But if we can get some neodymium out of them, well, I think it's certainly worth the risk."

Ben stood firm, and his frown deepened. "Captain, I advise against it. We can find our own source of neodymium. We don't need to put ourselves at the mercy of pirates."

Jake frowned. "Our own source? How? The way I see it this is us finding our own source right now. And we won't be at their mercy. Ensign Roshenko here can have coordinates entered for a gravitic shift if things look likely to get nasty."

Ben stuck out his lower lip and would have frowned further, if it were possible. "Fine. But don't say I didn't warn you."

"I wouldn't dream of it. Po?" He switched to his XO before Ben could respond to his jab.

"Ok," she said finally, nodding, "but let's get the coordinates from Volaski and run the destination through the computer. See what we can find out before we get to wherever he wants to take us."

And with that, Jake knew why he'd picked her as the XO. She was always thinking of the details he would miss in his drive to win. "Good thinking. Anyone else?" He looked around the bridge. He wanted the bridge crew to feel included. Like they had a stake in what the *Phoenix* did. Because in reality, they had committed their lives to the mission when that first QED torpedo struck the *Fidelius* three days ago.

"Really, people. I want to hear other opinions if you've got them."

"Captain," Ensign Ayala raised her hand to get his attention. "What is their motivation?"

Jake paused. "Money, I would think."

"Yes, but we're a dangerous customer. If the Imperials found out about them dealing with us, Admiral Trajan would send a fleet to whatever port these pirates frequent and punish them. Is it really in their best interest to deal with us?"

She was right. But unfortunately, there was no other source of neodymium around. At least, no sources of already-mined and refined metal.

"And Captain," she continued, "If it's neodymium we want, I suggest we try to get in contact with my people. I'm sure there's a few mining ships with the main flotilla that would have a store they'd be willing to sell us. As long as we hide our … less-than-pacifistic intentions."

He raised an eyebrow at her. "And how does one hide their-less-than pacifistic intentions sitting on the bridge of a warship?"

She slumped into her chair further, embarrassed. "No, you're right. Stupid idea."

He softened his face, but resisted the urge to wink. "Sorry, Ensign. Thank you for your input—I'm glad you spoke up. You raise a good point, we need to find out what the pirates have to gain by dealing with us. And Willow," he looked back at her, using her first name in the hopes she'd feel a little less alienated, "If you can think of any other way your people can help, I'm all ears. I know they're pacifists and won't fight alongside us, but if they could help us politically—I know they hold some clout in the Senate—then we would be indebted to them."

"Thank you, sir. I'll give it some thought." She brushed a lock of white hair out of her face and smiled.

"Captain, they're hailing us again," said Ensign Falstaff.

Jake glanced at Po with a raised eyebrow. "Impatient little buggers, aren't they? On screen, Ensign."

Captain Volaski reappeared before them, but this time he was not alone. A woman stood by his side, stern, proud, and wearing no-nonsense, unadorned clothing. "Mercer, I'd like you to meet Velar. She's plugged in to the world I'd like to take you to." He looked at her and motioned towards the viewscreen.

"Mercer," she said in greeting. "What an honor to have a

fleet Captain ask to visit my world."

Jake thought it odd she phrased it in that way. He hadn't yet asked to be taken to the world Volaski had spoken of, and he was not an Imperial fleet Captain, even if he was still by all appearances in the fleet, what with his navy-blue uniform and Imperial epaulettes.

"Nice to meet you Velar. I've spoken with my officers and we would be honored to be taken to your world for trade. Might I ask the name of said world?"

She maintained an inscrutable expression, neither smiling nor frowning. Just watching him. As if reading him, or waiting for Jake to say something she was expecting or looking to hear. "It is Destiny, Captain."

"I'm sorry, what is?" He squinted at her and turned his head slightly in misunderstanding.

"My world. It is Destiny. At the far end of the Filmore Sector."

"Ah, I see," he said, understanding what she'd meant. He'd never heard of such a planet. Then again, in addition to the Thousand Worlds of the Empire, there were hundreds of settled worlds that either had not fallen yet under the Empire's sway, or were too far out of the way for the Empire to bother.

Or perhaps, as the case was with a handful of worlds, it was simply too dangerous for even the Empire to attempt to subdue. Some pirate syndicates were notorious for laying mines, disguised as orbital debris. Several hapless Imperial battleships and dozens of merchant ships had been lost to mines over the years, and the Empire had finally given up certain worlds for good because of them.

"You know it? You will come?" She said, expectantly.

"I haven't heard of it, actually. Is it a very populated world?"

She shook her head. "Not really, no. Perhaps a few million people. The climate is not very hospitable in most latitudes. Dry and arid. But my family has lived there for six generations and it is home. You will come, then?"

She seemed oddly insistent. But lacking a good reason to say no, Jake nodded. "We will come. I'm afraid we don't have many Imperial credits to our name—I suspect the Empire has shut off our tab. But we have technology and other supplies your man on Destiny might find attractive. Send over the coordinates and we'll be on our way."

"Before we leave, Captain, I should prepare you to go down to the surface. You can't be seen looking like that." She glanced down at his clothing. "Imperial uniforms are not in fashion on Destiny. You're liable to get shot before taking a dozen steps there."

Jake looked down at his uniform, still smudged and blackened from the battle of the Nine. He hadn't had it washed yet. A few spots of stray blood stained his leg and arms, and he wasn't even sure if the blood was his or not. "Yeah, you might have a point there. But I wasn't planning on going down to the surface. I'd prefer to do all the negotiating from the comfort of my bridge and receive the shipment in our fighter bay."

She shook her head and held up a hand. "No, Captain. On my world, you do not negotiate from afar. No one will deal with you unless you come to them and look in their eye and shake their hand. Flesh to flesh. No one will trust you enough to do business otherwise."

Jake glowered at her. "Well if that's the case, why don't they come up to my ship and they can look into my eye up here? Why does the handshake have to happen down on the surface?"

"Because, Captain, you are the traveller. You are the one coming to our world, not the other way around. If our traders visited your world, we would expect to do no less than what we ask of you."

Jake paused to think, and finally nodded reluctantly. "Fine. We'll go down."

"And don't dress like you're some city lubbers from Earth, either. You'll stick out. You know what?" she nodded at him, as if trying to get him to mirror her motion, "Why don't I come over there and guide your clothing selection. You have printers on board?"

"Yeah, we have printers. But I think we'll manage just—"

Velar frowned at him—the first real facial expression she let through. "No, Captain Mercer, I insist. I will not take you to my planet and then have you draw attention to me and our supplier. It is unwise to draw attention to oneself on Destiny."

"Is it terribly dangerous?" Jake was becoming less and less convinced that he wanted to visit her world.

"Not for those who blend in. Those that stick out are a target for pirates." She glanced at Captain Volaski. "The less agreeable kind. Tell me, Mercer, can you receive our ship? It is not large."

She seemed absolutely determined to get on the *Phoenix*, and it bothered Jake. But they needed that neodymium. They would have to risk it, but he made a note to have Ben assign a security detail to the fighter bay while the ship was aboard.

"Yes we can. Though give us two hours to prepare for your visit. We have just left the scene of a battle with the Imperials and we need to memorialize our dead."

Her brow furrowed in what Jake could have sworn was sympathy, but he still couldn't quite read her emotions. "I understand. We will approach your bay in two hour's time."

Jake folded his arms. "When you get off your ship, be unarmed. No need to give my security chief an aneurism. Will it be just you, or do you require an escort?"

"I will come with Volaski, Captain, if that is alright with you." She glanced to her right at Captain Volaski, who nodded as if giving permission. Jake wondered what their relationship was.

"As you wish. Our tactical officer will relay instructions to your navigator for approaching the fighter bay. Mercer out."

Jake knew Ben would not be happy, and he was right. The moment Volaski and Velar disappeared from the screen Ben marched over to the command station where Jake still stood next to his chair. "Captain, a word?"

"Sure, Manuel," said Jake, using Ben's callsign in an attempt to lighten his mood. Judging by Ben's face, he failed miserably.

"In your ready room?"

The ready room. He'd still not even set foot in it since Captain Watson died. He'd been able to use the captain's chair in the bridge—he could hardly avoid it with his bridge duties—but somehow he'd managed to avoid setting foot in that other space. It reminded him of the cold, blue bodies lying in the makeshift morgue next to sickbay. All those bodies—all the ones they still hadn't had a chance to eject out the airlocks for a proper space burial. Not even a chance to have the memorial planned for earlier that day.

Jake followed his friend back to the hallway that led to the ready room, the bridge conference room, and the astrometric chart room, where the four walls of the tiny amphitheater turned into a scalable star map that helped the Captain navigate the known boundaries of the settled galaxy. Just over 1000 worlds had been settled by humans since the dawn of the space age, though dozens, perhaps hundreds more were colonized less conspicuously. Perhaps a world with a less ideal climate or atmospheric pressure or gravity would be passed over by average settlers, only to be scooped up by other groups more interested in escaping attention from civilized society.

As they entered the hallway, Jake looked back and motioned Megan to join them. Po was good at defusing Ben. Jake just tended to egg him on—a habit he would have to lose if he wanted to stay friends with the man as his Captain. She in turn motioned to her deputy she'd chosen, a young lieutenant from engineering. Lieutenant … Jake had already forgotten his name.

"Fitzpatrick, you have the bridge. Don't crash us into anything, please," she said as she followed Jake out the door.

"Jake, what are you thinking?" he said as soon as he walked through the conference room door. "This is insane! You're inviting pirates onto the ship? What the hell are you doing? What's wrong with you?"

As Po walked through the door she pointed at Ben. "You watch your mouth, Commander. Remember you're talking to the Captain—"

Jake held up a hand, interrupting her. "No, it's ok Megan.

When it's us three I don't want you guys thinking you have to salute me or some shit like that. It's just like old times. I can't do this without you, and I hope you feel the same about me. We're in this together. Ben," he continued, looking his friend in the eye, "I understand—"

"No, I don't think you do. Those people are murderers, Jake. They stalk the shipping lanes, waiting for unsuspecting merchants, and when they find an easy target, they pounce. If the merchant is lucky, they just get taxed," Ben said, making air-quotes around the word "taxed," "worst case, they get taken as slaves back to one of their hideouts. Actually, I guess worst case is they die, but who's keeping track at this point? Obviously not you. And if—"

"Ben, we need that neodymium. Bernoulli thinks we can have our short-range gravitic shifting capabilities restored within a few days of getting some. Just think of the advantage we would have over the Imperials if we had that!"

"We'll get it somewhere else! Jeez, Jake, why now? What's the rush? Let's lie low for a bit and get our bearings. Why do you feel the need to make a mad dash to some god-forsaken pirate infested rock just to get a few days head start on—"

Jake scowled and began pacing the room as he argued back. "Because, if we just sit around with our thumb up our ass, Trajan will find us. He'll find us sooner or later—you don't just hide a Freedom-class battlecruiser under a sheet. And when he finds us again, I want to be ready. And if that means facing down a few pirates in the meantime, well then I say bring 'em on." He turned back to face him, arms folded across his chest.

Ben smirked. "Heh, bring it on indeed, Jake. Is that what

you were telling yourself when you kicked the snot out of that drunk bastard on the shipyards?"

"As I recall you had a hand in that," Jake retorted icily.

"Yeah, and if I hadn't, you'd be either dead or in a full body cast."

Megan took a step between them. "And if he were dead Ben, then so would we all. We're here right now because of him. If we had have truly surrendered a few days ago, we'd all be dead by now. Don't deny it," she added as she saw his look of scorn.

Ben sat down in the captain's chair and fingered the armrest. Jake felt a sudden twinge of guilt—it should have been his friend who owned that chair. "You don't know that. We'd already lost most of the Nine by then. Trajan had already won his grand victory. The Truth and Reconciliation Committee would have demanded that we be released and stripped of our commissions or something. They wouldn't have let us be executed."

Jake shook his head and continued pacing. "No, you're wrong. Doubly wrong. First of all, Trajan would have just executed us then and there without even consulting the Committee. Remember, Senator Galba, the head of the Commission, was on the *Fidelius* when it blew, along with half of the other members. Trajan was behind it—I know he was— meaning not only was he willing to kill all of us, but he was willing to kill a bunch of senators to get to us. Second, take a look at it from the Commission's point of view. In their eyes, the Resistance just destroyed the *Fidelius* and commandeered nine Imperial battleships. We're war criminals to them, the symbol of their misplaced trust. They wouldn't let us live.

Don't you see the brilliance of Trajan's plan? He not only destroyed the Resistance, he destroyed our reputation. The Commission hates us now, and probably half the population of Earth, probably most of the citizens of the Empire, and the entire Senate—remember, we just killed three or four of their own."

He took a breath, satisfied that he'd seemed to shut Ben up momentarily.

"And furthermore, if we don't start getting out into the settled worlds and making allies, we're not going to last a month out here. We've got food, sure. But we'll run out. Water? Yeah, we've got purifiers and recirculators, but what if something goes wrong in one of the battles in the weeks ahead and we spring a leak? Where are we going to resupply our railgun ordnance? And anti-matter? That shit don't come cheap. We need allies, Ben. And these people are as good a place to start as any—didn't you see the way they charged the *Sphinx*? These people got a bone to pick with those bastards, and that's the kind of ally I want on my side."

Jake stopped pacing and looked down at Ben again, who only pursed his lips.

"Jake, he's just being prudent," said Megan, leaning up against the wall. "We agree with you. He's just saying, and I'm just saying, that we need to be careful."

Ben leaned forward and rested his arms on the table. "No, Megan, that's not what I was saying. I was saying it was an incredibly reckless and stupid decision to bring that ship on board. Have you even thought about how the *Sphinx* found us? And then how the pirates just shifted in out of nowhere? How fortunate! Do you really think those were just coincidences?"

Jake stroked his chin. "No, I don't. You're right, we should be cautious. But I stand by what I said. We need to make allies. And those weren't fake ion beams those pirates were firing at the *Sphinx*. They were shooting to kill, Ben."

Ben swore. "Fine. Let's get this over with."

Megan moved over to the console at the head of the conference table. She tapped a few buttons and spoke without looking up. "The ship is nearly here. Jake? How do you want to do this? Do you want to send me down there with a security contingent and meet this contact they have down on Destiny? I'm not much of a negotiator but I think I could hold my own."

Jake shook his head. "No, Megan. I want you with the ship. Ben and I will go."

"Oh, we will?" Ben said sarcastically.

"I need you with me, buddy," Jake tried to crack a smile and slapped Ben on the shoulder. Ben glowered at him. "Look, Ben, you're the best. If for some reason things go to hell down there, there's no one else I'd want at my side. Pick two special ops guys to go with us. And I've got one more person in mind," he said, tapping the comm button on the console. "Ensign Ayala, please report to the bridge conference room."

Megan and Ben both stared at him. "Captain?" Po said, looking at him askance. "Why Willow?"

"Because she's a Belenite. They're highly respected throughout the Thousand Worlds. Hopefully beyond the Thousand Worlds. And," he said with a grin, "it's superstition out on some of these worlds that if you're inhospitable to a Belenite guest that ill events will befall you."

"You really think these pirates are superstitious?" said Ben.

Jake smiled as he walked out the door. "One can only hope."

CHAPTER SIX

Senator Demetrius Corsicanus Harrison Galba stretched out his leg in the cramped bunk of Willow Ayala's tiny quarters. He judged the space to be no more than ten square meters. Not even a tenth the size of his second bathroom at the Senatorial Palace on Corsica. He sighed. The sacrifices he had to make in the service of the glorious Imperial Republic.

But he'd had enough. Four days of doing nothing but wait was starting to gnaw at him. He was a man of action. A titan of the Empire. A man to be respected and not trifled with.

He grimaced as he clipped his toenail. Dammit, he needed a surgeon. The blasted thing was ingrown.

And he was most definitely not someone to just wait around for some Belenite to feed him news in bits and pieces. Not even an exotic, sexy Belenite like Willow. Gods, she made him horny. He rubbed his crotch just thinking about her.

The Plan had gone astray. Trajan had miscalculated. The Resistance was supposed to be irrevocably crushed and discredited, clearing the way for the implementation of The Plan. But instead, the *Phoenix* had escaped, under the command of some rogue North American fighter pilot.

But the Plan would continue. He knew that. The Emperor and Admiral Trajan would not let such an insignificant turn of events deter them from the grander plan in place. Old Earth was but a piece of it.

And yet the *Phoenix* represented a dangerous variable. One out of their control. And he had to neutralize it. Too much was riding on The Plan to let one insignificant ship derail it.

But one ship could change the course of history. One man. One people. Galba knew that. He knew his history. Hell, hadn't Corsica been founded almost by accident? Because of a mutiny aboard a Joint European Colony ship nearly 400 years ago? Just one man, and his friends, had commandeered the vast colony ship, redirected it towards the newly terraformed American world of Commerce, and duly conquered it.

And renamed it Corsica.

The Americans didn't find out for three years, and when they did, they were already too tied up in another petty war with the Russian Confederation of Planets to do anything about it. By the time both sides lay in ruins, the Corsican Empire was already in its infancy, ready to spread its glorious influence out into the settled worlds.

Galba rubbed his crotch again, trying to focus his mind on the white-haired tattooed woman of his dreams, her lithe body, her round, petite breasts, her red lips almost lost in the tattooed forest creeping up on her face.

The door opened, and she walked in, breaking out into a grin as she saw his hand in his pants.

"Been thinking about me, Harrison?" She crawled onto the bed and sat on his thighs. Gods, he loved it when she did that.

"It's been eight hours. Eight hours, my love." He tried to frown, to sound angry. But his crotch screamed at him to soften his tone and lure her in.

She leaned forward, unbuttoning her uniform. "I know. I'm sorry. We just had another battle, you know. With the *Sphinx.*"

He ran a hand up her chest, between her heaving breasts, and stroked her forested neck. "I know. At least, I heard the klaxons and the pounding on the hull. Did we win?"

She laughed. "We? Yes, *we* did. Do you consider yourself part of the Resistance now?"

She took off her pants, and he wiggled out of his, and flipped around to lay on top of her. She was like an acrobat, displaying far more agility and strength than your average twenty-something young woman. He wondered at her history —he knew there was more to her than met the eye. She was a Belenite, sure, and from a rather prominent family. But his sources had discovered she might have contacts deep within the Belenite fringe group known as *The Red*, the group that wanted nothing to do with the pacifistic ways of the main culture.

But for now, he didn't care. He just cared about getting deep inside of her. And he did. And it was bliss.

Nearly half an hour later, nestled into the crook of his arm, she murmured, "how long do you think we can keep you hidden?"

Time to make his escape. "Actually, I was wondering if you could get me a uniform. I want to get out into the ship. I can't just live in your quarters for the rest of my life, my love."

She turned up to look at him, a skeptical look on her face. "And what do you think you're going to do? Even the lowliest midshipman will recognize you."

"We'll have to fix that, my love. Surely you know how we might alter my appearance?"

She rubbed his chest. "What are you thinking?"

Would she go for it? Belenites were pacifists. But it would be so incredibly sexy. "Well, I was thinking if you could … mark me. My face. Just a bit. Enough to throw off scrutiny. In fact, I imagine half the ship is injured in some way or another. I'd fit in nicely."

She rose up to a sitting position. "Are you really suggesting what I think you are?"

She wouldn't do it. He kicked himself for broaching the subject. "Well, if you're not comfortable, I understand…."

He trailed off, then added, "But it might be fun…." He winked, and added a sly grin—something he knew she had trouble resisting. It would be more than fun. He might even just get another erection.

Rolled eyes. She laid her head back down. "I'm Belenite, Harrison. It's not what we do." She kissed his chest. "Even for fun. *Especially* for fun. Violence is the watchword of the Empire, not of my people. I'm forbidden from drawing blood with my hands."

He sighed. "Very well. At least get me a uniform? I've been in these clothes for days now—I smell like a Trantorian miner."

Her fingers ran over his stomach and up his chest. What he wouldn't give to whisk the girl away to his seaside estate on Corsica. Watch her cook him scrambled eggs in his kitchen while naked. Lay on the brilliant white sand with the waves washing over their bodies, the troubles of the galaxy forgotten.

"Of course, Harrison."

He rested his hand on hers. "Violence in not our watchword, love."

"Oh?" she murmured.

"Peace. Stability. Those are our watchwords. Are there those in the Empire who tolerate violence? Yes. But no society is free of that guilt. Even your own, as you should know."

Had he gone too far? If he had, she'd lift her head up and glare at him with those fiery black eyes.

She didn't. She didn't even tense. "I don't know what you're talking about."

Oh well. Plenty of time to get at the truth later. For now, it was time to stop the *Phoenix*, and clear the way for The Plan.

CHAPTER SEVEN

Ten minutes later, Ensign Willow Ayala stood outside the doors to her quarters, wondering which way to go. She hadn't eaten in over a day, though that was usually not a problem for a Belenite, with their storied culture of multi-day fasts. Sleep was an enticing option, though with the Senator sprawled out on her bunk, clipping his toenails, that seemed unlikely. Maybe he was right. It might do them both good to get him out of her quarters. At least long enough for her to sleep.

But did he know? She hadn't told anyone on the ship about her membership in *The Red*. Sure, the Senator probably had access to Imperial intel reports, but even they shouldn't know anything about their order.

The order that would bring the Empire to its knees. At whatever cost.

She wavered on her feet and her hand shot out to stabilize her against the wall.

Damn. She really needed sleep.

Time to find the man a uniform and get him the hell out of her quarters.

CHAPTER EIGHT

Gavin Ashdown's morning was not going very well. As an assistant to the lead galley cook, he already occupied an unenviable place on the *Phoenix*'s totem pole, but to be the food server for the hectic stream of crew members rushing in and out of the cafeteria after an emergency like the one they'd had a few days ago was perhaps the worst job imaginable.

A constant stream of harried officers and enlisted men yelling at him to hurry with the trays or to bring more forks or to refill the coffee barrel passed though the cafeteria line. Hell, that wasn't even his job. Unfortunately, the kid whose job it was lay in sickbay with his head in stitches. The nurse assured the remaining galley crew he'd get better, but in the meantime they were short-staffed and facing an unruly crowd of hungry crew members.

Gavin would be lying if he said he didn't somewhat enjoy the hectic pace. After all, that was why he joined the fleet. For adventure. To see new places and travel the galaxy. To explore strange new dishes and seek out new ingredients and condiments. To boldly cook what no galley lackey had cooked before. Yeah, that was his life.

He rushed back into the galley storage larder and dashed back out with a bag of creamer, and tossed it towards the impatiently waiting Ensign. "Hey!" the Ensign yelled. "Aren't you even going to open it before you toss it in my face?"

"But that would have made a mess, sir." he retorted as he ran back into the galley, the Ensign's threats following him through the door. The cook was a sight to behold as he ran from one pot to the other, stirring the oatmeal and scraping the bottom of a pan to keep the eggs from sticking and checking on the progress of the hundreds of biscuits still in the oven.

"We need more eggs out there. The officers are getting a little surly," Gavin said to the cook, who grunted as he stirred the still soupy, yellow mixture.

"That's going to have to wait, kid. I don't perform miracles. Eggs cook when they cook." A cigarette hung out of the corner of the cook's mouth, which Gavin was sure ran afoul of several fleet regulations, regardless of which fleet they were currently in. Not to mention the health and sanitation codes of Earth and the Empire both.

"Can we just crank up the heat, sir?"

The cook scratched his crotch with one ungloved hand. "Just take the oatmeal out. That oughta tide 'em over."

Gavin sighed. He knew if he walked out there with just a pot of oatmeal, the crowd of hungry officers and enlisted men would run him out of the room.

"Hurry, kid, they can't wait all day," said the cook, an older, chunky man with a bristly mustache.

Resigned to his fate, Gavin hefted the giant pot out the

door and clunked it down on the serving table.

Eventually the breakfast crowd seemed to melt away into the lunch crowd, and before he knew it he was hard at work in the galley mixing up powdered mashed potatoes, boiling a vat of frozen green beans, and reconstituting what a container claimed was pork chops but which looked like limp, oily biscuits.

"Oh, dammit. The biscuits." He dashed to the oven and yanked the door down, only to be blasted with a wave of smoke in his face. 500 burned biscuits. He swore again to himself as he scraped them all into the trash and entered a command into the food printer to lay out another fifty perfect, even rows of dough balls onto the massive baking trays, and within a few minutes he had the whole lot baking again.

The cook barreled through the door, fresh off what Gavin calculated was his tenth break for the day. "What the hell is that smell? Did you burn my biscuits?"

"Technically sir, the oven burned them," said Gavin, trying to keep his tone engaging and playful. He'd only worked with the man for a week, and in that time Gavin had pinned the cook down as someone who was both quick to anger, but also quick to laugh. The trick was to get him to laugh before he swore at you.

"Dammit, Ashdown, I leave you for twenty minutes, and the kitchen is falling apart! Get a new batch in there now— we've only got a few minutes before the hungry asshats start streaming through the doors again."

"Already done, sir," he replied, subordinately. He knew his humor grace period had already passed, and there would be nothing but yelling for the rest of the night.

"And where the hell is Xing?" Jet Xing, the other galley assistant, was also on her tenth break for the day. She tended to make herself scarce whenever the workload was the heaviest and the cook was not around to supervise.

"In the bathroom, probably. Or her bunk." He knew it was not terribly classy of him to get Jet in trouble, but the girl deserved it. She was lazier than anyone he knew.

The cook rolled his eyes. "Come on then, lets get this all out to the tables. We've got five minutes before serving time."

Dinner dragged on for what seemed like forever to Gavin, but in reality only lasted just over an hour. It was full of more dashing back and forth to the galley, enduring the haranguing of officers and the impatient hounding of the enlisted men. The reality was that Gavin was the youngest crew member on the ship, and the people passing through his cafeteria didn't seem too amused that some teenage kid was holding up their dinner.

As the night nearly wrapped up, he was hefting another pot of mashed potatoes to the cafeteria table when he caught sight of some more officers. One in particular caught his eye. It was Commander Jemez. Gavin watched him as the man walked in, until his own foot caught on a table leg and he stumbled, sending the pot tumbling to the ground and white fluff flew everywhere. He glanced back up at Jemez and grimaced, and the Commander smiled wryly at him.

"Hey, let me help you with that," a friendly voice said next to him. Before he could stop her, the new XO, Commander Po, had stooped down to pick up the pot and reached for a stack of napkins on the table.

"Oh, sorry ma'am. You don't have to—"

She smiled warmly at him before she stooped down onto her knees and began wiping up the fluff. "Nonsense. You look like you've been on your feet all day. Sit down for a minute."

He didn't know what to say, so he kept his mouth shut and kneeled down next to her, scooping up the pile of mashed potatoes back into the pot. "Thank you, Commander. Very kind."

"Don't mention it." She winked.

What XO winked at their crew? Gavin was pretty sure he liked Commander Megan Po.

"Can I help you, Po?" A deep, sure voice asked above their heads. Gavin looked and saw officer's knee-boots, then looked higher and watched as Commander Jemez stooped down to join them. He'd never seen him up this close before. The man's physique took his breath away. Gavin made a mental note to start using the *Phoenix*'s gym. He'd played some sports as a teen, but had always envied his peers for their ability to bulk up with what to him seemed like scant exercise.

"Oh, Commander! No, you don't have to. We've got it, really." Gavin was beginning to feel his face burn. Not just the XO, but now two Commanders were stooped down helping him clean up his mess.

"It's nothing, yeoman. We're happy to help. You been on board long?"

The question took Gavin aback, since they'd all only been on board for less than a week, and he stuttered a bit before Jemez burst into an easy, pleasant laugh, pleased at his joke. "Kidding, Yeoman! Only kidding. Hey, what's your name?"

"Petty officer Ashdown, sir. Gavin Ashdown."

"Aren't you a little young to be serving in the fleet?"

Commander Po scowled at him. "Oh, leave him alone, Ben. Sorry, Gavin, our security chief here is just having a rough day and likes to take it out on the crew."

Ben slouched back on his lower legs and raised his hands, defensively. "Hey, I'm just making conversation. Trying to set the kid at ease." He turned to face Gavin. "Am I making you nervous down here, Ashdown?"

"No, sir. I'm glad for the help. And for the record, I am nineteen. Joined the fleet on my birthday two months ago."

"Nineteen, huh? I could have sworn you were seventeen."

"Ben," Megan said with an impatient glare. She turned to face Gavin and the warm smile returned. "Sorry, Gavin, Ben here thinks that he's thirty-five, when in actuality he's hardly older than you are. Twenty-four. In my opinion, far too young to be gallivanting about some dangerous frontier world with his best drinking buddy."

Ben snorted. "I'd hardly call the Captain my drinking buddy, Po."

"Well then what would you call him?"

A sheepish look came over Jemez's face. "My … wingman?"

Gavin felt like he'd stepped in the middle of a conversation he shouldn't be hearing. And yet he didn't feel like he could just walk away and leave them to clean up the rest of the mess. He focused on scraping up the rest of the potatoes as fast as possible.

"Thank you both for your help. I can take it from here. Really." He smiled awkwardly at Ben, and then at Commander Po.

"You sure?" said Po.

"Cause, you know, it's not like the XO is busy or anything," said Ben. The remark drew icy daggers from Commander Po's eyes, and Gavin couldn't help but chuckle. She turned her fearsome gaze to him.

"And what do you think you're laughing at?"

Gavin gulped. "Nothing, ma'am."

"Good," she said. Picking up the soiled napkins she stood up and walked away.

Ben reached over and touched Gavin's shoulder. "Good to meet you, Gavin. Hope to see you around," he said, and stood up.

"Me too, sir."

"Well, I know where you work now, so I'm sure we will." And with a smile and another squeeze on Gavin's shoulder, Ben returned to the line to get a bite to eat.

After tossing the dirty potatoes, he found another pot already made for him to take out—apparently Jet Xing, the other galley hand, had looked out to see Gavin's mishap and prepared another batch, and within another twenty minutes the two of them slumped into one of the benches of the mostly empty cafeteria.

"Saved your ass again," said Jet, shoveling a spoonful of food into her mouth. Her short cropped, nearly black hair spilled over onto her forehead in an unruly tangle.

"Huh?"

"Your spill there almost caused two dozen officers to go without potatoes. And you can't eat fake floppy pork chops without powdered potatoes." Jet's thick southern drawl sounded even more foreign to Gavin through the mouthful of food. "I call them floppychops." She grinned. "And," Jet continued, pointing her spoon at Gavin, "I think that Commander has the hots for you!"

"Who? Jemez?"

"No, dumbass. The hot mom chick. Po. She got all flustered when you kneeled down next to her."

"You're dreaming." Gavin started on his own plate, slowly, with manners for the both of them. He often considered that Jet's parents were feral squirrels that had passed their table habits down to their daughter. "Didn't your parents ever teach you manners?" It occurred to him that she'd never mentioned her family to him in the weeks that they'd served aboard the *Phoenix* together.

She shook her head. "Dead."

Gavin felt his face flush red.

"It's a funny story, actually. Wanna hear it?" she said through a mouthful of food.

"I … uh … sure." What does one say to an offer like that? He shook his head and tried to smile. Then frown. He wasn't sure if he should smile or frown.

Jet snorted through a bite. "Nah, I'll tell you later. Hey, you coming over to my bunk tonight again? You might think you're the shit at that videogame, but I've been practicing."

Gavin breathed a sigh of relief, and smirked. He'd played videogames since he was a little kid, and doubted the girl would ever match his talent, especially at *Galactic Conquest*, the starship game where the players conquer each other's planets and fleets with fighters and capital ships. Gavin was a veritable flying ace. At least virtually. "When have you been practicing?"

"During cook's smoke breaks."

Gavin swore. He knew Jet wasn't just in the bathroom all

those times. "Yeah, I'll come over. But don't think a few minutes of practice during the day will help you. I'm undefeated. I even played pro down in Denver at Vidcon."

"No you didn't," Jet said in between bites.

"Yeah, what the hell do you know?" Gavin said—he really had played in several competitions, but Jet never believed him when it came to his vid prowess. "Sure, I'll come over again. But we can't stay up until three like last time. Five o'clock comes too early to be doing that again."

Jet snorted. Gavin noticed she snorted a lot. "Yeah, I was falling asleep in the galley the next day. I think I dropped the entire salt shaker into the soup—people were giving me dirty looks when I asked them how it was."

Gavin chuckled. "Just don't let Cook catch you pullin' shit like that."

Jet gulped the last spoonful down, and licked her plate a few times for good measure. "Hey, did you hear? They're calling for new recruits for the fighter squad. They'll let anyone apply. You in?"

Gavin rolled his eyes. "Are you kidding? I just joined the fleet two months ago, and you three months ago. We're yeoman grunts. They don't take enlisted and just bump them up to lieutenants overnight." And he didn't think he'd be able to handle that type of action. He'd joined the fleet to see the galaxy, maybe see a little action, but not be in the thick of it with his life on the line every time he reported for work. The dangers of galley life suited him just fine.

Jet shrugged, and pulled at a wad of dried potato fluff in her hair. "Whatever. They put the call out, and I'm going. I figure my years of experience with the flight simulators on

those games will be just enough to put me over the edge …
why are you laughing?"

Gavin snickered and wiped a fake tear away. "I hate to
break it to you, but you kinda suck at those games. No
offense." He ran a hand through his shaggy hair and took
another bite of potatoes.

"And you think you're all that?" Jet shoved her tray
through the wall receptacle and stood up. "Come on. Let's go
play. Maybe I'll let you win a few games."

Gavin rolled his eyes. As if she could ever get even half
his score.

After cleaning up they tried to sneak out of the galley,
dodging insults and threats from the cook for trying to leave a
few minutes early, and ended up scrubbing the floor for an
extra half hour before finally getting back to their bunks and
settling down to play.

Awhile later, Gavin glanced up at the clock. And groaned.

Two-thirty. Dammit, not again.

CHAPTER NINE

Jake Mercer hated formality. Even more so when it involved an emotional subject. But there he stood, in his dress uniform in front of a fighter bay packed full of officers, flight deck hands, crew members, marines, technicians, and every other person on the *Phoenix* who managed to cram into the huge space. He supposed the room was large enough to fit 400 people, but it seemed they'd managed to pack in far more than that, easily over half the crew.

Half the living crew, that is. Behind him, behind the giant, transparent air lock door, each covered by a white sheet and a United Earth flag draped over the center of the group, lay the fallen. Captain Watson lay on a small table behind them all, just in front of the giant bay doors on the other side of which lay the void of space.

It was always so surprising to Jake how empty space was. As a boy he would look up to the sky and marvel at how full it seemed, laden with planets and clouds of stars, and later, as a fighter pilot, his assignments always kept him close to Earth, so he'd never had the chance to go out beyond the orbit of the moon.

But space was empty. Absolutely empty. The distance between stars so great that it was hard to comprehend. If it weren't for the miracle of gravitic drives, humanity would have been doomed to languish on the limited area of the Earth's surface, which would have seemed smaller with every passing decade. In the 500 or so odd years of gravitic shifting, humanity had settled at least 1000 worlds, and probably hundreds more that few knew about.

And they'd barely scratched the surface.

The gravitic shift technology had underscored quite starkly the vastness of space—the device only worked to send the traveller from one large celestial mass to another, in effect limiting the places explorers could reach since any mass under a certain threshold was off-limits, meaning that even in the settled sectors of the galaxy vast swaths of territory still lie unexplored.

And now, in a high orbit over the red giant star Laland 21185, they would commit the bodies of the fallen to the empty grave of space. On Jake's command, the *Phoenix* would accelerate to escape velocity for the few moments that would be required to open the fighter bay doors and release the air lock, sending the heroes to their cold sleep, destined to drift through the universe for millions of years until some star caught them in its sway and gave them a new, fiery burial.

Jake cleared his throat and stood at attention. The crowd of people stopped chattering and pivoted to return his stoic expression.

"Fellow officers, crew members, and friends. We gather today to salute the fallen. To remember the heroes, and to take our leave of them. Not forever, but until we meet them again in the eternal halls." He tried to keep the religious references vague, knowing that the persuasions of the crew ranged from Pagan to Christian to Buddhist to New Roman to none at all.

"They served with honor, in defense of freedom and liberty. They gave their lives so that we could carry their banner a little further, holding the shining light high so that others might also see, and have hope. Their sacrifice will never be forgotten."

He glanced around at them all, each of them weary from battle, repairs, and little to no sleep over the past few days. The heaviness showed in their eyes, and he knew that hope was flagging again. He knew they needed motivation. Inspiration.

They needed hope.

"Never again!" he yelled, and the nearest crew members in the front of the crowd jerked in surprise.

"Never again will we let the Empire crush us beneath their soulless grip! Never again will we run away from our home with our tails between our legs and let the Imperial bastards have their way with our world, raping it of our resources and our youth and our talent. For too long has the Empire conscripted our young people into its armies to dominate the Thousand Worlds. For too long have our daughters been kidnapped and sold away into the sex trade to live out their lives as the helpless toys of the rich on that syphilitic scab of a planet they call Corsica. For too long have we suffered under the arbitrary rules, and the cult worship of the emperor and the tyrannies of unaccountable bureaucrats and fleet admirals and generals. The midnight raids. The disappearances of those who dared to speak out. The murders. The intimidation. The

… all of it."

A brief smile tugged at one side of his mouth, but dissipated. "Well, fuck them all."

He continued his steady gaze at them. Staring them down. Daring them to give up, to give in. He caught Megan's eye, and she pursed her lips tightly. He knew exactly what she was thinking. She never, ever said anything about it, except for once or twice in the three years he'd known her, but he knew that her ever-present thought was of her children, held in her arms, limp and charred, the collateral damage of some Imperial strike against a suspected Resistance safe-house in San Bernardino. He spoke directly at her quivering eyes.

"And I promise you, I promise you all, that we will win. On all that I hold dear and holy, I promise you that we will chase the Empire from Earth all the way back to Corsica. We will find Admiral Pritchard, and rebuild the fleet. We will make allies, and friends, and whoever we can find common cause with. And when we've amassed such a fleet the likes of which as has never been seen, we'll descend on Earth and kindly ask the Emperor to get the hell off our world. And if he refuses— and holy shit, I hope he does—we'll blast his ass back to the old Roman Empire, and ensure the Corsican Empire never rises again!"

The fighter bay erupted in cheering. He waited for the hoots and hollers to die down before finishing.

"I stand in awe of you. As I've seen you perform your work over the last few days, I believe that you are every much a hero as those laying behind that door. They died for freedom, but you are living for freedom. You breathe freedom. You eat and you shit and you talk and laugh and cry freedom. My friends, the Empire will never even know what hit them."

He paused and looked down to the deckplate. Jagged edges still poked up in places from where Anya's fighter had shifted in her attempt to get the bay doors to automatically lower. The enormity of their task weighed on him, and he racked his mind for the right words. The eyes of everyone in that bay were fixed on him, and the ears of everyone on the entire ship was latched on his voice. He'd never sought to be the center of attention, but now, because of his choices, he was. Ben wasn't, and he was.

He needed to make his lie worth it.

"We've lost dear friends. Loved ones. Let's honor their memory by doing our duty. I may never be the leader Captain Watson would have been for the *Phoenix*, but I pledge to you my life and my breath and my sacred honor." He looked up at them again, staring Anya in the eye. She stoically met his gaze.

"I pledge to you I will not rest until this ship is safe, until the Earth is safe, and until all freedom loving people of the Thousand Worlds are safe." He turned to face a small group of marines. "Color guard, post the colors." He snapped a stiff salute.

The marine standing nearest the short, makeshift flagpole pulled down on the line with a steady, gloved hand, and raised the flag of the United Earth from half-staff up to the top of the pole, where it hung limply, like a blue corpse. He stood back, turned to the bodies behind the transparent shield, and saluted.

Don't let your voice crack.

"Open bay doors," said Jake, in as firm a voice as he could muster.

Behind the clear air-lock panel the giant bay door slid up like lightning into its receptacle, and the neatly arranged bodies and flag leapt up and shot out the gaping bay doors, tumbling end over end like tangled blue rag dolls as they faded slowly into the void.

When they were nothing more than tiny pinpricks against the backdrop of brilliant stars, Jake nodded once. "Close bay doors."

The door started to lower, slower than it had opened, and within a few seconds locked into place. Jake turned to face the crowd.

"You know your duty. Dismissed."

CHAPTER TEN

After the service, the deck crew barely had enough time to get the fighter bay back into order when Captain Volaski's ship approached the doors. It was barely small enough to fit through the opening, and Jake noted with a scowl that their fighters would not be able to launch while the ship was in the bay.

Velar and Captain Volaski seemed nice enough in person, and Jake's suspicions began to subside the more they talked. When Volaski descended the ramp from his ship, his heavy boots rang along the plate and the sound echoed through the fighter bay. To Jake's eyes the man looked straight out of history—cowboy boots, blue jeans, a simple brown shirt that looked like it had seen better days, the cowboy hat he'd worn before, and except for a vest pulled over the shirt he'd looked the same as he did on the viewscreen. Around his neck, barely visible under his collar, hung what looked like a thin wire necklace. Jake couldn't make out what hung from it.

Velar was dressed similarly, except that her head was bare and her hair pulled back into a short ponytail. She carried a large sack slung over her shoulder, which she tossed at Jake's feet.

"There. Wear those."

Jake eyed the bag on the floor. "I thought we agreed you would help us program our printers."

"This was faster, and it will look more authentic. These are used clothes, Captain. Torn, ripped, and dusty. You'll blend right in. However," she said, glancing at Ben and looking up at his hair, "whoever accompanies you to the surface should look rougher than your friend. Please, don't shave before we go, and definitely unslick your hair."

Ben grimaced and ran a hand through his perfectly coiffed hair. Jake glanced back at him with a grin. "Think you can manage? There's probably no such thing as hair gel on Destiny."

"I'll live," said his friend, stoically.

Jake felt his own face, and realized with a start what a sight he must be. He hadn't had time to look in a mirror for over two days, and his rough cheeks reminded him that he'd not shaved in well over three. Perfect.

"And you, Captain Volaski? Will you be joining us on the surface?"

The man tipped the brim of his hat, reminding Jake of the frontiersmen of the old west on Earth. "I'm afraid not," he said, with his vague Russian accent. "I have other business to attend to while on Destiny."

"What is the nature of your business?"

"What else? Profit. I have a caravan out there full of supplies to offload, and then a whole warehouse full of supplies to load up. We'll be quite busy while you negotiate with Velar's contact."

Jake pressed. "Mind telling me what you're selling?"

"I do mind," was his curt reply. There was only silence between them for about five seconds before Ben cleared his throat.

"Well, Velar, we certainly look forward to seeing your world. I hope you don't mind if we come armed? Two security officers, myself, and one other crew member will be accompanying the Captain, and I'd prefer not to travel without self-protection." His eyes pierced hers, but she did not blink.

"Of course, Mr...."

"Jemez. Commander Ben Jemez."

She spoke without a nod or a smile. "Of course, Commander Ben Jemez. I wouldn't dream of asking you to go to the surface of Destiny unarmed. That would be most foolish."

"To ask us? Or to go unarmed?" Jake tried to make a joke. By her expression he wasn't sure if she got it.

"Both," she replied with a no-nonsense glance.

Jake stooped down to rummage through the sack. Dusty old jeans, obviously worn shirts and vests, an array of beaten up boots and hats. He reached in and pulled out a Stetson hat and poofed out the dents in it. With a flourish he wrenched it on his head.

"Well this should be fun," he said with a smile at Po.

"Remember, sir, you're getting rare earths, not pretending to be a cowboy," she said. Po extended a hand to Velar and Volaski and continued. "Commander Megan Po, ship's XO."

After an exchange of greetings, Po folded her arms. "So, tell us about Destiny. You say it is lightly populated? How long have people lived there?"

Velar inclined her head towards Volaski and then back at the ship, and he walked back up the ramp and disappeared through the hatch, leaving the woman to answer their questions.

"About 150 years or so. It orbits a red giant, but is rather far away so life is concentrated around the equator. There's not much fresh water, so life can be hard. My life growing up involved a lot of work, even more dust, and little sleep. But I think I've done well for myself since then," she said, turning to watch Captain Volaski descend the ramp with another bag of clothes and boots, which he tossed to the floor at Ben's feet.

Jake raised an eyebrow. He had assumed Volaski was in charge, but it seemed more and more like the diminutive Velar was in fact calling the shots. "So, you've made a name for yourself on Destiny?"

"You might say that," she said with a wink, "but I try to fly under the radar. Too much unwelcome attention is bad for business."

Po stroked her chin, and said, "Are all those ships out there yours?"

Velar shook her head. "Not all, no. They are either mine, Volaski's here, or ships belonging to associates who often caravan with us. The shipping lanes are not safe, you know. At least not the ones we frequent. We try to stay away from prying Corsican eyes."

Po smiled, and extended her hand back out. "It has been my pleasure to meet you, but I have urgent duties to attend to before the Captain leaves."

Volaski bowed, letting his hand linger against hers.

"Ma'am, it's been my highest pleasure." Jake thought he was laying it on pretty thick, but then considered that that was how he probably interacted with everyone. With women, at least.

Po shot Jake a raised eyebrow of her own, but turned to walk away, her bun bobbing slightly with each step.

Jake tipped the brim of his hat, in imitation of Volaski. "Well then, guests. How shall we proceed? Will you give us the coordinates so we can all make the shift together, or do you need to go on ahead to make arrangements for us? Your call," he said, not sure whom to address.

Velar deferred to Volaski. Now Jake really couldn't tell who was in charge. "We'll go together. No sense in leaving you folks behind on your own. Pirates show up in uninhabited systems like these all the time. They make great hiding places from Imperial warships. I'm sure you'd do fine against any that come along, but no sense in risking it."

Jake nodded. "And the *Sphinx* might be back at any time with reinforcements. Though I guess that they'll have assumed we left by now. Very well. Transmit the coordinates and we'll be on our way." He turned to Velar. "Any idea what kind of merchandise your contact might be interested in?"

She inclined her head at the surrounding fighter bay. "I assume you have an assortment of electronics and weaponry?"

"We do," said Jake, though he was loathe to give away any of their arms, knowing that they would probably need as much firepower as they could get their hands on, eventually. But temporary sacrifices had to be made.

"Then I'm sure that will suffice." She extended a hand and Jake took it in his, bowing to her as her companion had. Velar glanced at Volaski in surprise. Jake figured she was used to traders being unaccustomed to the social pleasantries she was probably used to. What an odd group of pirates—they were nothing like Jake had expected.

"Captain. It's been a pleasure."

"The pleasure was all ours, Velar." He smiled as warm as he could, and turned to Volaski. "Captain," he said with a curt nod.

Before long, the ship lifted off the deck and flew out of the bay, pausing momentarily at the bay door as the transparent air lock bulkhead slid into place behind her. Moments later, she was through the out-bay door, heading towards the rest of the caravan.

Jake reached into the bag and drew out another hat, tossing it at Ben's chest. "Hey! Don't look so down. This'll be fun."

"Is fun what we're supposed to be having right now? We just buried 132 people," Ben replied with a furrowed forehead.

"Hey, I'm not going to spend the rest of my life moping. Live a little, Ben. Life is to be lived, not spent mourning the dead."

"Well I hope no one has reason to mourn us because of this little adventure," said Ben, picking up the sack at his feet.

Jake breathed out a puff of air as he hoisted the other sack over his shoulder. "Me too, buddy. Me too."

CHAPTER ELEVEN

Anya Grace had never hired anyone in her life. She hadn't even applied for a job before. Six years ago she'd turned in her application to the Anchorage Resistance fleet recruiting station, handing the form to the recruiting officer, who subsequently said, 'welcome aboard', without even looking at it. The need for new fighter pilots was so great at the time that just about anyone who could drive a hovercar without hitting a moose could be a pilot in the Resistance fleet.

Before then, she'd lived at home, in Alaska. Her mother had long since disappeared, and her brothers had grown creepier and more abusive by the day, threatening her with retribution from whatever Roman god was in charge of their version of hell—Hades? Thor? She could never keep them straight. She could never keep straight why they threatened retribution, either. Was it her refusal to worship their gods? Her short hair, which they deemed sinful? More likely, she surmised they were mad that she didn't respect whatever power or authority they supposed they had over her. They wanted control over her, and she wouldn't give it.

Not willingly.

Scanning the list of applicants, she crossed off several names. She'd crosschecked the entire roster against the computer's service records and decided against anyone born off Earth. At least for now. She needed to get a feel for who was trustworthy. Almost a third of the crew was from a world other than Earth, and many of them came from worlds with no history of rebellion, which might mean they were loyal to the Empire. Then again, since that same benevolent Empire had assigned them to the doomed *Phoenix,* Anya supposed that really there was no love lost between the non-Terran crew and the Empire.

But it always paid to be careful.

Flying a fighter required absolute trust from your co-pilots and fellow squadron members. Anything less would result in a sub-par performance at best. At worst, the result would be more needless deaths.

Scanning further, she crossed off a few more people with known health and psychological issues. Nothing could go wrong in one of those birds. Nothing. Any momentary lapse of judgment, any sudden medical issue that sprang up unexpectedly in the cockpit—all of those things would inevitably lead to death. A quick, gruesome death. They could take nothing for granted and leave nothing to chance. Eventually, if circumstances became increasingly dire and they needed more pilots, then standards could be lowered.

But not sooner.

She commanded the computer to rank the remaining names in order of their score on a rubric that combined overall test scores for reflexes and cognitive speed, their health and age—younger trainees always seemed to pick up fighter pilot skills faster and at a higher level than older trainees—and finally, the remaining miscellaneous skills the applicants had noted themselves, such as firearms training and wilderness survival. One never knew when circumstances would force the pilot to eject and crash land on some god-forsaken world where the only thing to eat was maggots, roots, and your own piss.

The thought whisked her mind back to Alaska, to the month her parents had left her in the wilderness. She'd mouthed off again, and rather than the usual teenage retorts, she'd insulted Minerva, her mother's favorite goddess. Within the hour she found herself dangling from a rope ladder hanging out of her parents' hovercar in the middle of Denali National Park at the peak of Moose's Tooth mountain. She'd screamed out for them to let her back in, yelling that the police would haul their asses to jail for child abuse, but she would not take back the insult.

She refused to apologize.

And as a result, they cut the ladder when she was two feet off the ground and shot away into the sky.

It was an interesting month, to say the least.

When the computer had finished its ranking algorithm, she glanced at the screen, frowned, and crossed off the last half. She clicked on the remaining seven names for further study.

Fifteen minutes later she rubbed her eyes in frustration— the bios and service records of each applicant left her with a sick feeling in her stomach. None of them would have been let within fifty meters of a fighter cockpit back on Earth. "This is going to be a long month," she said to her empty flight deck office.

The list of names and faces stared back at her. On a whim, she inserted several of them into the list of current pilots. Just to see if they fit. If they felt right.

"Quadri, Jason L. Grace, Anya T. Ashdown, Gavin C.," she said, reading the names and staring at their faces.

Did it feel right?

She blew her breath at a stray lock of hair in frustration. Out of curiosity, she opened her own file. These were Imperial records—they ought to have wonderfully kind things to say about her, especially given her prolific scorecard in bringing down Imperial bogeys during the war.

Scanning the service record, she sighed. Nothing incriminating at all. How disappointing. Just one censure. She smiled as she remembered that day, just two years ago. Her ass-wipe of an Imperial Wing Commander ordered her to report for duty two hours early, but only gave her ten minutes notice. Of course, she received the call with plenty of time as her barracks were only two minutes away from the fighter hangar. But she ignored it all the same. Just to piss the little prick off.

At the bottom of the service record, several administrative codes finished out the document. Length of time her name had been in Imperial records: ten years. That was no surprise, as most inhabitants of Earth were deemed high risk for agitation and rebellion. Cross referenced service records with other Imperial organizations: none.

She looked closer: it actually read *None**. Asterisk?

Bringing up the legend for interpreting the document she scanned for the meaning of an asterisk in that field.

Asterisk: has family or close friends with Imperial service

records in other organizations.

She tipped back in her seat, thinking. No, not one of her immediate, or even distant family had ever been employed by the Empire or served in any Imperial capacity. Nor her friends. Hell, she didn't even have any friends.

With a few clicks, she ran a cross referenced search against the rest of the Imperial database stored on the *Phoenix* computers. Surely the source of the asterisk would turn up.

Access denied.

Dammit.

She flipped off the computer and made her way to the fighter bay, mulling the new mystery over silently before she realized she was getting distracted. No. They were still in danger. She had to train those new recruits.

Mysteries could wait.

CHAPTER TWELVE

Gavin Ashdown could hardly contain his excitement. He hadn't even considered applying to the newly announced fighter pilot training program, but rather only did so because he was not about to let Jet score higher than him on a test of his hand-eye reflexes. The girl could hardly fly a virtual capital ship, much less an actual fighter.

And yet there before his eyes was the list posted on the outside of the fighter deck, and halfway down, the name Gavin Ashdown. Right below his own name, he spied Jet's as well, but didn't recognize any of the others. Oh well. At least there was one person he would know there.

But there was one other thing he realized seeing his name there, something he hadn't even considered until he entered his application. He was free. Free from the galley, free from officers and enlisted men grumbling about their food and about the service. Free from the cook.

Gavin bolted down to the mess hall and burst into the galley. "Did you see?"

The cook, holding a huge spoon dripping with tomato

sauce with his perpetual cigarette hanging out of his mouth, wiped his nose with a sleeve. "See what?"

"I was accepted! They're going to train me as a fighter pilot!"

The cook shrugged indifferently. "Don't get your hopes up, kid. They only put out a call for applicants. There's no way they're going to accept all of you. Hell, I'd be surprised if they pick more than one of you."

Gavin wouldn't let the man get him down. "Well even if they only take one, I'm going to be it. There's no way I'm spending the rest of my time in space working in this shithole."

The cook glared at him, then thrust a broom into his hand. "Watch your mouth. And get to work."

"But I'm not on for another half an hour!"

"Kid," he said, turning to sulk at him with his sunken eyes and sagging cheeks. "Do you think this is the face of someone who cares?" He pointed to the floor. "Sweep."

Gavin grumbled, but couldn't wipe the spreading grin off his face. The first training session started that afternoon, right after lunch. He did the math in his head. That meant exactly four more hours working for the sniffy old cook. Four more hours to freedom.

CHAPTER THIRTEEN

It wasn't easy, or pleasant, but Senator Galba managed to conceal half his face, and disfigure the rest of it. The first aid kit in Willow's quarters provided the gauze and bandages that covered his left eye and forehead, and his own fist proved handy for the black eye now gracing his right. His long, luxurious hair simply had to go, and Willow's hair clippers proved up to the task of giving him a nice, military-approved buzz cut.

No one could recognize him. And no one would.

He glanced down at his smart uniform, freshly stolen from the quarters of some dead Ensign down the hall by his love, and patted out a few wrinkles.

On second thought he balled up the material in his fist and put the wrinkles back. The more harried and disheveled looking, the better. He must not look like one of the senior ranking members of the Imperial Senate, but as a lowly tech worker on board a Resistance starship.

Tech worker—he smiled. He'd started out in tech, before pursuing his political ambitions. The grunt work didn't last five months, of course, since with one complaint to his father, he'd been elevated to a staff member position for some low ranking Senator. The elder Galba knew all the right people, having served for years in the Senate himself. Such were the perks of the aristocracy on Corsica.

But that tech knowledge just might come in handy. The doors to Willow's quarters slid open as he approached, and he turned left down the hall. First things first—he had to find a terminal and gain access to the ship's schematics and layout.

A sign he passed on his right called out to him. *Tech Supplies.* The placard looked askew, as if hastily glued to the door or possibly knocked loose during one of the many explosions during the previous week. The ship had been to hell. Galba smiled. It was up to him to make it worse. Make the Rebels feel the price of destroying all his hard work for the past five years.

Ever since the Emperor approached him and revealed The Plan.

The door slid open noiselessly; he hurried inside at the sight of another crew member turning the corner down the hall.

The lights flickered on as the door closed. There. On the shelf. A neat hand-held bag, complete with data pad and terminal access tools. Dozens of other boxes of supplies, chairs, and fire extinguishers lined the walls and floor—he even caught glimpse of a weapons locker in the corner as he waded through the sundry supplies to snatch the tool-bag.

Once back out in the hallway, he continued aft. A crew member passed, and nodded curtly at him, and Galba nodded back, avoiding the man's eyes. He smirked inwardly at the idea of the other man walking past the second most powerful figure in the galaxy.

Second most powerful? Had it come to that? At least. Sure, the Emperor had his consuls and secretaries, and regional governors, all trying to juggle the far-flung and sprawling Empire while maintaining stern relations with the rest of the Thousand Worlds. But he, Galba, was above them all. At least, that was what the Emperor had told him. Only he had been trusted to head up the Truth and Reconciliation Committee. Best to live up to the man's expectations.

The end of the corridor teed up against a larger hallway, this one with higher traffic. That wouldn't do. But sure enough, right where Willow had thought, there was a door marked *Systems Engineering*. He walked up and poked his head into the room as the door slid past.

Empty.

Willow said there were at least twenty of these rooms scattered throughout the ship, each capable of acting as a mini-command center in the event of a radiation leak in main engineering or other such eventualities. But for the most part, they were vacant. He just needed a computer terminal, he'd claimed, to amuse himself. Play some games. Distract from his boredom.

Now, time to find the nearest power conduit. Those made for rather attention-grabbing explosions.

Time for some games.

CHAPTER FOURTEEN

Megan Po jogged through the lower levels of the ship, nodding and smiling at the crew members she passed. She needed the exercise, and besides, what better way for the ship's new XO to get to know the ship inside and out, top to bottom? It was her duty. She plotted out a mile long course through half of the ship's lower decks, steering clear of the elevators and instead climbing the access tunnel ladders to reach another deck.

She'd seen some of the damage on an inspection tour she'd taken with Mercer immediately after their escape from the *Caligula*, but now, running through the forward section of deck twenty-six, she gaped at the wreckage still visible from the collision with the other ship. Automated hull repair robots were still busy at work patching the outer hull, but the repair crews had not even started on that deck yet, being too occupied with restoring weapons and gravitics.

She wondered if they'd ever be able to fix all the holes without docking at a real shipyard somewhere, but she knew that would be impossible with the Empire still hot of their tail.

But her run had one more purpose. She'd planned her route to take her past the mess deck. Deck fifteen. The one section of the ship dedicated to recreation, food, and entertainment for the ship's weary crew. The deck that the Fifty-First Brigade, commanded by Sergeant Tomaga, had been allowed to make use of during their stay.

Ben had been opposed to the idea, of course. Sensible, careful Ben. She smiled thinking of him. He reminded her of her own little brother back in California, prim, proper, serious, and an eye for style. She'd always thought his callsign 'Manuel' had been a mistake—Glamor-boy would fit him better!—but she knew she'd never hear the end of it. For all his fastidiousness, he had a macho streak, probably picked up from all the combat masters and marksmen he'd studied under while living in Texas with rich parents.

But Ben had relented to Mercer on the idea of giving the band of soldiers free reign of the mess deck. Mercer insisted that if they were to treat the soldiers like prisoners, that they'd have a hot mess on their hands pretty quickly, and instead wanted them to feel as at home as possible.

And now Megan was going to check up on their receipt of the extended hospitality. As she approached the entrance to the mess deck, two armed marines—stationed there as a precaution—saluted her, and she waved a salute back before going through the sliding doors.

And walked straight into a fight.

Luckily, it was an organized fight, as fights go. A circle of marines, split equally between the crew of the *Phoenix* and the Fifty-First Brigade of the *Caligula*, stood hooting and jeering at each other and the two men in the center. One man she recognized. Sergeant Jayce, who she'd met earlier during a tour. Tall, muscular, and remarkably sassy for a gruff, young marine, he'd shown her respect, but only just enough to keep from being thrown in the brig.

His opponent was one of the men of the Fifty-First. Vaguely Asian, the man was Jayce's equal in size, and possibly his superior in physique: the man tensed his washboard abdomen as he let loose a flurry of fists at Jayce, whose nose was bleeding. Jayce returned the blows, charging the man and colliding with him so they burst through the circle and slammed against the wall, where he proceeded to pummel the other man's stomach with a series of quick jabs.

It was a fight, for sure, but it was not a dirty, no-holds barred fight—Po recognized that at least. From the looks of it, the two men were engaged in some sort of match. A bloody match, but a semi-organized match all the same.

"ATTENTION!" she barked, standing just outside the circle.

Instantly, the yelling, the jeering, and the hollering all ceased: half the men and women in the circle snapped their backs up straight and stood at stiff attention.

The two fighters, however, continued pummeling each other, unaware of the change around them.

"Sergeant Jayce! Stand down. That's an order," she said again, in as stern and commanding a voice as she could muster. Her voice surprised even herself, and it finally got the attention of the two fighters, who stepped away from each other, bleeding, and glowering with stifled tension.

"What the hell is going on here?" she asked, glancing around the circle before resting her eyes on the bloody Staff

Sergeant Logan Jayce.

"A fight, sir," said the heaving man.

"Really?" She tried to keep her voice sarcastic, but not petty or girly. She knew the men would not respond to a high, snippy tone. "Looked like a bitchy hissy-fit to me."

A chorus of laughter came from the circle of soldiers standing at attention. She kept her steely gaze on the bloody men still gasping for breath, but inwardly delighted at the laughter.

"They insulted the Earth Resistance, sir. Called us all a bunch of cock-sucking motherfucking manwh—"

"I don't care what they called you, Sergeant. It may even have been true for all I know. But that doesn't give you permission to beat the shit out of them." She eyed the blood seeping from his forehead into his left eye. "Though it looks like it's not him I have to worry about."

She glanced around the circle of soldiers standing at attention. "So why haven't the rest of you joined in? He insulted all of us, didn't he? What are you waiting for?" She kept her tone ambivalent, trying to see what their reaction would be. Would they think about taking her up on the offer?

"Uh, sir, we're just blowing off some steam," said a tattooed young woman nearby—a private.

And Po understood. They were lucky to be alive, and they all knew it. But they also, each of them, were mourning the loss of their friends. And she knew the marines had born the brunt of it, being at the front line to fend off both Imperial boarding parties. Behind the gruff manner of the men and women standing before her, she could see the strain in their eyes, and behind that, the pain. They needed this.

"Just don't kill yourselves. Anyone who is not ready for duty because of this will find themselves in the brig for a few days. People, we're fighting a war here. Don't do anything stupid. And that goes for our guests, too." She turned to Sergeant Tomaga, who she now noticed outside the circle, still sitting in a chair. "If I find that any of you are causing my men trouble, we'll set you down on the nearest Imperial world we find. Somehow I doubt Admiral Trajan will be slapping your asses and sitting you down for a frothy craft beer." She turned to leave, but caught the eye of the man in a chair leaning back against the wall.

"Sergeant Tomaga. A word?"

She beckoned to the Imperial marine Sergeant, and he reluctantly rose to follow her to another area of the mess deck. The sounds of the resumed fight followed them as the two men started up again to cheers and hollers.

When they were out of earshot of the crowd, she turned to face the man behind her. Eyeing the vaguely Japanese sweep of his forehead and eyes, she wondered if he was from New Kyoto, one of the three triumvirate worlds—the original three planets that held a sort of special governing status in the Empire, though, ostensibly, each world was equal in all rights and privileges, provided that world displayed good behavior.

"You let this happen? Do you have any control of your men at all?" she snapped at him.

"I could ask the same of you, Commander Po. Did you not just let them resume their fight?" The man's voice remained neutral—speaking carefully as he thought she were judging his every word, including his tone. In reality, she was. She had to know how much they could trust the Fifty-First

Brigade, and how much to trust the Sergeant. That level of trust would determine whether or not they would indeed just set the Brigade down on the first Imperial planet they came across.

"True." She let out a small smile. "They seem to need a distraction. Still, I worry that it will escalate."

Tomaga lowered his chin and looked her in the eye. "I assure you, Commander, I will not let it get to that point. I know that we are guests on this ship and are at your mercy. I promise good behavior from my men, as I promised before," he said, in as calm and level a tone as she'd ever heard. She wondered just how nervous the man was. Or perhaps he was actually planning something. Getting in the *Phoenix*'s good graces just enough so they'd lower their guard. Just long enough to strike. A well-placed bullet in the head of Mercer, for example, or a surreptitiously placed charge at the base of the anti-matter engine.

She glanced back at the men fighting, who seemed to have slowed down, weary, bleeding, and squinting in pain. "So what set this off?"

Tomaga looked at the two men now slowly circling each other. Sergeant Jayce lunged for the other man's legs, and the pair went crashing back to the deck. "Your Staff Sergeant there insulted Private Ling. Private Ling responded with a series of insults that your man accurately described to you. The exchange was entirely mutual, Commander. You should know that Sergeant Jayce was the one who pulled the trigger that killed five of my men. Five men whose families won't even receive a body to cremate."

"And Private Ling? How many of ours did he kill?" she

retorted.

"Six," he said, adding with a shrug, "That's what Ling claims, anyway."

Megan wanted to blast a hole in the man's head herself. Six. Six more patriots killed by Imperial vermin. She wondered what in the world Jake was thinking letting the group escape with their lives.

But she caught herself. The Imperials might still have their lives, but that meant that half of her marines in the mess hall also had theirs. If Jake hadn't made his risky decision, there would be no boxing match on the mess deck, no cheers and jeers, no camaraderie among the crew. There would only be another pile of bodies blown out the fighter bay airlock the day before.

She watched the fight end as Jayce banged on the deckplate underneath him in a signal for mercy and Ling jumped off to the cheers of the rest of the Fifty-First Brigade. Before Ling returned to his buddies, he extended a bloody hand down to Jayce, who swore, but took the offer, and once hoisted to his feet strode back to the *Phoenix* marines, sniffing the blood still seeping from his nose.

A thought suddenly struck Po.

"Sergeant Tomaga. You and I both know that an idle marine can be a dangerous one. Almost more dangerous than one with a mission. What would you say to a few joint training exercises, perhaps with just a handful of yours and a handful of ours? It might go a long way towards lowering the level of tension between our men."

Tomaga stared at Po. "What makes you think we'd want to fight alongside you? Your rebellion goes against everything my people stand for. We like order. We like the safety the Empire provides the galaxy. The stability. The peace. All you people seem to want is war," he said, falling silent for a moment. "Why should we help you?"

Po shook her head and turned. She paced for a moment, stopping at a foosball table and idly spinning a few of the handles.

"I disagree with your characterization of us. We hate war, Sergeant. All we want is peace, and to be left alone. But that is not the point. I'm not asking you to help us. I'm asking you to help your men live. If tensions get out of hand, then we'll have to assign you all to the brig, which as you know was not our original agreement, but it is a step that I will take if necessary. And in response, you can either go willingly, or perhaps you choose to continue our aborted fight." She spun a few more handles, then glanced back up at him. "Or, we can get our men training together and let them shoot some bullets that aren't aimed at each other. Keep them busy and occupied. You might find that if we provide them with that, your stay on board may go much smoother."

Tomaga, lost in thought, walked over to the other side of the foosball table. "You play?" he said, indicating the rows of men attached to the steel shafts arrayed down the length of the table.

"Foosball? Yeah, I suppose. The Captain and Commander Jemez and I played a bit during our tour together in Viper squad." She looked up at him suspiciously. "What, you mean now?"

"Why not? If our men can blow off steam, then why not us?"

She couldn't even fathom what he was trying to do. Was he trying to make a genuine effort to get to know her? To lessen the tension? Or was this part of a gambit, to get in her good graces, hoping that she would slip up, grant him access to some vital part of the ship, or glean some sensitive information from her in a moment of unguarded weakness?

"I usually try not to socialize with enlisted men," she said, dodging the request.

"We're not even in the same fleet, Commander. I consider you no more an officer I should obey than a civilian. I was only offering—"

"Fine," she said, and picked up a ball and tossed it onto the table. "But only for a few minutes. I'm still making my rounds."

"Is the ship your patient?" said Tomaga, twisting several of the handles with a familiarity that suggested he'd spent many long hours playing the game.

"The ship. The crew. They're all my patients. My children, if you will."

"Interesting. I've never heard an XO talk like that." With a flick of his wrist he scored a decisive point, and tossed the ball back onto the table. "Do you have children of your own?"

Po's lips tightened, but she couldn't let the man see it. He couldn't know. He mustn't know. His question made her instantly hate him. Loathe him. With one simple question he embodied her sons' murderers. He was the Empire. She had to be a blank page to him. An iron plate. No weakness, or he'd take advantage of her. Of them.

She cleared her throat. "No. The ship is my family, Tomaga. Surely you can understand that? Is Earth so foreign to you that the idea of family doesn't register?" She said, trying to keep the coldness out of her voice.

"Not at all, Commander. It was just an innocent question. Nothing more." He eyed her, as if trying to read behind her face, behind her mask.

What the hell was she doing?

He scored again, the ball clattering into her goal. She smiled, and stepped away. "Excellent game, Sergeant. Thank you for taking the time. Please give some thought to my proposal. Now, if you'll excuse me," she said, turning towards the door.

"Commander," he called after her. She glanced back at him. "We'd be honored to join your marines for training exercises."

She let a thin smile through, and struggled to make it warmer than she felt. "Wonderful. I'll be in touch."

As she left the mess hall, she let out a held breath she hadn't even been aware she'd kept in.

What the hell am I doing?

CHAPTER FIFTEEN

Jake struggled into the jeans, but they simply were not going to fit. The brown shirt, the dusty old vest, even the worn leather boots were his size, but the pants seemed hopeless. With one more attempt, he strained, red-faced, huffing with exasperation as the door to his ready room slid open and Ben walked through, decked out in perfectly fitting, even stylish, frontier clothing. Jake rolled his eyes—even with dusty old second-hand clothing, Ben still managed to look like a French clothing model, only with far more muscle and far less pouting.

"Having some issues?" Ben raised an eyebrow, and fought to keep from smiling.

"I'm having about twenty pounds of extra issues. Hey, any more pants in that sack you took down to the marines?"

"Yeah. There should be a pair in there that'll fit you. What's the matter, Jake, have your thirties caught up with you?"

Jake glowered at his friend. "Jackass," he muttered, "I'm twenty-nine."

Ben couldn't stop the wry grin. "My mistake." But with a wrinkle of his nose he put on his customary scowl. "Jake, this is a bad idea. Fleet Regulation fifty-nine section A, paragraph two: No flag officers are to travel to planetside destinations known to harbor pirates, abductors, kidnappers, or areas otherwise likely to result in capture and demand for ransom, without a substantial security detail. And if you ask me it's a very sensible rule."

Jake scowled back. "You're quoting the *Imperial* regulation at me?"

"Do you want the old Resistance Fleet manual? The wording is nearly the same—as I said, it's a very sensible rule."

Jake sighed. "Can't get anything past you, can I?"

"Have you ever?"

"Ben, look. We need this neodymium, and these pirates aren't going to negotiate with anyone but the Captain." Right as he said it he nearly winced, knowing all too well that, after all, it *should* be Ben negotiating with the pirates. "And besides, you're coming with me. There's my substantial security detail. Better than twenty marines if you ask me."

Ben made a mock-embarrassed face. "Oh gosh. You're making me blush."

Jake stripped off the too-tight pants and pulled his regular uniform back on. "Hey, speaking of marines, are they ready?"

"Yeah. They'll meet us in the shuttle bay after we shift into orbit around Destiny's star. They'll have firearms for us and Bernoulli."

"Good." Jake sat down in the captain's chair to pull the dusty boots on. He realized that was the first time he'd actually sat in it. "How's the security force, Ben? What's morale like?"

Ben shrugged. "As good as can be expected. We lost over half our forces during the incursions by the two boarding parties. And now they're a little pissed that thirty-two of the guys who shot their buddies dead are now lounging around on the mess deck."

"Yeah, I don't like it either, but it was the best solution at the time. People lived because of it."

Ben eyed the captain's chair. "And people might still die because of it, you know. I don't think we can trust them. Sergeant Tomaga seems ok, but some of his men look a little sketchy. I wouldn't be surprised if many of them are through and through loyal Imperials."

Jake nodded. "Just keep armed guards posted throughout that deck."

"Already done." Ben's previous grin had disappeared, replaced by his ever-present no-nonsense scowl.

Jake wondered where they would be right then if he hadn't made his fateful decision. The decision that had robbed Ben of the chair he now sat on. Would they really be dead? Or just captured, waiting to be sent to the penal colony of Glazov? Jake supposed there was a chance that Ben might have actually pulled through with some brilliant plan—the man was very bright, after all, and as stubborn as they come. Just stubborn in the wrong way. Stubborn for rules. Decorum. Doing things the right way. Doing things the right way was not how you stayed alive.

The right way was not always the best way. The best way was to save as many lives as possible. But it was also whatever way that would make those lives worth living.

He eyed his friend, who he noticed was still staring straight at the captain's chair. "Ben, I know we haven't talked much one-on-one since everything went down. I just wanted to say that I'm sorry it didn't turn out how you thought it would." He paused, studying his friend's face. "He mentioned you, you know. Captain Watson. He praised you. Said you were the best officer a captain could ever hope for, and that you would make a fine captain yourself."

At least, Jake knew that was what the Captain was thinking.

Ben turned to leave, and looked down at the ground, shifting in his beat-up cowboy boots, studying them. "Jake, don't. I know what you're doing. I appreciate you trying to motivate me and help me feel valued, but it's really not necessary. What's done is done, and we've both got work to do. I know my duty and you know yours. So let's just do it."

"Fine." Jake stood up and walked out the door with his friend. He wondered if he would ever, someday, build up the courage to tell Ben the truth about what really happened in that sickbay. How would he react? It was easy to imagine Ben becoming a captain of his own ship one day, then maybe an admiral, until eventually the two of them would sit on some front porch somewhere in Florida as two dirty old men, hooting at the passing beautiful women and yelling at the kids to get off the lawn.

The comm officer looked up. "Captain, we've received the coordinates from Volaski's ship."

He nodded his acknowledgment. "Thank you, Ensign. Hail them."

"Yes, sir, opening a visual channel."

The viewscreen came to life, revealing the faces of Captain Volaski and Velar. "Mercer. We've sent you the coordinates. Are you ready?" said Volaski.

"We are."

"Good." Volaski nodded his approval. "We'll be under way then. We will shift to the star in the Destiny system, and then shift to the planet. We ask, Captain, that you park your vessel over Destiny's north pole. It would be best if no one noticed you were there—wouldn't be good for business."

Jake demurred. "That wasn't part of our original plan, Captain. Parking over the north pole will require a tremendous amount of energy to counteract gravity. We'll have to have our gravitic drive engaged at a constant ten percent or so." The alteration in the agreement unnerved him a little, and he questioned whether they should even go through with it. But the bridge crew were all looking at him. He couldn't change his mind now—he'd look indecisive. Wishy-washy. Captains couldn't afford to appear wishy-washy. Not the good ones, anyway.

"Velar and I discussed it just moments ago and we think it will be for the best. Will that be a problem?"

Jake tried to look nonchalant. "Of course not, Captain. When we arrive, my team and I will disembark on a shuttle and meet your ship. We'll follow you down through the atmosphere."

"Sounds like a plan, then," said Volaski, in his thick Russian accent. He bowed slightly before glancing towards Velar, who simply nodded once. "We will talk to you at Destiny, then. Volaski out."

Jake turned to Po and Jemez, who stood behind his console at the XO's station. "What do you think?" he said.

Ben raised his hands in a shrug. "You know what I think, Captain. And now they've altered the plan. It looks even more suspicious to me."

Everything looked suspicious to him, Jake thought. But he was grateful for the consistent advice, at least. "Megan?"

"We'll monitor you from the ship. I've checked the computer records for data on Destiny, and they've got a healthy magnetic field like Earth, and a fairly active star. The ionic activity at the poles will mask our presence, like Velar and Volaski are hoping, but it will also impede communications, and our ability to track you."

"But it can be done?" he asked. No sense in tempting fate.

"Probably. We'll know when we get there, but I'm guessing we'll be fine. And using the pole to mask our signature will allow Lieutenant Grace to get her newbies out on birds right away. She's itching to get them out of the simulators. Up there will be the ideal place to run through fighter maneuvers—fewer eyes to see what we're up to."

"All right then." Jake turned to navigation. "Ensign Roshenko. Lay in the course and make the shift when you're ready."

Roshenko's fingers pecked at the console. "Ready sir."

"Take her away, Ensign."

With a punch of Roshenko's finger, the view on the screen changed in an instant from a flotilla of small freighters and frigates with a red dwarf star in the background to a brilliant yellow-blue star. Destiny's star was a tad larger than Sol, and hotter—its radiation peaking in the green-blue range rather than the green—and Jake guessed that the sky on Destiny might reflect that, perhaps appearing as an even deeper blue than Earth's skies.

"We've arrived, sir," said Ensign Roshenko.

"And Captain," began Ensign Ayala at the tactical octagon,

"the rest of Volaski's caravan is shifting into orbit with us."

A low rumble in the deckplate came and went. Jake cocked his head. "What the hell was that?"

In answer, Alessandro's voice boomed over the speaker. "Friend! Our gravitic drive just got spanked! And spanked hard, friend. Long range shifting is out. This could take days to fix. With some pure neodymium we'd be in the clear, but as it is the temporary solution I came up with at Earth has failed."

Jake shook his head. "Thank you, Bernoulli. Bridge out." Great. One more thing to worry about. He turned to Ayala. "Scan all orbits of the star. Any contacts?"

Ayala punched several keys on her board. "Nothing yet, sir. But I'll notify you if we find something."

Jake keyed open the commlink to engineering. "Bernoulli, how long until the gravitic capacitor banks recharge up to what's required for the next shift?" The gravitic drive and its capacitor banks had been hit pretty hard, and Jake supposed it would take longer than usual to build up a sufficient charge.

"Give it half an hour, friend," said Alessandro over the speaker. "I've got them mostly repaired, but there's a few caps I've got my eye on. They should hold for now, but they're leaking current. We'd do well to pick up some new ones on Destiny if we can manage it."

"We'll keep it in mind, Alessandro. Meet me on the flight deck when we've shifted to Destiny. Mercer out." He turned to Po. "Have you been down to storage yet? Find us some bargaining chips?"

She nodded. "Chief Petty Officer Zaxby is stuffing the shuttle full of electronics as we speak."

"Good." He turned to sit in his chair. "Looks like we're

good to go then—"

"Captain! I'm reading an unidentified contact," said Ayala, the alarm in her voice creating a pit in Jake's stomach. They weren't ready for another confrontation. The ship was dangerously low on railgun ordnance, and the repair crews were still busy just patching the hull, not to mention all the damaged weapons turrets and other tactical systems.

"Is it just one of Volaski's?"

"Negative, sir, they're all accounted for. This one's new. It's bigger than they are—not as big as us, but still nothing to sneeze at."

"Do you have a visual?"

Ayala shrugged, the tree tattoos on her neck bunching up as she did. "It's still over 10,000 klicks away in a more highly inclined orbit around the star, but it looks like they're shifting course to match ours. They'll be on us in ten minutes or so."

Jake stood back up. "I want a reading on that ship. Scan them for armaments, defenses, everything. Still no idea who they are?"

"They're not sending out any transponder codes," said Ayala.

"Captain, Volaski's ship is hailing us."

"Onscreen."

Volaski and Velar reappeared on the viewscreen, now with worried faces. "Captain," said Velar, "it looks like we have an unexpected visitor. I take it you've never seen a November vessel?"

So. It was a November clan ship. He'd never seen one, but he'd heard of them. Fast and deadly, was the reputation. Not like an Imperial capital ship, but with the *Phoenix* in her current state, it might not matter. "So they're with the November family? This isn't their space, what are they doing out here?"

Velar answered his question. "Destiny is outside the Empire, Captain Mercer, so anyone comes here as they please. We don't often get November clan ships here, but they have been known to come to trade occasionally, and while we're wary, we've never had any problems with them. Except this one seems to have taken an interest in us."

Velar's face, usually unreadable, now displayed nervousness. Clearly, she hadn't been expecting this. Somehow, that made Jake trust her a little more. If she'd made some sort of deal with the Imperials to somehow betray them, the ship bearing down on them now would be several Imperial fleet capital ships and not a November vessel. Somehow, her nervousness soothed him.

"Very well, Velar. You apparently have dealt with them before. How do you recommend we proceed? I'd rather keep a low profile here, though it seems they've seen us already. Are there likely to be hostilities with us around?"

"No, I doubt it. The November clan is an old pirating family, and a sworn enemy of the Empire. If they know your story, it's certain they'll not attack," she said. "But I'd be careful if I were you. They might see that you're damaged, and think you're a very attractive target. A capital ship might be too tempting to pass up. You'd fetch an extremely high price on the black market."

Great. Not just the Imperials to worry about. Having the November family hovering like vultures, waiting for the *Phoenix* to present a weak face before swooping in was not another thing Jake needed on his plate at the moment.

"Ensign. Hail them."

Ensign Falstaff pressed a few buttons and glanced up at Mercer. "They've responded, sir. Audio only."

"This is Captain Jacob Mercer of the Earth Resistance Fleet Ship *USS Phoenix*, to the November fleet vessel. Please identify yourself."

A pause, and then the speakers crackled to life, the interference from the star readily apparent from the static. A male voice answered, speaking in a strange accent Jake couldn't completely pin down. Indian? Not quite. "*Phoenix*. So it's true, then."

Another long pause, and Jake wondered whether the voice was going to continue when the speaker came on again. "We'd heard rumors, but we suspected it was only the Empire playing its tricks again to lure us out into the open."

Jake cleared his throat. "To whom do I have the pleasure of talking to?"

"Nathaniel Raza, of the November clan. You are on the run then? From the Empire?"

Jake glanced up at Megan and Ben. "I wouldn't say on the run, no, but I would prefer not to run into them." He didn't want to give the impression of weakness. To be on the run was to imply weakness.

"I understand, Captain. I would not prefer to run into them either. Though if we did, I think I would prefer it now with you sitting here than to any other time. I think between the two of us we could make short work of any Imperial ship. Don't you?"

"Yes, Mr. Raza, I suppose we could," Jake said with a laugh. "So what is your business here in the Destiny system?

Do I gather correctly that you were told about us?"

"Told about you would be a stretch. I just heard rumors through my contacts that there was a renegade Imperial capital ship on the run and that Admiral Trajan was hunting her down, and would probably pay a mighty price indeed for information leading to your capture."

The way the man said it made Jake nervous, though angry might have been a better term. "So, Mr. Raza, do you intend to go collect a reward?"

Laughter snorted through the speaker. "You are kidding, right? The November family is an honorable one, Captain Mercer. We don't deal with the Empire, and we don't deal with the slavers and the lawless bands of criminals that frequent these parts. To turn a fellow freedom fighter like yourself over to the Emperor would go against everything the November family stands for."

Something nagged at the back of Jake's mind, but he couldn't quite grasp at it. "You say you don't deal with criminals, but isn't the November family a crime syndicate? Don't you deal with black market goods and harass legitimate businessmen and merchants?"

"We deal in items the Empire has deemed criminal, yes, but the ramblings of a man who considers himself an embodied god do not define for me what is and is not evil. The Emperor could outlaw water, but would that stop us from drinking? He could outlaw thoughts but would that stop me from thinking? He could outlaw fecal matter, but would that stop me from shitting? There are many things the Emperor forbids which we find useful, and profitable."

"And the merchants you levy your special tax on? The one

where you claim to provide special protection? Back on Earth, we might say that you make them an offer they cannot refuse."

The man laughed long. "So we do. But we only tax those businessmen we know to be in league with the Empire, or those that benefit from its corruption, its oppression, and its violations of fairness and freedom. Those merchants that struggle and try to scrape by in spite of the Empire? We are rather their champion, Captain, not their enemy. We are not some Italian mafia. We don't kill for sport or on a whim. But those that benefit from the Empire's oppression have a great deal to fear from us indeed."

The thought niggling at the edge of his memory clicked into place. "Mr. Raza, you wouldn't happen to know anything about the *USS Fury*, would you? Admiral Pritchard's ship?"

Silence.

"The galaxy is a big place, Captain Mercer, and the Empire has a big fleet. Is Admiral Pritchard a name I should recognize?"

He was hiding something. He'd paused too long, and his voice sounded far more suspicious than it should. Jake couldn't put his finger on it, or even say why he thought Raza's voice sounded suspicious. It just did.

"He's not Imperial, if that's what you're implying. No, Admiral Pritchard is the Earth Resistance Admiral who fled from the Dallas massacre three years ago. Surely you've heard about Dallas?"

"Yes, of course we've heard about Dallas. Half of us were expecting Old Earth to go the way of Belen. But I have no idea as to your Admiral Richard."

"Pritchard," corrected Jake. "Hmm, interesting. It was just

that I had heard that the last time he was seen by anyone was in November clan space. And that it didn't go very well for him. You're telling me you know nothing of it?"

Another long pause, and Jake could hear Raza talk to a companion, but not quite loudly enough to hear.

"Sorry, Captain, that I can't be of more help. But a lot goes on in November space that the Empire doesn't know about. Perhaps it might be to your benefit to return to our outpost with me? It is not far from here, about ten light years."

Ben caught Jake's eye and slowly shook his head. Jake couldn't agree more. No sense in being led like a lamb into the den of one of the galaxy's most feared families, in spite of the claims of innocence put forth by Mr. Raza.

Jake shook his head. "I'm sorry, sir, but we have business here on Destiny. Perhaps another time."

"You're always welcome, Captain Mercer. Any enemy of the Empire is a friend of mine. And of my family. Perhaps there at my outpost we can have a more in-depth discussion about your Admiral friend—a discussion I'd rather not have on an open channel in the Destiny system. Destiny is not the safest, my friend, and you would do well to be careful, whatever your business is."

"I intend to. Exactly where is your outpost located?"

"Classified," said Raza, and Jake could almost hear the man grinning as he said it. Crime syndicates didn't exactly have a government classification system, but Jake understood the man's meaning: none of your damned business.

"I understand, Mr. Raza," said Jake.

"But if you should ever need to get in contact with me, shift into the Szabo system, and wait in orbit around the star there. November ships use that star as a waypoint for gravitic shifts all the time, and if you ask for me, I'm sure one of my fellows will know where to find me."

It was odd. It was almost as if the man were inviting Jake to come with him, or at least to come find him. As if he had something of importance to tell him....

Or perhaps he was only trying to lure the *Phoenix* into November space and waylay her, like they were rumored to have done with the *USS Fury*. Perhaps that was what he was doing, dropping just a hint that he might know Pritchard's whereabouts so that Jake would follow Raza straight into an ambush on the other side of a gravitic shift.

"Very well, Mr. Raza. Thank you for the advice. Now, if you'll excuse me, I have some business to attend to on Destiny. I assume you've been there? Any advice I should know?"

A chuckle. "Yeah. I hope you like dust. And horse shit."

"We had heard about the dust," said Jake with a nod.

Raza continued. "And keep your weapons with you at all times, Captain. Like I said, Destiny is not the safest place in the Thousand Worlds. I'm surprised you're even headed down there." He coughed, before finishing. "Good luck Captain. I think you'll need it. Raza out."

Jake breathed a sigh of relief. "Well that went better than I expected."

Ensign Falstaff spoke up again. "Sir, Volaski's ship is hailing again."

Jake nodded, indicating to the young man to open the channel.

"Captain Mercer," said Velar, "I trust you will not take the man up on his offer?"

"So you were listening in on my communication?" Jake said.

"Yes. One can never be too careful around the November clan. And I assure you, Captain, it's best to be careful around that lot. They're all smiles and friendly out here, away from their space, but once you get into November territory things change. When you shift to their space, you are instantly surrounded by a small fleet of missile frigates, stripped of whatever valuable cargo you have, and sent on your way far poorer than how you came in, if you leave at all. In your case, I doubt you would," she glanced at Volaski, who nodded in approval. "But come. My world awaits. It is not much, but it is home, and I know you will like it for the short time we will have you there. You have the coordinates for the northern pole?"

"We do. Our gravitic capacitor banks will be fully charged momentarily. I'll send word when we're ready to shift. Mercer out."

Po grumbled behind him. "Pirates. What a tangled web we've got here. Trust Velar and Volaski, or trust Mr. Raza of the November family?"

Ben answered, shaking his head and poking a few buttons on his security station. "Neither one, if you ask me. The only good pirate is a dead one."

Jake grinned back at him. "Oh, admit it. You're loving dressing up like a cowboy and heading down to a frontier world."

Ben grumbled, and shifted on his feet. He tried to frown, but couldn't help the tug on his cheeks. "Only if we actually get to ride horses."

NICK WEBB

CHAPTER SIXTEEN

The shuttle ride down to the surface proved rougher than Jake was accustomed to. He wondered if the ship had been damaged during the battle at the shipyards, but Bernoulli shook his head.

"Destiny's sun is extremely active," he said, scratching at his half-mustache. For some odd reason that Jake still hadn't had the mind to ask about, Alessandro Bernoulli kept one half of his mustache perpetually shaved off, and the other half— the right half—properly groomed. "The gamma rays have the most pronounced effect on the gravitic field—they're most likely to penetrate the hull and disrupt the dopants in the crystal lattice. But you'd be surprised at the effect neutrinos can have as well—gravitic fields are basically neutrino exclusion zones, which is why we can't shift too close to a gravity well, because that gravity well is usually a star. In fact, there is a delicate balance between shifting too close to the star and run the risk of neutrino saturation of your field, and too far away and not having enough energy to even make it. You might say that—"

"Alessandro," Jake held up a hand. "Less is more, buddy."

Alessandro laughed. "Ha! Friend, you ask, so you should expect the answer!"

"I expect an answer, Alessandro, I just don't expect to fall asleep during the answer," said Jake as he took off his left boot and shook it. A small pebble fell to the floor with a clatter, and he wondered how it even ended up in there—as far as he knew, there were no pebbles on the *Phoenix*. It must have already been in there.

"Interesting, Lieutenant," said Ben, furrowing his brow like he did whenever he started thinking about something. "So would that make shifting to high orbit around a black hole difficult? They are neutrino emitters, if I'm remembering my astrophysics class correctly."

"Jemez, I didn't know you took astrophysics. What gives?" Jake glanced up at his friend as he pulled off his other boot. He continued in an attempted backcountry accent. "I knew you were all into this book learnin', but astrophysics?"

"I did finish college before I joined the fleet, you know. Some of us had lives before the war."

Bernoulli shot Ben an amazed look before turning to Jake. "Friend, you take this bullshit attitude from him?"

Jake raised a hand. "Ben and me go way back. He just dishes it out as good as I give it to him."

Ben smirked. "Way back means three years. Jake here was my Wing Commander when I first started with the Viper squad," he said. "And somehow he thought that bringing the newbie along to help him win a bar fight would be a great way to break me in."

Jake chuckled. "It sure did. Just look at you now! Strapping young lad."

Alessandro laughed. "It is good. Is good. But yes, Commander, you are quite right. My associates and I at CERN were working on a solution to the neutrino flux problem when we stumbled upon the Milan Approximation, but high-neutrino-flux gravitic shifting is still a hot area of research right now. I'm sure the person to figure it out will win the next ten Nobel prizes at once. It would mean we could travel not just to the center of our own galaxy with as much energy as it takes to shift to Vega, but we could shift to the center of the Andromeda galaxy as well."

Ben rubbed his chin. "Did you say the Milan Approximation? Are you telling me that you came up with it?"

"Well … not exactly. Me and a few others were primarily resp—"

Jake made a raspberry sound. "Don't listen to him, Ben. The Milan Approximation is sitting its ass approximately right there," he said, pointing to Alessandro's chair. "Would have been called the Bernoulli Approximation if our friend here didn't hate the limelight so much."

Alessandro shrugged. "I would have had to give speech. I hate speeches. Especially in front of people."

Jake rolled his eyes. "You've got no problem delivering speeches to me."

"But you're not people, you're just Captain Mercer," Alessandro retorted. "And besides, you ask for it. Didn't you realize that I make those speeches to you during our chess games just to keep you distracted? Most of what I tell you is complete bullshit—all I'm really doing is planning out my next ten moves."

The two marines, dressed in the frontier attire like the rest of them, chuckled at Bernoulli's remark. One of them, Corporal Suarez, checked the sidearms strapped underneath his vest, and tightened the long knife strapped to his shin underneath the dusty old black jeans. Sergeant Avery, a grim-faced, experienced spec-ops soldier sat next to him, peering out the window at the thickening atmosphere.

The ship trembled a little harder. Jake peered out the window through the atmosphere to the land below. "Ben, buddy, are you even flying this thing? Or are we falling?"

"It's on autopilot. It's just a normal reentry, nothing the computer can't handle."

"Yeah, but all the same, let's just make sure we don't crash land in one of those wheat fields or something. Or is that just dust?" He watched the ground approach them with gut-wrenching speed. Jake knew, intellectually at least, that the gravitics would kick in 1000 meters from the ground and they'd decelerate from five or so kps down to just dozens of klicks per hour, but the approach to the ground still always made Jake nervous—at least when he wasn't at the controls.

"The computer can fly this thing better than you or I could even dream of, Jake," his friend said.

"I doubt it. Computers have glitches. I'd rather control my fate with my own two hands on the stick and not some piece of silicon."

"There's a higher chance of your brain glitching than the triply redundant auto-pilot software." But Ben knew about Jake's squeamishness with computers flying ships, and took the controls in his hands. "Starting our deceleration curve. Don't worry, Captain, we'll all live to see the *Phoenix*."

"We'd better," Jake said, "or I'll kick your ass."

The shuttle landed just behind Captain Volaski's ship, which had parked in a giant, dusty field next to what would have looked like a spaceport, except for the sagebrush caught in all the fencing and the dust piled high over the landing lights and signs. Stepping out of the shuttle, Jake instantly saw that Velar was not exaggerating—he didn't see how the main export of Destiny was anything other than fine, brown dust.

"Captain, welcome to Destiny," said Velar, sweeping her arms wide and greeting them with a grin. It was the first time he'd seen her truly smile.

"Thank you. It's a lovely world...." he trailed off as he coughed, having inhaled a mouthful of dust as the wind picked up. Glancing upwards, he saw that the sky glowed a little more violet than the Earth's atmosphere, but just barely. The sun felt hot on his skin, and the light coming from it seemed whiter somehow, like the florescent lights that lined the hallways of the *Phoenix*. The glare from the sand was almost intolerable.

While the sun felt remarkable hot against his skin, Jake noticed how cold it actually was. Not cold enough to be terribly uncomfortable, but enough to make him want to start walking briskly to warm up.

"So, not a farming world, huh?" said Jake, noticing the unending white-brown landscape all around them, punctuated only by occasional scraggly brush and the rare, squat tree.

Velar shrugged. "It does rain here—you'd be surprised at what the summer months look like. A monsoon sweeps up out of the ocean like clockwork at around the point the sun reaches its zenith. The year is only eleven months long, so I'm sure that will take some getting used to. But for me, it's home."

That was an odd way to put it, as Jake had no intention of getting used to the month cycle on Destiny, but he brushed the comment aside and glanced up at Volaski who was descending his ship's ramp.

"Captain Mercer, I trust you're all armed and ready to go into town?"

Jake patted the sidearm under his vest and nodded. "We're ready when you are. Is your contact far away? We'd like to get this over with if you don't mind. We try not to spend too much time in any one system. Too tempting of a target, you might say, and not just for the Imperials."

Volaski nodded. "I understand. Right this way. We'll take ground transport to the town." He led them to a small, tattered building that housed half a dozen ground vehicles, each with large, deeply grooved tires, which Jake supposed would be useful for driving through the mud during the monsoon season. Volaski sat in the driver's seat of one while Velar took the wheel of a second car.

"You'll have to split up for a moment. We can't fit you all in one," said Velar. She fumbled with the ignition controls, and a low rumble sounded from the front hood.

"Are these things gas-powered?" asked Jake. He hadn't ridden on a gas-powered ground vehicle for ages. His mom's neighbor, an older fellow with an eye for antique technology, kept a twenty-first century gasoline vehicle in his garage, but he'd never seen it run.

"Methane, yes," said Velar. "Destiny has methane in abundance—it's about .5 percent of the atmosphere. Too low of a concentration to react with the oxygen, but high enough that we can easily distill it out of the air. And it means that

Destiny is far warmer than it should be, given its distance from our sun. Methane is an excellent greenhouse gas."

"No carbon dioxide?" asked Alessandro. But then he nodded to himself, as if understanding.

"Barely," continued Velar as she put the vehicle into gear with a grinding thrust of the shifter. "There is no native multicellular life on Destiny to speak of. Just the cyanobacteria that is the source of the planet's oxygen. Most of the carbon is in the form of methane, which suits us just fine. We've never lacked for power here."

As they spoke, the barren landscape flew past, and the passengers bounced up and down over the unpaved dust. Jake held his vest over his face to filter out most of the grit, but he still felt a veneer of powder coat his teeth. He turned to Bernoulli and the marine in the back seat, Corporal Suarez.

Suarez nodded his youthful face at him, indicating his readiness for whatever they might encounter in the town, which now loomed just ahead of them. It was actually a small city, though without any tall buildings—just an assortment of ramshackle homes and businesses that stretched out to the low, distant hills.

"Looks like it's seen better days," said Jake, eyeing the tattered remains of a few buildings on the outer edge of town. A few stray dogs bolted through a front door hanging by one hinge.

Velar nodded. "It's the price we pay for privacy. The standard of living would certainly improve if the Empire were here, but, and I think you'd agree, we wouldn't want it any other way."

The vehicles ground to a halt outside what looked like a

vast warehouse building, at least 200 meters long. Hundreds of other vehicles were parked haphazardly in front, in no discernible order. In fact, everything on Destiny seemed to be a free-for-all. The streets were a maze, the houses built at odd angles and with no obvious regularity. Jake spied a few men ambling down the street, guns openly hanging from their belts.

"Here we are. This is one of the central markets where the merchants gather to trade and sell," said Velar as she jumped out of the vehicle.

"Is your contact here?" asked Jake.

"No," she replied, to Jake's surprise. "I just need to pick up a few supplies here. You're welcome to come inside, of course. Have a look around." She eyed him with a sidelong glance, looking down at the bulge beneath his vest, indicating the sidearm underneath. "Or not, if you'd prefer not to attract attention. But you might find something useful for the *Phoenix*. The pirates, as you call them, often come across rather interesting technologies that haven't filtered their way out to the Empire or to Earth yet."

Jake nodded. "Sure thing. Meet you back out here in half an hour? Is that enough time?"

"That should suffice, Mercer," and she led them to the front entrance, which was guarded by two masked men with assault rifles, who—Jake wasn't exactly sure if it was the message the market's management intended to send—were sound asleep in chairs propped up against the walls.

Volaski stayed in the vehicle. "I'm trying to figure out a shipping schedule," he said, studying a data pad and waving them off. "I'll wait out here."

They followed their guide into the warehouse. Velar

disappeared into the milling crowds of merchants and customers, and Jake supposed that there must have been an additional parking field out behind the building since the hundred or so vehicles out front could not have accounted for such a large number of people. Everyone was dressed like Velar, and Jake noticed, like himself and his men. Rough, dusty, worn clothing and a sea of hats. Banners indicated the location of merchant's tables; the entire warehouse was alive with shouted negotiations and haggling.

Besides English, Jake saw a smattering of other languages covering many of the signs: Spanish, Chinese, or some other Asian language—he could never tell them apart—and even what looked like Russian on a banner that hung limply and bedraggled between two posts.

"Well, Alessandro? This is your playground. Lead the way."

Bernoulli grinned. "With pleasure, friend. I bet we can find some caps the right size, or if not quite right, I can string together a bunch in parallel," Alessandro pushed ahead into the crowd. Jake noticed some people stare at the man's half-mustache, but otherwise he seemed to blend right in.

Ben leaned over to him. "Hey, Jake, I'm going over to the wall down there. Looks like a fun assortment of knives and plasma-based small arms that might be helpful."

"A winning combination. Take Corporal Suarez with you," he pointed at one of the marines, and glanced at the other one. "Sergeant Avery, stay with Alessandro and me." He leaned in close to the man, who, though empty handed, kept one hand very close to one of his sidearms. "And be vigilant. Stay on the lookout for anything out of place—anyone staring at us for too long."

Sergeant Avery nodded his grizzled face once. Jake was glad Ben had chosen him. The man did special ops in the North American Marines before joining the Resistance, and served in the special forces there for many years and many successful missions before being assigned to the *Phoenix*.

Alessandro, however, had no inhibition whatsoever. He plunged into the crowd, not even noticing anyone who bumped into him, keeping his gaze locked on an array of tables in the center of the huge warehouse full of electronics, parts, and other odd pieces of equipment that Jake couldn't recognize.

"Friend! We're in luck! And so soon, too." Bernoulli reached down to pick up a massive block. It looked like a white brick, except two fat metal prongs stuck out the top. He read the inscription on the side. "One megafarad. Perfect. We can link up fifty or so of these in parallel and we've got ourselves another cap."

The merchant who owned the tables waddled over. A heavyset man in his fifties, he grinned as he watched Bernoulli examine the white brick. "Straight from the factory in the Manchuria system. Came in just yesterday. They sell for fifty thousand off-world, but I can give it to you for thirty."

Alessandro nodded. "A fair price, I'm sure. But I don't think it's quite what I'm looking for."

A scowl crossed the man's face. "Well then be a little more gentle with it, sir, and save it for the next paying customer."

Bernoulli set the cap down gently before facing the merchant again with a sly smile. "Really what I need is, oh, say, fifty of them. Do you have that many in stock today?"

The merchant's eyes grew large, and Jake could almost see

the man crunch numbers in his head. "Fifty! What on Old Earth do you need fifty for? One or two is plenty for a standard sized freighter. Unless you have one of the really old models of gravitic drive?"

Alessandro chuckled. "No, state of the art, in fact." Jake glared at him, and Bernoulli caught his eye. "Let's just say I have friends who find themselves in need of them. A lot of them. Seems there's an entire merchant fleet of freighters out in the Vitari Sector that needs new cap banks. The whole lot of them flew too close to some star there and the induction currents from a coronal mass ejection blew out the banks of every ship. They're stranded until I get out there to them. Profit highs for me and you both if we can meet the demand."

Jake reminded himself to never believe a word Alessandro said ever again. The man lied like it was the most natural thing in the world.

If it were possible for the merchant's eyes to grow any larger, they'd fall out. He fumbled in his pocket for a data pad and punched at it feverishly. "Well, I can give you thirty now. And if you wait another few days I can get you the other twenty. And a whole lot more if you need them." He glanced up with a hopeful expression. "Twenty-five each?"

Bernoulli shook his head with a scowl, and wiped his half-mustache. "Ten thousand."

"Ten! That's what I paid for them! I won't go any lower than twenty-thousand. Final offer." He shoved the data pad into his pocket and folded his plump, hairy arms.

Bernoulli glanced up at Jake, who nodded. He was sure they could scrounge up a million bucks or so on board. Every Imperial fleet ship embarked with a small supply of hard cash for emergencies, for just such situations—dealing with people who would not take Imperial credits.

Alessandro nodded and said, "Deal. When we offload our equipment we're selling, I'll come back and make the payment. Probably later today," he added, with another glance at Jake, who inclined his head again. He was pretty sure they could finish their deal with Velar's contact by then.

The merchant agreed, and the three of them continued browsing the various wares until Velar was finished with whatever her business was. Jake noticed that many of the merchants wore a sort of band around their necks, just like Volaski, as if it were some sort of neckwarmer or fashion statement—though he doubted that anyone on Destiny had even a remote interest in fashion. He glanced around the nearby tables and down the narrow pathway between them at all the customers browsing the merchandise. Sure enough, many of the customers wore them too. He made a mental note to ask Velar about them.

Alessandro sidled up to him. "Hey, friend, come take a look at this." He pointed over to one of the tables piled high with numerous instruments.

"What is it?"

"If that's what I think it is, we might find them handy, though I can't believe they sell them here. They're incredibly dangerous." They approached the table, and Bernoulli bent down to inspect a pile of electronic devices.

Jake read the sign above the table. The larger script was in Russian, but next to it were the words, *Uncommon Defense*. The name of the shop, most likely, though Jake supposed that a few tables set up in a warehouse didn't really deserve to be called a shop.

"Gentlemen," said a woman in a thick Russian accent. "You have interest in my product, yes?" She eyed them up and down. Standing at over six feet, Jake almost had to look up to her. A full, ill-fitting jumpsuit didn't quite reach down to her ankles, and a bulge under her long vest indicated the presence of at least a sidearm, though judging by the length of the bulge she could very well have an assault rifle hidden under there.

Bernoulli cleared his throat and looked up at her with a grin. "Hello, sweetheart." Jake shot him a glance, as if to say, careful. Bernoulli continued, "Vesuvius mines? I didn't know cloaked anti-ship mines were legal these days. Much less that they were still in production."

She furrowed her bushy eyebrows, and cast them a suspicious look. "Most customers don't mind. You? If you mind, you're welcome to get hell out." She pointed to the next table as if telling them to move along.

Alessandro held up his hands. "Sorry, honey, I didn't mean to offend you. I was just pleasantly surprised, is all. Does the cloak work? Most cloaks only go into the infrared these days, but does it do optical? Radar?"

Jake peered at the diminutive, cylindrical black shapes. He supposed the black would be enough to hide it from most optical sensors, given its size, which meant that a good infrared cloak and proper stealth geometry would be sufficient to escape most detection. He remembered reading about Vesuvius mines in the academy. When the Empire first starting spreading its influence 150 years ago, they outlawed the sale and manufacture of the devices, on pain of detention in the Glasov penal colony. Most offenders never returned.

She grunted. "They do well enough. And the antimatter is fresh. Very low leakage, too. Less than an attogram per day. You can lay these in almost any orbit, and when target matching specifications appears nearby, it will do a slow release of the anti-matter into the microthrusters and steer into the ship. Explodes on contact. Taking half ship with it, of course."

Bernoulli nodded. "Almost a good thing the Empire banned these things, right? They lost dozens of ships in the early days of the Empire before they tracked down the manufacturers and … dealt with them," he finished with a grimace.

She shot him another dirty look, but Jake interrupted her retort. "And how much are you asking, ma'am?"

"Fifty thousand. No less. I have regular customers, so don't try to low-ball me." She glared at him, and he stroked his chin. They would give them a leg up if Trajan ever tracked them down. A few of those sent surreptitiously floating towards the Imperial ships and any fight would soon be over.

"Fine. We'll take five."

One thick eyebrow rode high on her forehead, and she smiled—the first time she did anything besides frown. "Really? Well then, I had you pegged as no-good window shoppers. Very well, Five it is. Cash? I don't take no filthy Imperial credits."

Jake nodded. "Yes, of course cash. Though we'll be picking up a large shipment of goods here later today, and I think we'll take these then. No sense in carrying them around with us all day. Is that fine with you?"

She grinned, and yellow-stained teeth peered through her parted lips. "Very fine. Come back when you're ready."

They continued walking down the narrow aisle, looking at the various goods displayed, and Jake could definitely tell they had entered the contraband section of the warehouse. Besides the mines, several tables displayed glittering heaps of cocraina, the latest drug craze sweeping the Thousand Worlds, which the Empire had sensibly banned. Others held weapons that could be disassembled into constituent parts so innocuous and discrete that they could be smuggled into just about any location, including, presumably, detention facilities and penal colonies.

Out of the corner of his eye, behind them, Jake saw an urgent movement. He glanced around and looked into Ben's serious eyes, followed by Corporal Suarez.

"What is it, Ben?" he asked as his friend came in close to his ear.

"We've got tails," he said, nodding his head behind him, and to the side, towards the next aisle over. Jake looked up and saw a man in a heavy coat peer at them, walking slowly towards them. Two more men in the next aisle over stared at them as well, and as Jake turned, he saw that just further down their same aisle another pair of men in similar thick coats slowly approached. Jake didn't need to ask Ben what he thought they carried underneath.

"What do you think, Avery?" said Jake, leaning into the sergeant. The man had extensive spec-ops training, and might have some insight.

"Tight, confined, public space. They're not likely to pull guns on us, but then again, this isn't some market on the east coast of North America, this is Destiny. They might not feel so inhibited here." He glanced to the next aisle over, the one closer to the wall they had entered from. "That aisle looks clear. Lets jump the table and get outside."

Jake furrowed his brow. He didn't want to leave without their guide. He looked up and down the aisles for Velar, but didn't immediately see her.

"Fine. Let's move. Get to the vehicles," he said finally. And the moment they hopped the nearest table to get to the wall, the heavy-coated men sprang into action, all simultaneously revealing their assault rifles.

CHAPTER SEVENTEEN

Senator Galba was used to acting. He'd spent his entire Senate career putting on a good show for the people, for the Emperor, for his aides, for his fellow senators, and for all the myriad of women he'd conquered. He knew how to say just the right thing for the right ears. How to ingratiate himself, or make others cower in fear, or covet his attention. Usually, just a simple touch on the elbow, a wink, and a sly smile was enough to get him whatever he wanted from just about anyone.

"No, sir, just doing a quick inventory of some critical supplies. On the XO's order." He tried to stare straight ahead, like a good soldier, without looking the officer in the eyes.

"I wasn't informed. Which department did you say you're in?" The Chief Petty Officer looked him up and down. At least, that was the rank Galba interpreted from the insignia on the man's shoulder. He really had no idea. The man could be a private, for all he knew.

"Operations, sir. But I was, err, requisitioned to repair duty after all the craziness the other day. Damn Imperials." He knew how to talk like a commoner. Gods knew he grew up with enough of them. Of course, even the commoners in the seaside resort of Capricus on Corsica were gods among men in comparison with the riffraff on Old Earth, or any other backward world in the Empire. He scratched his balls for good measure.

The other man paused, but nodded, then looked closer at Galba's bandage covering half his face. "You ok there? Lose the eye?"

"No, thank the gods. Doc says it'll be fine in a few weeks." He froze on the inside, though, as he realized he just slipped in a reference to the gods. The Roman gods—the gods of the Empire. But to his relief the man gave him a sly smile.

"Oh, you're a believer, huh? Don't run into to many others like us in the Resistance. Gods, I hate the Empire, but at least they know their stuff with religion. Hey, don't I know you? Did you serve down on Earth? In the North American Brigades?" The officer squinted, waving a finger at him as if trying to pull at a distant memory.

He was obviously just remembering Galba's face from the news broadcasts. The Senator weighed his next move carefully. "Huh, no actually I was in the Euro Brigades. Just as a tech. But our division saw some action over in D.C. during D-day. Were you there?" It was only partly a lie. He knew from his studies of the Old Earth Resistance movement that there was a lot of shuffling around of Rebel divisions in the days leading up to D-day, including several European brigades seeing some intense action at the Imperial Government Satellite offices in Washington. Of course, he was safely light years away at the time.

Thankfully, the man nodded. "Yeah, that's it. I was

stationed in Baltimore, but we saw some action down south. Man, the fuckers sure don't know when to stop, do they? We'll have to chase them all the way back down to that rat infested shithole of a world they call home. Corsica? Fuck. More like Forsica. Ha ha—get it?"

Galba did not get it, but guessed at the man's meaning, and cringed inwardly at the crude lower-class attempt at humor. His friends at the Capricus Beach Club would howl with laughter at him for getting himself into such a ... detestably common conversation. "Right, sir. Very good, very good. Well, I should be getting back to work. Can I help you with anything while you're here?"

The officer glanced at the shelves. "Yeah. I'm looking for some spanners and a few omni-gauges."

Galba stepped over to a shelf and opened a box—one he'd already rifled through an hour ago. Hefting out a few spanners he held them out to the man. "These work? And I think we've got some omni-gauges over here.…"

A minute later the man had gone, leaving Galba to his work. He breathed a sigh of relief and sat back down at the computer terminal he'd managed to hack into from the access port on the wall. Apparently, his secret diplomatic codes hadn't been locked out yet, and hopefully no one on board knew to look for them yet in the security reports. They'd find out eventually, of course, unless he could hide his tracks.

But hopefully it wouldn't matter.

With a few more keystrokes he initiated the coolant build-up. Even after hundreds of years of engine technology, the damn things still needed cooling, and the most reliable source was still water.

Main engineering would never even know what hit it.

With a grin, he slipped out of the room, tool bag firmly in hand, and melted into the stream of crew members who rushed down the corridor towards some new emergency.

Time to find Willow and establish an alibi. His groin clenched—with any luck, an alibi with a happy ending.

CHAPTER EIGHTEEN

Gavin Ashdown could hardly believe what he was doing. Overhead, through the transparent composite viewport, wheeled a field of brilliant stars, and to his side, the polar region of the planet Destiny. He almost giggled—he never giggled, but he couldn't wipe the grin off of his face as he pulled up on the controls and spun the fighter around to face the direction he had just come from, and punched the accelerator.

"Dammit, Ashdown, is that all you've got?" came Lieutenant Grace's angry voice over the speaker. "My great-granny Meredith could pull a tighter turn than that. And she's dead. Pull your head out of your ass and get in the game!"

"Yes, sir," he said, and attempted the 180 degree flip again, setting his nose towards the horizon and then simultaneously firing his forward dorsal thrusters and his rear ventral thrusters: with a flip of the wings, spun the craft around in as tight a radius he could manage, and gunned the gravitic drive when his orientation righted itself.

"Better, but still pretty shitty. Keep at it for the next few minutes while I tell your friend how awful she is."

Gavin chuckled. He supposed Jet Xing had it worse than him—she was good at the videogames, but never like Gavin. She just didn't have the feel for the three dimensional space, nor the reflexes. And furthermore, she didn't take well to people yelling at her. Threw off her groove, she claimed. He could imagine the sneer on her face as Lieutenant Grace shrieked at her over the comm, and how it would only aggravate her and make her lose concentration. And the callsign that Gavin had tagged her with hadn't helped.

"How's it going over there, Floppychop?" he murmured into his comm.

"Up yours, dipshit," came Jet's annoyed voice. Gavin smiled at himself. She'd get used to the name eventually, and talk to him again.

He performed five more 180 degree flips before Grace's voice thundered over the speaker again. "Ashdown! Get your ass to the flight deck!"

At first, the hairs on the back of his neck prickled, and he looked all around at each viewport, peering out to see the cause of her yelling. "Why? Is something wrong?"

"*You're* wrong, newbie! You're all wrong. Get your ass in the conference room within five minutes, or you'll be scrubbing galley floors again so fast your head will explode. Literally. All over the floor. And then you'll have to clean that shit off the floor too. Move!"

With a sigh, he pulled on the controls until the nose pointed towards the maw of the flight deck on the rear of the *Phoenix*, and received his instructions from the deck chief concerning his landing order. At least he remembered that. The first time he came in for a landing, he forgot to check with the chief, and nearly crashed into another fighter making its own approach.

When the bird came to rest, he wrenched the cockpit door open and hopped out and dashed towards the still scorched and pockmarked door to the anteroom.

"Gavin! Wait up!" He glanced back and saw Jet Xing. His competitor. He threw her an insincere, thin-lipped smile. No need to play nice with the enemy.

"What do you want, Floppychop?"

"Looks like you pissed off Lieutenant Grace again. You keep this up and I've got this thing in the bag," Jet said as they walked through the entryway to the anteroom.

"Screw you, Jet," said Gavin. He wiped his sweaty forehead, making his blonde hair stick out from his head at an awkward angle. "The day Grace gives that spot to you is the day I kiss your ass."

"That oughta be fun," Jet quipped, and hung up her helmet in the bullet-strafed locker in the anteroom. "Get ready to pucker up, dickhead. You've got about as much chance of landing that spot as landing your dick in Lieutenant Grace's runway."

"Yeah, screw you." Gavin shut his locker and ambled towards the door to the conference room, Jet close behind. He noticed the deep pockmarks in the doors and walls of the conference room, which left him with a pit in his stomach every time he saw them.

"What, you offering?" Jet laughed in her high-pitched, whiny voice, and Gavin rolled his eyes. Whereas before they'd been tentative friends, playing videogames together for long hours into the night, now the kid seemed to Gavin like a petulant little cocky douchebag who needed to be put in her place. As he sat down in the stadium seating of the conference room and glanced up at a glaring Lieutenant Grace, he hoped she might provide it.

"Come on, newbies, sit your asses down and shut the hell up." She glanced at her watch. "Four minutes, thirty seconds. That was cutting it kind of close, dontcha think?" She stared at the lot of them: three marines who occasionally glanced down at their rippling arm muscles, two shuttle pilots who in Gavin's opinion probably had the fighter pilot positions in the bag, and of course Jet and Gavin, who both still had a few lingering pimples.

Jet raised her hand. "Lieutenant, I think I can safely speak for all of us when I say tha—"

"Floppychop, when I want to hear you talk, I will ask you a question. Until then, shut your pie-hole." She stared at her with her fiery eyes until she looked down. Gavin grinned. Grace turned to him. "And what the fuck are you smiling at, Ashdown? You think I'm funny?"

"No, sir," said Gavin, sitting up straighter in his chair.

"Damn right. I'm the least funny thing you newbies have to worry about right now. There's far funnier things. Exploding propellant tanks, miscalculated gravitic coordinates, misfired torpedoes, enemy railgun fire, friendly railgun fire, ion beam cannon fire that can literally boil the shit out of you, burning up in the atmosphere, colliding with suicidal bogeys, psychotically insane Imperial admirals, Commander Jemez's luscious lips, Doc Nichols's scalpel, unexpected depressurization, electrical overloads, and last but not least, the incompetence of the people seated next to you." She took a deep breath.

"Corporal Taylor," she addressed one of the marines in the front row, "we're back in here because of you. Tell me what you did wrong."

Taylor, a burly, crew-cut marine in his mid-twenties or so, stiffened in his seat. He hesitated. "Uh, sir, I think I—"

"Wrong answer. Can anyone else tell Macho here what his problem is?"

Silence. Gavin had no idea—at the time of Taylor's supposed mistake, he'd been practicing his own 180s.

"You said 'I think I—.' I gave you specific instructions out there that I expected you to follow to the letter. You will think when I tell you to, and that will only happen when I'm convinced that you have the capacity to do so. I said to do five 180s. You did seven. A little thing, right? Wrong. The Wing Commander—me—gives the orders for training exercises. If you're out there doing some crazy shit that I don't know about, at this stage you're likely to slam into another fighter who actually is carrying out my orders." She folded her arms and rested her gaze back on Corporal Taylor, who shrunk a little further into his chair. "Let me be clear. You do what I say, when I say it, exactly how I say it, with no stunts, bravado, or any dicking around, period. If this happens again, you're out. No second chances. You're out. Gone. Do I make myself clear?"

"Yes, sir," said Corporal Taylor.

"I said," she repeated, looking around at the rest of them, "do I make myself CLEAR?"

"Yes, sir!" they all shouted.

"Good." She returned to her podium and examined the console on top. "Next up, we've got basic target locking and pursuit maneuvers. We'll be using dummy rounds, but lucky for you, the likelihood that you will actually need dummy rounds is vanishingly small, given that you all probably have the targeting skills of a virgin in a whorehouse."

They all chuckled.

"Did I tell you to LAUGH?" Lieutenant Grace shouted again.

"No, sir!" they all shouted back at her.

Gavin started to feel like he was back in basic training, only better—this time, someone was actually expecting him to perform. Back in basic, the drill instructor, a lazy, petulant Imperial wanker who looked as if he'd rather be back on Corsica getting ready for retirement than training a bunch of Terran miscreants, didn't seem to have the heart or the urgency that Anya Grace now injected into the pilot training. This seemed to matter more, and it excited him. A few months ago, when he signed up at the recruiter's office, he'd only dreamed of a free ride to tour the galaxy, paying his way by cooking slop for soldiers. Now, after surviving the battle at the shipyards and getting his first taste of piloting a fighter, he dreamed of something more.

To matter.

Gavin listened to Lieutenant Grace explain the procedure for getting a target lock, and even practiced maneuvering the imaginary controls in front of him.

"Ashdown, what the hell do you think you're doing?" Grace had stopped talking and now bore her eyes down on him.

"Uh, practicing what you're teaching us, sir."

"With what, newbie?" She folded her arms.

"With … uh, with my imaginary controls, sir."

The room erupted in laughter, and even Lieutenant Grace smirked for a moment. She glanced down at Corporal Taylor and, smiling, remarked, "Funny, isn't it?"

"Yes, sir," the boar of a man said, turning back to grin at Gavin, who shrunk a little lower into his seat.

"Yes, funny," she repeated. "Funny how, at this point, it seems newbie Ashdown might be the only one to make it through this training program." She let the words mingle with the dying laughter, which faded away to silence. "People, if you don't breathe being a pilot, if you don't dream of it every night, if you don't shit, fart, and drink being a fighter, if you don't think about this every waking hour, you're going to fail. And then you will die."

The room was so silent Gavin could hear the fighter deck work crews through the two sets of doors that separated them from the bay. Grace continued, pointing straight at Gavin, "Take a page from newbie here, and start getting your heads out of your asses and into the game. Do that, and you just might be joining him with an officer's commission in a few days." Gavin could feel Jet glare at him, from two seats over.

Corporal Taylor cautiously raised his hand, and Grace nodded once to him, permitting him to speak. "Uh, sir, did you just say a few days?"

"Are you deaf, Corporal, or did your vagina suddenly shrink to the size of an acorn?" He did not respond, so she continued. "In case you haven't been paying attention, we're at war. We've got the entire Imperial fleet breathing down our backs looking to smear our asses into the closest god-forsaken desolate moon they can find. We don't have the luxury of time. Under normal circumstances, you would all have had months of classroom and simulator instruction before I let you even touch one of my birds, but you've already been out in them twice today. Average cadets don't graduate from flight school for two years, and half flunk out."

Corporal Taylor went on. "But days, sir? Aren't we liable to get ourselves killed?"

She cast a cold glance at him. "You either die strapped into the coffin of your barracks, or the coffin of your fighter. At least in the fighter you might take out a few of them with you." Pivoting, she stepped back around her podium and looked at the console again. "Any more dumb-ass questions?"

Gavin, slowly and tentatively, raised his hand. Lieutenant Grace looked a little annoyed at him, but said, "Yes, newbie?"

"Do you really think we'll be seeing combat in a few days, sir?" As excited as he was to be doing something that mattered more than slopping mashed potatoes onto platters, the thought of live combat—other people actually shooting at him, Gavin Ashdown, terrified him.

Without skipping a beat, she said, "You've seen our situation. What the fuck do you think? Would you rather go back to the mess hall to scrub floors and play your videogames at night?"

"No, sir," he said.

She smiled, the first time she'd done anything but frown the entire day. "Good. Then let's get back out there and blow some shit up."

As if in answer, the deck rumbled and shook, as if rocked

by a massive explosion several decks down. Gavin glanced over at Jet, whose jaw momentarily hung open.

Anya hit the comm button on her podium. "Lieutenant Grace to Bridge. Commander, are we under attack?"

"Stand by, Anya, we're not quite sure.…" Po glanced over at the tactical octagon. Willow was absent—hopefully resting —and the station was manned by several ensigns and yeomen from the second shift. "Sensors?"

The Ensign at the sensor station shook his head. "Nothing unusual, sir. No ships anywhere near us."

"Anya," began Po, "We're clear. No enemy craft nearby."

"Well, shit. I was hoping for some fun. Grace out."

Po rolled her eyes at the bravado, and hit the comm button. "Engineering, this is Commander Po. Anything I need to know about?"

Shouts and cursing drifted through the speakers, and momentarily the deputy chief engineer's voice piped through. "Yes, sir. We've had a backup in the main coolant line. It ruptured on deck fourteen, aft."

"Damage?" She glanced back at the operations center.

Operations. That was supposed to be her station, before all hell broke loose. That was where Captain Watson was going to assign her. Instead, she was sitting in the captain's chair while her brash young friend was cavorting around in a cowboy hat down on some god-forsaken dustbin.

"Part of deck fourteen is flooded, sir. Only minor injuries reported so far."

Po turned back to the comm. "Chief Simmons, engine status?"

More muffled swearing from the speakers. "Sir, without

that main coolant line, we're down to the backup line. I wouldn't dare do any shifting without the mains. We're ok to use gravitic propulsion, but one long distance shift will melt down the drive."

Po leaned back in the captain's chair. "So. Looks like we're stuck here for the time being. Chief, when you can, run some diagnostic checks to see what the cause was."

"Aye, sir!"

She didn't dare suspect one of the crew. The ramifications of sabotage were almost unthinkable. And since they'd all only been together for just over a week, nearly everyone was suspect.

Unless Tomaga was responsible. But how could he or any of his men have done it? They were confined to deck fifteen. Could one of them have slipped out unnoticed?

She turned to the comm officer. "Ensign, get me Sergeant Jayce."

After several moments of furrowed brows, Ensign Falstaff looked up. "I've found him, sir."

"Yeah? What's up, Commander?" Jayce's voice huffed through the speaker. He sounded out of breath.

"Caught you at a bad time, Sergeant?"

She could hear him spit, and she imagined some new brown spot on a brand new deckplate somewhere. "Just running these training drills you requested, Sir. With my boys and the Fifty-First."

"Sergeant, please report to the Captain's ready room in an hour. Bring Sergeant Tomaga with you."

Another spitting sound. "Shit, that motherfucker? He's been giving me grief all day, sir."

"Fine. Report in an hour, and we can work out your differences then. Po out." She sighed, and reached back to another loose strand of hair that had fallen out of her perpetual bun. Between a crazed Imperial Admiral hunting them down, Jake hanging out with pirates on the dusty planet below, possible sabotage, a half-broken ship, non-working engines, and a band of possibly hostile marines on board, she wasn't sure how much longer it'd be before the shit hit the fan.

Judging by the previous week, it wouldn't be long now.

CHAPTER NINETEEN

A bullet blasted a chunk of concrete out of the wall next to Jake's head. He flinched, diving further beneath the cover of the steel table he'd overturned. In response, Ben popped his sidearm over the table's edge and emptied the gun in the direction of the nearest attacker.

"Who the hell are they?" hissed Ben as he yanked his weapon back down to the relative safety of cover.

"Thugs, I'd reckon," Jake deadpanned. Sometimes Ben asked stupid questions.

"Thanks." Ben glared, and checked his ammo, wincing in disappointment at what he saw. "Jake, I'm almost out, and those guys have assault rifles. We've got to get the hell out of here!"

"Working on it," he said, and turned to the other overturned table not far away where their two marines and Alessandro had hunkered down. He pointed at Avery and held up his hands, indicating for the man to use whatever special ops training he'd had to think up some plan of escape. Avery only shrugged.

And he was right to do so. They were pinned down, and Jake knew it. At least six men with more powerful weaponry than they had now ringed their two tables in a large semicircle, about fifteen meters off, hunkered behind their own tables. Everyone else in the vast warehouse had either fled in terror, or hid behind whatever cover they could find for themselves, quaking in fear.

Avery peeked around the corner of his table and popped off three quick rounds. Even though his ears rung from the firing in the closed space of the warehouse, Jake could hear the cries of a dying man. He nodded at Avery—at least there was only five now, that they knew of.

Jake could see Alessandro fiddling with something in his hands. The man stared intently at an odd black shape, vaguely familiar. Before he could think too much more about it, another hail of bullets leaped out from their pursuers and Jake hunched over even further. The other marine popped around their table and showered the nearest target with rounds of his own, which bounced harmlessly off the steel tables.

"Get down, friends!" yelled Alessandro, and Jake suddenly recognized the black cylinder in his hands.

One of the anti-matter Vesuvius mines they'd promised to buy earlier.

An anti-matter bomb.

"What the hell do you think you're—" Jake yelled, but it was too late. With a grunt, Alessandro lobbed the small black cylinder as high and as far as he could throw. The rest of them had no choice but to lie flat on the ground and wonder if they'd be alive in a few moments.

A gargantuan blast rocked the building, and tables, chairs,

and scattered merchandise went flying, pelting the walls and ceiling. But it wasn't nearly as large as he would have expected from an anti-matter bomb, even if it only had a few nanograms of the stuff.

Jake shook his head, and squinted through the smoke. He reached down and yanked at Ben's arm.

"Let's go."

They sprang to their feet, joining the other three who'd already started running for the exit, which they dove through just as it was pelted with another volley of rounds. Jake looked around, and saw an old, dusty board on the ground, which he seized and shoved through the two handles on the door. It wouldn't hold them for long, but it might buy them ten seconds or so.

Running towards where they'd left the vehicles, Jake immediately saw something amiss. Volaski and his car were gone. A tickling feeling of suspicion spread over Jake as he jumped into the other vehicle and cranked the engine—luckily it required no key or identification. It roared to life just as the door burst open and an assault-rifle-toting figure bolted from the warehouse.

Jake gaped. "Velar?"

"Go!" she shouted, and pointed towards the setting sun. She dashed towards them. Jake put the vehicle into gear, and, checking to make sure the rest of his men had jumped in, slammed on the accelerator.

Another man darted out of the warehouse and aimed his assault rifle at them, spraying rounds, several of which hit the side of the vehicle. Velar spun around and, aiming her own rifle, felled him with a blast through his temple, which sprayed the wall behind him with blood and bits of gray chunks.

That was enough to convince Jake of her intentions, and he wheeled the vehicle around towards her.

"What the hell are you doing?" Ben shouted in his ear.

"We might need her to get out of here," he replied, as calmly as he could.

"You still trust her?" Ben's voice sounded incredulous.

"No. But I doubt she'd splatter the brains of one of her men all over the wall of the warehouse. For the moment, we're on the same side." They pulled up alongside her and she jumped on the rear fender and aimed her rifle again at the door of the warehouse, which billowed smoke from Alessandro's handiwork.

"Move!" she shouted, again, pointing towards what Jake guessed was west.

He slammed down on the accelerator again, not looking back, but he could hear the firing of her rifle, and the side-arms of everyone else in the vehicle, spraying their pursuers with rounds. After half a minute or so, he'd put enough distance between them and the warehouse that the gunfire died down and he finally yelled out the question that had been burning in his mind for the past two minutes.

"Bernoulli, what the hell did you do? That was an anti-matter mine. It's meant to take out a capital ship. What the hell were you thinking?"

Alessandro beamed at him, and extracted a tiny vial from the front pocket of his vest. He held it up to Jake's eye, and grinned.

Jake swore. "Is that what I think it is?"

"Five nanograms of anti-boron?" said with a grin.

"Alessandro," he said, turning to face his friend, "you're the craziest-ass bastard I've ever met."

Alessandro poked the vial back into his pocket. "Honestly, friend, you really think I'd lob an anti-matter bomb at someone so close? I'm not that dumb, you know."

"Alessandro, dumb is the last word I'd use to describe you. Crazy, yes. Dumb, no. So, if the anti-matter is in your pocket, what the hell blasted back there?"

Jake swerved through the wide dusty streets, avoiding the piles of trash spilling out onto the road and the stray pedestrian.

Alessandro shrugged. "Just the initiator. It takes a pretty strong implosion to initiate the anti-matter interaction. You had nothing to worry about, friend." He hesitated a moment, before adding, "except for the obviously deadly explosion that the initiator is capable of. I suspected we'd be ok, but one can never be too sure with explosives. I've got friends at Los Alamos, you see, and—"

Jake interrupted, trying to think and follow Velar's periodic pointed driving instructions simultaneously. "Are we safe with that thing on your pocket? I mean, is it contained enough?"

"For now. It is not optimal, but it is not likely to explode in its current state."

"You're not assuaging my concern, buddy," said Jake, spinning the wheel to turn down a street indicated by Velar, who had jumped into the backseat, crouching in between the legs of the two marines, half turned to watch behind them and working on getting Jake to drive where she wanted.

Alessandro continued, "The chances of a critical runaway matter interaction in this state is less than one in one hundred per day. We're perfectly safe."

The blood drained from Ben's face as his jaw hung slack, but Jake only said, "I don't like those odds, buddy, but I guess they're better than our odds back in that warehouse." He turned to look in the back seat. "Velar? Where are you taking us? Why aren't we going back to our shuttle?"

She kept her eyes trained on the road behind them, scanning for pursuers. "To my home. I don't think we'd make it to your shuttle. Obviously, someone knew we were coming and tipped off their men."

Jake felt Ben eyeing him from the passenger's seat, and he knew exactly what his friend was thinking. And he was right. They had no idea if Velar could be trusted at this point. But she was currently their best option, and Jake suspected that even Ben knew that.

"We've got a tail," said Avery.

Velar offered her rifle to Avery. "You look a little more comfortable with guns than me." He took it, and passed his sidearm to her, which she took and aimed at the vehicle now gaining on them.

"Where am I going, Velar?" Jake shouted.

"Keep going west. Head for that hill you see on the edge of town—my home is just behind that."

The pop of Avery's rifle interrupted her, and a hail of bullets whizzed past their head, riddling a building just ahead of them. Jake swerved down a side street and stepped on the accelerator, dodging tables set up by street vendors and other parked vehicles. Broken-down, dilapidated brick buildings flew past and dust swirled in his face as the wind picked up. He squinted to see.

"Velar, where the hell did Volaski go?" Jake asked, though he suspected he might not like the answer.

"I don't know." She continued staring behind them, resting her gun on the back of the seat.

"Could he be responsible for this?" Jake wondered if she would even tell them if he was. He realized he still had no idea what the relationship was between the two. Was she his boss, or was he hers? Or was their relationship one of mutual convenience?

"Unlikely," was her only response. But it did not satisfy Jake.

He cranked on the steering wheel, turning onto another street heading west, the low sun in their eyes. The bright, bluish sun had dipped very low in the sky, which now glowed red and purple with the dying light. "Unlikely my ass. Talk, Velar."

She sighed. "I can't imagine him doing something like this. It's far more likely that one of the syndicates was alerted to your presence. Have you got a bounty on your head or something?"

"Probably. But I wouldn't think Admiral Trajan would be able to get the word out so fast," he said, but instantly kicked himself inside for saying the Admiral's name—best not to freely give up too much information to the woman behind him. He still had no idea who she was, beyond the fact that she claimed to be able to get them some rare earths for their gravitic drive.

The pops of more rifle fire sounded behind them and Jake swerved, pounding down on the accelerator. The brick buildings whirred past and he worried that someone might not see them coming and step into their path, but fortunately the roar of the engine was loud enough that people a block ahead turned and ran out of the way before they sped past, followed closely by the pursuing vehicle.

"Bernoulli, got any more of those mines?"

"Yes, but I don't think I could safely remove the anti-matter with all this jolting about."

A bullet whizzed past Jake's head and shattered the windshield in front of him. "Avery!" he yelled. "Take them out!"

"Working on it," came the man's harried reply, and he popped off several more rounds into the tailing vehicle. Finally, Jake heard a crash, and looked back to see the pursuing car slam into the brick wall of a building halfway down the street. "Got the driver, sir."

"Nice shot, Avery," Jake said, and breathed a sigh of relief. The hill loomed ahead and the buildings began to thin out somewhat. Jake veered down a street that looked like it led to an open, dusty field, and aimed for the south side of the hill, which looked a little less populated.

Before long, after passing another dozen structures ranging from corrugated tin roofed shacks to a few stately, swanky mansions, they found themselves in front of a large, iron gate that Velar pointed to.

"That's it," she said, and stood up in the back seat, waving her arms to some unseen gatekeeper. It swung open, and Jake revved the engine to drive into the courtyard of the sprawling compound laid out before them. The gate closed with a rattle behind them.

"Well. That was fun," said Jake. "Any more surprises I

should know about?" He turned back to look at Velar, whose gaze was fixed on one of the marines next to her. Not Avery, but the other one—Corporal Suarez. Red covered his shoulder, and he leaned back into his seat with clenched teeth. Jake swore. Avery had already tossed his rifle aside and stripped off his vest to press into Suarez's bloody shoulder.

"Get him inside. We have medical supplies there," said Velar, who jumped out of the vehicle and waved at a man that appeared at the entrance to one of the brick buildings. He was dressed like Volaski, and had the same sort of electronic gadget circling his neck, almost like a necklace, or a communications device. Running over, Velar directed him to lift Suarez out and carry him inside.

"We'll be safe here, Mercer. At least for the moment."

Jake nodded at the man assisting Sergeant Avery with the bleeding Corporal Suarez. "These are your people?"

She nodded. "Yes. I run my business from this compound, and it is adequately defended. We should be fine until we can get you back to your ship. Come." She motioned to them, and Jake followed close behind, glancing back at Ben.

Ben's eyes told Jake all he needed to know.

Jake nodded, but pointed towards the building Velar was taking them into. He agreed with his friend's reluctance, but it was their only choice at the moment.

He made a mental note to start listening more closely to his paranoid buddy.

CHAPTER TWENTY

Senator Galba ducked behind a corner at the approach of the footsteps. He wasn't sure why—he supposed his nerves were just getting to him. Leaning up against the hallway's bulkhead, he placed a finger against his neck and felt his pulse.

It pounded. Just like his head. The migraines were getting worse—if only he were back on his beloved Corsica and had access to his personal physician.

The footsteps grew louder, echoing off the composite wall panels. He crouched down to lay his tool bag on the floor and turned his back to the intersection with the other passageway where the steps were coming from. Busying himself with rifling through the bag—or at least making the best effort to maintain the appearance of busyness, he waited as the steady clicks grew louder.

They paused at the intersection. He resisted the urge to turn around to see who it was. Probably some nameless blue-shirted ensign or yeoman, staring at him slack-jawed, an expression frustratingly common to all Old-Earth inhabitants.

"Can I help you?"

The voice was young. And female. He risked a glance backward, careful to show only the bandaged half of his face.

Young, and female, yes. But otherwise nothing to look at. Frazzled red hair. A horse-shaped jaw. Flared nostrils. He shuddered at the thought of bedding her. Turning back to his tool bag he sighed.

"No, yeoman," he hoped he got the rank right, "Just trying to find the damn omni-spanner. Carry on."

The steps started again, slower.

"Good luck," came the young, hesitant voice once more, and then she was gone.

He took a deep breath and lurched at the wall panel to pull himself up. His knees creaked and his head throbbed. Great gods, he was far too old to be crouching down like that.

Satisfied that the young redhead was long gone, he returned to the hallway he'd fled from, and aimed towards engineering. This time he'd have to be a little more ingenious. He hadn't thought about the fact that there would be redundancies in the coolant lines.

Still, he'd caused some damage. He'd knocked out the ship's long range shifting, at least. Time to knock out the rest of the navigation system. That way, the next time Trajan came looking for the *Phoenix*, it'd be a sitting duck.

And he'd be free.

And The Plan could continue.

He grinned to himself. Of course, the Emperor and the Admiral were probably still well engaged in carrying out the other aspects of The Plan. Even though the Resistance was essentially crushed and discredited, pockets remained on Old Earth. Pockets of independence. Gumption.

And ironic that out of all the planets the upstart young Captain could have fled to with the *Phoenix*, he'd chosen Destiny. Home to the Twilight Project. One of the vital elements of The Plan. For his own sake, the blustery young fool had better steer clear of Dr. Stone and his research at the Imperial Cybernetic Institute.

The Institute was well hidden though. And Dr. Stone had the sense to stay out of the public eye. Especially with his … aberrant habits. The man liked to bleed things. Animals. People. Whatever. And control them. The perfect man to head up the Twilight Project. But it was good that the Emperor had shuffled the good Doctor and his Institute off to some anonymous frontier world where no one would notice his abominations. Where he could conduct his research in peace.

Before long, the hallway ended in a set of metal steps that descended to the deck below, and he stepped slowly down. The recreation deck. Right above main engineering. He turned the corner down the hallway that ran parallel to what he knew would be the vast engineering bay below, and walked smack into another man.

"Damn you, watch the hell where you're going," he snapped, stooping over to pick up his spilled tool bag. The other man reached down to retrieve a few tools that had cluttered to the floor near his own feet. The hand bore bloody scars and gashes. No doubt from the battles of the previous week, supposed Galba.

"Maybe if you didn't walk with your head straight down you might see where you're walking, old man," the stranger said, a familiar accent to his voice. Galba glanced up.

He was Asian-looking, and the accent was distinctly inner-

Empire. Maybe even Corsican. The man's face was bruised and beaten, one eye puffed up purple and the other nearly swollen shut. He offered the tools to Galba and sneered a smile. "Here. Be more careful next time, crewman."

Galba accepted the tools and turned to continue down the hall, towards the emergency access room that lie at the end of the deck, but stopped, and glanced again at the sneering face. "Where are you from, soldier?"

Indeed, the man wore an Imperial marine's uniform, bearing insignia that the Senator recognized as special ops. Some type of urban assault battalion.

"Provincial World Number Eighty-Seven," said the man in a slow, dry voice. "Private Ling. And tell me what pussy-barren province of Old Earth you crawled out from."

Galba ignored the insult, knowing that it was intended for some yokel Resistance tech, not for him, a Senator of the Empire. What was more interesting to him was the presence of an Imperial marine on board a Resistance ship. "Eighty-Seven? Yonggan? I know it well!"

Private Ling looked at him suspiciously. "And how would a syphilitic Terran rat like yourself know anything other than the fuckhole that is Old Earth?"

Galba glanced down to his feet, remembering he was supposed to be playing an uneducated, uncivilized tech. "Oh, just stories. Maps. I like geography, you see. Look at pictures of other—"

"You like looking at pictures? Did the pictures have words? Did you read them? Or did you pay your whore of a mother to read them to you?" The private spat on the deckplate at Galba's feet, and, even though the Senator knew the words were not truly meant for him, he momentarily snapped.

"No, Private. On the serendipitous occasion when I can draw my attention away from far weightier affairs than you can hardly fathom, I order one of my Yongganian harem girls to read a book to me. So wipe that snide, frontier-world smirk off your face and kindly step out of my way. My time is far too important to waste on one more word on a conversation with someone registering half the intelligence of a kitchen table leg."

He brushed past the gaping man, and strode down the hallway towards the intersection he knew would take him to his destination. The emergency access room where he could find auxiliary controls for engineering.

The voice called after him. This time with far less sanctimony and pride. "You look like someone I know."

Galba slowed, but didn't turn back. "Oh?"

"Yeah. Someone famous. You famous, tech?"

Shit.

He stopped, and half turned, letting the marine see only the bandaged half of his face. "Do I look famous to you, soldier?" He paused, letting the question linger as he reached a hand up to rub his newly shaved head. Gods, he missed his hair. The glorious hair that was the legend in every harem on Corsica. "Would a famous celebrity be fixing fucking hull breaches on some damned ship?"

He turned back down the hall and continued. Private Ling didn't respond, but as far as Galba could hear, the marine didn't move, either. The Senator turned the corner at the intersection, stepping over a fallen girder, and left the other man behind.

Dammit. That was too risky. Too risky. If the man discovered his identity, if he even suspected it, and mentioned it to his buddies, it would be all over.

But what the hell was an Imperial marine doing on board the *Phoenix*?

One more thing to ask Willow the next time he let her ride him.

CHAPTER TWENTY-ONE

Megan Po was starting to regret her invitation to the Fifty-First Brigade. It seemed like such a good idea at the time. Build unity between the two marine contingents. Defuse tensions. Keep the Imperial visitors occupied—less time for them to get into trouble.

What had happened instead was a constant butting of heads between Sergeant Tomaga and the *Phoenix*'s ranking enlisted officer, Sergeant Logan Jayce. Jayce was a hothead, and while he respected authority for the most part, he resented being told to work with people who had killed his buddies, for obvious reasons.

And Sergeant Tomaga was the stereotypical Corsican Empire soldier. Stiff. Abrupt. Dispassionate. Efficient. All things that Sergeant Jayce was not.

And Jake Mercer is neither, she thought with a grin. Maybe that was why Captain Watson had ultimately chosen him as his replacement.

The ready room doors chimed, indicating the presence of the two men, and Po waved the door open. Sergeant Jayce swaggered through the door, his left eye still purple and his lower lip still cut from yesterday's fight with Private Ling. Sergeant Tomaga followed several paces behind, entering more deliberately, and warily, than Jayce. Po noted that the man was probably still quite ill at ease on what to him was an enemy ship.

"Gentlemen, have a seat," she said, indicating the two chairs against the wall. "Bring them up to the desk, if you don't mind." She sat in the captain's chair, realizing that she'd now sat in it about as much as Jake had. Tomaga lifted his chair and placed it firmly near the desk. Jayce simply grabbed his and swung it sliding over the floor until it came to rest on the opposite side of the desk from Tomaga.

"Commander, I'm not sure what you were thinking having these bastards train with us today. I reckon they'd best be tossed out the—" Jayce began, but Po's stern eyes interrupted him.

"Sergeant, when I want your opinion I'll ask for it." She maintained her steely gaze into his eyes until he shoved out his chin.

"Yes, sir."

She nodded once in approval. Realizing that she probably had a very narrow window to gain the trust and confidence of the type of soldier Sergeant Jayce was, she knew that to be soft with him or show weakness would undermine every future order she gave him or his men. "Sergeant, if you can't obey my orders with exactness when I give them, without any bullshit, then it's you I'll be tossing out the airlock. Or at least a few weeks of galley duty. Is that clear?"

His chin stayed thrust out, but his answer came more

quickly than last time. "Yes, sir."

"Very well." She turned to Tomaga. "Sergeant, I'm under the impression that you've been rather difficult to work with. Please explain yourself."

Sergeant Tomaga, seated, with his back rigid, didn't so much as blink or change his cold expression. "Then you heard incorrectly, Commander."

Her only reply was to meet his cold gaze with a fiery look of her own.

A crack in his expression was the only indication that he understood her implied meaning: respect her, or face the consequences. "If you could be more specific, Commander. I can address your concerns more easily if I know what I've been accused of."

"Sergeant Jayce tells me that you refuse to allow your men to take orders from him during the intra-ship combat exercises. I thought we had a deal. You and your men train with mine, and as a reward I let you have access to more of the ship than just the mess deck, among other, less tangible results," she dipped her chin and softened her tone, very slightly, "like trust."

Tomaga nodded. "It is against Imperial fleet regulations for a staff sergeant to take the lead of combat exercises when outranked by a master sergeant," he said.

"But we are not on board an Imperial vessel. And besides that, I ordered it. As far as I remember, master sergeants are obligated to obey Lieutenant Commanders."

Tomaga grinned, ever so slightly. "Ah, but Commander, you yourself just pointed out that I am no longer on board an Imperial vessel, and so I am not obligated to obey your orders.

Or am I wrong?"

Po sighed. She felt like she was arguing in circles with the man. "Sergeant, let's cut the obtuse nonsense. We agreed you would take part in the exercises. As part of those exercises, I've designated that Sergeant Jayce will be the lead. Those are the ground rules. If you don't accept them, then I'll just confine you and your men to barracks, dammit. I'd rather not do that, but I will if you force my hand."

She had to tread carefully. While she knew she had the upper hand, it was also readily apparent that the presence of Tomaga and his men presented a clear and present danger to the safe operations of the *Phoenix*, and that, if provoked, they could certainly cause no small amount of chaos.

"Very well, Commander Po. But on one condition."

"I'm listening," she said, steepling her hands under her chin.

"That I will also have the opportunity to give orders to your men. If the Fifty-First Brigade sees only Sergeant Jayce ordering them around over my head, then they will most likely carry grudges. But if Jayce and I share responsibilities, then they will respect you, and him."

Damn. He was right, of course, as Tomaga outranked Jayce. But it was risky. She still didn't know if she could trust the Imperial soldier or not. It was true, if he'd wanted to disrupt operations on the *Phoenix*, he'd had ample opportunity over the past few days to do so already. But he could just be positioning himself and his men to cause as big a disturbance as possible. Maybe even the destruction of the *Phoenix*, for all she knew.

But no. Those men were conscripts. They had families

waiting for them. Many had small children. Most soldiers conscripted into the Imperial fleet were not true believers, but rather well-trained prisoners with guns who had little to gain and a lot to lose by disobeying their Imperial officers.

And yet these were a cut above the average Imperial battalion. Tomaga was shrewd—that much she recognized. Shrewd and able. She could see him thinking, strategizing, planning, with every thing he said or did. The question was, was he strategizing for the safe release of his men, or for the capture or destruction of the *Phoenix*? She suspected the former, and not just suspected, but believed it. It made no sense for those men to continue the fight.

"Very well, Sergeant Tomaga. Tomorrow, you will lead the training exercises. With a condition. Before the exercises, you will discuss your plans for the day with Sergeant Jayce. Agreed?"

"Agreed, sir."

Po nodded, then turned to Jayce, who had merely smirked at Tomaga the entire time. "Sergeant Jayce. You will be as accommodating towards the Fifty-First Brigade as you can. Cut the macho shit. Understood?"

The smirk turned back into the glower of before.

"Yes, sir."

"Dismissed."

She let out a deep breath as they left, and held her head in her hands. After a moment of collecting herself, she reached up and stuffed a stray strand of hair back into her bun, and left the ready room.

"Ensign Ayala, status report?"

The bleached-white haired young woman in the captain's

chair stood at attention as Po walked onto the bridge. Megan wondered whether it might not be a better idea to find some lieutenant down in the operations center or weapons bays to reassign to the bridge—some might find it unseemly that an Ensign was constantly being given command of the bridge.

But these were not normal times, and Po needed to leave the bridge with someone that she trusted, and somehow, the wispy, tattooed, wiry young woman from the ill-fated world of Belen had gained her confidence. Something about how she carried herself. Or was Po just treating the young woman like a celebrity, like everyone else seemed to do?

"Sir, damage repair crews are reporting that the holes in the forward section are nearly covered over and we'll be able to raise the emergency bulkheads within two hours."

The thought of the grim task that lie ahead made Po a little envious of Jake and Ben down on the surface. There were at least twenty more bodies stuck behind those emergency bulkheads, victims of both the Imperial attack, and Captain Mercer's rash but necessary strategy of ramming the *Caligula* a few days prior. At least all her two friends had to deal with at the moment was dust.

"Very well. Engine status?"

"Same, sir. Long range shifting still out, but gravitic thrusters holding steady. We're maintaining a position 1000 klicks above the north pole of Destiny," said Ayala, stepping aside from the captain's chair as Po approached.

"And contact with the ground team?" Her voice lowered, as if expecting bad news.

"The ionic and magnetic interference from the pole is making it difficult to track them. They haven't attempted to hail us since they landed last night."

That was damn peculiar. Jake had suggested the *Phoenix* not constantly try to raise them on the comm to avoid undue attention, but they had not had contact with the ground team for nearly twelve hours, and Po was starting to worry.

"Thank you, Ensign. Resume your post—" she glanced up at the young woman, whose lined eyes had started to sag almost imperceptibly. "Ensign, how long have you been at your post?"

"Twenty hours, sir. And I even grabbed a quick nap a few hours ago. I'm fine, really." She stifled a yawn.

"Nonsense. Get to bed." Po silently kicked herself for not drawing up a better bridge crew rotation—not that she'd had time to do so, what with ship repairs, Fifty-First Brigade management, shuffling the rest of the ship's crew around in the wake of so many lost, and just the general rigors of command that Po had still yet to become accustomed to.

"But who will replace me, sir?" She waved her hand back to the tactical octagon, which was staffed by an assortment of enlisted crew members and another ensign. "The only other officer trained for tactical is still asleep. Ensign Walker won't be reporting for duty for another three hours."

The urgent voice of the one of the tactical crew interrupted her. "Sir! We have multiple contacts approaching us. They're coming from the surface."

"Identify them," said Po, sliding into her seat. Ayala stole back to her post.

"One of them is our shuttle. The others look like two of Volaski's," the red-faced technician said, squinting at his console.

The first good news they'd had all day. Po made a note to herself to scold Mercer for not informing her of his return to the ship. But later, when the bridge crew wasn't watching.

"Hail them, comm," she said.

"Channel to the shuttle open, sir," said Ensign Falstaff.

"Captain Mercer? Is everything all right?"

Captain Volaski's voice came over the speaker, to Po's surprise, and she slowly stood up. "Commander Po, your Captain is still down on the planet. There is something we need to discuss."

"Volaski, what is the meaning of this? Why are you on our shuttle? Did Mercer authorize this?" A pit had grown in her stomach. Something was dreadfully wrong.

Volaski hesitated. "We have a situation down on the planet. Perhaps it is best we talked in person. May we board the *Phoenix*?" His voice sounded strange. Not like how he sounded before, when he was confident, almost exuberant.

Po turned to look back at Ben before remembering that he was with the Captain on the surface. As she scanned the bridge, she realized she was alone. There was no one on the bridge to offer advice, to tell her she was crazy for suspecting Volaski of doing something to the landing party. She glanced at Ayala, who seemed to read her thoughts.

Ayala, with wide eyes, slowly shook her head.

Good. I'm not crazy.

"Volaski, I see no reason that we can't talk on this channel." She folded her arms.

A sigh. "Commander Po, I'd really prefer not to discuss such a delicate matter over an open channel. Even over the northern pole where I doubt anyone can hear us—you are surrounded by enemies, and any communication over an open line is inadvisable."

Po cleared her throat. She felt like she was being talked down to, and it galled her. "Captain Volaski, what makes you think I will bring you and your men aboard my ship when you have presented me with no evidence that you haven't stolen that shuttle and now mean to steal the *Phoenix*? Give me something to work with, Captain, or else I'll be forced to shoot you out of the sky and go down to retrieve the Captain myself."

Volaski swore. "Commander, your landing party has been attacked by an unknown band of mercenaries. Velar was with them, but I've lost all contact with her and all of her people."

The pit in Po's stomach tightened, and threatened to rise into her chest. "Attacked? Did you witness it?"

"Just the first shots. They were in a marketplace when all of the sudden I heard gunfire, and decided to high-tail it out of there before...."

"Before what?" prompted Po.

"I prefer to face the danger from the comfort of my ship than from behind an assault rifle. When I heard the attack, I'm ashamed to say I headed straight back to the shuttle, and when your team didn't show up, I came straight up here. Please. We must discuss this in person—Destiny is home to any number of crime syndicates that would love to get their hands on your Captain, your crew, and your ship. You have no idea what kind of price the *Phoenix* alone would capture on the black market, to say nothing of the Captain. There's word the Empire has put out a generous bounty on Mercer, and you, for that matter."

A bounty on her head. Po never thought she'd see the day, and to her surprise, she laughed.

"Fine, Captain, you may come aboard. But just you. Bring the shuttle into the fighter bay, and exit alone. None of your men come with you. Is that clear?"

"But, Commander—"

"Is that clear, Captain Volaski? There will be no negotiation on this point. You come alone, or you don't come at all and I'll be forced to retake our shuttle by force. Your choice, sir."

She knew her game was risky. Threatening a pirate with violence could pay unfortunate dividends down the road, especially if the man was telling the truth. If he was lying, well, best to play it safe.

"Very well, Commander. Alone it is. But just be aware that if anything happens to me, I've got a small fleet of freighters and frigates that will come knockin' at your door."

"Understood, Captain. Po out." She nodded to the comm, and the Ensign cut the channel.

She glanced back at Ayala. "What do you think, Willow?"

Ayala bit her lip and closed her eyes, as if deep in thought. "If he's telling the truth, we're going to need his help."

"And if he's lying? If this is just a ruse to get us to lower our defenses and capture the *Phoenix*?"

The Belenite opened her eyes. "Well, I think you astutely avoided that possibility, sir, by forcing him to come alone."

Po shook her head. "No, Willow, I'm afraid I did not. That shuttle could be holding at least twenty well-armed men, for all we know."

Ayala's face fell into a frown. "I didn't think about that."

"If we're going to stay alive out here, we've got to be constantly vigilant." Her dark thoughts turned to her husband, who'd said the same words the night before the Empire attacked their neighborhood in San Bernardino, suspecting it to be a hotbed of Rebel activity. He'd always carried himself with a certain bravado—similar to Jake, now that she thought about it—and the night before the attack he'd sounded supremely confident that they'd have some advance warning of any Imperial activity.

He was wrong. And his error didn't just cost him his own life. Few errors of that type do. She forced herself to focus on the matter at hand, rather than go down that road of dark memories.

"Sergeant Jayce, Sergeant Tomaga, this is Commander Po. Please report to the fighter deck, with ten marines—five from the *Phoenix*, and five from the Fifty-First Brigade. Come heavily armed, please. Po out."

Ayala murmured, "Do you think it will come to that?"

"I sure hope not. But if it does, we'll be ready."

CHAPTER TWENTY-TWO

Suarez's wound wasn't bad, but the man would definitely need surgery to repair his rotator cuff according to the medic at Velar's compound. Jake wondered what sort of business Velar ran that would require the presence of an on-call medic. In fact, the place seemed to be teeming with people. Men and women, young and old. Even several older children could be seen at times. Destiny must be like a true frontier town like in old times, where it was a family business and everyone helped, even the young.

The old medic sniffed, and scratched underneath the electronic-looking ring around his neck as he peered into the gaping wound on Suarez's shoulder. It had finally stopped bleeding, and whatever the medic had given him for pain seemed to have worked, since the marine no longer winced whenever he moved.

"I can't guarantee a clean scar—I'm a little short-staffed and surgery isn't really my specialty, but I can patch that cuff up nice and good. You'll be ready to work within a few weeks."

Jake shook his head. "Doctor, we're not planning on

sticking around long enough for it to matter." He thought it was a little odd that the man was offering to perform surgery on Suarez's shoulder. "I'd rather leave it up to our doctor on the *Phoenix*. He's an accomplished surgeon. But thank you, anyway, for the offer."

The man peered up at him, somewhat wryly. "Suit yourself." He stood up and packed his medic bag. "I'll be around. Just let me know when you want your surgery," he said to Suarez. "Keep it bandaged in the meantime, and put that antibacterial cream on again in a few hours."

He strode out the door, and Velar came in to take his place, accompanied by several aides—gruff men who looked like guys that Jake wouldn't want to meet in a bar fight. At least not sober.

"Mercer, I think the men who followed us are gone. We need to figure out how to get you to your ship. I finally located Volaski, and he's keeping your shuttle safe. Will you authorize him to pilot it over here?"

Jake eyed her warily. "Sure. How soon can he get here?"

"It will be several hours. We'd prefer not to fly it until morning—the local authorities are a bit jumpy about off-world vessels flying around the city at night. Will you relay your command authority to him?"

Jake paused, debating whether it was safe. But there was no other choice that he could see. "Can't you just fly us out to the shuttle? Surely the authorities wouldn't mind a local flying around at night?"

"You'd be surprised, Captain. Destiny is not Earth. You have to earn trust here. Or take it by force. Fortunately, I've earned a bit for myself, but it doesn't transfer to you just because you know me." She reached down to her side and lifted a canteen up to her lips that had hung at her side. Drinking deeply, she glanced at them and said, "thirsty?"

Jake nodded, and looked down at Suarez, whose mouth was bone dry between the chase and the shock of all the blood loss. Velar nodded to the two men beside her, one of whom opened a cabinet drawer, extracted a few canteens, and filled them at the sink in the corner of the room. The man distributed them to the visitors.

"Thank you," said Jake, and held one up to Suarez's lips. Alessandro gulped the water down, and Avery sniffed at his before likewise drinking. A bit dribbled down his chin and wet the dusty clothes given him by Velar.

Only Ben set his aside before turning back to Velar. "You've got to be kidding yourself to think that we'd give Volaski the command authorization for the shuttle."

Velar held up her hands. "Suit yourselves. I can transport you all back to the shuttle in the morning by ground car, but there's no telling who may try to stop us. I've called a few contacts since we arrived here, and word on the street is that you'd fetch a high price. Some Admiral is out to get you people and is willing to pay dearly for it. He's even willing to work with the syndicates."

Ben sneered. "Like you?"

Velar shrugged. "I suppose, if you want to think of me like that. I assure you, Captain," she turned back to Jake from glaring at Ben, "that my business is entirely legitimate."

"And what business is that?" Jake asked. He shook his head. Being shot at, and the general lack of sleep from the past week was starting to take its toll.

"Uranium. Destiny has rich uranium deposits, and I run one of the larger mining operations. In fact, this compound sits over one of the smaller mines. The larger ones are on the eastern edge of the continent, where the two continental plates are pulling apart, exposing virgin deposits."

Jake glanced down at Suarez. The man had fallen asleep. Finally. He struggled to keep his own eyelids open. Struggled a little too hard, in fact. Then he glanced at the canteen still in his hands.

"What the fuck did—" he lurched. Black clouds seemed to swirl at the edge of his vision. He was vaguely aware of Ben catching him before he fell into the table of equipment that the medic had left behind. He turned to Velar, and with a thick tongue said, "You'll regret—"

But before he could finish the sentence, his eyes closed—the smirking grin of Velar's face the last image engraved on his mind.

CHAPTER TWENTY-THREE

Ben glared at Velar, who still smirked. Gently, he lay his friend down on the floor and stood up, watching Velar's two assistants warily. Behind him, he heard two dull thuds. Avery and Alessandro had fallen into the rear wall. He glanced back at the guards. They had each extracted a sidearm—high caliber, by the looks of them, and both were now pointed at his head.

"He's right, you know," said Ben, trying to formulate some kind of strategy, and yet knowing there was little hope of not only overcoming the two armed guards, but the rest of the guards of the compound who were probably similarly armed. "You'll regret this. The Resistance doesn't look kindly on people who—"

Velar guffawed. "The Resistance is dead, Commander. It's all over the news broadcasts. Just yesterday I watched as Imperial police squadrons raided the offices of former Resistance members, hauling them off in handcuffs. Truth and Reconciliation is over. The Resistance blew it. Everyone in the Thousand Worlds saw the little stunt that you tried to pull in orbit over Earth last week, and I'm afraid you'll find that public sentiment has turned against you."

Ben eyed the nearest gun pointed at his head and judged the distance between them. "We've still got the *Phoenix* in orbit. They'll send a force down, and when they get here, you'll wish —"

"Wish that I'd just killed you? No Commander, you see, the people who try to rescue you will eventually find themselves joining you in my mines. Just think of it: how many men and women on your ship? You just might be able to double my workforce. And it's far better than what Trajan was going to do to you. In time, you'll come to see me as your savior, rather than your captor. Without me, you'd be dead already."

Ben snorted. He took the barest step towards the nearest guard while motioning his arms in an expression of disgust. "Please. You honestly think I'll ever be thankful to you? You're deluded—that's what you are." He turned to one of the men— the one to Velar's right. With another furtive step, he came ever closer to the one on the left. "So, what, is she paying you? Or are you slaves, too?"

Ben noticed the electronic neckband on the man, and finally understood. Slaves indeed. Spying a thin, translucent wire that ran from the collar to the skin, he finally realized what the devices were. "How can you live like this," he said to the guard, trying to fill his voice with pity. "You're a slave? To her? Why don't you just kill yourself and be done with it—not let her cut your balls off and have you at her beck and call. What, does she make you polish her boots, too?" The man took a step forward, and the hand holding the gun quivered. In the tense moment, Ben managed another stealthy shuffle in the direction of the other guard, who was now just feet away. Just another step....

"Stay where you are," barked Velar. Her voice had decidedly changed since the pretense of friendship had fallen. Both of you. Commander, if you take another step, I assure you it will be your last." She pulled her own gun out of her overcoat and pointed it at his head. With her other hand she extracted what looked like a comm device, which she fingered on and held up towards him. "The command authorization please, Commander."

"You're a deluded bitch if you think I'll give that up willingly." He sneered at her. They'd fought their way through literally dozens of Imperial ships, managed to convince a hostile marine brigade to lay down their arms and had narrowly averted the catastrophic damage from the fire they'd taken during the battle over Earth, and now here they were about to be taken hostage by a slaver. It irked him, to say the least.

Velar responded by pointing the gun down at Jake's prone head on the floor. "The command authorization, Commander. Quickly, please, or your Captain dies. And then you."

Ben swore, but took a deep breath, praying that Po would have the sense to see through whatever Velar and Volaski were planning. "Fine. Command authorization Jemez delta one five nine echo zed. Transfer command of *Phoenix* shuttle to arbitrary control."

Satisfied, Velar thumbed the comm off and returned it to her pocket. She nodded once to the man at her right—the one Ben had insulted. He withdrew another gun from his jacket, this one a bit larger, and Ben recognized it as something a little less deadly than the other firearm in the man's hand.

This one fired darts, and within seconds Ben writhed in pain as the dart released its charge of tranquilizer deep into the flesh of his thigh. He fell to his knees.

The same guard stepped forward, and, looking at Velar, said, "May I?"

She shrugged her indifference and turned to leave.

The guard swung hard with his gun, and Ben, with the last bit of consciousness he had, felt the blow hit his left temple, and he knew no more.

CHAPTER TWENTY-FOUR

Volaski entered the commands into the shuttle navigation computer to approach the *Phoenix* fighter bay and make a slow, deliberate landing. He knew what he had to do—he'd been rehearsing the plan in his mind for days now. And yet he still couldn't help but think of other ways—other things he might say or paths he might take to accomplish the mission.

But his path was set—it was too late to change his mind. The opening doors to the fighter bay loomed large through the front viewport, and Volaski turned to look at his navigator.

"You ready, Mott?"

The other man jabbed his fingers at a few buttons on the control panel. Clearly, the man was not ready—he'd been against the plan since Volaski had presented his men with it days earlier. Too risky. They were sticking their necks out way too far.

"You sure 'bout this, Vlad? With all that these ex-Imperials have been through, I don't think they're going to take our shit."

Volaski nodded. He agreed. Captain Mercer had seemed easy-going enough. Trusting, even. But his two companions,

Commander Jemez and Commander Po had seemed far more leery when he met them. The distrust showed in their eyes and sounded in their voices. He'd have to use that.

"No, I'm not sure." He turned back to his own controls. "But what choice do we have?"

He absentmindedly reached under the heavy folds of his thick shirt and fingered the electronic collar around his neck underneath. His collar. He hated the term. Dogs wore collars, not men. How many years had he worn it now? Ten? Twelve? After the fifth year, they all seemed to blur into one long nightmare.

Mott eased up on the controls and slowed their approach to the fighter bay, which loomed ahead. "We always have a choice, Vlad."

Volaski shook his head. "The alternative to obeying is death. For us, and our families. Don't think I haven't thought this through. I know the stakes."

The giant bay doors passed out of view and the vast fighter deck lay out before them, looking even more put together than the last time he'd seen it the day before. The repair crews must have finally made it to the fighter bay.

"Oh, I believe you've thought it through. I'm just not so sure about your choice."

Volaski grimaced. Neither was he. "So are you saying you don't believe Velar when she says that if we can bag this ship, it'll earn us our freedom?"

Mott set his chin. "No."

"Yeah, me neither." He glanced back into the passenger compartment and nodded at the men huddled there. Volaski's most trusted fighters and officers. Each of them outfitted with body armor, assault rifles, and a grim determination to carry out the brutal task ahead.

It would not be easy. But it would be worth it. Freedom always was.

CHAPTER TWENTY-FIVE

Po watched as the shuttle set down gracefully on the fighter deck. Volaski was at least a good pilot, if nothing else. She peered up at the walkway ringing the bay, halfway up the giant walls, and nodded to Sergeant Tomaga and then again at Sergeant Jayce, who had both donned battle-scarred ASA suits and trained their assault rifles on the entrance hatch of the shuttle.

Po realized this would be a very inopportune time for Tomaga to show his true colors if he was indeed playing her. Just like that, it would all be over, the *Phoenix* lost. But her gut told her otherwise. Tomaga may guard his emotions and mind well, but he couldn't hide the look in his eye—he was absolutely loyal not to the Empire, but to his men. She could see it in his interactions with them, and knew that his first priority was to get them to safety.

The door opened, revealing Volaski standing at the hatch opening. He started walking down the ramp slowly, before it had stopped moving. When he reached the bottom he turned back to the cockpit and signaled for his co-pilot to shut the door.

Well, at least he didn't come out with guns blazing. Po nodded her approval to herself, and took a few steps to the man, who greeted her handshake with a grim smile.

"Commander Po," he said.

"Captain. Is this private enough for you?"

She watched him look up at the marines flanking the ship at every angle. "A little crowded in here. Mind if we talk somewhere else?"

She regarded him. If he was planning on storming her fighter bay or ambush her during their meeting, he sure wasn't placing himself in a very strategic position.

"Conference room good enough?"

"That will be fine."

She waved her arm back to the bullet-riddled doors to the fighter bay's anteroom. "Follow me," she said, before turning to Ensign Ayala, who had accompanied her. It felt good to at least have someone at her side, even if she was only an Ensign with less than two years of experience in the fleet. As they passed through the fighter bay, she suddenly realized that not all of the senior staff was on the planet below. "Ensign, get Lieutenant Grace. I'd like her to join us."

"Yes, sir," said Ayala, and the white-haired woman spoke softly into her commlink as Po turned back to Volaski, who followed behind as they made their way through the anteroom to the conference room.

"I trust your men on the shuttle will be quite comfortable while they wait?" she asked.

Po watched as he gave a start, a nervous shadow passing over his face. She went on. "Surely you'd realize we would scan the shuttle before you landed. Or did you think you could hide the presence of sixteen well-armed men accompanying you?"

"I assure you, Commander, they are there for all of our protection. Yours included."

"I'm sure," she said, flashing a tight smile. "Just be advised that if the door to the shuttle opens again before you get back on it, an entire battalion of marines will make your men regret it."

Volaski hesitated. "Understood, Commander."

Strange. He seemed so demure. Hesitant. Uneasy. Quite unlike the man she'd met before. Earlier, he was far more brash. Commanding. On the viewscreen when they'd first seen him, he was a man in control. A captain not just in command of his ship, but a rather respectable fleet.

The doors to the conference room slid open and Anya Grace ambled in. "What's up, Po?" As usual, her uniform top was tied around her waist by the sleeves, revealing her tattooed arms and shoulders. "I'm knee deep in training newbies how to not crash into the hull so this better be important."

Po waved her to a seat. "Actually, I thought it would be a welcome break."

Grace flipped the chair around and straddled it. "Yeah, you're right. I'm telling you, Po, these newbies are really making me nervous. And I don't get nervous, remember? Just an hour ago one of them nearly punched a hole in the wall out there because he accidentally hit the gravitic accelerator during landing, the little fucktard." She trailed off when she saw Po indicate Volaski, who had taken a seat next to Ensign Ayala.

"Lieutenant Grace, this is Captain Volaski of the ship ..." she broke off, realizing that she didn't even know the name of his ship, much less any of his affiliations.

"*The Gamble.* That's my ship. And the fleet out there, well, that actually belongs mostly to Velar, though she lets me command the day-to-day operations."

"Velar? So she's the head of your organization?"

A look of disgust passed over his face. "She is. But not by our choice. You see, Commander, we're all permanent indentured servants to her and the syndicate she runs."

Anya blew air through her teeth. "Permanently indentured? Don't you mean slaves?"

Volaski nodded. "Yes, that is another way to say it."

Anya went on. "Come on, Captain, you look like a big boy who can handle himself. How is it that little old Velar has you and your men under her fingers?"

Captain Volaski reached up to his neck, slowly, apparently so as not to alarm any of them. Pulling down his shirt collar, he revealed the strange electronic device looped around his neck Po had glimpsed before. "A Domitian Collar. You've seen these, I presume?"

Po shook her head, but Ayala said, "I have. If you try to take it off, it kills you, right?"

He nodded.

Ayala turned to Po. "The Domitian Collar is an old Imperial tech that was banned soon after the destruction of my world. After the Thousand Worlds witnessed the horrors of the Belen diaspora, public tolerance for barbaric technology like this lessened. The Imperials don't use them now, as far as I know. Only slavers."

Volaski released his shirt collar, concealing the Domitian device. "And not even all slavers use them. But Velar has few scruples, and will not hesitate to do whatever she feels is necessary to keep control over her people. And those people now include your Captain, Commander Po."

The pit in Po's stomach returned. "They're captured?" She nearly stood up, but forced herself to remain calm. No need to clue Volaski as to how she really felt.

"Yes. Don't worry, they're safe. They're far too valuable to just kill. The government on Destiny is starting to crack down on the slave trade so it's become increasingly harder for Velar to kidnap her regular rotation of vagrants and young, single women. She's had to resort to kidnapping off-worlders, and, given your ship's new reputation, she felt it would be a singular opportunity to nearly double her workforce by kidnapping all of you."

It didn't make sense. Why in the world was Velar's second-in-command on the *Phoenix* telling her all about the inner workings of his boss's operation? "So, Volaski, why are you here? Why are you telling me all this?"

"Simple, Commander. We're slaves. And we want out. You and your ship represent the first opportunity to escape that we've seen in years. If we don't get out now, with the *Phoenix*, we never will."

Anya Grace blew the bangs out of her eyes. "Bullshit. It's a trap, Po."

Volaski shook his head. "I assure you, Commander Po, that I want nothing more than to see Velar hang, and to be a free man again. She's had me under her thumb for over ten years."

Po shrugged. "Why haven't you left before now? You've got ships. Surely you could just find some place to remove that collar and then be on your way," said Po.

"The Domitian Collar is a devilish little device, Commander. If I try to remove it myself, or any other technician for that matter, without the proper deactivation passcode, it sends a little signal to the tiny speck at the end of this fiber-optic," he indicated a miniscule little transparent line that ran from the collar into the back of his neck.

"If I try to even pull this out, the little chip at the end will … well, let's just say that even the milligram of explosive embedded within it will have quite a deleterious effect on a man's head."

Anya made a face. Po said, "I see. And if you were to just leave the system? I presume it has some sort of timed proximity response?"

Volaski nodded. "Unless Velar is with me, I have roughly twenty-four hours to get back to the planet."

"Roughly?" Grace looked skeptical.

"Yes, roughly," he eyed her. "Velar never tells us exactly how long. She feels it inspires a certain amount of terror to never know exactly when one's head will explode. It's kept her workforce in line for years." He turned back to Po. "But that's not all. For many of us, she knows where our families live. Mine is still on Destiny, and she has hinted that there might be similar devices hidden somewhere in our homes as well. If we try to escape, not only do we die, but we simultaneously lose our loved ones, too."

Velar's insidious schemes turned Po's stomach. But, no. It was all too convenient. "So, let me guess. You want us to lead another mission down to the surface to not only rescue our people, but to rescue yours?"

Volaski nodded. "Something like that, yeah."

Po pressed further. "And why us? Why haven't you just overthrown Velar on your own? Why now?"

"Because, Captain, if my men and I were to try a full frontal assault on Velar and her faithful slaves, we'd be instantly killed with the flip of a switch. But if some of your marines lead the assault and distract her from us, we'll have a much better chance. With her distracted, I can hit the critical Domitian infrastructure in her command center and set us all free."

Grace stood up, shaking her head. "He's full of shit, Commander. He's pulling your chain. Sounds like a ploy to capture yet more of us, and then, when we've only got a skeleton crew, that's when they attack and enslave the rest of us and take the ship. Well, fuck that."

Po's eyes narrowed. "Why is our shuttle full of your armed men?"

Volaski nodded. "As I said, they are for my protection, and yours. And they are at your disposal in this operation. I've discussed this with them, and they all agree that the risk is worth it."

"Are their families at risk too?"

"Some, yes. Not all."

Po didn't know what to do, or even if she could trust him. Anya clearly thought they couldn't. And for good reason—the man could be lying. The device around his neck could be a prop, and he could be luring them all down to a similar fate to the first landing party.

"So what's your plan? Just waltz into Velar's headquarters, shut the devices off, and be on your way?"

"It won't be quite that simple. But we have the element of surprise. She is not suspecting this—not in a million years. She can't understand this."

"Understand what?" Po shifted in her seat.

Volaski looked into her eyes, and rested a clenched fist on the conference table. "That we're willing to risk our lives, and the lives of our families, for freedom." He pounded the fist once for emphasis.

Po watched his fist. His eyes. His legs. Anything to read his body language—to try and discern his true intentions. "Has anyone tried before?"

"Just a few, and they died horribly. But it was always the new ones, and the single ones—the lone freighter pilot with no attachments. The newly captured merchant who didn't know any better. Surely, Commander, you can understand the stakes involved when there's more than one life on the line. Especially when those lives are young. Commander, I have two children at home that I haven't seen in ten years."

Charred little bodies flashed into Po's mind, and she shook the image from her head. Her eyes drilled into Volaski. Could he know? Was it possible? Had he studied her past, and found the one thing that might let him in? That might get her to trust him? Just a mention of his made-up little children and he'd be in her good graces?

No. It wasn't possible. A motley crew of slavers on Destiny would not have access to Imperial fleet records.

Unless Trajan had sent Velar all of their personnel files. Unlikely, but Po didn't put it past the man. He'd gone to great lengths to arrange the ill-fated battle at the shipyards; doing something like this would be almost inconsequential.

She decided to just confront the possibility head on. Maybe put the man on edge. "Did Trajan put you up to this?"

A look of surprise covered Volaski's face. "Admiral Trajan? Why, yes, he did."

Po raised her eyebrows at his confession, but he continued. "Soon after you escaped Earth, he sent out private messages to all his contacts with the syndicates. Velar received one, and I can only assume that others on Destiny got similar messages, since soon after your landing party arrived it was ambushed, but not by us."

Po watched his eyes. They darted between her and Anya, who paced back and forth nearby, perhaps in an attempt to put the man on edge. He ignored Ensign Ayala entirely. Had he ever seen a Belenite before? "What did Trajan promise you?"

Volaski snorted. "What else? A very large payment. And possibly your ship. He was vague on that point, but he was clear that if we took your entire crew as slaves, we would not only be highly paid, but that the Empire would look the other way on the slave trade in this sector, giving Velar and the other syndicates free reign."

Po pressed on. "And Velar believes him?"

"She is wary, but this is too good of an opportunity to pass up. If we refuse, the Empire swoops in and takes her out. Simple as that. They've only let her live this long because she is willing to do the odd job here and there for the Empire. We're not the November clan, or any of the larger, wealthier syndicates. We're small fry, and Trajan knows it. And he's had other business on Destiny. So the rumor goes."

The rumor? What sort of business?

Anya, still pacing, turned to Po. "You can't trust him,

Megan. Let's just take him and their men hostage, and their ships, and use them as bargaining chips."

Po nodded. "The thought had crossed my mind." She turned back to Volaski. "Any reason why I shouldn't?"

Volaski cleared his throat and leaned back in his chair. "Your Captain will die. The landing party will die. Velar has no compunction about putting a bullet in their heads if she thinks it will encourage you to cooperate. For now, they are safe. But if she doesn't immediately get what she wants, she will start killing your crew, one by one, until only the Captain is left. And then she'll just call Trajan and hand Mercer over to the Empire if she can't get you to come down with a handful of crew."

"So, she's expecting you to return with a shuttle full of *Phoenix* crew members? As more slaves?"

"Yes. Those men in the shuttle were under her orders to secure the *Phoenix* once I leave with another group of you."

The enormity of their problem weighed on Po. Refuse Volaski, and her crew members die. Trust him, and risk all of them dying. Or worse, living for the rest of their lives as slaves to some small-time syndicate on the dustbin called Destiny.

"Commander Po, this is the bridge," a voice sounded over the comm.

Po moved over to the wall to access the comm receiver there, out of others' hearing range. "Go ahead."

"Sir, we're not sure, but we think sensors have picked up a large gravitic signal. Something big just entered orbit around Destiny. It's hard to tell for sure, but the signal matches the signature of the *Caligula*."

Damn. They weren't even going to wait for Velar to uphold her end of the deal.

And they were probably going to give the woman more than she bargained for.

CHAPTER TWENTY-SIX

When Jake woke up, his head hurt. A lot. He struggled to open his heavy eyelids, and reached up to rub them when he realized he couldn't even reach his face. He pulled.

A chain tugged back at his wrist.

Shit.

Forcing his eyes halfway open, he peered around. Alessandro lay next to him, chained to the wall, and against the other wall lay the heaping forms of Avery and Suarez, similarly bound. They had the same collars around their necks as the medic and Velar's two grunts, and a little dribble of dried blood marked both of the men's necks.

He reached up to his own neck, and felt the collar there. A thin wire led from the collar to the back of his neck and he winced in pain as he realized that it ran under his skin.

That's when the headache kicked in. He could almost feel the end of the wire sticking deeply into his brain. He wondered exactly how far it went in. Wrapping his fingers around the wire he tugged at it, wincing as the pain of one hundred tiny daggers seared into his head. Pulling harder, he grit his teeth and prepared to yank the thing out before pausing to consider his actions. With no idea what might be at the end of the wire or what it could be wrapped around, he decided to let it be.

He looked back down at the sleeping forms of his crew and a sudden realization dawned on him. Ben. Where was Ben?

"Avery!" he whispered, as lowly as he dared. "Avery, wake up. Bernoulli! Suarez!"

The others seemed to be still sound asleep, deep under the effects of whatever had been in those canteens. It started to make a little more sense to him now. That room—it was probably a prisoner prep area of some sort, where Velar brought her victims to rest, perhaps after a contrived chase. He thought back to the bandits with the guns at the marketplace who had chased them all the way to the compound, and wondered if they had been in on the whole thing. And then, once the unsuspecting prisoners felt somewhat safe in that room, that's when they were given something to drink from the tainted canteens.

But Ben. Ben didn't drink—he just set his canteen aside and started confronting Velar. Something Jake should have been doing himself.

His head pounded, he raised a slow, groggy hand up to his face to rub his eyes. What the hell did they do to him?

Dammit. Ben was right. He was right all along. The man never trusted anyone, and Jake had believed all along that it was one of his friend's faults. But now, it turned out that if Jake had have deferred to his Ben's judgment, they'd never be in this mess.

Why did I take this command away from him in the first place?

His decision to lie to his friends and assume command of

the ship started to seem incredibly foolish. Who the hell was he to think that he could do a better job than either Ben or Megan?

Doc Nichols. The doctor supported him; he approved of his erstwhile decision. He'd seen decades of service in the Imperial and Resistance fleets, and he should know a good officer—a good captain—when he saw one. Shouldn't he? Didn't he say that Captain Watson was a friend, but that the man was not the most competent of captains?

No, those were not his words. He said the Captain lacked imagination. Initiative. Drive. Those were things Nichols he saw in Jake. Well, not so much saw in Jake, so much as *didn't* see in Ben.

And the man was right. For as long as Jake knew his friend, Ben had never been one to creatively think his way out of situations or to do anything other than quote the regulations. Hence his callsign: *Manuel,* a semi-racist play on the word *manual.*

Looking around the room, he tried to focus his mind on his situation. Yes. Time to get his bearings. Know his surroundings so he could formulate a plan. Get them out of there. That's what he did, right? That was his talent? Getting out of trouble? He sure as hell could get into it, so he must have some experience getting out of it.

Each brick wall was studded with rings, through which the chains that bound all of their arms and legs passed. A table was against the third wall, next to which rested a set of shelves that held several more menacing-looking collars like the one around his neck. A set of tools lay scattered about on the table, including a scalpel, several small drills with multiple, bloodied attachments, and one end of the table looked as if someone had bled heavily on it, and someone had hastily tried to clean it away, with mixed success.

The fourth wall held only a door. No other openings into the room could be seen. Not even so much as a ventilation shaft. Still wincing in pain, Jake struggled to his knees, and attempted to raise his body upright in a kneeling position.

His head spun, and he lay back down.

"Avery," he croaked.

"Yeah?"

Jake glanced over at the marine, whose head was in his shackled hands.

"You ok?"

Avery rolled his head around, and Jake could hear a succession of distinct pops from his neck. "Yeah. I'll manage." He fingered the wire sticking into his neck and started tugging on it. "What the hell is this?"

"I don't know. I wouldn't mess with it though, we've got no idea what's at the end of it."

Avery scowled, but released the wire and stood up with a grunt. He wavered on his feet for a moment before steadying himself against the wall. "What's the situation, Captain?"

"I just woke up a few minutes before you. Commander Jemez is gone. Haven't seen him." He felt a little sick, but shoved the feeling of nausea deep down inside. Ben was alive. He knew it. The man was built of stronger stuff than he was.

Avery examined the iron brackets on the wall, testing their strength. "Do you think the *Phoenix* knows we're captured?"

Jake shook his head. "I've got no idea how long we've been out. Feels like a few hours, but it could have been days for all we know."

The other two men started groaning. Jake reached out and wiggled Alessandro's boot. "Hey, Bernoulli. Wake up. Time to get moving."

Alessandro opened one eye—the same side as his half-mustache. "Have you brought me on vacation, friend?" he said, groggily.

Jake couldn't help but chuckle. "Best vacation ever. No obligations, holed up with the three most standup guys you could hope for, and I imagine there will be room service later."

Suarez grunted. He sat up and touched the collar around his neck with his good hand. The other arm was wrapped tightly to his chest, supposedly to keep him from moving the shoulder. Jake wondered if they had gone ahead and operated on it, since it appeared their hosts were not planning on returning them to the *Phoenix* anytime soon.

The *Phoenix*. He hoped that Megan had the sense to keep the pirates off the ship, no matter what offers of help or threats they made.

Suarez wrapped his hands around the wire sticking into his neck. "Bitches aren't going to collar me," he said.

"Suarez, NO!" Jake yelled, but before Avery could reach over to his companion, Suarez yanked on the wire as hard as he could.

POP.

Suarez's head snapped at an angle, his eyes screwed up into odd directions and turned crimson red, and two bursts of blood shot out his nose.

He slumped back to the floor, motionless.

Jake's nausea returned and he doubled over and vomited

onto the floor.

Avery jerked against the chains to reach towards his friend but it was no use. There was no point.

Suarez was dead.

CHAPTER TWENTY-SEVEN

"Commander?"

Po shook her head. It was all coming so quickly. The landing team unable to communicate. Then Volaski saying that they were captured as slaves, to be sent to work in some god-forsaken uranium mine. Then the pirate captain claiming a change of heart, and that he wanted to help the *Phoenix* recover her crew. And now the *Caligula*. The fighter deck conference room seemed to spin around her.

She leaned in towards the comm. "I'll be right up, Ensign. Maintain position, and cut all active scanning of the planet and the orbital space above it. Cut all systems that could give away our position, except gravitics. In fact, lower our position by Z minus 1000 klicks."

"Aye, sir," came Ensign Roshenko's reply.

She cut the comm and turned back to Volaski, Ayala, and Lieutenant Grace. "I'm afraid something has come up. Captain, please follow Ensign Ayala and me to the bridge. Grace?" She glanced at Anya, who had risen from her chair in half-alarm. "A word?"

She led the woman to the anteroom and spoke in hushed tones. "Is your fighter crew ready?"

Anya whispered back. "No. But they're what we've got. They'll hold up in a fight with any pussy-ass pirates. Why? What's up?"

Po leaned in close to Anya's ear. "The *Caligula* just shifted into orbit."

"Shit," breathed Grace.

"They probably haven't spotted us yet due to our position over the pole, but they will. Eventually."

"Are we fixing for a fight, sir?" Anya almost looked eager. But Po knew better than to fall for the bravado.

"No. But get your crew ready just in case." She turned back to the waiting Ayala and Volaski.

"What's the likelihood that they're just here by chance, sir," said Ayala as they made their way to the bridge, after Po had filled them in.

Po glanced sidelong at Volaski, who shook his head. "Zero."

The atmosphere on the bridge was far tenser than when Po had left it. The tactical station was a hive of activity as the officers and technicians there scrambled to get a passive sensor reading on the *Caligula*, and the operations station struggled to coordinate the shutdown of the nonessential systems that might be detectable.

"Status?" said Po as she approached the command console. She motioned to one of the two marines stationed at the door to stand by Volaski and watch him.

Ensign Roshenko looked back at her. "We've lowered our altitude. Now hovering 2000 klicks above the pole."

"Science, what's the likelihood that they can read our gravitic signature from wherever they are, given our position over the pole?"

A young man at the science station hesitated. "It's hard to say, sir."

"Best guess, Ensign." She eyed the man—not quite a boy, but young nonetheless. Probably a Los Alamos volunteer—the weapons lab had sent a steady stream of scientists to be officers in the Resistance fleet back in its heyday, and this man fit the bill—he looked a little awkward in his uniform, as if unused to formal authority.

"Maneuvering gravitics certainly leave a smaller trace than shifting gravitics, sir. The energy consumption is smaller by several orders of magnitude. But it's still a gravitic signal, after all. The ionic and electromagnetic interference of the pole might mask us, but then again, it might not."

Po grit her teeth. No, that was unacceptable. They had to get rid of their gravitic signature. But there were only two ways to do that. Either put on a burst of speed to enter a stable orbit, or….

"Ms. Roshenko, lower us to the ground."

Ensign Roshenko spun around again. "Sir?"

"You heard me. Take us to the ground. Quickly."

Volaski still hovered near, under the watchful eye of his marine escort. "Commander, the Admiral knows you're here somewhere. Down there you'll be a sitting duck for whatever he decides to throw at you."

She didn't even look at him. She was still too angry that it was his syndicate that got the *Phoenix* into their precarious position, in spite of his assurances that he just wanted out like them. "They know we're at Destiny, but they don't know where. If we can get down to the surface before they find us, it'll buy us some time."

"And when we get down there? Are we just going to twiddle our thumbs while the Admiral decides whether he'd rather take us out with nukes, or just conventional torpedoes?" Volaski had turned to her in a confrontational manner.

Po didn't even look at him, but stared straight at the viewscreen, watching as the distant surface loomed larger. "Control yourself, Captain. This is the only way we buy time without directly engaging them. And we are in no shape to do that at the moment. Helm, are we moving?"

"Yes, sir. Halfway to the surface," said Roshenko.

The science officer cleared his throat. Po struggled to remember his name. "Sir, uh, there is no surface there. It's ocean."

She spun around to him. "It's not ice?"

"It looks like the northern hemisphere is in the last few weeks of summer. Nearly all the ice has melted." The young Ensign looked as if he loathed being the bearer of yet more bad news to the frazzled Commander.

Po steeled herself. She must not look frazzled. She had to appear in control and in charge and on top of things and put together and….

"Take us down anyway. Put us under the water, and then maneuver us under one of the chunks of ice, if there are any."

The entire bridge crew turned to look at her.

"Get to work, people. You heard me." She didn't even look at them.

The science officer hemmed and hawed a little. "Uh, sir,

these ships weren't exactly designed to go underwater."

She walked up to talk to him more directly. "Any reason we can't …" she peered at his name insignia, "Ensign Szabo?"

Ensign Szabo shrugged. "Well, for one, the hull was meant to withstand positive internal pressure. If we go much more than a few meters under water, the pressure differential will go negative. A lot. The hull wasn't designed for that. It's not even in the specs what it will—"

"Ensign, it's not in the specs because no one has ever needed it. We need it. I'd reckon that if our hull can withstand the vacuum of space, that it could handle a little external pressure."

He shook his head. "Yes, but sir, the pressure differential between space and us is only one atmosphere, with the force gradient pointing outward. Under water the pressure will be many times higher than atmosphere, and the force gradient points inward. There's no telling what will happen."

She sighed, quietly, so that the young man wouldn't hear. "Thank you, Ensign Szabo. Take us under, Ensign Roshenko. Keep us as close to the surface as possible, and get us under ice."

"Nearly there, sir. Another ten klicks. Decelerating now. Five, four, three…." She began to slow the countdown.

"Sensors, still no sign of the *Caligula*?" She kept her gaze on the viewscreen, which displayed the vast, ice-pocked ocean now surrounding them.

"None, sir. But there's only so much passive scanners can pick up," came the reply from tactical. She wasn't even sure who had responded. It felt like she was in a tunnel—just her and the viewscreen, watching as the ocean reared up at them.

The voices around her faded into the background and she braced herself for the moment the hull would contact the water. She wondered how the gravitic compensators would handle it.

A gentle wave, and it was over. They were floating on the surface, but steadily sinking.

"Push us under, Roshenko," she said, fighting to keep her voice steely and calm.

Glancing at Roshenko, she saw her hand shake as she touched the controls that would take them under the surface. She walked up behind her and rested a hand on her shoulder.

"We'll be fine," she said, with a small smile. She desperately wanted to believe it. Roshenko's shoulder felt tense. Po didn't blame her, and yet also inwardly marveled at the Ensign's steely resolve, in spite of her shaking hands. Any other Ensign fresh out of the academy would have broken under the pressure about two battles ago.

The science officer, Szabo, called out, "Two atmospheres of pressure, sir. We're now past the hull rating."

The picture on the front wall changed as the water engulfed the camera on the front of the hull, replacing their view of the vast field of ice islands with a blue, turbulent vortex, pierced by low, streaming shafts of weak sunlight that managed to shine through the maelstrom of water.

Szabo continued. "Four atmospheres." They watched the maelstrom of water and light turn darker. The deckplates moaned and the girders behind the walls creaked.

"Six atmospheres. Eight. Ten. Sir…." Szabo began, but Megan cut him off.

"Maneuver us underneath that ice sheet, Ensign," said Po.

The entire bridge crew waited with baited breath as the water began to settle, and Ensign Roshenko—a bit calmer now with Po's hand on her shoulder, pushed the ship under one of the larger sheets of ice. Something snapped behind one of the walls, making everyone on the bridge jump. But no explosions. No water rushing in. After another minute, it was all over. The water on the viewscreen cleared, and Roshenko breathed a sigh of relief.

"We're there, sir."

Po turned to the science station, shooting a quizzical look at Ensign Szabo.

He studied his console, tapping a few buttons. "Hull is holding, sir. Pressure at twelve atmospheres at the bottom of the ship. Two at the top."

A collective sigh swept through the bridge. Po felt like a *Caligula*-sized weight had just been lifted from her shoulders.

She'd done it.

For now, at least.

Po backed up to the captain's chair, and as she did so, her mind turned back to her friends down—now up—on the surface. She had absolutely no desire to make that chair her own. "Good job, everyone. Now, let's get to work trying to detect that ship, and our people. I want some answers."

CHAPTER TWENTY-EIGHT

Captain Titus leaned over the command console, studying the readout. He glanced up at the one-eyed man sitting in his chair. The captain's chair. "We've shifted into orbit, sir." He looked over at the tactical station. "Any signs of the *Phoenix*?"

The Lieutenant sitting over the technicians at the station shook his head. "Only about a dozen or so merchant frigates."

Admiral Trajan, who had remained uncharacteristically quiet for the past several minutes, finally spoke.

"They won't be in orbit, Captain. They're far too cautious for that."

Captain Titus felt his brow furrow in surprise. "Oh?" He turned back to tactical. "Does Destiny have a moon I'm not seeing?"

The officer at tactical shook his head, but Trajan responded for him, apparently already quite familiar with the Destiny system. Titus wondered again what had brought him here before. "No moon, Captain. Check the poles." He turned in his chair to face tactical. "What's the interference like at the poles?"

The officer studied his readout. "Heavy interference, sir. Ionic storms are generating a significant EM noise signal."

Trajan nodded, and looked back at Titus, who kicked himself for not thinking of it before Trajan. Yet another instance of the Admiral making him look foolish in front of his own bridge crew. "Incline our orbit to take us over the south pole, Captain. If they're not there, take us over the north."

"Yes, sir," and he nodded to the helmsman in confirmation. Turning back to Trajan, he cocked his head. "Do you suppose Velar and her gang could have secured the ship by now?"

Trajan paced the bridge. "I doubt it, Captain. Mercer is far more capable than you give him credit for. But who knows? Maybe our work here is already done."

The helmsman announced, "Orbit adjusted, sir. We'll pass over the southern continent in a few minutes."

Titus glanced over at tactical. "Engage all visual and infrared cameras. Cover every portion of the sky—they could be above us, below us—I don't want to just stumble on top of them and blow our surprise."

"Yes, sir. Cameras engaged," came the reply.

For once, the Admiral seemed to be in a pensive mood, and the bridge fell back into silence. Whenever Trajan was present, Titus didn't feel like it was his purview to initiate conversation.

He glanced at the Admiral. His one eye was shut. The gash over the other half of his face had begun to heal, though the man had scoffed at the idea of going to sickbay to have the doctor look at it. The man was fiercely independent—Titus surmised that the Admiral refused to believe that he needed anyone around him, including the doctor. Including Titus. He suspected that every one of the bridge crew was a giant disappointment to the man, who probably would have staffed the bridge with robots if he had his druthers.

Several silent minutes later the helmsman spoke up again. "Now passing over the southern continent. We'll be at the pole in fifteen seconds."

Titus glanced at tactical again. The man shook his head.

After another minute, the helmsman cleared his throat. "We've passed the polar region."

"Nothing, sir. No sign of the *Phoenix*," said Captain Titus.

Trajan steepled his hands in front of his chin. "Scan all orbits of Destiny. Look for a debris cloud."

"You think Velar might have just destroyed them?" asked Titus.

"No, I don't. But we may as well exhaust the possibility."

Another silent two minutes passed, and the tactical officer spoke up again. "No debris clouds so far, sir."

"And we'll be approaching the northern polar region shortly, sir," said the helmsman.

Trajan murmured to himself, "Mercer, Mercer. Where have you gotten yourself to?"

Titus cleared his throat. "You don't suppose they've landed somewhere? Hidden themselves under some foliage or covered the ship with camouflage or the like?"

"It's possible," Trajan said. And he nodded. "Indeed, if we don't find them in orbit, either as an intact ship or a debris cloud, we're forced to consider the possibility. Either that or they've flown out to hide behind one of the gas giant planets

—but that is unlikely." He sat pensively for a few more moments before standing up briskly out of his seat.

"Comm. Open up a channel to Velar. You'll find I've placed the appropriate frequency on your console display."

The comm officer's eyes darted over to a section of his console, and he nodded in recognition when he found it. "Channel open, sir."

"Velar of the Urensys syndicate, this is Admiral Trajan of the Imperial Fleet. Is now a good time to talk?" His voice sounded perfectly polite, as if the man actually cared—as if he were calling on an old friend. Titus realized the man could hit all the right notes—pitch perfect—without actually feeling any sentiment behind what he was saying. A true psychopath, indeed.

The main speaker on the bridge came to life. "This is Velar. Greetings, Admiral Trajan. Welcome to Destiny. I must say, I hadn't expected you so soon. Is there a problem?"

Trajan smiled. "I was about to ask the same of you, Velar. Tell me, do you know the whereabouts of the *NPQR Phoenix*?"

Vague, inaudible voices muffled in the background before Velar replied. "The last I saw of her, she was hovering over the northern polar region. They seemed to think they could avoid being seen there."

Trajan glanced at the sensor officer. The man shook his head. "We're passing the north pole now, sir, and still no sign of them."

Admiral Trajan began a slow pace around the command console, and Titus stepped back to avoid being caught in the middle again. The vulture was swirling.

"They apparently have moved on," Trajan replied. "Tell

me, Velar, Do you suppose they were warned of my arrival?"

The response was immediate. "Absolutely not! I run a tight ship here, Admiral. None of my people would dare betray me...."

"I don't doubt it," he said, cutting her off. "Still using the Domitian Collar, I suppose. Barbaric, but yes, it does get the job done." He continued pacing. "Do you have any guests there?"

"We do. The former Captain, his First Officer, and the Chief Engineer. And two marines," she added, "one alive, and one dead."

A dangerous smile broadened on Trajan's face, which combined with the cavernous pit of the eye would be enough to give a brave man nightmares. "Quite a quarry you've got yourself, madam."

"And does our deal still stand? We get to keep them and the rest of the crew, right?" She sounded nervous. Titus smiled inwardly. She had every right to be. If it were up to him, he'd bomb the entire slaver complex without any further conversation.

"Yes, it stands. But we have no deal if the *Phoenix* has escaped with nearly her entire crew still aboard."

Titus could almost hear Velar sweat. "Understood, Admiral. I'll get the word out. My people will find them if you don't. Not to worry. The *Phoenix* is as good as yours."

Trajan's pace came to a head back at the captain's chair. "It *is* mine, Velar. Don't forget that."

"Of course, Admiral. I didn't mean otherwise—"

"I know what you meant, Velar." Trajan looked peeved. "Just hear me now. If that ship is not found in the next twelve hours, I'm afraid our deal may have to be altered."

A long pause.

"Yes, Admiral. Velar out."

Trajan turned to Titus. "Captain, prepare a squadron of fighters to patrol the orbits of Destiny. I want that ship."

"Yes, sir." Titus spun on his heel to motion to the Wing Commander behind him, and pointed at him, indicating he carry out the Admiral's orders.

"Comm officer?" Trajan said, peering over at Ensign Evans.

"Yes, Admiral?"

"You'll find another set of carrier frequencies there on your panel. I need to speak to Dr. Stone."

Ensign Evans studied his console, and nodded. "Yes, sir. Entering frequencies now."

Titus could hear the Ensign mutter into his headset, talking with some communications operator on the other end, when finally a sterile voice sounded over the speakers.

"This is Dr. Velasquez," said the female voice, without a hint of emotion. "Dr. Stone is indisposed at the moment. May I pass along a message?"

The look in Trajan's eye could melt right through a solid composite metal hull. "Indisposed? He had better hope he is indisposed with research, Dr. Velasquez, and not his hobbies. I've come to retrieve the Cybernetic Institute's first deliverable. I assume it is ready?"

With hesitation, the voice continued. "I—I'm not entirely sure. Please stand by, Admiral."

Dr. Velasquez's voice cut out, leaving an uncomfortable silence reigning on the bridge. Trajan was seething, that much was clear. Titus only rarely had seen the Admiral actually angry. Usually, the man was calm and collected, even as he ordered soulless, horrific acts.

Titus cleared his throat. "Sir? Would it help if I sent down a contingent of—"

"No, Captain, it would not. I already have an entire squadron of marines and technical staff down there as a permanent reminder to the good Doctor of our arrangement."

"And that arrangement...." Titus trailed off as the eye came to rest on him.

"Is none of your concern at the moment, Captain," Trajan replied icily.

Titus clammed up immediately, breathing a sigh of relief as the speaker blared to life again, saving him from the conversation.

"Admiral, th—this is Doctor Stone." The voice was high, and nervous. "I have good news, Admiral. Lymphatic response is normalized, and the protease catalytic enzyme response is now off the charts! The next step is to normalize the synaptic response in the cortex, and stabilize the electromagnetic response of the—"

"Doctor, Doctor, Doctor. Do you think you can fool me?" Trajan asked, dangerously.

"E—excuse me, Admiral?" The man sounded like he'd swallowed his tongue.

"I know about you, Doctor. My men have described to me your ... habits. And I've looked the other way because until now you've delivered. But if I find that the Empire can no longer trust you with its science funding, you'll find that I have no problem *cutting off* the dead weight, if you know what I mean."

"But Admiral, I assure you that—"

Trajan stood up and interrupted. "Do you have the first deliverable ready?"

"Yes! Yes, I do. At least, part of it."

"Part of it," Trajan repeated, in annoyance.

"Yes. You wanted to test it, correct? Well it is definitely in the testing stage. I can't deliver the amount requested, b—b— but...." The man hesitated, the nervousness in his voice coming loud and clear through the speaker. "But would .1 kilos be sufficient?"

Trajan pursed his lips, and sat back down again. "Will that be enough to perform a dozen or so tests back at the testing center on Corsica?"

"Yes! More than enough. I'll— I'll, I'll package it up right away and have it ready for you whenever—"

"Very well, Doctor. The Emperor will be most pleased with your progress, I'm sure. He follows your research personally. Did you know that?"

"Uh ... no, sir. I didn't," the man stammered. Titus imagined a half-balding man in a white lab coat with flop sweat running down his temples.

"Oh, yes. He does indeed. Your research is extremely important to him. He is a man of science, after all." Trajan sat down, and his voice took on a softer, more reasoned tone, apparently trying to calm the scientist down. "An enlightened man, he is. Emperor Maximilian was still in his graduate program in Biology when his father, Emperor Justinian, died and he inherited the throne. I assure you, he understands what it takes to make the great strides you've made."

"D—does he?" Doctor Stone was starting to sound a little more at ease. "Then, perhaps I can ask a small favor? To help the research along? I seem to be running low on subjects."

Trajan stirred in his seat, a look of annoyance crossing his face. "And what of the last shipment of Terran girls I arranged last year?"

A long pause. "Used."

Trajan sighed. "Very well. The Commander there will send his men to the streets and pick out some new ones. How many?"

Stone hesitated. "Twenty?"

"Twenty missing girls is not easily covered up, Doctor."

"On Corsica, sure," came the curt reply. "But on D-Destiny? That many disappear every week. The slavers are quite active here.

Trajan nodded slowly. "Done. Anything else, Doctor?"

"Th—that should be it. I await your shuttle to transfer the deliverable."

"Excellent. Trajan out."

The Admiral glanced up at Titus, as if sensing a question. "You look concerned, Captain. Tell me what's on your mind."

Titus cleared his throat, and swallowed, not wanting to raise the subject on the bridge in front of the crew. But the Admiral seemed eager to address his questions. Especially the most obvious question of all.

"Sir ..." he began, choosing his words carefully. "Do we—that is, does the Empire engage in kidnapping?"

"Kidnapping?" Trajan looked genuinely surprised. "Kidnapping? Of course not, Captain. Though I can imagine how you'd be left with that impression. No, the Empire does not kidnap. Do we reassign children of dissidents? Yes, naturally. Do we send entire families to the reeducation centers? When the corruption runs deep in a family, yes. Do we kidnap? No. Most assuredly."

"Yes. Well—" Titus began.

"Then what was that conversation about, you're wondering?"

Titus nodded. "Yes."

"A good question. With an easy answer. You see, the Doctor is working on a special vaccine to prevent an incurable new disease that is raging through the frontier worlds. He requires subjects to test it on. The most vulnerable to the disease are the weak. The destitute. The street people. So naturally, they are the ones we'd want to help first. We only bring in those most at risk. For their own good." He lowered his chin and stared at Titus. "Isn't that rather beneficent of us?"

"Yes. Yes it is, sir. But what did Stone mean when he said the previous girls were … *used*?"

Trajan nodded. "He is a scientist, Captain. And scientists have such a utilitarian way with language. I'm sure he just meant that, as a testing resource, the pool of subjects had been used up. What he probably should have said is that all the girls are now immune from the sickness that will surely sweep through this world within a few months. Years at the latest."

"I see," said Titus, unsure of what to make of it. The explanation sounded plausible. But he'd never heard of a sickness sweeping through the frontier worlds.

Trajan nodded, as if reading his mind. "Yes, the existence of the threat has been classified. To keep hysteria from spreading. No sense in allowing panic to set in. No, Captain, the Emperor would much prefer to keep this under wraps. To cure the epidemic before it ever really gets started, and surely before it becomes common knowledge."

Titus inclined his head in acquiescence. "Very well, sir. Shall I prepare the shuttle, then?"

Trajan stood up, and straightened his uniform. "Thank you, Captain. I was just about to ask. Such foresight. Really, I could not ask for a better assistant," he turned to the rest of the bridge, raising his voice, "Or a better crew." He said something similar the week before, praising the bridge crew for all to hear. Just before he blew the Chief Engineer's brains out. Trajan turned back to Titus. "I'll be in my quarters. Find that ship, Captain."

"Aye, sir," he replied as the Trajan stalked out the rear door of the bridge. He turned to the Wing Commander. "Prepare a shuttle. Send it to the Cybernetic Institute down on the planet to receive delivery of … a deliverable."

How odd. A vaccine. Being developed at an institute for cybernetics.

It didn't add up.

But it wasn't his job to add it all up. It was his job to find the *Phoenix*. He turned his attention back to his console, and got to work.

CHAPTER TWENTY-NINE

The deckplate creaked, and Senator Galba held his breath. He'd heard the klaxons, and the announcements to man emergency stations, but there was never any mention of what was going on.

Turning back to the half-disassembled console panel, he poked his probe back into the circuitry. It'd been so long since he'd worked with electronics. Forty years? Forty-five? His father was insistent that he learn a trade. As insurance. Just in case the family's fortunes fell. And so he spent two years as an apprentice tech in the Imperial Senate Office building.

He grinned to himself. That's when he bagged his first woman. She was young, like himself, tall, shy, and lit up whenever he casually tossed a compliment her way. Ah, the way they'd steal away to that utility closet during lunch….

The deckplate groaned again, and he glanced up at the walls and ceiling nervously. The ship seemed to be protesting some kind of strain. Some intense pressure. With a press of a button, he flipped on the power to the terminal and navigated to the ship's tactical situation software, hoping to see the source of the moaning of the deckplates. Heh—it reminded him of tall, shy tech-girl. She always moaned. Not like Willow, who only cursed like a marine whenever she got frisky.

Within minutes, he found the source of the ship's problems—about ten meters of ice water covering the hull. What in the world was the Captain thinking?

The Rebels must be hiding. But who could they be hiding from?

There was only one answer to that question.

And so he shifted to his new task. If he could force the *Phoenix* to come out of hiding, the game would be up.

All it would take was a simple power buildup on one of the hull's gravitic plates. That would serve both his purposes: disrupt gravitics, and possibly cause a hull breach, forcing them to surface.

Within minutes it was done. Careful to make the buildup escape attention of any engineer who might be monitoring, he set the charging rate low. It would take hours. Maybe days. But the damn thing would blow eventually, and then it'd be all over.

The Plan would continue.

And he could retire to his Corsican beach house. Finally.

The door slid open without a warning. Dammit—he thought he'd locked it.

"Need any help, Senator?"

Wonderful.

He snapped his head around towards the door and saw Private Ling's bruised and battered face. A smile tugged at the marine's lips.

"What in the blazes are you talking about?" said Galba.

Ling stepped into the cramped utility room. "It struck me

a few minutes ago. You look exactly like that one Senator. You know, the one who heads up the Truth and Reconciliation Committee? The one trying to improve Empire-Old Earth relations?"

Galba rolled his eyes and turned back to the console, stuffing a few wires back into their places and shutting the back panel. "You're seeing things, Private. But don't worry...." He turned back to face the young man and flashed a big smile. "I get it all the time. In fact," he grunted as he stood up, and leaned in closer, "You'd be surprised how much pussy I can get when I impersonate a Senator." He waggled his eyebrows at the young man as he stepped towards the door.

"So ... you're not Senator Glib? Gliba?" The young man looked positively disappointed. Good.

"Alas, my friend." The door opened and Galba stepped through. "But if I see him, I'll let you know. So long!"

He turned and hurriedly walked away before the marine could change his mind about his identity. Something would have to be done about it, of course. He supposed he could tell Willow. See if she could finger the marine for the previous explosion. She had mentioned last night in bed that the XO was hot on the saboteur's trail.

"Hey! Stop!"

Galba froze, and turned his head, cautiously. Private Ling stood behind him, arm extended.

"You forgot something."

Galba paced back, and took his tool bag from the offered hand.

"Thanks, soldier," he said, nodding once before turning to resume his retreat.

"No problem," Ling called after him.

He turned the corner, and quickened his pace through the common area, past other Imperial marines sprawled out on couches and chairs, and headed for the stairs.

CHAPTER THIRTY

Jake was numb. The image of the twin blasts of blood streaming out of Suarez's nose refused to leave his mind; neither would the image of the eyes jerking into an unnatural, twisted gaze. He didn't get much time to dwell on the death immediately afterward, as Velar had rushed in and, using some device in her pocket, made the rest of their heads nearly explode in pain.

It didn't kill them, of course, but Jake dropped to his knees with his head between his hands and writhed. The pain lasted for what felt like hours, but probably was only a few seconds. Time seemed to dilate with incomprehensible pain, it appeared.

"First lesson. Don't touch the collar," said Velar, as she waved two of her guards over to collect Suarez's body. As they dragged his limp, ghoulishly staring form out the door, she continued. "Second lesson. Do exactly what I tell you, and you will be rewarded. Disobey, and you'll be punished. Severely, and without delay. That jolt I just gave you was but a taste. A sample, if you will. Don't make me actually punish you." She smiled. It was an ugly, smug smile.

"My people will find us, and they'll take you down, bitch," Jake croaked.

"Oh? I doubt that. Captain Volaski is onboard the *Phoenix* as we speak. He should be joining us shortly with another group of senior officers and marines to *rescue* you." She laughed. "And after that group is subdued your ship will be mine for the taking. Chew on that as you spend your first day of the rest of your life in my uranium mine."

"Where's Ben? Why is he not with us?"

She fingered the hidden device in her pocket. "He was not as cooperative as you. I had to keep him isolated."

Jake bared his teeth, and tried to keep the snarl out of his voice. "I swear to you if you hurt him, I'll rip your fucking throat out."

A laugh was her only reply.

She turned to leave, but glanced back at Jake with menace in her eye while she patted the bulge in her pocket. "Don't tempt me, Mercer." The door closed behind her. A tiny trail of blood marked the path where Suarez's body had been dragged.

Another body. Another one of his decisions had led to another cold, lifeless body. His head sank down in his hands. Not another one. How much longer could he keep this charade up? Why not just throw the responsibility onto Ben when they all escaped, and let him deal with the body count? Let him make the hard decisions? He'd be good enough, wouldn't he?

He glanced around at Alessandro and Avery. The scientist looked to be in shock, and the marine looked like he was suppressing a rising rage. "Avery?"

The marine grunted. "I'm going to kill the bastards," he

said. "I'm going to wrap ten of these things around her neck, set them to the highest setting, and then shove my fist down her throat." He set to work examining the chains around his wrists, looking for a way to unlock them.

"I know, Avery. She'll pay. But first we've got to get out of here."

Alessandro, who hadn't said a word the entire time, looked up at him with dazed eyes. "You really think we'll get out of here?"

Jake forced a stoic look, setting his jaw and nodding. "We have to, friend. You want to die here? I sure as hell don't. Come on buddy, it's just another chess game. We've just got to find their weakness and then catch them off guard. Just like you've done to me every morning for the past few weeks." He tried on a grim smile. It felt false, and flimsy, but it was all he had.

Fuck Velar.

"If you say so, friend." Alessandro started fingering his Domitian Collar, searching for any kind of functionality on it.

"Careful there, Bernoulli," said Jake.

"It must have some kind of access port or settings panel."

"It's probably run remotely."

Alessandro nodded. "Sure, but any device will have manual factory resets and calibrations buttons."

"Any normal device, sure, but these aren't exactly the latest entertainment gadget."

A wan smile of defeat passed the man's face. "All the same, friend, it's something to do."

Jake couldn't argue with that.

Nearly an hour later, two guards showed up and ordered

them to their feet. With rough manners, they bound their hands together, but removed the chains binding them to the walls.

"Move," one of them said, pointing with his assault rifle at the door. Jake eyed it, and his reflexes nearly made him leap for the weapon, but he restrained himself. *Later,* he thought. When their chances were better. When he'd found Ben.

They followed the guards out the door, into a long, cluttered hallway. Most of the lights were out, and those that were on, flickered pathetically. At the end of the corridor, another door led out into another passageway, but this one was made of rock—not the wood and brick of the previous one. Clearly, they were underground. The damp, musty smell belied the stagnant air and unwashed bodies.

"How far down are we?"

"Shut up. No talking." The guard eyed Jake, and pointed to his own collar in warning.

"What, do they prevent us from talking too mu—" and suddenly his head snapped to the side and he shrieked in pain. The flash subsided as he panted, but the fiery daggers inside his head throbbed for a few more seconds, before ebbing slowly away.

"Yes," said the guard.

Well that's going to put a damper on our escape, he thought.

CHAPTER THIRTY-ONE

The guard led them to an elevator shaft that plunged them down another several hundred meters or so, and the air soon became thick and warm. The smell of unwashed bodies intensified and rose up to meet him as a dense, ripe wall as they exited the elevator and plunged into a mass of people. Some laid against the walls, as if sleeping. Others huddled sitting on the ground in tight, silent circles, while still others fiddled with mining equipment. Both men and women—at least there were no children down here, Jake noted with a feeling of relief, until he saw a young man who couldn't have been more than fifteen sitting up on one of the iron girders spanning the length of the low, jagged rock ceiling. The teen swung one hanging leg back and forth as he eyed the newcomers.

The guard pointed to another man—better dressed and not as thin as the other slaves, but gaunt nonetheless.

"Boss," said the guard to Jake, still pointing at the other man, and then turned to leave with his companion.

The man the guard called boss walked over to them. He walked with a limp, and his bland, pale skin spoke of years beneath the surface. Stringy hair grew in tufts on his balding head and spilled over onto his tattered shirt. But compared to the rest of the people there, he looked veritably healthy. "Oh good. More grunts. Listen, friends. The rule here is that you work. If you make your quota, you earn your food and I don't get punished. If you don't make your quota, I get punished. If I get punished, I take it out on you tenfold. Understood?"

Jake, his head still sore from the last shock from his collar, decided to risk speaking again. "You sleep without a guard?" He glowered at the filthy man, who advanced on Jake until they were eye to eye.

"Funny. I don't want to be here anymore than you do, so just shut it, ok? We all work, we all live. Simple. And if you think about doing anything to me, you'll have to deal with *him*," he indicated the boy up on the girder and laughed gruffly. "Jeremiah doesn't take well to people jostling me around." He picked up a heavy-looking piece of machinery and shoved it into Jake's chest. "Take it. I'll teach you how to use it, and then you teach your friends." He glanced at the other two, pointing at the floor. "You there. Pick those up."

Avery bent over and with a grunt, picked up a device that looked identical to Jake's. Alessandro hoisted his up, as if it were just a small power tool. Jake rolled his eyes at himself as he wondered how the scientist lucked out with the light one. The tools looked identical, but Jake's must have been thirty kilos at least.

The man they called boss dug into his front pocket and extracted a whistle, which he blew. Jake was not prepared for the sound, since the rock walls seemed to magnify the shrill noise, and he nearly dropped the hulking piece of mining equipment onto his toes. "Break's over! Move!" The boss pointed down the long, sloping passageway, and with an assortment of grumbles and groans, the crowd got to its feet and started shuffling down. There must have been nearly one hundred people, Jake guessed. The boy sitting on the girder dropped down to the ground and tailed after another slave—a gaunt, haggard man who glanced back squinting at the newcomers. Had they been recognized? Impossible. No one here would know anything about the *Phoenix* or the Resistance.

Jake, Avery, and Alessandro followed the boss close behind. Every now and then, a passageway would branch off the main one, and a small group would peel away and follow it. They passed a few motorized carts—empty, but soon to be filled with valuable ore, which Jake supposed would be hauled to the surface for processing. He wondered why they didn't just dig a large open-air pit and make the process more automated.

He didn't feel like asking. People with power couldn't abide questions.

At the junction with another branching side-passage, the boss stopped, and pointed down it, indicating that they follow the winding path. Jake went first, and occasionally, a pale, flickering light would come to life on the low ceiling just as it became too dim to see one more step ahead of him. After nearly five minutes of trudging along with the mining equipment, he ran into the blank wall at the end of the passageway, and nearly dropped the heavy load.

"Careful!" The boss smacked Jake hard in the back of the head with a small, tubular electronic device he'd been carrying. "That thing is worth more than your life, I can guarantee that."

Jake bent his knees and set the equipment down before

reaching around to rub his ankle. The tendons still had not healed properly ever since the run-in with the surly drunk in the bar on the Earth shipyards. It seemed like ages ago, though he realized it was only a little over two weeks.

The boss growled. "Hey, this isn't rest time! Pick it back up! I've got to show you how to use it, and then I've got to go patrol the hallways for slouchers."

Alessandro hemmed. "Excuse me? How many words?"

The boss screwed up his face and glared at Bernoulli. "Huh?" He turned back to Jake. "What the hell is he talking about?"

Alessandro paused, as if choosing his words carefully. "How many? Before the shock?"

Realization dawned on the boss's face. "Oh. I don't know. Fifteen or twenty. But after awhile you get more. It discourages revolt. Helps the lower class slaves stay demoralized."

"And you?" Bernoulli asked.

"Me? Ha!" The man pulled the cap off the electronic device he held in his hand. "I get however many I want. I need them to tell dumbasses like you what to do." He pointed at Jake. "You. Point that thing at the wall, and engage the power."

Jake looked down and examined the giant tool in his hands. Indeed, at one end of the grimy object, an array of three metal rods protruded, each covered with wires wrapped as if they were massive solenoids. Several large, unmistakable switches dotted what Jake supposed was the top, and the largest one sported a fading symbol that he recognized as the Russian symbol for "power on."

He flicked it, and when he held it properly around the worn rubber grips, found the trigger. When he pulled it, a blinding beam of ionized, electrified gas shot out the front, slamming into the rock wall ahead of him. A blast of heat, and the occasional white-hot spark of rock hit him in the face.

The boss yelled. "Careful! You'll lose your eyes if you don't close them and look away." Jake powered the device down and looked at his handiwork, while the boss grumbled his disapproval. "See? All you made was a hole in the wall. You've got to take out wedges. Small enough to carry, but big enough to make the trip down the passageway worth it. You've got six hours to haul out one ton of ore each."

Alessandro's head snapped to glare at the boss. "One ton! If I carry twenty kilos per load, that's fifty tri—" his head lurched back and he screamed, apparently having hit his word quota.

"Yeah, that's right smartypants. Fifty trips. Some people can do it in forty. But," his face descended into a distasteful grin, "the women take longer. Sixty. Sometimes seventy. But God help me if it ain't fun to watch."

Alessandro had set the extractor down and was now furiously rubbing the back of his head, panting and sweating as if he'd run a mile. Jake thought he heard the man mutter an expletive under his breath. He wondered how low they could speak without triggering the collar's sensors. He reached down to pick up Bernoulli's extractor, and, tugging at it, realized it was just as heavy as his own. Huh. The scientist must be far stronger than he realized.

The boss held up the cylindrical device. "This is an omni-scanner, which we use as an ore discriminator. When you haul a piece back to the bins, you scan it first. If the concentration of Uranium is at least one percent, you dump it in the green bin. If it's less, you dump it in the red bin. Remember, green good, red bad. Got it?"

They all nodded wearily.

"Good. Then get to work." He handed the cylinder to Avery, and strode back down the passageway and out of sight.

Avery turned to Jake. "Well, Captain?"

Jake only grunted. "You heard him. Let's get to work." He hoisted the extractor back up to his chest, aimed at the wall, and imagined the white-hot beam slamming right into the hull of the *Caligula*.

CHAPTER THIRTY_TWO

Po had to sleep. She had lost track, but she was sure it had been over thirty hours since she last slept. Sooner or later, it would catch up with her, during some critical moment when an error of judgment would mean life or death for every crew member in her charge. She shuddered to think of it. These people trusted her. Ostensibly looked up to her, if the rumors were true. She couldn't let them down, and therefore, she had to sleep.

At least, that was what she told herself as she marched down the hall towards her quarters. Since they were currently underwater and the pilots had no way to train, she'd left Lieutenant Grace with the bridge, rather than the less-experienced Ensign Ayala. She figured a few hours in charge of the whole ship might do the Wing Commander some good. Give her a different view of things.

The ship groaned. She could almost hear the deck girders creak as she walked down the hallway, stressed from the incredible forces pushing against the hull. Spaceships were not built like submarines. The science officer told her that the hull plates on the lower decks were likely experiencing over ten times atmospheric pressure—far more than the ship was designed for.

Four hours. She allowed herself four hours to sleep. What could happen in four hours? Surely nothing Lieutenant Grace couldn't handle. The woman was capable—she could give her that. In the week or so she'd been the Wing Commander, she'd whipped it into better shape than Po imagined Jake would ever have done had he remained its leader. He was far more suited to command of the ship than he was of the squadron, even though he'd commanded Viper Squadron back on Earth for over two years. She thanked her stars that Captain Watson had chosen him.

Collapsing on her bed, she called out to the computer: "Wake me up in four hours."

"Acknowledged," the disembodied voice replied.

Her mind drifted to various images as she tried to sleep, and before long she realized that she was dreaming, though only half so. Klaxons reverberated in her mind as the images of the battle over Earth replayed before her. The *Caligula*, firing a steady stream of railgun fire, the *Fidelius*, with its contingent of celebrities, politicians, and other citizens of Earth, blown to pieces by a well-placed torpedo. The turncoat Ensign who'd fired the fateful shot, before raising a gun to his own head and splattering half the bridge with his brains. The former XO splayed out on the floor with a metal rod sticking out of his temple.

The klaxons. The yelling. The screaming. It all flooded back to her. That night. That night in San Bernardino. Her home. Their home. She ran down the stairs and peered out the window, looking up at the night sky. The bombs showered down; the force of one landing in the street knocked her away from the window and hurled her into the opposite wall. She got up. Blood in her mouth. She tried to run upstairs, but the blast had collapsed one of the exterior walls into the stairwell. She ran back downstairs and outside, hoping to scale a ladder up to the kids' room. Rick was up there with them. They'd be safe. They'd all be safe until she made it.

She found the ladder, and set it up, not heeding the aircraft that shot by overhead, showering that section of the city with bomb after bomb. Why were they attacking so indiscriminately? Didn't they know there were children there? Innocent people that had nothing to do with the Resistance?

A bomb struck and blasted her with a massive shock wave. She flew off the ladder and into a nearby tree that broke both her fall and her arm. But it didn't matter. The pain didn't matter. The jagged radius bone sticking out of her forearm didn't matter. Fire ravaged the house—what was left of it. She screamed. Oh, how she screamed. She ran towards the burning structure, but a neighbor tackled her and restrained her. Hours later, she entered, after the fire crew had snuffed out the dying flames. She found them. All three of them, huddled together. It had happened before, and now it happened again, accelerated, pausing at certain moments to etch certain images deeper into her mind.

She knew it was a dream, but she couldn't stop the image from replaying. She knelt down and held them. Burned, desiccated bodies are so much lighter than normal, healthy ones—it is odd what one thinks about when in shock. The klaxons. The alarms. The inhuman screams coming from her own throat. It all mixed together. She looked down at the bodies; her throat constricted around a cry.

The faces. The faces were not *them*. They were other people. The two fighter pilot recruits. Ashdown, and Xing.

The klaxons. She jolted up in her bed, shaking her head and trying to figure out what was real and what was dream. The images were old—just memories. Nightmares, not dreams. But the sound—the alarm was new. She rubbed her eyes and tried to clear her head.

"Commander? Are you there?"

She recognized the voice. Lieutenant Grace. The sound of the voice was almost unrecognizable over the klaxon of the red alert. Sweat stained her undershirt and she grabbed a soiled uniform top from the floor to mop her face.

"Po here. What's happening, Anya?"

"An explosion on deck thirty-one, sir. And after the explosion, the hull buckled down there and flooded the entire deck before the emergency bulkhead came down. We've got casualty reports."

"I'm on my way," she said, trying to not groan as she struggled to her feet.

So much for sleep.

CHAPTER THIRTY-THREE

By the time Po reached the bridge again, the klaxon had stopped, but the bridge crew was in a frenzy. The operations station flurried with activity as the ops crew did their best to manage and coordinate the emergency response to the hull breach, and the security station was already organizing an investigation into the cause of the explosion.

"Was it intentional? Or just caused by the water pressure?" said Po as she walked through the door to the bridge.

"We don't know yet, Commander." Anya stood up from the captain's chair and stepped back as Po approached the command station and examined the console. She scanned through the data for the number that mattered.

Nine.

Dammit. Nine more. At least, the nine crew members stuck behind the emergency bulkhead were presumed dead—unless they'd all had time to reach an ASA suit or somehow found a pocket of oxygen trapped behind a bulkhead.

"Have internal sensors been able to scan for life signs?" said Po, turning back to the ops center.

A young technician shook his head. "No, sir. The salt water is interfering with sensor readings."

Another voice sounded over the comm. "Bridge, this is Chief Simmons in engineering. Sir, that blast knocked out our gravitic thrusters. Conventional only until we get that gravitic field projector repaired.

As the man spoke, Po could hear the deckplates groan under her feet as the strain from the pressure warped the girders and support structure of the ship. How much more could the ship take? If there was a saboteur aboard, now was the time to find out, before they could kill another nine people. Or ninety. Or all of them. How many were left? 670? Or was it 663 now?

"Thank you, Chief. Keep me apprised of progress. Po out."

She leaned in towards Lieutenant Grace, keeping her voice low to avoid the bridge crew overhearing. "Do you think one of Tomaga's men could be responsible? I've got Volaski locked down in the brig, so I think we can eliminate him as a possibility."

"What about his men aboard the shuttle? Could they have triggered it remotely somehow?" Grace puffed the hair out of her eyes.

"Possible. But I don't want to remove them from the shuttle—they're all armed, and we can't trust Volaski that they want to help us. For now, we've got to keep them in their makeshift brig."

"We can disable all shuttle functions remotely. That would ensure they're not using the shuttle's functions to screw with the ship," suggested Grace.

"Good idea." Po bowed her head, thinking. "Anya," she said, turning to Lieutenant Grace, "we need intel. We need to know the second the *Caligula* leaves so we can get out of here."

Grace nodded. "Sounds reasonable."

"We at least need to know its position so if we have to break the surface, we can do so when the *Caligula* is on the other side of the planet. And I think the only way we're going to know that is to shift a fighter out there. Who do you trust?"

Without skipping a beat, Anya replied, "I trust me."

Megan shook her head. "No. I'm not letting another senior officer off this ship. We can't afford to lose you. Choose someone else."

"Fine. I'll send Lieutenant Quadri. And I'll stick the newbie with him as his gunner. Ashdown. He's the least disappointing of the bunch."

Ashdown. Po's back stiffened. She remembered his charred face from her dream, still fresh in her memory. "Very well. Go."

Po waved her hand to the back of the bridge, indicating to Grace to get a move on. As she watched her Wing Commander leave, she waded in among the chaos of the ops center.

Time to track down the saboteur.

CHAPTER THIRTY-FOUR

Gavin almost danced he was so excited. Strapping himself in next to Lieutenant Quadri—a dark-haired, lean young man himself, probably no older than twenty-five by Gavin's eye—he engaged his console and began going through his pre-flight checklist he'd learned over the past week.

"What the hell are you doing?" said Quadri.

"Doing pre-flight."

"Newbie, this is an urgent mission, not a training run. There's no time. Engage the sensors, but passive only, and keep your thumbs ready to twitch in case we need to shoot our way out of a tight spot. Just leave everything else to me. Got it?" His dark eyes scanned over him and Gavin nearly wilted under the stare.

"Yes, sir."

Quadri nodded his approval, and thumbed open his comm channel. "Bridge, request permission to leave P-town."

Commander Po's voice sounded over the main speaker. "Permission granted, P-one. Make your shift just fifty meters or so above our current position. Just above the ice. Then scan the sky before you head up there. Po out."

Quadri keyed the coordinates into the console and looked over at Gavin. "Ready, kid?"

Gavin grinned.

"Wipe that smirk off your face. It's bad luck." Quadri looked back down at his console. "Engaging in three, two, one…."

As Gavin watched, the view of the fighter deck disappeared, replaced suddenly by the spectacular sight of an endless field of ice sheets, fragmented by deep blue, icy cold water under a pristine purple-blue sky without a single cloud. Too cold for clouds. He peered down below the craft at the ice sheet that hid the *Phoenix*, and gaped in awe. There was a thick, white layer of frost on the top, making the sheet completely opaque. There was no way any orbiting ship would be able to see under it.

"Ashdown?" Quadri glanced at him, with an expectant look in his eyes.

"Oh, right. Scanning…." Gavin flicked on the visual scanners, which made high-resolution, filtered images of the sky above them. After a minute, the computer gave him its conclusion: the orbital space above the north pole was clear. For now, at least.

"We're clear," he said.

"Sky acknowledged as clear, engaging engines now. Hold on to your butt—I'm taking us out fast with conventional thrusters. Too risky for gravitics."

Gavin nodded and immediately was thrown hard back into his seat. The bow of the ship pointed up and they began to pick up speed at an alarming rate. He felt his cheeks sag backward towards his ears, and found it difficult to breathe. He reckoned they were pushing four g's.

The leading edge of the fighter started to glow red. Gavin checked the altimeter and saw that they'd already passed three klicks. Quadri pulled back on the accelerator, reducing their acceleration to near zero, and the fierce glow on the leading edges of the bow and wings faded to a dull red, and then to nothing. Gavin saw the planet fall away beneath them, and the view of the blue sea speckled with the ice islands morphed into a sight that he still found breathtaking—the curvature of the planet, and the clouds far below, marking a distinct line between the green-blue of the lower atmosphere and the purple-black of the upper atmosphere and space.

"Fifty klicks," said Gavin. "We're good to accelerate again —the atmosphere's pretty thin."

Quadri hit the accelerator, throwing Gavin once again back into his seat. He fingered his console, initiating a passive EM and infrared scan in all directions from the ship. He had no idea what orbit the *Caligula* might be in, so he might as well scan all of them.

An indicator flashed at him. "Contact. Coming up fast behind us!"

Quadri glanced at his console in alarm. "What is it? Hurry! Tell me what it is!"

Gavin fumbled with his controls, trying to remember his scant training. "Uh, ok, trying to read the transponder…." Where was it? Which button? He breathed relief as he saw the appropriate control, and read off the resulting code out loud. "Merchant freighter out of the Oberon system. Registry code HY11 dash fourteen dash—"

"Ok, ok! I don't need a speech. Just tell me if the contact is Imperial or not."

"You don't think the Imperials might have enlisted the help of all the merchants freighters in orbit to look for us? I hear the Empire can be persuasive," said Gavin, trying to keep the edge of sarcasm out of his voice.

"Yeah, you're right. I'll incline our orbit away from them." As Quadri pulled at the controls, the ship rotated, and accelerated to the east.

Gavin felt vindicated and grinned as he scanned his console for more results. "So what's the plan here? We scan for the *Caligula*, but what then? Won't they be able to see us as we see them?"

"Yeah, but we're faster than the are. If they try to give us trouble, we'll just shift to the opposite side of the planet and make them catch up. We just need to keep an eye on them, and shift back to the *Phoenix* when we see them doing anything suspicious. You know, like fire missiles down at her, or something."

"Got it." Gavin got the feeling he was in for a long ride.

Or not. "Contact. This one just appeared out of nowhere. No, wait. Three contacts!"

"Get a read on them, newbie."

Gavin's heart froze. "Uh, Quadri, they've got an Imperial code. They're fighters. But…." He shook his head, trying to figure out his readings.

Quadri's voice had reached a crescendo. "But what?!"

"But," he began, gulping, "these fighters have a code that matches the fighters on the *Roc*. Wasn't she destroyed back at Earth?"

Quadri shrugged. "Looks like one survived. And the Empire stripped out her fighters. Gavin," he turned to Ashdown, "this is bad news. Those fighters have the exact same capabilities as us. A regular Imperial fighter? Sure, that's no problem. But three of our own? That's a problem."

"What do we do? Do we shift back to P-town?"

Quadri smirked. "To hell with that. We're taking the bastards out."

Gavin's frozen heart gave way to a deep knot in his stomach. He saw Quadri fire up the gravitic drive, and they accelerated up to match the speed of the incoming fighters. With a gulp, Gavin readied his triggers and prepared to get missile locks.

Quadri let out a war-whoop as he flipped the ship ninety degrees and blasted out of the pursuit plane. In a split second, he tapped on the gravitics to shift them Z minus 500 meters, and suddenly Gavin saw the underbelly of one of the fighters loom up fast in the viewport. His twitchy thumbs squeezed the trigger, and the fighter exploded in a fiery cloud.

"Nice shooting, kid. Hey, you're not as bad as Grace said."

Gavin laughed. "Yeah, that was pretty—"

"Don't get cocky. There's still two more. We're only lucky that these pilots probably haven't developed any tactics based on the short range gravitic shift."

A blinding flash ahead of them suggested otherwise, and Quadri hit the shift controls to get them out of the way of the suddenly incoming fighter. "Shit!"

Their fighter flipped one eighty, giving Gavin a momentary view of the craft that had strafed them, but he missed his shots.

"It's ok, kid, we'll just wear them down. Try to keep up."

The star field flipped again, making Gavin's stomach lurch. He had to keep telling himself it was all a video game. It wasn't real, he told himself. Just a game.

Red streaks strafed past the viewport by Gavin's left shoulder. He caught his breath in his throat.

Just a game. Just a game.

CHAPTER THIRTY-FIVE

Titus glanced up at the Admiral. "Sir, our fighters report they've engaged a craft from the *Phoenix.*"

"Excellent, Captain. Keep me apprised of their progress. Sensors," he called behind him, "The *Phoenix* is here somewhere. Find them."

The sensor officer nodded, and busied himself with the console. Titus wasn't sure what else the man could be doing, other than what he already was doing. The sensors only had so much bandwidth and could only scan a certain portion of the space above the planet at a given time.

"Use whatever resources you need, sensors. If you think an extra five technicians will help you get the job done, then just say the word," Trajan said.

A look of surprise crossed the sensor officer's face. A whole team of technicians helping him with his job? "I'm not sure I'd know what to do with them, sir."

Trajan's eye darted towards the man, who looked away in what Titus could see was revulsion. The sensor officer apparently had not grown used to the crater of Trajan's left eye. Titus wanted to reach out to the man and warn him to keep his emotions in check around the Admiral—he'd never seen him lash out at anyone because of the eye, but he didn't want any preventable outbursts, either.

"I'm sure you'll think of something, sensor officer," said Trajan coolly, and turned back to face Titus. "Captain, send word to astrometrics to devote every telescope, every camera, every device that can detect a photon, neutron, proton, neutrino, or muon to scanning the star field for the *Phoenix*. That fighter came from somewhere, and if I don't have it in my possession soon, I swear I'll bomb the planet into oblivion." The Admiral gripped the armrests of the captain's chair until his knuckles were white.

Titus was taken aback. He'd never heard the Admiral raise his voice, or sound even remotely flustered. He'd always been the model of absolute control. But Trajan's tone suggested he was quickly losing his patience.

"Perhaps, sir, we could press Velar to lend us more direct assistance. Perhaps we could even enlist the help of the merchant ships in orbit."

Trajan steepled his hands in front of his face. "Yes." He breathed in deeply through his nose, and released the held breath through his mouth with a sigh. "An excellent idea, Captain. Good work. I will contact Velar from the ready room. You will handle the communications with the merchant ships from here." He stood up to leave. "And Captain," he said before turning, "Did you manage to send condolences to the family of the Chief Engineer yet?"

Titus's back stiffened. What an odd question. And the meaning was unmistakable.

It was a warning. Titus had crossed a line, somehow. He should have kept his mouth shut when Trajan was expressing his impatience. And now, the implied threat was obvious.

"Yes, sir. I did," said Titus. He racked his brain for something else to say to placate the man. The lunatic. "But I neglected to send any bonus pay. Shall I do so?"

Trajan paused, with his back turned towards the Captain. "No. Funds are tight right now. We can't spare anything away from destroying the Resistance." He started walking towards the door. "Carry on, Captain, carry on."

Titus rubbed the back of his neck and breathed deep. They had to find that ship, for the good of his own crew. They might not survive Trajan losing his patience in the future.

CHAPTER THIRTY-SIX

Gavin whooped as the second fighter from the *Caligula* burst into a fiery explosion, which was quickly snuffed out by the rarified atmosphere of the upper exosphere of Destiny.

"Cut the noise—we ain't done yet, Newbie," said Lieutenant Quadri, who hit the gravitic shift initiator, shifting them in the blink of an eye to tail behind one of the two remaining fighters. Before Gavin had a chance to even aim, the ship shifted away.

"They're learning," he said, as he squeezed off a few rounds at the fourth fighter, which flitted momentarily into view.

"Yep," said Quadri. "I guess we'll just have to step it up a notch." Without even a lurch, the ship stopped its forward motion and plummeted down towards the atmosphere. "What's our capacitor charge?"

Gavin glanced at his console. "Only fifty gigajoules."

Quadri swore. "Only two or three more shifts until we'll need to recharge. Let's make them count. We'll wait until one of them shifts to take us out, then we'll move. Be ready."

"Got it." Gavin gripped the controls and held his thumbs nervously over the triggers. Really, it was just like a video game. The gravitic drive accelerated all parts of their bodies at once, removing any sensation of g-forces. It seemed to detach him from the physical reality of their swerves and plunges, serving to make it seem like he was still sitting in Jet's bunk, whipping his friend at yet another round of *Starfighter*.

Out of the corner of his eye he saw a flash of movement —one of the fighters had shifted into place just a few dozen meters away, plunging down through the atmosphere to match their speed. With a flick of a finger, Quadri shifted them over to trail the other fighter, which Gavin sprayed with a barrage of fire. It exploded with a puff of debris. Gavin peered down out his viewport to watch the body of the pilot fall into the atmosphere—he couldn't tell if the man had ejected, or if the blast had killed him and knocked him out of the wreckage of the bird now spiraling down through the atmosphere with its owner.

Quadri breathed deeply. "Ok, *now* you can celebrate."

"What about the other one?"

"He shifted away when he saw his buddy skydiving."

Gavin whooped again. "So, you're telling me that we just took out four fighters all by ourselves? Is that what you're telling me?" he asked, his voice rising in excitement.

"Looks like it, Newbie." Quadri pulled up on the controls and pointed them back up to the line of the atmosphere wrapping the planet and gunned the accelerator. "Don't get all cocky on me."

"No, sir. Of course not, sir," he said with a mock salute.

Quadri continued, "I mean, it was pretty badass and all—

I've got to admit. So when we get back, the story for the rest of the P-town jocks will be that we took out eight."

Gavin chuckled. "Right. Got it." He looked back at his console. "Caps are back up to one hundred gigajoules. When do you think we should go back?"

"When we find the *Caligula*. I'll adjust our trajectory to take us on a highly inclined orbit—we should be able to scan most of the space above the planet that way. We'll find her soon."

"And then?"

Quadri blew air out of his mouth. "Hell if I know. Then it's time for Commander Po to come up with another crazy-ass plan."

Gavin shrugged. "Hiding under an ice sheet doesn't seem that crazy to me," he said.

"That just shows you've never served in the Imperial fleet. They don't do shit like that there. That's the point of the Empire—order, rules, control. That's why they never could just let Earth govern itself. We like to show our crazy too much for their liking. And Captain Mercer and Commander Po have just a bit too much crazy for the Empire's liking. Why the hell do you think they're spending so much time chasing us? We're just one ship, after all. The Resistance basically got crushed back there at the shipyards battle, and yet here they are chasing us down."

Gavin turned to Quadri. "So you think they're just chasing us because of those two?"

"Of course. Mercer is turning into another Pritchard. And they can't afford another Pritchard."

"But isn't he dead?"

Quadri smirked. "Dead? You must have never met Pritchard. The man is a certified genius. No sniveling Imperial admiral could outwit him. No, Newbie, he's out there somewhere, biding his time until just the right moment. He'll come back with some fleet he's pulled out of his ass and save Earth. You just watch."

Gavin shrugged again. "Yeah. Here's hoping."

CHAPTER THIRTY-SEVEN

Captain Titus turned to the communication station. "Ensign Evans, send out a wide band broadcast to every ship in orbit."

After a moment, the comm officer said, "You're live, Captain."

Titus cleared his throat. "To all merchant vessels in orbit around Destiny. This is Captain Titus of the *NPQR Caligula*. I would understand if you felt unnerved by our presence here, as this is not Imperial space. To be honest, I have no interest in staying longer than we must. But I am looking for a hijacked Imperial vessel. The *NPQR Phoenix* is in the vicinity of Destiny, and we will be eternally grateful to the merchant or syndicate who manages to find it, and tell me her location. There may even be a reward involved," he glanced back at his XO, who grinned.

He continued, "But rest assured that whoever does not help in the search will be added to our list of merchant vessels engaged in illicit activity, and will be targeted or detained by any Imperial fleet ship in the future. We have scanned the orbit of Destiny and already have a log of every ship here, so don't think you can slip out unnoticed. I await all of your responses. Relay them by text to my communications officer. Titus out."

"Sir!" the tactical officer yelled out. Titus spun to face him. "One of our fighters has returned, sir."

"Just one?"

The officer nodded. "They're messaging us that the others were destroyed, and they barely managed to escape intact."

Titus shook his head. The pilot was lucky Trajan was not on the bridge. "Order him to return to the fighter bay for a debriefing. I want the report in twenty minutes."

"Yes, sir."

So. The *Phoenix*'s fighter fought off four of their own, destroying three. Three next generation gravitic drives lost, out of twenty-three transferred from the *Roc*. He made a mental note to instruct the Wing Commander to develop new tactics involving the new drives, since the *Phoenix* fighter most likely had been practicing with it for weeks now.

"Sir!"

Titus spun again towards Ensign Evans. "What now?"

"Sir, I've got a merchant vessel—well, more like a pirate ship—that claims to know where the *Phoenix* is."

"Where?"

"They haven't told me yet, sir. They want to talk to you."

Titus nodded. "Patch me through."

A ragged voice sounded over the speaker. "Titis?"

"Captain *Titus*," he corrected. "To whom am I speaking?"

"This is Captain Vorat of the cruiser *Ragswain*. I can take you to your ship."

Titus nodded. "Good. How shall we—"

"For a price." Vorat interrupted, his voice degenerating into a spasm of violent coughing. It sounded as though he had a vicious cold.

Titus nodded to himself. "If you give me information that leads to the *Phoenix*, you will be rewarded. But until then, you receive nothing until I see evidence of your knowledge. What are the coordinates?"

Vorat laughed. "No, I'm afraid it doesn't work that way. I don't fear you. Put me on whatever damn list you want, I never go into Imperial space anyway. No, I want pressed bars of gold. I know you Imperial boys all carry a supply on your ships. You know, for just such occasions as this?"

He was right, of course, but the presence of emergency funds on Imperial capital ships was supposed to be classified information. Especially that they had pressed gold bars.

"Fine. I'll give you two kilograms of gold."

Vorat laughed even harder, then coughed even more violently. Titus cringed at the awful, phlegm-filled noise.

"*Two*? That is what, just one pressed bar? No, Captain, I was thinking more along the lines of twenty pressed bars."

"I haven't got twenty."

Vorat sniffed. "Then I'll take whatever you've got."

After a moment's pause, Titus shrugged. Surely the *Phoenix*, at a build cost of over a quadrillion credits, was worth more than the five million that ten pressed gold bars would set them back. "Ten. That's all a capital ship carries." It was a blatant lie—capital ships like the *Caligula* carried one hundred at least, but that seemed to satisfy Vorat.

"Ten it is. We'll be at your ship shortly to collect payment."

"No. Information first," said Titus, sitting down in his

captain's chair.

"Ha! You expect me to spill my peas first, and then let you shove a torpedo up my ass as you go collect your precious ship?"

Captain Titus shrugged. "Fine. I'll send half to your ship by shuttle, and then you will escort us to the *Phoenix*, at which point I'll transfer the other half. How's that?"

Clearly, this was more what Vorat had in mind, as he responded immediately. "It is well. I'll be there in ten minutes."

Titus drew a hand over his throat to signal Evans to cut the comm.

Pirates. Thank Athena for the Pax Humana, or their filth would still have free reign over all the Thousand Worlds.

CHAPTER THIRTY-EIGHT

Ben groaned. He tried to reach up to his head to rub his piercing headache away, but found himself unable to do so. Strange—his shoulders hurt too. No, they screamed at him. Hot, fiery pain flared in his arms and shoulders, waking him up enough that he finally opened his eyes and looked up.

He was hanging. Dangling about a foot off the stone floor by his wrists, which were bound by chains attached to the ceiling. He let out a sharp puff of air as he tried to move, and the pain in his shoulder erupted into daggers pressing deep into every nerve.

Trying not to move again, he looked down. He was naked, except for the collar around his neck that he'd seen many of Velar's people wear.

Velar. Where was she? He strained his neck around to glance at the space surrounding him. It was a simple, brick walled room, with nothing other than a few sets of chains hanging down from rivets in the ceiling. There was only one small light fixture, and one door in front of him. He strained his head to look behind, but the pain was too intense.

And he was alone. Gritting his teeth, he tensed his shoulder muscles and, in spite of the searing pain, yanked as hard as he could against the restraints holding him in.

They felt hopelessly solid. He lifted himself up a few inches and let his weight down precipitously again in another quick tug. Again, not so much as a creak from the rivets sunk deep into the dusty wooden beams. He groaned in pain.

"Mr. Jemez, my monitor informed me that you're awake," said a voice behind him. Velar. He heard her footsteps approach and she appeared to his left holding a small electronic screen. She flashed it at him with a vague grin. "The collars keep me apprised of all my slaves' progress. You received quite a nasty knock there. I do hope you're not in too much pain—my customer wants you in tip-top shape for when he gets back from his trip. Shouldn't be long now."

Her customer? He'd thought he was destined to spend the rest of his life toiling away in her uranium mines.

"Where are my people?" he managed to croak out, suddenly realizing that his mouth was bone dry.

"They're safe, if that's what you're worried about. Well, except for one of your hired muscles. He tried to remove his collar rather abruptly and it didn't end well for him. Which reminds me—please don't try to remove your collar," she said, a sly grin stretching into a cunning smile. She added, with a wink, "It won't end well for you, either. Leave the fiber-optic implant alone, and you'll be just fine. It can handle snags and incidental contact, but if you attempt to rip it out, the bomb inside your head will utterly destroy your brain. And slaves without brains are not much use. You see, Doctor Stone prefers his slaves to give themselves to him completely, of their own free will."

She started pacing around him, stretching up a hand to his bare chest and stroking it gently. He recoiled at her touch as if it were a viper. "Doctor Stone—he's brilliant, by the way, the finest nano-cyberneticist in the galaxy—he's paying top coin for this body. He expects you to resist at first—in fact, that's how he gets his cheap thrills—but his ultimate pleasure is that you give yourself to him completely and utterly, trailing after him like a dog, not even thinking about your own wants or desires, but focused singularly on him and his ... needs."

"It'll never happen," he said. He tested his feet, trying to raise them but realized that they were also chained down to the floor. He sighed—no way to lash out with his legs and knock her out.

She noticed his slight movement. "You may try to resist all you want—in fact, the more noise and thrashing you make when he arrives to inspect you, the higher price you'll fetch. Just this immaculate body alone will be enough to land you the highest price I've ever commanded for a slave." She stroked his abdomen, looking at him hungrily. "I've half a mind to keep you for myself.... Pity that he likes to mar things so." Her voice drifted off in almost a sing-song tone. "I hear he likes knives. And other, more creative tools."

A beep from the data pad drew her attention. "Velar, Doctor Stone has arrived."

She held her pad up to her face. "Good. Tell him I'll be there shortly."

Ben willed moisture into his mouth and tried to speak again. "You won't get away with this. Po will find you. The *Phoenix* still has its guns. She'll blast the compound to hell before she let's you keep us."

She raised a lazy eyebrow. "The *Phoenix*? No, I'm afraid my most trusted slave of all is currently on board your ship, preparing to take it over. No, Jemez, soon Po will be joining you. We've got quite a shortage of good, strong-bodied women in our pleasure house—I'm afraid our customers have been going through them at an alarming rate. Costs me a fortune to keep the place stocked with local girls. Sometimes I even have to buy girls from Old Earth through my Imperial contacts." She walked behind him.

He heard her footsteps pass through the door, which closed almost too softly to hear. When she'd gone, he immediately started thrashing against the restraints, tensing his abdomen and pulling up on his feet as hard as he could, to no avail. There was no escaping the chains. Not yet—not until they dared to release him.

And he'd have to be ready. Doctor Stone did not sound like pleasant company.

CHAPTER THIRTY-NINE

A day had passed since the explosion, and Po had worked for hours, going back and forth with the science, ops, and security teams about every possible scenario that might have caused the rupture, but the source evaded them.

And with the emergency bulkheads holding back over ten atmospheres of pressurized seawater, there was no chance of investigating the central location of the hull rupture—not in person, anyway, and likely not with the automated hull repair droids. They were not designed for operation under water and had not budged from their housing.

To the acting head of security she said, "Well at least evacuate everyone away from the outer hull. Get them all within the first sets of emergency bulkheads—if this happens again, at least we can avoid casualties."

Ensign Szabo at science piped in, "If this happens again, we're risking a progressive collapse of every deck, not just at the source. That explosion and the subsequent water penetration weakened the structural integrity of the ship—its like an egg with a piece of the shell missing. We're nowhere near as strong as we were a few hours ago, and even then the risk of hull breach was high. Commander, I'm not even convinced that this explosion wasn't just caused by the extreme pressure acting on some power conduit or hydraulic system somewhere."

Commander Po approached the science station from the captain's chair. "Then how long do you think we have, Ensign?"

Ensign Szabo shrugged. "No idea. But every hour we stay under here, the more likely our hull gets corroded. The more likely our conventional thruster ports get rusted out. More stress on the hull means more micro-cracks in the support girders running the length of the ship. It's a crapshoot, Commander. Every hour we're here is a gamble."

"And yet every hour down here is another hour that we're alive." She knew the words were correct, but she realized that hiding was not a long-term solution. The *Caligula* would either find the *Phoenix* and drop a few megaton nuclear bombs on them—which, given their immersion in water would likely crush them—or they would just camp out until the *Phoenix* surfaced and destroy her in orbit.

Something had to give.

"Ayala, you've got the bridge." She turned towards the tattooed, wispy-white haired Belenite at tactical and thumbed her towards the captain's chair.

"Aye, sir," said Lieutenant Ayala, who stood and tentatively sunk into the chair in the center of the bridge. Po almost thought she looked apprehensive. Guilty? For what? She shook her head once out in the hallway. Clearly the lack of sleep was getting to her, making her suspect even the most loyal officers of nameless crimes.

As the elevator doors closed, she tapped on her data pad and turned on the comm. "Sergeant Jayce and Sergeant Tomaga, please report to the brig. Immediately."

Something had to give. And if that meant she had to finally place trust in two people that could undo everything they'd worked for over the last week, then so be it.

But it wasn't just the last week. The shipyards operation had been planned for years. Ever since Pritchard disappeared. The D-day commemoration was to have been the breakout moment for the Resistance. The moment when all their years of suffering and fighting would come to a head and pay off. And now look at them. Hiding in a half-broken ship under the ocean of some god-forsaken world while their Captain, Security Chief, and Chief Engineer were held hostage by some petty slaving syndicate. How did it come to this?

"Open his door," she said to the security officer standing guard at the console in the brig.

"Yes, sir." Volaski's door slid open and she walked in, seeing him rise from his bunk.

"Commander Po?" His Russian accent hung thick on his words, as if not speaking for half the day made him unaccustomed to talking like the rest of them.

Po stopped in front of him and put her hands on her hips. "Captain Volaski. How badly do you want to see your daughter again?"

The man shrugged. "Badly. But if you do not trust me to lead you to your men down on the surface, then I suppose we are still at a stalemate."

Po sighed. "Recent events have changed our situation. We

can't stay under the water forever. We need to find our people and get the hell off Destiny. And we need your help to do it."

Volaski smiled. "I agree."

His smile unnerved her. In spite of his claims that he'd changed, that he only wanted to be free again, something about him nagged at her. He was not completely forthcoming, that much was clear. But she did not get the sense that he was blatantly lying to her. He really *did* want to be free. No one could hide that desire. To want to be free was to be human.

"What I don't get is how you actually pull this off. The *Caligula* is in orbit. If you help us, they're bound to find out. They have no qualms about blasting an entire planet to its core just to enforce their will, and to punish traitors. If you do this, you are a traitor to the Empire."

"I've never been a friend to the Empire, Commander Po, so it's no skin off my back, as they say. Trust me. I can disappear. They need never find me." He glanced at the door as two more men appeared.

"What's the trouble?" said Staff Sergeant Jayce as he swaggered into the cell, a bulge in his cheek from some chew. Tomaga followed close behind.

"The trouble is on the planet. How do you gentlemen feel about leading a rescue mission on Destiny?"

Jayce shrugged. "Bring it."

Po raised an eyebrow, and then turned to Tomaga. "Sergeant? We could really use your urban warfare expertise."

Tomaga kept his expression vague. And yet she could see him calculating, thinking. Was it worth it to him and his men to help? She hoped he saw the obvious—that if he didn't help, he most likely would die with the rest of them. "I will help," he said. "As a show of good will. In the interest of our new friendship."

"Good. Volaski? How many soldiers has Velar got in her employ down there?"

The pirate shrugged. "At the compound? Fifty at least. But between my men, yours, and the element of surprise, we should do well. The only problem will be these collars." He tapped the electronic device around his neck. "She can kill me and all my men in an instant with a press of a button. By this point, your Captain too. Your boys will have to pin her down quickly before she has a chance to do anything. Really, without some kind of plan, it's a huge risk."

He was right. Po realized that they still had a ways to go on planning this rescue. "And? Do you have any ideas?"

Volaski smiled again, this time more jovially than before. He was apparently quite pleased with himself. "I do. I know the frequency domain her remote controller operates on. If we jam that frequency space with a whole lotta white noise, then our collars will be unable to see any signal she sends out. At least until she figures out what we're up to and changes the signal frequency."

"You don't think she'll have foreseen something like that? If it's as simple as broadcasting white noise…."

Volaski held up a hand. "First of all, it'll take a powerful signal. Only your ship could generate something that large— none of mine can. Second, Commander, you don't realize what it is like to be a slave after so many years. At first, a man will constantly be looking for ways to escape. But after awhile, after seeing so many of your comrades die in the attempt, you become resigned, and after that, complacent. All of her top lieutenants, including me, have become quite complacent over the years. She treats her top people rather well—not like the uranium miners. You'd think we were family. Trust me, she won't be expecting this."

Po shuddered at the thought of thinking of your captor as family. Stockholm syndrome? She wondered if some of Velar's top people suffered from it. Tomaga cleared his throat. "Captain Volaski, what is the situation on the ground? Will the *Phoenix*'s men be held in buildings on the surface? Or do you expect them to be in the mines?"

"The mines. Velar will want your men as far from the surface as she can manage—that's where we send all new recruits, as we call them. It makes escape during the first few years far less likely. Later, as a slave proves their loyalty, they can graduate to the upper levels of the mine—maybe even see a little sunshine, you know? The best get transferred to the surface to work up there."

Jayce grunted. "What weapons have they got?"

"Assault rifles. Plasma RPGs. The usual."

Jayce spat a brown wad into the corner of the brig's cell and turned to Po. "Sounds like fun. How many men can I take?"

Po wanted to grin. She liked Logan Jayce, insubordination and chewing tobacco notwithstanding. "How many do you need?"

Jayce glanced at Tomaga. "I'd say at least thirty."

Po nodded. "Done. Get your men ready. Sergeant Tomaga? Please choose a few of your most capable people."

"They are all capable."

"Then choose fifteen of your best," she replied, more

curtly than she intended. She knew this was a big risk—they still had no idea who the saboteur was. For all she knew, it could be Tomaga himself. Though how he would have escaped attention didn't make sense.

He nodded. "Very well."

Po continued, "And Jayce, I want no casualties among the slave population. If they're not holding a gun, you don't shoot, is that clear?"

He almost looked disappointed. "Clear, sir."

"I'm sure we'll be on some camera somewhere, and I don't want a gruesome aftermath transmitted to every viewscreen in the Thousand Worlds. The Empire's propaganda machine would eat that up. We need friends now more than we need new enemies."

Jayce pounded a fist into his palm indicating his readiness. "Got it, sir. Kill the people with guns."

"I'll be back on the bridge. Please escort Volaski to the fighter deck when you've finished making your plans and preparations." She turned back to Volaski. "Captain, I've decided to trust you. Please don't misplace that trust. You'll find that a scorned Earth Resistance officer is far more terrifying than any old Imperial capital ship."

"Thank you, Commander. Believe me, your trust is well-placed. No one wants to see Velar's downfall more than me."

She looked him squarely in the eye before turning back to the door. "You've got one day, gentlemen. Let's make this count."

The door to the brig slid shut behind her as she let out another sigh. This was risky, and she knew it. Could she trust Volaski? Could she trust Tomaga? Were both of them playing her? If they were, she hoped with a grim smile that at least the betrayals would cancel each other out—that's how it worked, right? Couldn't they just kill each other off?

She scolded herself for such thoughts. Definitely not enough sleep.

CHAPTER FORTY

Ben's heart froze slightly as he heard the door creak open behind him and heavy footsteps approached. These were not the soft footfalls of Velar, but the quick, heavy boots of some larger person—erratic and nervous, by the pace of the steps.

"Oh my," said the man's voice. "Velar wasn't toying with me. You really are something."

Ben thought back to what Velar said. The man liked resistance. He liked feisty and would pay top coin for it.

And he liked knives.

Ben supposed the only way to spite Velar at this point would be to fetch her the lowest price possible. He closed his eyes and willed himself to say nothing. Give the man no interaction. No pleasure. Nothing.

"I hear you're a regular old Imperial space jock. Such an— such an—such an ... illogical profession. So much danger. It's a wonder you're still alive." The stuttering man came up close behind. "But, mmm, those make the best slaves. Hard to break. So hard to break. Neural pathways strong and resilient. Bodies," he touched Ben's back, "usually nice and toned," he paced around to face Ben, who cracked his eyelids open slightly.

He felt hot breath on his cheek. "Are—are—are … you afraid, slave?"

Ben opened his eyes fully and stared at the sallow face peering into his. Not with defiance, nor with submission. But with the most nonchalant, uncaring gaze he could muster—as if this were just another day for him.

The man—medium sized, slightly cross-eyed, scarred and with a completely shaved head, reached into his pocket for something, and extracted a small electronic device. Leering at Ben, he pressed a button.

Fiery needles pierced into every nerve of Ben's body, which involuntary thrashed against the chains.

"You like it?" The man excitedly fingered the controls and ramped up the intensity.

Ben thrashed harder. The pain seared itself into his muscles, his stomach, his head, his eyes. Everything erupted in blinding pain. Then, abruptly, it ceased, replaced with a dull, lingering ache.

The man stepped up close to him, standing just an inch away. He whispered into Ben's ear. "Y—y—you're going to love our time together." He smiled a toothy grin. One of his lower teeth was missing. The dental care on Destiny apparently wasn't the best.

Ben kept his mouth clamped shut. He wouldn't give the sick monster a thrill of any reply. Not even defiance.

The man whispered again in his ear, "All I want is for you to serve me. This doesn't have to hurt, you know. N—n—n … not much, anyhow. I have a lot of experience stimulating pain receptors. It seems the synapses are quite susceptible...." He trailed off, reached down to his pad and pressed the button again. Ben felt his body thrash with blinding pain again, pounding up against the man who had not backed away. Still, in spite of the searing pain, he kept his mouth clamped shut.

The man flashed an hungry, greedy smile. "Stoic? Splendid. You'll do. You'll do nicely. I'll be back. D—d—d—don't go anywhere."

He stepped away and paced quickly back to the door, much more quickly than he'd entered. Excited, it seemed. Ben could kick himself if he could. It seemed his plan had backfired. The man would probably pay double what Velar had demanded, dammit.

CHAPTER FORTY-ONE

Willow slid into the captain's chair as Po rushed out the door and stared up at the screen, blue with the light filtering through the thick sheet of ice above them. A few fish fluttered past the camera, and she wondered how cold of water the little things could stand. Had they originated there on Destiny?

No, of course not. The most advanced form of life found on any planet outside of Old Earth was the most rudimentary cyanobacteria. In fact, only worlds teeming with cyanobacteria were able to be settled, since otherwise there would be no oxygen. These fish were surely imported from Old Earth. Like the trees. Like the birds.

Like the people.

Every world was the same. Explorers come. They find a planet with gravity similar to Old Earth, temperature similar to Old Earth, cyanobacteria-generated oxygen levels similar to Old Earth, rotation cycle similar to Old Earth, and once those basic necessities were met, the planetary engineers and xenobiologists would arrive to prepare the world for human habitation. The first vegetation was always chosen and engineered very carefully, for it must survive on whatever nutrients the cyanobacteria and the soil could provide. Next came the trees, and bushes, simple plankton. Things that could process the nutrients left by the higher order life.

And so it went. Each level feasting upon the order below it.

Like the people.

The Empire fancied itself as the alpha. The top of the food chain. But it was an imposter. A parasite. A weed. And weeds are uprooted and cast aside to dry upon the rocks, shriveled by the summer sun.

She closed her eyes and smiled. The summer sun on Belen was beautiful. So claimed her grandmother.

Opening her eyes, she grinned up at the fish swimming by, and silently wished them well. In her mind, she told them the secret. So many secrets to tell them, but she told them only one. The secret only the initiated among the clans of Belen were worthy to know.

Secrets were a sin—that much was passed along to her from her ancestors, blessed be their name. But some secrets were worth forgoing celestial nirvana for. Secrets that would ensure the continued life of her people.

Like the existence of her brethren. *The Red.* Her order. A sacred fighting force. They would fight the Empire until it sat upon its knees, begging for mercy.

And then *The Red* would dispatch it with no mercy. Staining their own hands red, if need be, that sin above all sins.

But that was not the secret she told the fish.

Glancing down at her console, she monitored the ongoing repairs of the most recent explosion. Good. In spite of the considerable damage, and the lost lives, the hull integrity was holding.

"Science. Can we pump that water out?" She stood and strode back to the science station, leaning over Ensign Szabo's shoulder.

"I doubt it sir. The pumps were designed to expel water to vacuum. Not to ten atmospheres, which is the pressure at the top of the ship's hull."

Willow nodded in disappointment.

"What about ... what about pumping it to other decks?"

The Ensign turned, looking incredulously at her. "Sir?"

"Some of the underutilized decks. At least then the flooded sections would become accessible, and we could get crews in there to at least repair the weaponry. If we stumble upon the *Caligula* up there, we'll need all the firepower we can get."

The science officer glanced down and studied the ship schematics, tracing a finger along certain decks and various sections. "Maybe, sir." She glanced up. "There might be a way. Let me work on it."

Ayala nodded again at her and started to step away.

"Great idea, sir," the woman added, "I see why the XO picked you."

Ayala stepped back to the captain's chair. "She picked me because she was desperate, Ensign. Just like us all."

Another secret was that the Belenite High Command was also desperate. Desperate for a suitable replacement world. A civilization simply could not live out among the stars, in orbit around god-forsaken worlds, scrounging for raw materials and water and food.

The Belenites put up a good front. A good show. The entire population of the Thousand Worlds held them in the highest esteem, holding them up as Moral Authorities, since they had suffered so much at the Empire's hand and yet refused to settle down on the worlds offered to them by their same old persecutor.

But they were a dying people. And the High Command knew it.

And Galba knew it. He'd assured her that he would do everything in his power as a senior senator. He claimed to have the ear of the Emperor, after all.

Unless he was lying, just to get her in bed. She smiled inwardly at herself. No. He was a horny old bastard, but he had a dear heart.

Unless.

She tapped her head.

Unless. Could he have been responsible for those explosions? He was so insistent about getting out of her quarters.

One more mystery to discover. Knowledge to press him for, after she pressed against his flesh ... his glorious flesh.

And eventually, she might even tell him *her* secret. The secret she just told the fish. She glanced up at the screen. They were gone, fled, replaced by a field of blue water, with white streamers of sunlight filtering through the creamy ice sheet.

Gone, just like the fish on her world. Like the trees.

But the secret was that they had lost something original. Native. Something unique in the galaxy. Not some transplant from Old Earth.

That was the great crime the Empire must answer for.

Genocide.

Something Galba could help her with, in her quest to extract expiation from the Empire.

And then the trees could rest in peace at last.

But first the ship needed safety. And she had to eliminate Galba as a suspect, for her own peace of mind, at least.

Turning to the navigation station, she gestured at Ensign Roshenko—the long-haired, calm young woman. Nothing seemed to faze her. She could handle the ship for an hour while she handled Galba. "Roshenko. You've got the bridge. I'll be right back."

CHAPTER FORTY-TWO

Jake, Alessandro, and Avery decided to work in shifts. Two of them would handle their heavy ore extractors while the third marched back and forth down the winding rock passageway, carrying the hunks of raw ore back to the carts. Jake found that the passageway was just a little too short for his liking, as he regularly scraped his head against the jagged ceiling, eliciting a constant stream of carefully counted curses as he hauled his loads.

The work seemed endless. The shift was only six hours long, and he was used to far longer in both the Imperial and Resistance fleets, but somehow, the tedious nature of it all seemed to lengthen the time. Or perhaps it was knowing that Velar could kill them on a whim by activating their collars. Or maybe the knowledge that the boss could inflict horrendous pain on them if they didn't produce their quota. He never liked working under a deadline.

But really, it was none of those things. His ship was up there, somewhere, in danger. Ben was missing, and probably in mortal danger. He'd endangered everyone with his risky choice to come down to the surface in a vain hope to find more neodymium for the gravitic drive. More people would die because of his decisions, and he hated it. And knowing that he was powerless to do anything seemed to stretch the hours into days, and the days into months.

But he'd had no choice, really. What else could they have done? Hadn't their long-range shifting capability cut out after that last shift? If they hadn't have shifted here, to Destiny, and instead shifted somewhere else, some place with absolutely no possibility of finding any neodymium to fix their drive, then their position would have been far more precarious. They'd be stuck in the middle of nowhere. Perhaps orbiting some star somewhere. If they were lucky, maybe they would have been able to use their gravitic thrusters to find their way to some planet in orbit of said star, but the chances that planet would be inhabited were slim.

People had found out long ago that while planets were plentiful, oxygen atmospheres were not. Only about one in 10,000 planets had developed their own cyanobacteria and had had time to break down enough carbon dioxide into oxygen to support human life.

His mind kept wandering as he trekked down the passageway. His feet hurt from all the walking. A dull ache had settled in where the wire was implanted into his skull, and the memory of the two shocks he'd received so far seemed enough to make the rest of his nerves extremely testy.

As he approached Alessandro and Avery, he stumbled over a rock he must have dropped during his last trip and fell against the cold, jagged wall.

"Dammit!"

"Friend! You ok?" Alessandro turned off his extractor and set the hulking piece of equipment down.

"Yeah, fine," he said. "Just can't seem to keep my feet under me. You got anything else for me?"

Alessandro grabbed his arm and helped him back to his feet. "I cut smaller pieces. Easier to carry."

Jake shook his head, mindful of exceeding their word limit —the collars seemed to only allow maybe fifty words per minute, which Alessandro kept getting remind of. "No, too small, won't make quota."

The scientist shook his head. "Ten percent decrease in weight, production rate increases fifteen percent."

"Had time to think?" said Jake with a small grin.

Alessandro tapped his head. "It is what I do."

"You just think about math all day?" Jake grunted as he sat down next to the wall.

"Math. And pussy. Everyone knows science gets the ladies all hot and horny."

Jake snorted, and waited a minute before responding, fearing the shock. "Well how about thinking a way out of this, huh? So does that trend continue all the way down? What happens when our loads hit zero? Does our production hit a billion or something?"

Alessandro picked up the omni-scanner and examined the latest rock he'd blasted out of the wall. "Obviously not, friend. I'm sure the production efficiency reaches a maximum, and then plummets precipitously as your body has unrealized capacity." He continued scanning the rock as Jake rubbed his head. The pain seemed worse.

"You sure you're ok, friend?" Alessandro's half-mustache

bristled as he glanced up at Jake.

"Really, I'm fine. It just seems like this thing kills whenever you've got that scanner running."

Alessandro turned the scanner off, then on again. Then off. Each time he did, Jake felt an almost imperceptible pulse, and when it turned on, the pain indeed seemed to intensify. "You don't feel that?"

Lieutenant Bernoulli shook his head, but Avery cocked his. "Yeah, I think I do," grunted the marine. "Barely."

"Very interesting." Alessandro held the stubby cylinder up to his face and clicked the thing on. He waved it all over his head, but the blank look on his face told Jake that he still felt nothing. "I wonder if the electromagnetic signal is interfering with your collars. I can't feel it affect mine."

"Obviously it's because your brain is so much bigger than ours, it takes a lot more oomph to get you to notice," surmised Jake.

In reply, Alessandro touched several buttons on the front of the cylinder. "I'll increase the gain." He waved it over his own head again.

"Shit!" Avery's hand slapped his forehead, right as Jake felt a stabbing pain behind his own.

"Yes, friend, yes! I feel it!" Alessandro seemed far too excited, especially given the amount of pain Jake and Avery were experiencing.

"Fine! Shut the damn thing off!" Jake waved his hand blindly in front of him as he closed his eyes against the pain.

Alessandro shut the scanner down and sat staring at it in his lap.

"Well?" Jake said.

"Well what?"

Jake rolled his eyes. "Don't tell me you just did that for fun."

"It was a mystery. I wanted to test the hypothesis."

"And what was your hypothesis?" Jake rubbed his forehead.

The squinted eyes of their scientist seemed to penetrate into the scanner as he turned it over and over in his hands. "That the field generated by this thing can interfere with our collars."

"Obviously. But Bernoulli, tell me. Does that help us? Come on, we've got to make this quota or we'll be in a world of pain in a few hours. Remember what happened to that other crew yesterday? They screamed for nearly an hour."

"I believe it does, Captain." Bernoulli called him Captain. He never called him Captain—he always said friend, or Jake. The man stood up, brandishing the scanner. "I need to study this to be sure. During our next break, can you make sure I get time? Warn me if the boss notices? If I can just get inside this thing and examine some of the circuitry I can— shit!" His head snapped down to his hand and he grunted. He'd exceeded his word limit. Again.

Jake cocked his head at his friend. "Sure thing, Lieutenant." He stooped to pick up the rock Bernoulli had just scanned. "Which bin?" He looked at Alessandro, pointing at the rock.

"The rejects," said Alessandro, without taking his hand off his face.

Jake turned and began his long, stumbling walk back to the main passageway that held the ore carts. Surely, he thought, if the man could figure out a new solution to the gravitic field equations, he could figure out how to disable their Domitian Collars.

Because if he didn't, he wasn't sure they would ever get out of there.

Unless Po came through, somehow. But why should she come get him? He was a liar. He'd stolen his command from his best friend. Was Ben really his best friend? No, Crash was. But Crash was most likely dead. The last he'd seen of the *Roc,* it was being boarded by Imperial troop carriers. Crash was dead.

But what if they'd somehow escaped too? They could meet up. Share resources. Combine forces. Track down Pritchard and live off the land for a few years while they planned their next moves.

Jake's head spun. The hunger, thirst, and fatigue were clearly starting to affect his mind. No. Crash was dead. Pritchard was dead. Po would not risk another mission to the surface. She was far more sensible than he. She'd have the sense to get the hell out of there while she still could and save the ship.

It's what he should have done in the first place, right after the *Sphinx* shifted away. He should have taken Ensign Ayala's advice, and gone to look for her people. They had neodymium, she'd claimed.

He stumbled again on another loose rock, this time falling flat on his face since he was hefting a piece of ore in front of his chest.

He wiped the blood from his nose onto his sleeve. The sleeve of the jacket Velar had given them. Slave's clothing, he now realized.

"Dammit!" he said to himself. Why hadn't he seen this all coming?

CHAPTER FORTY-THREE

It wasn't until Ben woke up that he'd understood he'd been drugged again. He shook his head, trying to remember the last moments of being awake. Footsteps from behind—Velar's, he'd thought—and then something touching his arm. It pinched. Like a needle.

She'd said something. It enraged him, but he couldn't remember. Something about retiring.

He tried to move, but found that he couldn't. Not one limb responded. No pain—not like last time—but nothing moved. He opened his eyes and looked towards his chest.

Straps. About two dozen straps holding down his chest, arms, legs, and abdomen. Everything except his head, which he let clunk back down on the table he was tied to. He wondered how much money he'd finally sold for.

Velar. That's what she'd said. *One more sale like you, and I can retire early.* He swore at her, and thrashed against his chains. Another voice. That man. The one who'd bought him. The sadist—or so Velar had let on.

He swore again to himself. How the hell had he gotten in

this position?

The answer was obvious, of course. Jake was always getting the two of them into trouble. It seemed like half the bars they went to over the past two years had kicked them out at some point for fighting. When he met Jake, he seemed like the perfect friend. Older, a little more experienced, a bit of a loudmouth. Not the kind of people he usually gravitated towards.

Ben was not a loudmouth. He preferred to speak softly and carry a big fist. All those years of jujitsu, wrestling, and plain-old Irish boxing were not for nothing. At the time he learned them all, he'd only planned on winning. He wanted to be a superhero—someone who was never at the mercy of anyone or anything. And so he studied. He read every book. Mastered every skill he could think of. Wilderness survival. Bow-hunting. Hell, he even learned a little black-smithing. Anything and everything he thought might come in handy one day. Anything that would help him stay one step ahead of the game. Keep him out of anyone else's mercy. No situation would catch him with his pants down.

He glanced back down at his body. Still naked.

He sighed, and glanced to his right.

The room he was in seemed more like a dungeon. Chains hung from rivets on the steel crossbeams of the ceiling and iron shackles dangled from the brick walls. Various cages and tables were scattered around the room, along with other implements of what could only be torture and several items of a less savory nature. Seemingly out of place, computer terminals sat on a lab bench, accompanied by an array of scientific equipment. Test tubes, scopes, microscopes, and several other pieces that Ben couldn't identify.

He closed his eyes and concentrated. What does the field manual say about capture? Surely there were protocols to follow, weaknesses in his captors to exploit? He strained to remember.

And then he did. That was the one section of the manual he'd skipped. At the time he couldn't even fathom a situation in which he'd need that knowledge.

He was never supposed to be at another's mercy. He was never supposed to be caught.

A rustle. With a start, he looked to his left, where he thought the sound had originated from.

Another man. At least, he looked somewhat like a man. He was tied to a wall, but minimally, by just a single, long chain. Deep, savage scars were cut across his face and chest, which had only somewhat healed. Many of the wounds looked fresh, but the deepest ones looked older. The man was naked; his thighs and abdomen appeared to be similarly ravaged by scarring. His eyes sagged, and he squinted at Ben, as if searching him for something.

"Who are you?" said Ben.

"Shhh!" The man held up his middle finger to his lips. Ben wondered why he used the middle finger, until he saw the stump of the index finger, which looked red and inflamed, as if only recently healed over. "We're not supposed to talk to each other," he whispered.

"We're not? Says who?" Though Ben knew the answer before the man replied.

"*Him*. The master. He gets very angry if he's disobeyed."

"How long have you been here? What's your name?" The

evidence of their captor's cruelty stood hunched before his eyes, but still Ben did not want to believe he was in for a similar fate.

The man looked reluctant to speak further. His eyes darted left and right before glancing furtively back at Ben. "Number six. That's my name. That's what he calls me. I've been here for … for … forever, I think."

Forever? "He's messed with your mind, friend. Don't believe him. Tell me, how long have you been here? Do you remember your life before you came?"

The man shook his head violently. "Mustn't think of that. Master tells me not to. There is no before. Only now. Only now, if I am to feel peace. There is no peace for the wicked. I was wicked, but my master saved me. I'm whole now. Pure. See? My master purified me." He held out his ravaged arms.

Ben felt sick. Their captor was indeed a psychotic lunatic. Somehow, he'd ruined the man—the shadow of a man—chained to the wall. He wondered how long the man had been here. How long did it take to break a man? Ben swore he'd die first.

"What's your name?" Ben repeated.

"Six. I told you. Six. And you're Seven. I heard master call you that."

"Screw that. I'm Ben. Ben Jemez. Hey, can you reach me? That chain of yours is pretty long."

The man covered his ears with his gnarled, beaten hands. "No. He speaks impurities. Can't listen. He'll sully me. He'll lure me in. Mustn't listen."

Ben let out a sigh. He closed his eyes and tried again. "Listen, Six. I've got a ship out there waiting for me. A big one.

If I can just let them know where we are, we'll both be safe. I'm with the Earth Resistance. We take care of our people—if I get out of here, I can take you with me. You'll be safe. I just need you to reach over here."

The man's hands edged away from his ears. "Earth? Did you say Earth?"

Progress.

"Yeah. I said Earth, all right. You been there?"

The man's hands hovered near his ears, as if undecided whether to plug them again. "I remember Earth. I think. From another life. Before I was born to this life. Earth, and the Resistance, and ships, ships, ships, great Jupiter there were so many ships. And that madman. Pritchard. Who ended it all for Earth."

Ben's eyes opened with a start. "You knew Pritchard? Were you with the Resistance?"

Six laughed. A coarse laugh. Bitter. "Resistance? Resistance was pointless. Futile. Resist? To what end? In submission there is order. You'll submit to the Master, too, and you'll find peace."

Ben snorted. "Peace? You think you've got peace? Have you looked in a mirror lately?"

"Servants don't look in mirrors. Our Master's face is our mirror. If we see joy in his, then we feel joy. If we see anger, we feel anger at ourselves for causing it."

"You're really messed up, aren't you?" Ben wiggled against the straps. His shoulders still felt incredibly sore. Probably a by-product of hanging from the chains for so long. He took inventory of the rest of his body, focusing for a moment on each limb, flexing and relaxing, searching for any give in the restraints. Nothing. Each strap had been wrenched down tightly. Whoever did it knew what they were doing.

Six hesitated, starting to speak but stopping multiple times. "Are … is your ship still here? In orbit?"

"Yes," said Ben. In truth, he had no idea where the *Phoenix* was, but he had to believe they hadn't left him. How long since he'd been captured? A few hours? A day? A week? With no idea of how long he'd been under, it was difficult to tell with any certainty.

"Mine left me here. The bastards left me. But no, it was a blessing. A wonderful chance blessing. If they hadn't have left me, I'd never have my Master."

Ben tried to get the man to focus on his old ship. "They left you here? What ship was it? Why did they leave you?"

Six continued without answering, as if unhearing. "I was furious, at first. My fury could hardly be contained. My fury!" He chuckled at the word, though Ben couldn't see what was so funny about it. "My master expunged my fury. He purified me from it. He helped me to—"

Ben interrupted, not interested in hearing Six sing praises to his twisted Master. "And the ship? Was it a big one? An Imperial ship?"

"Imperial, no. Not Imperial. I resisted, like you, once. It was the *Fury*. That devil of a man was my master. That soulless shell that left me here."

The *Fury*? Had it really stopped here? The coincidence seemed far-fetched. And yet, why would the poor man make it up. And the devil he referred to … Admiral Pritchard? Was it possible that a Resistance officer would think of their hero that way?

"Do you mean Pritchard? The Resistance Admiral?"

The man sneered, the jagged scars on his face bunching up into hideous folds. "The same. He left me here. I came down like a good tech. They told me to find some food to barter for. We were running low, you see. But we couldn't just come down to any old planet. We were on the run. Pritchard said no one could know where we were. And so he kept us to the backwater worlds. The spaces in between worlds. The voids. Until we ran out of food. Then we came here. And I woke up in this room." His voice drifted off, and he added, in a wispy voice, "I suppose I do remember my birth. Funny. I must be the only one to remember his own birth. I was born there," he pointed up towards Ben, "on that very table. The blood stains from my birth stayed on the floor for months afterward. I think. Time passed so slowly back then."

Ben's heart sank as he realized just how far the man had deteriorated. Was he too far gone? Could he come back? "Look, Six, you've only been here, what, two years? Three, tops? You've got to pull yourself together. We can get out of here. I just need you to come over here. Can you reach?"

"There is no peace for the wicked," said the man, with an air of finality, and he dropped his head to his chest and said no more.

Ben let out a long, slow breath, trying to breathe in a rhythm—to stay focused. He glanced around the room. Various tables held all sorts of wicked looking steel equipment that his mind couldn't even fathom the use of. Whips and flogs hung from the wall, as well as chains, shackles, various clubs, crops, hammers, mallets, and straps. A few power tools even lay here and there—several drills, and Ben could only imagine what their captor did with those.

And against another wall, a stark contrast. Sleek scientific equipment. Computer terminals. Vials. Chemicals. Even what looked like a scanning muon microscope. A lunatic. And a scientist? It didn't make sense.

Stone walls and hardly any lighting gave the room the distinct impression of a dungeon—the rank smell of urine and the faint whiff of blood didn't help. The room looked as if it could hold up to ten prisoners or so, and Ben wondered how many residents had occupied it over the years.

"How many—" he began, but a noise distracted him. Someone was coming. Against the far wall, a door opened, and in walked the man who'd purchased him, dressed in a white lab coat, as if just coming back from his laboratory. Ben wondered what sort of research the man did. Nano-cybernetics? Is that what Velar had said?

"You're awake. Good." He stopped at a table and picked up a vicious-looking knife, and continued on towards Ben. He turned to Six. "Has he talked at all?"

"Yes, Glorious Master. He tried to pollute me, but I resisted."

Stone stopped, and turned towards Six. "Did you talk back?" His voice had assumed a dangerous tone. The stuttering seemed to disappear when he talked to the man on the floor.

Six cowered. "Only to tell him to stop. He was polluting the air with his ramblings, and I made him stop."

"I told you to stay quiet."

The broken man cowered further.

"But I see you were trying to help me. Good slave. I'll give you your punishment later, for disobedience. But then I'll reward you for your good intentions."

"Thank you, Glorious Master."

How had the man sunk to this? Ben swore he'd never descend to the poor fool's level. He'd fight to the end. He'd rather die than end up like Six.

Doctor Stone turned back to him, and sniffed, wiping his nose with a lanky wrist. "And n—n-n-now, Seven, we come to your first lesson. It is the easiest lesson there is, but I've found that m-most of my subjects have trouble with it." He moved closer, resting a hand on Ben's shoulder. "Especially the s-s-strong ones, like you. Six only resisted a few days. I certainly hope I'll get much more fun out of you. Hades knows I paid for it."

He lifted the knife against Ben's chest, who took a breath and held it. The knife dug into the flesh, cutting downward, and to the side, hopping over the straps as he came to them. "Oh my," said the man. "Like a virgin canvas. And what a canvas. Not a hair, not a single hair. You keep yourself clean, don't you, my b—b-beautiful thing."

Ben's eyes, though shut, watered—not so much out of pain, though it was certainly intense, but out of rage. Several swipes later, the man drew the blade away.

"There. Now I've marked you as mine. No one will want you now. No one will ever want used property." He set the bloodied knife down and picked up a whip that had rested out of sight on the floor. Chunks of glass and metal were embedded in the single thick strand of hide.

"Your first lesson. Your name is Seven, and mine is Master. Call me Master."

He waited.

"Do it. I am your Master and you must address me as such." A pause. "Speak, slave!"

Ben kept his eyes closed. He would not so much as give the man the satisfaction of even a glance.

"You will be here a very, very long time." Stone continued, softer now. "There is no sense in resisting. Your ship has already left. There was no sense in risking more lives to save yours. They left you, Seven. Forever." The stuttering seemed to fade away as the man's confidence grew. He dropped his voice to a near whisper. "But you've found salvation with me. I will save you from your filth. And in time, I'll introduce you to my research."

Ben thought of his time in the Imperial Academy on Earth, trying to stay focused on happy memories. For the first time in his life, he had felt accepted by his peers. At least at first, before the whispers and furtive glances started up again. Those same worried looks had followed him all through his teenage years—all the people his age were jealous. Jealous of his talents, his strength, his body, his brain, everything. He graduated, and was assigned to Viper squad, and finally, for the first time in his life, he found friends.

Real friends. Jake. Megan. Some of the others. They liked him. Respected him.

He focused on them, and tried to ignore the sound of the whip.

"Very well, Seven." Ben could almost hear Stone smile. "This is the best part anyway."

CHAPTER FORTY-FOUR

Jake let his body down on the cold, stone floor with a grunt and stretched out next to Alessandro. They'd made their quota, but only just. The boss had examined their cart, and clucked his tongue when he saw the readout. "You warts are cutting it pretty close." But a quota was a quota, and he waved them on through to the main entry chamber where apparently there would be some water. And maybe even some food.

Alessandro hunched over the omni-scanner—he'd found a tiny piece of metal wedged into a crack in the floor and somehow he'd managed to remove the scanner's casing. Mumbling to himself, he poked and prodded at the circuitry, reading off numbers and integrated circuit board serial numbers—Jake wondered if he was as good at electronics as he was at gravitic field theory. If he even knew half as much of the one as he did of the other, they would be in business.

"You know what you're doing?" said Avery, hunched over and holding his head in his hands—obviously he didn't want anyone to see he was talking, much less talking to Bernoulli.

"My father repaired viewscreens, Avery." Alessandro

sniffed, and wiped his nose with a dirty sleeve. The shaved half of his upper lip had begun to show a shadow, and his mustache, at least in the weak lighting of the chamber, looked almost like a regular one. "I spent hours disassembling and reassembling the old ones that he gave to me. The ones too old or obsolete to repair."

Jake eyed the other slaves around them. Up above, on his rafter, the boy Jeremiah was perched in his usual spot, gnawing on some hard biscuit thrown out by the boss's henchmen. The other people just lay there on the ground, silent, but with a few whispers here and there. Most had given them a wide berth—he wondered if the boss or Velar had warned them all to stay away, or if it was customary to avoid the new arrivals.

One man kept glancing furtively at them and then looking away whenever Jake caught his eyes. It was the same man who'd eyed them before. The one that Jeremiah had trailed after. After the third or fourth round of this, he leaned over to Avery. "Watch over Bernoulli for me, would you? I'll be right back."

Before Alessandro could protest, Jake rolled over onto his knees and grunted as he stood. Approaching the man, he stopped short. The man glanced nervously at him and almost looked ready to bolt. Jake took one small step backwards—no need to make him too nervous.

"Hi. Jacob Mercer." He held out a hand to the man still sitting on his haunches. A grizzled old face peered up into his, and a distrustful look gave way to surprise. Jake wondered if it was at all common for the slaves to talk to one another, but surmised that the boss had to give some kind of leeway to all his fellow slaves, or he'd be faced with a crowd of angry men and women who would have no problem wrenching the collar controller from his hands, setting it to maximum, and pointing it straight at their tormentor's head.

"Tovra. Did they capture you in a raid, or were you dumb enough to come down to the surface?" Tovra's face, though worn and pasty, was the face of a man who couldn't be older than forty or so. Yet the years of slavery had taken their toll. Loose, haggard skin hung from his neck and cheeks, and hardly any fat or muscle showed under his tattered clothing.

"I'm going to go with dumb," Jake replied with a wry grin. "You? How long have you been here?"

"Shhh!" Tovra's finger darted up to his cracked lips. "Bad luck to talk about our time here." He scanned the far wall, looking for the boss and the guards, but they had disappeared. "I seen hundreds come and go through here."

Jake took a few steps closer and sat down on the bare, rocky ground next to Tovra. With a grunt and a curse, he swept a small stone that had dug into his rump and tried sitting again. "Hundreds, huh? People leave here often?"

Tovra sniffed. "Only in body bags. A couple get promoted to groundsworkers—usually the ones who do favors for the guards."

"What kind of favors?"

The man rolled his eyes back into his skeletal head. "You don't want to know."

"Ah. So just like any old prison."

"Worse. In regular prisons, there are ostensibly rules against mistreatment of prisoners, even if the rules aren't always followed. Here? We're property. They protect us as we are an investment, but not beyond that. If we break, we're replaced. Simple as that."

The man didn't sound like a regular old toothless grunt. His vocabulary was too big, and his accent reminded Jake of the more cosmopolitan planets like Earth, Corsica, or New Kyoto. Not a backwater like Destiny.

"You from around here?" he asked.

"Sound like it?"

"No."

Tovra laughed. "Good. Then I haven't lost my Oberanian accent."

"Oberon? The moon in the Sol system? Around Uranus?"

Tovra scowled. "Sol? Hell no. The Oberon system. One of the last few places outside the Empire that still has art, culture, science—you know, civilization?"

"I've heard of it."

"Oberon?"

"No. Civilization."

Tovra's scowl softened into a wry grin that matched Jake's. "I like you. I take it you're from the Sol system? Earth?"

"That's right. North America, if that means anything to you."

"It does, it does." Tovra scratched his long, filthy beard. "My ancestors were from there. Emigrated way back in the twenty-fourth century, when the Oberon system was settled. A good chunk of the settlers came from already settled parts of the Thousand Worlds. Young families seeking to start up a brand new world by themselves. Sounds wonderful, doesn't it? To start all over again, on a new world, unsullied by Empire or syndicate or crime. Only hard work standing in between you and a blessed life of luxury?"

Jake wondered how the man was able to speak so many words without the shock. Did old-timer slaves get a higher quota?

"Huh. I'd always heard that the first settlers to any world always had a rough go of it. You know, what with the lack of buildings, roads, irrigation, bars—that sort of thing—shit!" The shock came like a dagger to the brain and he winced.

Tovra snorted, ignoring his pain. "Well that's because you're a lazy Terran who thinks life should be served to him on a gold platter."

Jake glanced back at Alessandro, who continued to work on the omni-scanner as Avery kept watch. So far, no one seemed to have noticed the activity—the boss had reappeared, and looked to be preoccupied with portioning out the rations. "So, why hasn't Oberon been conquered? If it's as rich and beautiful a world as you say, wouldn't the Empire have taken it over by now? You know, for its own *protection*?" He emphasized the last work with sarcasm.

Tovra's eyes flashed with excitement, as if he were about to divulge a great secret. "That, my friend, is a good question. One I happen to know the answer to since I captained a small frigate in my day. Tell me, how massive is Sol?"

"Uh … roughly one standard solar mass?"

"No shit?" Tovra glared at him. "Of course it is. It set the standard. Corsica's star is maybe 1.5 solar masses. New Kyoto is .9. Guess how big Oberon's star is?"

"Two solar masses? Three?" Jake stabbed blindly at numbers, wondering where the man was going with it. The pain slowly ebbed away from his head.

"Point one. As in one tenth the size of Sol. Only you

hardly notice because Oberon orbits so closely to the star. Imagine looking at your sun, but through the reddest glass imaginable. That's Oberon's star. Red as a campfire. In fact, our eyes have started to adapt over the centuries. We see better in red light than offworlders."

"Fascinating," grumbled Jake, though really he was gazing hopefully at the rations table, which was now teeming with slaves eager for a bite to eat.

"But the mass is not the only part. Guess how far it is away from the nearest star? I'll answer for you since you seem too hungry to think. Ten light years. Ten! Do you know how much energy it takes to shift from that star to ours?"

Jake thought a moment before understanding the man's point. "Yeah, you're right. That's more energy than most capital ships have. Even a Centurion Class cruiser. I bet only the ships with the largest power plants relative to their size would—"

"Precisely! That's why Oberon remains free, because it is isolated. For the Empire to invade would require immense resources. And so they let us be. Makes you wonder why more pirates and resistance movements haven't tried exploring the Void."

The table of food was almost empty. Luckily, most of the slaves had retrieved their rations and had sat down to eat. "Uh, sorry? The Void?"

"The Void. The giant molecular cloud in between Antares and Vega. Absolutely empty. Or so they say. Oberon is right on the edge, and there's a legend on our world that tells of desperate people fleeing into the Void and finding sanctuary there. A haven. Or maybe even heaven—you know how wild stories tend to escalate." Jake could tell from Tovra's face that he was kidding, but the idea of an unreachable region of space —a protected sanctuary—appealed to him.

"So tell me, has anyone on Oberon tried to—"

A sharp voice pierced the dank air of the cavern. "Hey! What are you all doing? It's grub time!" The boss was walking angrily over to Avery and Alessandro, who tried to stuff the pieces of the omni-scanner in one of his pockets. Jake jumped to his feet and intercepted him.

"Problem?" he said.

The boss spluttered. He looked drunk. "Yeah. Your friend there. What's he up to?"

"Looks like he's resting. You taking issue with that?" Jake said dangerously.

The boss put a hand into a pocket and sneered. "Don't tempt me, maggot." He glanced up to the girders lining the ceiling, at Jeremiah, who sat on the one right above them watching them closely. "Or you'll answer to *the prophet* up there." Jake wondered at the nickname—if it was some kind of epithet or something.

With one hand Jake motioned to Avery and Alessandro to go get their rations, but he stayed with the boss—he needed to make sure the drunk man forgot about Alessandro and stayed focused on him. He took a menacing step closer. "You listen to me you little rat." He towered over the man, who only came up to Jake's shoulders. "You may like playing with your little toy there, but don't think for a second that I won't rip your fucking head off with my bare hands if you cross the line with us."

A momentary look of terror passed over the boss's face before he fumbled with his pocket, yanked out his collar controller, and clamped down on one of the buttons.

Nothing happened. Behind the boss, Jake saw Alessandro holding the omni-scanner once again, manipulating its controls with a look of triumph on his face.

The boss glanced down at his controller again, and clamped his thumb down on one of the buttons more firmly. In response, Jake yelled, and tried to give the best impression of writhing pain that he could. He breathed a series of short, shallow breaths, all the time keeping an eye on when the boss's thumb left the button—he had to make this absolutely believable.

And he made it a mental note to promote Alessandro if they ever got out of there.

The boss sneered, a bit of drunk spittle clinging to his chin. "There. I told you before, don't speak out of turn. Next time I'll just leave the damn thing on and you can sweat it out for a few hours. How would you like that?"

Jake rubbed his head in false agony. "Yes, sir. I'll behave."

"Good. Now go get your grub—I can't afford to have you maggots collapsing on the job."

As the boss left, Avery and Alessandro fell into step next to him as he hobbled over to the ration table. He leaned over and mumbled in Alessandro's ear. "Al, you're a certifiable genius."

The man leaned over and whispered back, "Friend, tell me something I don't know."

CHAPTER FORTY-FIVE

Captain Titus surveyed the viewscreen on the front wall of the bridge. The ship—Vorat's tiny freighter—blasted away from the *Caligula*'s main fighter deck several gold bars heavier. It was show time. Either the man was lying, and Titus would blast the fool out of the sky, or he was telling the truth and the *Phoenix* was just one orbital adjustment away.

Ensign Evans called out. "Sir, Vorat is hailing us."

Titus waved a hand, indicating to the Ensign to pipe it through.

Vorat's voice wheezed through the comm. "Captain Titus? Is your ship ready?"

"We are. Transmit the coordinates and we'll all be on our way."

A long pause.

Ensign Evans nodded. "Sir, they're coming through. Uh, sir, these coordinates put us right back at the north pole."

"Indeed. Well, perhaps we didn't look closely enough."

Vorat replied, after a hacking cough. "You're right Captain, you did not. You didn't look down. Way down."

Titus paused. "Are you telling me that the *Phoenix* is down on the surface?"

"Further."

Further?

A sitting duck. Titus couldn't have hoped for a better outcome. They'd be able to drop a single nuclear warhead. The *Phoenix* wouldn't have time to get out of the way if it were at rest in some underground cavern.

Vorat continued, "Let's just say your little bird has become a little fish."

In the ocean? Was it even possible? Could a ship survive underwater without imploding? Titus started to have even deeper misgivings about having transferred five gold bars over to Vorat's ship.

He motioned to the helmsman to follow the coordinates. "Take us there, Ensign."

"Sir, we'll be there in just a few minutes—we weren't that far away to begin with," replied the helmsman.

Even better. He turned back towards the comm.

"Ensign Evans, inform Admiral Trajan that we may have located the *Phoenix*." He didn't often want his superior looking over his shoulder, but this was a moment he wanted Trajan to witness: the moment that he, Captain Titus, found their quarry.

"He's coming, sir," said Evans from the comm station.

Titus finally smiled—possibly the first time he'd done so in days—and lowered himself into the chair. The captain's chair. *His* chair. He wanted to make sure Trajan saw him in it when the moment of triumph came, to leave no doubt in the man's mind about who had found the *Phoenix*.

"Just another minute, sir," said the helmsman.

The door to the back of the bridge slid open and Trajan strode through.

"You have news for me, Captain? Something that couldn't be delivered to me personally? It had better be good." The Admiral stopped near the tactical station—not close enough to warrant Titus standing up. Well, technically, military protocol dictated that the entire bridge crew stand upon the entrance of an Admiral to the bridge, but Trajan had long since dispensed with that formality. It lowered efficiency, the Admiral claimed.

"Good news indeed, sir. We are seconds away from the *Phoenix*. Or so this merchant claims," he replied, motioning to the viewscreen. Vorat's ship was still barely visible ahead of them, a tiny speck against the backdrop of stars.

"Seconds? Very good Captain. And have you paid him already?"

"Half. Five gold bars."

"Five?" Trajan's eyebrow raised up—the one over the pit, which Titus thought odd.

The Captain's stomach knotted slightly. "Yes, sir, five. I thought the information worth the price."

"And how do you know he isn't leading us on some wild chase? He could disappear in an instant and we'd never be the wiser." Trajan's single eye penetrated Titus's face with an intensity the Captain was not accustomed to. He forced himself to meet the gaze.

"Well, sir, we're about to find out. Helm?" He turned to the station next to the command console.

"We're there sir."

"Full stop. Sensors," he looked back at the tactical station, "scan the surface. What do we see?"

"Ocean, sir. Nothing but a sea of broken-up ice sheets."

Trajan wheeled on Titus, his face turning into a deadly sneer.

"And beneath the ice," Titus continued in a hurry.

A pause.

The sensor officer glanced up, and smiled. "The *Phoenix*, sir. Right where the merchant claimed."

Titus stood up. "*Under* the water?"

"Yes sir. Under one of the ice sheets."

Titus turned to Admiral Trajan. "Sir? Shall I order nuclear strike?"

Trajan, without missing a beat, took the situation in stride. "No. I want that ship intact. But we can disable it. Fire two torpedoes—the water will transfer enough of the shock to the ship that we just might disable their gravitic drive."

Titus motioned at the tactical station to execute the order.

It wouldn't be long now before he'd get his bridge back.

CHAPTER FORTY-SIX

Gavin turned to Quadri. They'd orbited the barren planet below for several days, shifting back every eight hours to piss and grab a quick bite, but never seeing even a hint of the *Caligula*. But his sensors had finally picked up a gravitic signature.

"I think we've finally got it," he said excitedly.

Sure enough, the passive sensors determined that the giant mass ahead of them was indeed the *Caligula*. Gavin focused the fighter's optical scanner on the other ship and brought it up on his viewscreen.

"What's she doing?" asked Quadri. "Just orbiting? Looking for us?"

"Looks like it. But wait," he paused, peering at the grainy, pixelated image on his screen. "It looks like there's another ship there. It was docked with the *Caligula*, but now it's leaving." He stared harder, then tapped a few buttons.

"Read their transponder," Quadri suggested.

"Doing that now. Hmm. Looks like a merchant freighter. And now the *Caligula* is changing course to match the freighter." He glanced up at Quadri, unsure of what it might mean.

Quadri on the other hand, leaped into action. "We're getting out of here. Prepare for gravitic shift back to the *Phoenix*."

"Why? Have they found us?"

"Of course they have. That merchant ship must have seen us go down into the atmosphere, and has now sold that information to the Imperials. Remember the communication that they broadcast to the whole system? Asking for help, and that whoever brought info would be highly paid?"

Gavin shook his head. "They didn't say highly paid."

"Yeah, well, we can't take chances with this." Quadri tapped a button, and within a second the view of the stars and the brown planet below was replaced by the fighter deck. Gavin forgot to flinch—he'd half expected to just materialize right inside a bulkhead or a technician by doing a blind shift like that. Collecting himself, he watched as the pilot lowered the fighter down to the deck, hitting the ground with a clang.

"Commander Po, this is Lieutenant Quadri. Sir, we're about to have company."

CHAPTER FORTY-SEVEN

Willow sprinted down the corridor, skirting around piles of debris, fallen girders, and ceiling panels that had come loose in the battles of the previous week, jostling into other crew members who were walking at a more sensible pace, and pounded down the stairs to the next deck.

Best to be back on the bridge before the XO returns. Po was generous, and good-natured, but Willow didn't want to test the woman's boundaries. She wasn't the XO because she was a nice mom figure. The XO's fighter piloting skills were legendary. Second only to the Captain's, and perhaps Lieutenant Grace's as well.

By the time she reached deck four, her heart pounded, and she slowed to a jog, wiping the first bead of sweat from her tattooed brow. Two more decks. At the bottom of each stairwell, one had to run a short length of hallway to the next stairwell leading down to the deck below. It annoyed her, now that she was in a hurry, but knew that otherwise the gravitic fields generated within the deckplates wouldn't reach all the way to the top of a multi-floored stairwell.

And wouldn't that be convenient, she thought. One could jump off the top few stairs, float down, and not worry about landing until the last few stairs at the bottom. But wait too long before arresting the fall, and the landing would get painful. She supposed that was why each deck's stairs led to only one floor above and below it, to prevent stupid crew members from trying their luck at jumping down ten floors at once.

And with a gasp of breath, she brushed through the sliding door onto deck six, where her quarters were. Hers, and half the other ensigns on the ship, though a quarter of them were dead and another quarter never even assigned to the *Phoenix* in the first place. As it was, deck six tended to be quiet.

She burst into her quarters, and looked around.

He was gone.

Swearing—something she never did—she reached over to the bed and squeezed the rumpled covers, just to make sure he wasn't buried under them, fast asleep. Then she rose up on the tips of her toes and peered up onto the top bunk, just in case he were hiding up there.

"Looking for me?"

She half jumped, and spun around, only to find him standing in her bathroom, dressed only in one of her robes. Water dripped off his chest hair, and he grinned at her, toothbrush in hand.

"Harrison!" Her voice suggested anger, but she blew out a puff of air in exasperation, and then let a smile tug at her cheek. "What are you doing?"

"Freshening up. I had to borrow your toothbrush. Do you mind?" He held it up to her, and she shook her head.

"Yeah, sure." She stepped into the bathroom and shut the

door behind her. "Look, we've got to talk. Things have been happening. Maybe you've heard—"

He interrupted. "Yes, we do have to talk. I've been out and about for short periods of time, you know, just to stretch the old legs, and I've discovered something you should probably know."

She raised her eyebrows. "Really?" Leaning back against the towel rail, she folded her arms and inclined her head, trying hard to look him in the eye and not at his hairy chest. Gods, she loved that hair. Every Belenite she'd ever met was slippery as a dolphin. "Go on."

He set the toothbrush down and took a step closer. "You do know that there are Imperial marines on board?"

"Yes, I know that. The Captain made an arrangement with them during the battle to spare their lives. And many of ours."

He nodded. "Sure. Very noble of him. But little does he know that there are true believers among them. Imperial die-hards. Men that are waiting until just the right moment to strike. When the *Phoenix* is at her most vulnerable." He held up his hands, suggesting ignorance. "Who knows? Maybe one of them has already struck. Why, what were you going to tell me, my love? Has something happened?"

She squinted at him, unsure of whether this was an act, whether he was trying to deflect her suspicions. "Interesting you should mention it. I was about to tell you of two separate incidents, possibly involving sabotage. One was a runaway coolant buildup. The other was a very inopportune power surge that has crippled our gravitic thrusters. Both very suspicious. Are you suggesting one of the Fifty-First Brigade is responsible? Have you talked to any of them?"

Galba looked down, as if studying his feet, then nodded slowly, as if coming to some sort of decision. "Yes. I had hoped not to betray confidence, as I didn't think the young man was actually going to do anything. I thought he was just venting. Complaining about being held hostage here—in his words, mind you."

"Who? Tell me," she said, letting her voice rise.

"Now, before I do, promise me no harm will come to the boy. I promised him I wouldn't tell a soul."

She took a step forward, coming up close to his body, but not quite touching. Not yet. She would give herself to him, but only for a price. Only for knowledge. Knowledge led to power. And in this instance, safety.

"Harrison, people have died already. Two people died in that first explosion. Nine more in the next. I promise nothing. Tell me who it is, and what he did. Now." She pointed a stiff finger at his face.

He sighed. "Very well. Private Ling. You'd recognize him if you'd seen him already. His face looks something awful. Seems to have gotten into a fistfight with one of your boys a few days ago. I was walking the lower decks yesterday, and I saw something funny going on in one of the utility rooms. Near deck fifteen, where I understand the Fifty-First Brigade is being held. I entered, and there he was, opening up the back of a computer terminal. I asked him what was going on, and he claimed he just wanted to hack into the libraries and check for porn. Said he and his buddies were going crazy without any … relief. We talked for a while. Seemed like a fine young marine. Gregarious. Gritty and bold, like any marine I've ever met. But something struck me as … off. He seemed nervous. Kept glancing at the door during our conversation. Finally, he said he had to go, and so I left with him, and came back straight here. You see—"

Galba trailed off. He'd sounded more and more agitated during the speech, and now he hesitated. Senator Galba? Hesitate?

"Go on, Harrison. What is it?"

The Senator swallowed. "I think he may have recognized me. Willow, if he talks, and Mercer finds out I'm here, I'm as good as dead. Out the airlock with old Senator Galba. There's no way I'll be able to convince him I had nothing to do with what I'm sure he thinks is Trajan's devious scheme."

"Did you?" She kept her arms folded and dropped her chin.

He held up his hands, as if feigning innocence. "Would I do something like that? I've worked for reconciliation for years. It was supposed to be my crowning achievement. Instead, I'm locked away on some renegade starship. Doomed to hide in the shadows until you help me escape."

She laughed and finally uncrossed her arms, letting a hand drift lazily down his chest. "Oh, is that what you think I'm going to do? I'm afraid you're all mine, Harrison. Now get on that bed."

A greedy smile passed his lips and he allowed her to lead him back into the cramped bedroom and onto the bunk where he sprawled out on his back, naked and excited front exposed, grinning from ear to ear.

"Just promise me one thing, my love."

"Anything," she said, crawling on top of him.

"Promise me you'll be generous with Ling. Not too harsh."

She kissed him. Violently. Not too violently. Belenites must not draw blood, after all. But she kissed with passion. With teeth. With tongue.

"I promise," she breathed into his ear.

And she meant it. She'd be very generous with the boy. He'd get nothing he did not deserve.

CHAPTER FORTY-EIGHT

"Company?" Po gripped the armrests of the captain's chair.

"Yes, sir. The *Caligula* is bearing down on our position—they're being led by a merchant freighter."

Po leaned forward in her chair. "Did you monitor any communications between the ships?"

"No, sir, but it seemed odd that the *Caligula* would be trailing a freighter so closely, aimed directly at our position. I assumed the worst. They should be here in ten minutes or so. Unless they've sped up...." He trailed off.

"Thank you, Lieutenant Quadri, you made the right call. Po out." She jumped out of her seat and continued talking. "Commander Po to Sergeant Jayce. Sergeant, you've got five minutes. Are you ready?"

"What the hell, Commander, five minutes?" came Jayce's harried reply.

"You heard me, Sergeant." We've been spotted and we've got to get out of here. I want your team gone in five minutes or this mission ain't happening. Understood?"

Po could hear the man grumble under his breath, but he managed to find some intelligible words. "Yes, sir. Five minutes."

"Po out." She strode over to the helm. "Ensign Roshenko, take us up."

"Up, sir?"

"You heard me. Through the ice. Our cover is blown."

"Yes, sir. Engaging gravitic drive." The Ensign's voice trembled slightly as she keyed in the commands, and with good reason. Under the water they were sitting ducks. One tactical nuke would be enough to finish them off. Even a few conventional torpedoes would cause severe damage—the water would propagate the shock wave from the blasts far more efficiently than empty space or even air.

"Quickly, Ensign, but not too quickly."

"Yes, sir. Engaging at .1 percent."

Out of the corner of her eye, Po saw Ayala rush onto the bridge and take her position at tactical, but her attention was drawn to the horrendous sounds screaming out from the walls. The deckplates groaned as they protested the sudden changes in pressure and stress on the hull. "This ought to look pretty impressive for anyone watching," she said to herself. Someone at tactical must have heard her, as the front viewscreen suddenly displayed the feed from one of the cameras on the front of the ship.

A maelstrom of swirling, bubbling water, ice, and air danced across the screen, accompanied by the giant cracking sounds of the ice sheet breaking into thousands of chunks which slid off the top of the hull and into the raging water left behind the *Phoenix*.

"The phoenix is supposed to rise from the ashes, not the water," said Ayala, whose voice had taken on a sing-song, mystical quality.

"We may yet get the opportunity to rise from ashes, Ensign, but let's hope that day is much farther off than today," replied Po, who monitored the progress of the ship over the shoulder of the helmsman.

"We're out, sir," said Ensign Roshenko.

"Sensors?" Po spun around to the tactical octagon.

"Coming online now, sir." Ayala studied her board. "Quadri was right. The *Caligula* is bearing down on our position in low orbit. They'll be here in two minutes." Ayala's head snapped up. "And sir! A torpedo! It's right on top of us, impact in four seconds!"

Po slapped the helmsman's shoulder. "Go, Ensign. Full speed, up and opposite the direction the *Caligula* is approaching from."

The raging ice field below dropped far behind them as the *Phoenix* darted away and upward, and the viewscreen showed the torpedo impact the water, detonating with tremendous force, right where they had been just moments before.

"That blast would have propagated through the water and collapsed every bulkhead," said Ensign Szabo, with a low whistle.

Temperature alarms began to go off as the atmospheric compression along the leading edges of the ship made parts of the hull glow a dull orange.

"Sergeant Jayce, are you ready?" said Po into her comm.

Jayce's voice boomed over the bridge's speakers. "Nearly. Team is loading onto the shuttles now. We'll be gone in two."

"Thank you, Sergeant Jayce. Good hunting."

"Sir!" said Ensign Ayala, sounding agitated. "The *Caligula* has sped up. They're nearly on top of us."

"Are we clear of the atmosphere yet?"

"Almost," the helmsman replied.

Po grit her teeth. "We're cutting this one pretty close." She paused, lost in thought for a moment. "Helm, turn us directly towards them. Collision course."

Every head on the bridge turned towards her. Silence reigned for a scant few seconds, punctuated by the regular beeps of the stations and the groan of the ship's trusses and internal structure as it accelerated upward, a fiery comet racing through the atmosphere. She read the incredulous looks in their eyes—the shock, the fear. Clearly they all remembered the last time their Commander had ordered such a tactic. "Sir?" said Roshenko.

"Just do it. No, we are not committing suicide again, but our Captain's tactic last week is no doubt still fresh on their minds. They might actually think we'll do it again. When they swerve away, gun the engines to the opposite direction they swerve and accelerate to maximum. And tactical," she turned back to the octagon, "rain hell on them when they do."

CHAPTER FORTY-NINE

Sergeant Jayce glanced out the window to the busy fighter deck. Technicians and flight deck team members scurried like a hive of ants around the giant bay, struggling to get everything in order for the imminent takeoff. Luckily, he'd already been assembling his team in the bay before the Commander called with her impossible request to be out of there in five minutes, but ordering his team to the shuttles was the easy part. The hard part was goading the deck crew to get the shuttles ready for launch in far less time than they were used to.

Softies, he thought, as he checked his packs of ammunition on his belt for the fifteenth time. Never seen a day of real combat in their lives, most of them. Not like Jayce. Not like his people, and from what he could tell, most of Sergeant Tomaga's too. In the few days he'd had to train with them, he'd learned they were elite shock troops, specially trained for urban combat situations. They weren't the cream of the crop, by any means, that honor belonged to the fabled Imperial T-corps—battle hardened soldiers called upon by the Emperor for the most sensitive of missions—but the Fifty-First Brigade held their own during the training sessions, and they'd come to a wary sort of detente with Jayce's men.

The deck beneath them shuddered. An explosion? Maybe the *Caligula* had resorted straight to nukes. But that wasn't his battle. His battle lay on the surface, with his Captain. Rescue the Captain and the team, said Commander Po. At any cost.

Well, not quite at any cost. Safeguard the other slaves. They were too valuable, especially as propaganda for the Empire, should any of them get killed. *Screw that*, he thought. He'd not point his rifle at any of them, of course, but if they got in the way, or interfered, his first priority was his Captain, and his men.

"Why aren't we gone yet!" he yelled at the navigator, a slight older thin man from the small team of shuttle operators on board. Washed out fighter pilots, most likely. Couldn't make the cut to be a jock, and doomed to spend the rest of his career ferrying passengers with real jobs.

"We've not been cleared, Sergeant."

"Get us the hell out of here! We're late," said Jayce.

The rail of a man shook his head. "Sorry, sir. Can't do it. Not until I've got—" he peered out the viewport at a woman running towards the shuttle, flashing some sort of hand signal. "Oh. We're good to go now, sir. Hold on."

Captain Volaski leaned over the pilot's shoulder. "You entered the coordinates I gave you?"

"I did. Engaging gravitic thrusters—" Jayce felt the faintest bump as the shuttle pulled away from the deckplate. "And preparing to shift in ten. Nine. Eight." The pilot counted down, flipping the comm open to the other two shuttles to allow them to synchronize their departure. The shuttle to their left held Sergeant Tomaga and his men. To their right floated the shuttle containing Volaski's people. Jayce had convinced the pirate to ride with him, ostensibly to make navigation to Velar's base easier, but more for the fact that Jayce didn't trust the man in the slightest. The old pirate looked shifty and dour. Like a man who acted as if he was being watched and was thus on his best behavior.

"Two. One. Shift." The pilot tapped a button and looked up.

The frantic interior of the fighter deck disappeared in a blink, replaced by a star field. Jayce craned his neck down and saw the dusty brown planet far below. The pilot aimed the bow of the ship towards an unremarkable brown spot on the planet's surface and gunned the gravitic accelerator.

"Beginning our descent," said the pilot.

Volaski leaned forward again, tapping Jayce on the shoulder. "Here, let me talk to Velar. She'll be expecting me. If I don't check in, she'll blast us out of the sky."

"She has orbital defense cannons?" Jayce began to wonder if it wouldn't be wiser to mount a ground assault.

"Nothing that fancy, no. We're just a mining operation, remember? But she's got a few turrets, and by my count just three shots would do it." He smiled wryly at Jayce, and motioned towards the comm. Jayce flipped it on and motioned Volaski to have at it.

The pirate captain leaned farther forward and entered in a comm band frequency. "Velar, this is Volaski. You copy?"

Several moments passed, but a woman answered the hail. "Velar here. Status?"

"I've got three shuttles coming down. Full of *Phoenix* crew members. Their best and brightest."

Jayce snapped his head back to Volaski with a start and reached his hand down to the sidearm strapped to his thigh. Volaski didn't seem to notice. Was he betraying them? If he was, would he be this obvious about it?

"Good. You're cleared to land in the courtyard. Commence with the plan once you're here. Velar out."

Jayce grabbed Volaski's shirt and wrenched the man towards the floor until he gasped. "What the hell is that supposed to mean? What plan?"

Volaski heaved, trying to breathe properly. "Velar expects you to attempt a rescue." He struggled against Jayce's firm grip, but to no avail. "I was sent to appear to assist you with the rescue, and once you were all within the compound you would be incapacitated and sent to the mines as slaves."

Jayce loosened his grip, but only slightly. "And remind me again, how can I trust you? How do we know you're not going to just deliver us into her hands like you did the Captain?"

"Because. When we approach the compound, rather than land in the courtyard we're going to take out their turrets, and then land in three separate locations, just like we planned."

Jayce swore and spat a brown wad into the corner, but kept a firm grip on Volaski, whom he held to the deckplate. "Why the hell didn't you tell us about Velar expecting us? Seems like a pretty important detail to leave out."

Volaski seemed to force himself to breathe. "Because, if I told you before, I didn't think you'd trust me."

Jayce sneered. "I don't. And now I trust you less."

"I understand," said Volaski calmly. "But I couldn't take that chance. I knew that if we could just get out here on the shuttles that you wouldn't change your mind. Really, this changes nothing. We still go in guns blazing. The only difference is that Velar will be even more taken by surprise than you planned on. Trust me, she doesn't see this coming."

Jayce held the sneer, but released his grip, allowing the pirate to pull back and smooth out his jacket. "I'm warning you, pirate, if you double-cross us, I'll put a bullet in your motherfucking head."

Volaski pulled at his sidearm and checked its clip. "Believe me, Sergeant Logan Jayce, I have no intention of betraying anyone today but my captor of twelve years. Velar is the one who'll see the inside of a cell for the next fifty years. Gods know she deserves it." He peered out the viewport to his right and looked down. "We're nearly there. Pilot, can you handle the missile controls while you fly or shall I target the turrets?"

Jayce waved him off. "I'll handle it. Just tell me where they are." As he pulled up the missile fire controls he began to get the feeling in his stomach that he always got before battle. The tense, hyper-alert sensation that came with the rush of adrenaline. He was built for battle—he lived for it. But it still made him edgy. And now, with the new revelation from Volaski, he felt even more on edge than usual.

CHAPTER FIFTY

Jake couldn't sleep that night. He couldn't tell if it was the fact that he was laying on bare rock, if his muscles were too sore from all the mining, or if his mind was simply too full to calm down enough to drift off. Stretching out on the flattest, least jagged section of floor he could find, he tried to keep his eyes closed and his mind clear.

But he couldn't stop thinking about Alessandro's achievement. Jake could hardly believe it—the man had worked on that omni-scanner for less than an hour, and had somehow managed to broadcast a signal that interrupted the pain signal sent out by the boss's controller. The man with the half-mustache continually amazed him. One of these days Jake was sure that Alessandro would rip off a mask and reveal himself as a sentient AI or something.

But it wasn't just Alessandro's work that kept Jake up.

Tovra.

The man had roused in Jake an idea. Tovra spoke of the Void—the giant molecular cloud that was impossible to scan, and yet by everything Tovra had said it was most likely teeming with brown dwarfs and rogue planets. Maybe even a full-fledged star or two, completely veiled from outside eyes by the thick cloud of molecular dust—left over from the primordial supernovas that formed it.

Jake's idea was simple. Hide in the cloud. Use it as a base of operations against the Empire. They couldn't be hopping from one world to the next out in inhabited space—eventually their luck would run out. Indeed, in Jake's mind it already had, and they'd only even visited one planet so far. Granted, it was Destiny—a hellhole of a world if he ever saw one, and he could kick himself for letting Velar and Volaski convince him to come, but it certainly didn't bode well for the future. How long until Admiral Trajan had a fleet waiting for him at the next world the *Phoenix* shifted to?

"Friend. You awake?" Jake heard Alessandro's voice whisper at him from several feet away.

"Yeah."

"What do think we should do with this thing? The omni-scanner?"

Jake grinned in the darkness. "I thought you would have had our escape completely planned by now, Bernoulli. And come up with a new solution to the gravitic field equations. And proved Fermat's last theorem. And maybe even come up with a recipe for—"

Alessandro's quiet laughter interrupted him. "I'm sorry, friend, I can't help it. That theorem was proven over 600 years ago."

"It was?" Jake chuckled. "Well that just shows you why I became a space jock instead of a mathematician."

"Or a historian," Alessandro added.

"Right."

Alessandro shifted on the floor next to him. It was nearly pitch black: the cavern was lit only by a small utility light hanging against the far wall, ostensibly only there so that the mass of slaves could use the buckets lining the wall to relieve themselves in the middle of the night. At least, Jake assumed it was night. There was really no way to tell buried under one hundred meters of rock and dust.

"Look, friend," Alessandro continued, "I'm no tactician. I can juggle an equation and fix electronics, but I leave the escape plans to you. I just don't have the head for it."

"Yeah, I've been thinking about that. Your little handiwork there is sure going to help, but there's more than the boss to worry about. He's got two cronies with whips. And even if we get to the surface who's to say that Velar's transmitter isn't more powerful than the boss's? And she could do more than make us feel pain. With a flick of a switch, we're dead—" His head jolted as he hit his word limit, but the image, still only a day old or so, of Suarez's cross-eyed blank stare after the bomb in his head had done its job haunted his thoughts. Maybe that was the real reason he couldn't sleep. Another man down. Because of him. Because of Jake. Because he'd lied and stolen command from his best friend. He let the pain wash over him like a refining fire. His penance. He deserved it.

Alessandro pointed the controller at his own head, and started talking. "Actually, friend, we're safer than you think with regards to that. You see, the omni-scanner is not just interfering with the pain signal sent by the boss or Velar. It's actually interfering with the processor in your head. If I'm right, it can only handle so many commands at once, and so I sent it a stream of idle commands. About fifty trillion of them. They may even still be in the command buffer, but it's more likely that the processor resets after a certain number of identical commands. So if it looks like Velar is going to kill us, I can just resend the commands and we'll be safe for a time."

Jake shrugged. "Sure, but that doesn't mean she can't just shoot us."

Alessandro fell silent for a moment. "There is that. Also, did you notice how many words I just said?" He held the omni-scanner up to his eyes. "I think I just disrupted the algorithm that tracks my quota."

Jake smiled. He wasn't sure how his friend had managed the past several days having to rein in his speech. "I was thinking maybe we could cause a distraction once we're back on the surface. Like maybe rig an explosion, like you did with those mines. I'm sure that'll grab their attention long enough for us to jet."

Someone coughed nearby—their cold hacking indicating the years of inhaled dust from the mining operations. Jake imagined himself in twenty years, still drilling away into the rock wall, old, toothless, haggard. He shuddered and vowed that it wouldn't be.

"I had two more mines, but they took them when I was out cold," said Alessandro. In the dim light of the single fixture, Jake could just make out the growing shadow on his face that seemed to now blend in with the mustache, making it look almost whole.

"Don't worry about it. I'm sure we'll—"

Alessandro grabbed Jake's shirt. "Hold on!"

"What? What happened?"

"I've still got it!" Alessandro seemed excited about something.

"The mines?"

"No, friend, the capsule I took out of the mine I threw. The anti-matter!"

It slowly dawned on Jake what Alessandro was suggesting, and he couldn't decide if he was crazy, brilliant, or just really tired. "You're kidding."

Even in the darkness Jake could see the wide grin brimming out onto his face. "I never kid. Ok, I always kid. But not about this. I never kid about anti-matter!"

"But what kind of an explosion would that generate?"

"Enough to take out a starship."

"So ... exactly how does that help us?"

Jake wasn't understanding. An explosion that large would not only take out the mine, it would destroy the entire compound above them, and likely any building for miles around.

Alessandro hesitated. "I, uh, well I haven't thought that far ahead yet."

But the man was right. A picogram of exploding anti-matter, or however much was in that vial, would surely be enough to distract their captors long enough to escape the compound. And once they were out? Then what?

Jake knew what happened next. He had to find his best friend. They'd heard nothing about Ben since they arrived in the mine—none of the other slaves had seen anyone new come in recently, and the boss wasn't much for conversation. He owed it to his friend. Even at the risk of his own life and the lives of the two men resting nearby.

"Captain?"

Jake's head snapped to his left, from the direction of the raspy voice that called to him. Who in the world was calling him Captain? Avery was snoring loudly to his right, and Alessandro lay near his head. But the voice....

"Tovra?"

As his eyes focused on the man's face, he recognized the Oberanian he'd talked to earlier in the day.

"Why are you calling me Captain?" he whispered.

Tovra chuckled. "Because. You're from Earth, you speak in an authoritative, almost cocky tone, and you're here. I assume some Imperial commander has blacklisted you and arranged for your retirement. Am I wrong?"

Jake hesitated. "Cocky?"

Tovra brushed aside his question. "Look. I've heard some of what you've said. I know you're planning something, and I want in. I can help—I've been here for ages and I know things. Things that might be useful to you."

Jake weighed his next question, then decided it was alright to trust the man. "Like where we can set off a minor anti-matter explosion without killing all of us, and yet big enough to distract them while we escape?"

"That depends. Is your ship still in orbit?"

"I'd assume so. Why? Can you help?"

"I think so," breathed Tovra. He glanced nervously over his shoulder towards the light, as if looking for trouble.

Jake watched him warily. "And what is it you want in return."

"Safe passage is all. Back to the Oberon system. Trust me, you'll be safe there too. At least for the short term. You'll be able to rest, repair your ship, stock up on supplies. We've had recent problems with our aggressive neighbor, the Vikorhov Federation, but our fleet keeps them from doing more than beat their chests. Trust me, you want to go to my planet. You'll find refuge."

Jake nodded. "Very well, easy enough. That's assuming we can even get out of the Destiny system. We were here for supplies to refit our gravitic drive, but our transaction hit a snag."

"What kind of supplies?"

"Raw materials. Refined Neodymium."

Tovra looked at Jake askance, as if he'd just overlooked something plainly obvious to the other man. "You do realize where we're being held, right?"

"A uranium mine." Jake paused. "But, that doesn't mean…. Does it?" It seemed a little too good to be true.

"Of course it does. Lanthanides, Actinides, they're like birds of a feather. Where you find one, you find the rest of them. Especially on a chunk of heavy rock like Destiny. All those reject bins we've been filling? Where do you think those end up? We refine them right here, in some other building in the compound. Neodymium, dysprosium, ytterbium … you name it."

Alessandro, who had been listening in silence, interrupted. "How many nines?"

"Excuse me?" said Tovra.

"How many nines? Of refinement? How enriched is it? You know, is it ninety-nine percent? Ninety-nine point nine? How many?"

"Oh." Tovra paused to think. "Well, honestly I don't know.

Does it matter?"

Jake slowly nodded his head towards Alessandro, warning him not to reveal too much information. Especially not about their next generation gravitic drive.

The scientist hesitated. "Oh. Well, it could be. My engines are new, and I want to put only the best material in them, you see...."

Jake picked up where he left off. "Doesn't matter. We'll take what we can get, and if need be we'll rig something on board to purify it to Mr. Bernoulli's specs."

"Of course," said Alessandro and Tovra at the same time, though probably for different reasons. Alessandro aimed to change the subject while Tovra simply wanted the conversation to steer in the direction of taking him along on their escape.

"Well, Tovra, you've got yourself a ride. Just to Oberon, correct? Not to this Void you were talking about?"

"What void is this?" asked Alessandro.

"The molecular cloud between Antares and Vega," began Tovra, before coughing and holding his chest through his tattered shirt. Clearly, the years were taking their toll. "It's impossible to get a good view of what's inside, but my people believe there to be a haven in the deep interior that one can shift to if one knows the coordinates. A place safe from the Empire. From the pirates. Some even say," he lowered his voice to a near whisper, glancing around before turning back to Jake, "that there is a planet there with original vegetation. Native life. Not like all the rest of the Thousand Worlds with their transplants from Old Earth. All alien. Like nothing we've ever seen. Greener than you can imagine. Waterfalls. Forests." He sighed. "Peace. Verdant peace."

Jake shrugged. "No one has ever found a planet with anything more than cyanobacteria on it. The governments of Earth agreed long ago to leave them be if they ever found any. But it's never been an issue. Alien, you say? I think in the 500 or so years we've been in space we would have found aliens by now."

Tovra let out a ridiculing breath. "No, not *aliens*. Not bug-eyed long-limbed green men. I'm talking about the vegetation. The animals. Like nothing we've ever seen. Many on my world are proposing a formal expedition to the government, but it's probably folly. Especially with the recent Vikorhov aggression —we need all the ships we can get to convince the Vikorhov Federation we're not worth their time." He coughed again, and wiped his hand on his threadbare pants. "But no. I ask only to go to Oberon."

"But didn't you tell me that not even the Empire can reach Oberon because of its size?" said Jake.

"The capital ships, no. Most ships can't make it under normal circumstances. Your engine to mass ratio must be—"

"But Oberon has a fleet, doesn't it? It controls several systems in that sector if I remember my galactic history right. How do they get their capital ships in and out?"

A gleam in Tovra's eye. At first Jake didn't think the man would answer, but, glancing over his shoulder again he began in whisper, "It's a secret. Our gravitic deck devices—you know the ones that create the artificial gravity within the ship? Basically a gravitic thruster projecting negative thrust across a two dimensional space? You know how they work, right?"

"Of course I do!" Jake said, waving a hand. He had no idea how they worked, but he thought it best to maintain his air of authority—of cockiness—that Tovra thought he had. "Explain it to him Bernoulli."

Bernoulli, liberated from his word quota, jumped right in. "The device projects the gravitic field at a target, and all the target sees is a giant mass in the direction of the source. It affects every piece, every atom, every subatomic particle of the target at the same time, which is why there is no sensation of acceleration when one is attracted towards the origin of the gravitic signal. In fact—"

"That's probably good, buddy," said Jake. He knew that his friend could easily talk about gravitics for hours, in spite of their circumstances.

Tovra nodded. "Exactly. Oberon Prime—the star—is extremely low mass, sure. And that prevents most ships from shifting to it. But the government of Oberon, unbeknownst to just about everyone, has designed a network of gravitic generators orbiting the star. Every month or so the generators all align to a specific direction and project a gravitic field at a specific vector away from the star. The signal is so strong that it basically collapses the regular four-dimensional space within the core of the beam, enabling it to travel far faster than light. Any ship near that beam, for light years around, can use it to shift to Oberon Prime. Like a beacon. The ships suddenly see the star not as a puny red dwarf star, but a supermassive behemoth."

Tovra's use of the word *behemoth* brought up images in Jake's mind of the flaming hulk of the former Imperial ship that had nearly killed him three years earlier. He shook his head. "And if it's so secret, how do you know about it?"

"I told you. I was a captain of a merchant freighter."

Jake shook his head again, this time in disbelief. "Uh huh. You just said it was some big state secret. How would a common merchant know about it?"

Tovra shrugged. "State secret? Yeah, kinda. I was put through a rigorous security examination and background check. I passed, and so they told me." Jake studied the man's eyes. They looked honest, but there was something else there. "Really. The Oberanian government depends on the merchant fleet to keep the home world supplied with raw material. Common things like iron, aluminum, copper—they don't exist on Oberon. At least, not in large enough quantities to mine. We depend on shipping from the surrounding systems, and merchants like me met that need. And so, once a month, on the very first day, at noon standard Earth Greenwich time, the beam shines out from Oberon, towards Vega. It's masked with random noise so that passersby won't notice. But those who are looking for it can find it."

Jake squinted. Something about the man's disposition had changed. A subtle change, sure, but Jake could feel it. But if the man could help them out....

"So tell us, Tovra, what do you know? How do we get out of here?"

"Well that depends," Tovra smiled, "I assume by your performance earlier today that your friend here has figured out how to defeat the Domitian Collars?"

So, he'd seen that. The man noticed a lot. Jake nodded.

"Well, if you can get us out of this cavern and up the elevator shaft, I can take it from there. I made it, once, but this damned collar was my undoing." Tovra fingered the nicked and worn device hanging around his bony shoulder.

"What exactly can you do for us?" Alessandro said.

"I overheard you talking about needing a way to make a distraction with that little vial of yours. Anti-matter, huh? Potent stuff. Probably don't want to be setting that thing off on the ground."

The meaning of Tovra's words sunk into Jake. He nodded in understanding. "Sure, ok. How do you propose we launch the thing?"

"It just so happens that this compound has defenses. A few laser turrets. A missile battery. Pretty standard stuff. But what most people don't know is that there is an old railgun in one of the ore storage buildings."

Both Jake's and Alessandro's eyes went wide. A railgun? Here? Those things packed a punch. "Are you sure? Does it work?"

"Yes, and yes, I'm pretty sure it works. Velar set up the thing years ago to defend the compound from any attack by capital ships in orbit, back in her more paranoid phase. But she found that even owning it brought more attention than it was worth. So she stowed it and powered it down. I'm betting that if you fire that vial through the roof, it would explode pretty much on contact."

Jake stared at him. "And? That helps us how?"

Tovra sped up, apparently sensing that he was losing his audience. "But the thing will be flying so fast that it'll be a mile up before the shock wave bursts though the container. Railguns fire things pretty fast, you know. Escape velocity. Maybe higher."

Jake glanced over at Alessandro for confirmation of what Tovra had suggested they do.

"You know, it sounds absolutely insane," said Alessandro, "but it just might work."

"I was afraid you'd say that, buddy."

A shadow darkened Tovra's face. Something was blocking the pale light cast by the hanging receptacle.

"I thought I told you rats no talking," a voice growled. The boss. His voice sounded tired to Jake's ears, and, possibly worse, extremely annoyed.

A well-aimed boot connected with Jake's stomach. Knocking the air out of him. But something inside Jake snapped. Something primordial and raw. Now that he knew the virtual handcuffs were off, he felt overcome by the same violent energy that had overtaken him at that bar on the Earth Shipyards a few weeks ago. The same energy that left that unfortunate, boorish drunk laying in a heap with a broken everything.

With a grunt Jake swung his foot towards the man's leg and the boss fell, grunting in surprise. Jake grit his teeth against the sudden jolt of pain up his leg. His sprain from his motorcycle crash several weeks earlier still had not completely healed, and the swipe at the boss's legs didn't help. The boss twisted around to reach in his pocket for the Domitian device as Alessandro fumbled in his own pocket for the modified omni-scanner, but Jake had already tackled the boss and started pounding his face with balled fists as the man held up his hands to ward off the attack and shouted for help.

From across the giant cavern the boss's two henchmen came running, brandishing wicked-looking batons that looked like they could split a skull open with one swipe. Tovra rose to his feet to meet them, but Jake continued pounding on the

CHAINS OF DESTINY

boss, knowing that if he escaped he'd bring back plenty of reinforcements.

The two henchmen were nearly there, and out of the corner of his eye Jake saw Tovra tense up, crouching down slightly as if preparing to charge. He wondered how the frail man would stand a chance against the burly guards running towards them, now only ten feet away.

Jake had forgotten completely about Avery: the man snored like a boar and hadn't made any sign of waking. But Avery sprang up like a coiled snake as the men passed, lashing out with his feet to drop one of them and slamming his fist into the nose of the other. Even in the dim light Jake could see blood spurt out of the man's face as he risked a quick look in Avery's direction before turning back to the boss.

A fist smashed into Jake's face and he saw stars. He looked down. The fist hadn't come from the cowering man underneath him, holding his hands up to his bloody face to ward off Jake's attack.

Stars flared again. The fist had struck the side of his head hard, and a third punch swiftly followed the second, this time grazing his nose and snapping it to the left. He jumped off the boss and faced his attacker.

It was the boy. Jeremiah. The one that tailed Tovra and whom others had mockingly called "the prophet." Though scrawny, obviously malnourished, and small for an eighteen year old, there was fire in his eyes, and he lunged at Jake with a fury that seemed almost unnatural. Jake dodged a few punches, but his ankle still smarted from knocking the boss's legs out from under him and he fell backwards as Jeremiah leapt with superhuman ability onto Jake's shoulders.

He landed with the boy on top of him and a flurry of fists came beating down.

"Ha! Good, boy, good," Jake heard the boss say. Luckily, he still had his arms raised in front of him and most of the blows glanced off of them, but a few made it through. The boss continued, "The picobots may not have completely worked on him, but it's made him remarkably susceptible to suggestion. I've placed an order in him to protect me from all bodily harm, even at the risk of his own life. Good, Jeremiah, good—"

Jake heard a thud, and he risked a glance at the boss. He'd been knocked over, and Avery now stood over him, a boot placed firmly on the man's throat. "Call him off. Now! Or I'll break your neck," said the burly former special forces officer. He wiped some blood off his hands and Jake noticed the sprawled, broken bodies of the two henchmen lying nearby. At least one of them was still breathing, but Jake wasn't so sure about the other.

The boss wheezed and coughed at the pressure of the boot and started to resist, but the boot clamped down harder, the heel digging in to his neck. Jeremiah continued pounding on Jake, who couldn't manage to dislodge the youth, and several more blows had gotten through his outstretched arms, aggravating the profuse bleeding from Jake's nose.

"Boy! Stop! Stop at once! Ah, fuck it!" The boss grit his teeth as Avery's boot ground deeper into his neck. Jeremiah was not stopping. Jake saw Alessandro approach the enraged youth from behind and made as if to tackle him, but in a blink Jeremiah twisted around to meet the man with a fist to the face and the scientist went sprawling backward onto the ground.

But it was enough. With the boy off-balance for a split second, Jake shifted his weight and Jeremiah toppled off. There was a tussle of thrashing arms, legs, and heads, and Jake's ankle screamed at him in pain, but eventually he came to rest on top of the boy and pinned his thin arms to his side.

"Hey! Hey! Stop it! Wake up!" Jake maneuvered the boy's arms so that he kneeled on them, freeing up his own hands. He slapped the boy once. Jeremiah roared and thrashed even more. Veins throbbed in his neck and spittle flecked out of his foaming mouth. His sandy brown hair smeared with blood at having his head on the rocky floor.

"What the hell have you freak shows done to him?" Jake yelled back at the boss, prone on the floor underneath the weight of Avery's boot. He now noticed out of his peripheral view that most in the cavern had awoken and stood around them in a giant circle of several hundred people, staring at them with gaunt eyes, made even more haggard by the dim light.

"The picobots didn't take. They didn't work like they did for others. I can place orders in him, but only when he's calm. Not when he's riled up like this," spat the boss.

"You bastards," breathed Jake. How could people do this? The boy was, well, a boy. Eighteen, and technically an adult, but how long had he lived in the darkness? Under a whip and a Domitian Collar? His entire childhood? The thought of it made Jake's head spin with the cruel injustice of it all. These people must be stopped.

"Jeremiah," said Jake, in as soft a voice as he could muster given the circumstances. "Jeremiah, wouldn't you like to get out of here? I can get you away from him, you know. Jeremiah, listen to me," he elevated his voice slightly to make himself heard over the boy's howling.

"It's no use, rat. If you want him to shut up you'll have to kill him. For all the good it'll do you. I've got reinforcements showing up in a minute anyway and then all you fuckers are dead," the boss spat.

"Shut it," said Jake, but then turned back to the thrashing boy. "Jeremiah, listen to me. I can get you out, but you've got to calm down." He paused and thought for a moment. "Don't worry, I won't hurt him, so you don't have to hurt me. I promise I won't hurt the boss. You don't have to defend him from me."

Almost like cutting the strings of a marionette, Jeremiah relaxed and stopped screaming. Panting and sweating, he looked up at Jake and their eyes met.

"P—p—promise?"

Damn it. Jake really wanted to rip the boss's head off, but now his hands were virtually tied. Again. And now in a completely unexpected way. The boy was hardwired, it seemed, to protect his captor. They had to get the kid out of here. Jake looked around at the crowd surrounding them. They had to get *all* of them out, but there was no way. The poor souls would have to make their own fortune.

But he'd at least give them a fighting chance.

"I promise, Jeremiah. I won't harm the boss. We'll let him go, unharmed, as soon as we can get up the shaft. Back up to the real world. The sunlight. You remember the sun, right?"

Jeremiah thought for a moment, and then nodded apprehensively. "It's hot, right? White hot. That's all I remember. Father would make me work in the white hot all day. And then I was here."

Dear God. Jake shook his head at the barbarity of the hunk of rock they called Destiny. For the briefest of moments he entertained the idea that maybe it would be better if the Empire controlled the world after all. Controlled all worlds. At least then kids wouldn't be sent to work in mines, never to see the sunlight again.

But no. The Empire had done far worse, and he couldn't forget it. The girls abducted, destined for pleasure houses. The political prisoners. Children—toddlers—taken to Glasov along with their parents. And he'd never forget the look in Po's face and the tone of her voice when she described finding her children's and husband's bodies, blackened and scorched from a midnight Imperial strike in San Bernardino.

The Empire must die. And he would kick the stool out from under it as it hung.

"That's right, son. It's hot. But it's nice. Nicer than down here. You'll see. I can take you up there and you'll never be forced to work again. I'll feed you real food. You'll have a soft bed. You can run. And climb. You like climbing, don't you? But I need you to calm down and promise you won't hit me. Can you do that?"

Jeremiah nodded. Jake stood up, and pulled the boy to his feet. For the barest moment, Jake could swear a smile threatened to cross the boy's mouth, before Jeremiah's face contorted, and he breathed out, almost in a whisper, "You'll die. You'll die before the end. You'll liberate, but in the darkness you'll die alone."

Jake froze.

The boss, who'd been silent until then, snorted. "Ha!

Jeremiah the prophet indeed! He's right, you know. I called for help just before I ran over here. You're all about to die. Let me go and I'll let you live," he sneered.

Was he bluffing? Jake shook his head. There was no time to debate. No time to think it through. They had to get out of there, and fast.

"As I promised Jeremiah, I'll let you go. But not until we get in that elevator shaft. Alessandro," he looked at his friend, who was still nursing his bloody nose, "get the Domitian controller device from him. It's still in his pocket, I think." He pointed to the boss, and Alessandro fished in the man's pocket until he pulled out the familiar hand-pad.

"All right. Let's move," said Jake. He wrapped an arm around Jeremiah's shoulder and led the way out of the cavern and towards the elevator shaft. Avery jostled the boss to his feet and pushed him forward. Most of the other slaves followed in a huge crowd behind them. Out of the corner of his eye, he saw a few bedraggled slaves descend on the still breathing henchman, but he averted his gaze at what happened next.

Once at the shaft, Jake wrenched the door open and indicated for the others to enter. Avery maintained a firm grip on the boss's arms from behind. Jake took the Domitian device from Alessandro, and walked up to a tall, gaunt man who'd followed them.

"Think you can use this?" Jake asked.

The man glanced at the boss, and back to Jake with a smile. "I think I can manage it." He examined the device Jake shoved in his hands. "How long do you think we should wait to come up? What do you think we should do?"

Jake shook his head. "I'm sorry. You're on your own. I can only look after my people. I'll do what I can to clear the way, best I can do is say you're best off if you work as a group." He raised his voice to speak to all of them. Hundreds of people staring with sallow, sunken eyes. "They can stop one of you, two of you, but they can't stop 300 of you. Work together and you might live."

The man nodded and turned towards the boss with an evil grin on his face, as if his wildest, most vengeful dream were about to come true. Avery shoved the boss out into the crowd, which had begun to hoot and shout at their former captor, and they both dove into the elevator shaft.

The boss's face was the last thing Jake saw just before he shut the door.

He'd never seen fear like that in his life.

CHAPTER FIFTY-ONE

Captain Titus gripped the arms of his chair. It wouldn't be long now—just moments ago the tactical officer had fired the two torpedoes, and they now sped away towards the sea of water and ice at the north pole of Destiny. He glanced around the bridge—officers and enlisted men alike sat staring at the viewscreen at the magnified image of the torpedoes speeding towards the surface—some with their jaws slightly parted as they waited with baited breath.

Finally, victory was in sight and they could have their ship back. They could return to their normal duties. The regular patrols. Destroying or taxing the occasional pirate, ferrying various senators to conferences, the shore leaves. Not this mad quest to suppress a minor rebellion—a rebellion that was already and hopelessly crushed.

"Science station, would the *Phoenix*'s scanners be able to see anything above the ice? I assume the salt water will make that impossible...." Trajan asked the officers huddled near the rear of the bridge.

"Aye, sir. Highly unlikely that they're seeing this," said the head scientist on the bridge rotation.

"Excellent."

Everyone on the silent bridge, even Admiral Trajan, stared at the screen. And then the unthinkable happened.

A giant sheet of ice, and the water surrounding it, bulged upward.

And then the ice sheet cracked, falling into the raging water all around it, revealing a huge ship, rising slowly above the torrent underneath.

"Impossible," muttered Titus.

The *Phoenix*, rising from the water, suddenly and improbably shot upward.

The sensor officer looked up. "They're under conventional thruster power. No gravitics."

Maybe they've lost their gravitic drive? Capital ships only rarely blasted off from a planet with conventional thrusters.

"Helm, move to intercept. They're not getting away this time," said Trajan as he rounded the command console and came near the captain's chair. Titus sighed internally and stood up, just in case the Admiral wanted to sit.

"Battle stations," said Titus. He pointed a gloved finger at the tactical station and the officers sitting there. "Prepare railguns and laser turrets. All flight crews to the fighter bay."

Titus watched as the *Phoenix* grew larger on the screen as the *Caligula* matched its course. Suddenly, the other ship turned and aimed straight for them. A collision course.

Trajan raised an eyebrow—the one over the hole, which, rather than indicate surprise like a normal eyebrow raise only highlighted the absence of sight underneath. "Interesting. Mercer is on the surface with his Security Chief and Chief

Engineer. This must be his XO. Megan Po."

"Is she the suicidal type, sir?"

Trajan didn't look at Titus as he stared at the screen. "No, she's not. She's out for blood. She hates us. Hates the Empire, and will do anything to see us bleed. But not, I am quite sure, throw away her crew's lives with a suicide run. She's far too much of a protector than that. A motherly figure."

How on Corsica can he know that? Titus stroked his chin in wonder, and watched the other ship draw closer. It wasn't veering away.

"Ready railguns," he said. The tactical chief nodded his acknowledgement.

"One hundred kilometers and closing fast," said the sensor officer.

Titus turned expectantly to Admiral Trajan, who remained motionless and silent at his side.

"Seventy kilometers. *Phoenix* maintaining her course," the officer continued.

Titus leaned towards Trajan, whispering so that only the other man heard. "Sir?"

Trajan merely shook his head.

"Fifty kilometers, sir."

Titus approached the command console in front of the viewscreen and watched the readout indicating the rapidly closing distance between the two ships.

"Twenty kilometers."

"Fire," said Trajan. "Full spread. Railguns and lasers."

The ordnance leapt out the front bow of the massive ship, shooting across the narrowing space to the *Phoenix*, slamming into her pockmarked hull, which answered with volleys of its own. The *Caligula* rocked as the railgun slugs slammed into the hull, still ravaged and tattered from the battle not two weeks ago.

"Five kilometers. Collision in five seconds...."

Titus couldn't take it. "Helm, veer off to starboard. Tactical, transfer targeting options from the forward crews to port and aft."

Trajan snapped around to pierce Titus with his eye. "What do you think you're doing?"

The viewscreen now showed the port side of the *Phoenix* as it soared past, guns blazing. "Saving our lives, sir. They were about to hit us."

"*No,* they were not. They would have veered off, Captain." His sneer turned to a cool tone, "The next time you subvert my orders on this bridge you will be dismissed to your quarters. Is that clear?"

Titus swallowed hard, but nodded. "Yes, sir."

"Helm," said Trajan, turning to the navigation station, "Change course to pursuit. Tactical, aim for their gravitics and thrusters. They're not getting away again."

CHAPTER FIFTY-TWO

This is it, she thought. Po gripped the arms of her chair—Jake's chair—and watched the *Caligula* grow larger and larger on the screen.

"Eighty klicks, sir," said Ensign Ayala.

"Helm, prepare to veer away, heading…." She checked her board: "Two-sixty degrees. Gravitics?" She glanced at the operations station with a pleading look. The solemn shake of the head by the ops officer told her that the engines were still out. "Very well. Lieutenant Grace, this is Commander Po. What's the situation down there? Are our jocks ready to fly?"

The entire bridge could hear Lieutenant Anya Grace cuss out some deck hand before answering. "Yeah, we're getting there. Jayce's boys just left. Kicking my crew's asses now to get them out. When are you thinking?"

Po grimaced. "Gravitics are still out, conventionals only. The *Caligula* can easily outrun us. The only area we've got them beat is fighters. Theirs are no match for yours."

"I'm touched, sir," came Grace's semi-sarcastic reply. "We'll be ready in a few minutes. Grace out."

"Forty klicks, sir," said Ayala again.

"Prepare to change course on my mark." She turned back to the tactical octagon. "Weapons ready. Fire when we're in range. Target their offensive capabilities only—we need to make every shot count, people, we're running low on ordnance."

"Thirty klicks."

Po felt the knot in her stomach tighten as she had a moment of self-doubt. Had she underestimated the ability of the conventional thrusters to get them out of the way in time? Should she be high tailing it out of orbit and hope the *Caligula* doesn't follow? The uncertainty and the apprehension gnawed at her, but she refused to let it turn into fear. There was no time for fear. Too many people depended on her for that.

"Helmsman, ch—"

Ayala interrupted her. "Sir, the *Caligula* has veered off."

Perfect, Po thought. "Ok, Roshenko, we're in their heads now. They think we're crazy enough to kill ourselves. Let's use that to our advantage. Reverse course. Take a heading opposite theirs and get us into a high, stable orbit. Let's make them chase us."

Everyone gripped their consoles or chairs as the *Phoenix*'s thrusters pushed the ship into a wide arc. Usually, with gravitic propulsion, there was no sensation of changing inertia; conventional thrusters offered no such comfort.

"Doc Nichols here—what the hell are you doing up there, Commander?" Nichols's harsh smoker's voice blared over the comm.

"Sorry, Doc, I should have warned you we're only on conventional. Things are about to get pretty rough. Prepare for casualties."

"More? I've got patients tumbling off their beds from the inertia, and now you tell me we've got more coming?" The bridge crew heard several profanities under the doctor's breath.

"Sorry, Doctor, just trying to keep us alive. Hope you understand. Po out." She swore. "As if I didn't have enough to worry about."

The deckplates started to shake, and the groans of the internal support trusses made Po's neck hair stand on end. "Hold together, baby," she whispered to the ship.

"Sir, the *Caligula* is changing course to match us," Ayala announced over the rising din of the protesting groans of the ship.

"Very well." She turned to her comm. "Grace, Commander Po. Scramble the fighters as soon as you can. Your orders are to terminate their offensive capabilities first, then their engines, then their lives."

Anya's harried voice sounded over the comm. "Does it have to be in that order?"

Po couldn't help but smile at her Wing Commander's retort. "Funny, Grace. Get to work. Good hunting, Lieutenant."

CHAPTER FIFTY-THREE

Ben had lost track of time, which, in his delirious frame of mind, he found very fortunate. Whatever setting the freak show had put the collar to seemed excessive at first, as the pain was unbearable.

The collar seemed to produce pain in waves up and down his body, penetrating every joint, muscles he didn't know he had. Unfortunately, it seemed to have the greatest effect on his head, and the first several hours of it had made Ben want to put a bullet through his own brain—if only he could get his hands on a gun.

But after what he could only guess was most of the day, he'd hung there from his wrists, bleeding from the carving the man had made on his chest and back, writhing and contorting with the most cruel pain he'd ever felt. Cruel, because there was no stopping it. It just came, grabbed hold of him, chewed him in its relentless, cold mouth, and he was powerless to even struggle. And somehow, after a few hours, it became manageable. For the first part of the eternity that he hung there, he'd tried to negotiate with the pain. Convince it to go and come again later. To at least spare him a few moments of calm clarity. But it refused, and like most unpleasant things it had become familiar.

Had he fallen asleep? How was that even possible, through that kind of searing pain? A voice. A voice calling him. Now he was sure he was hallucinating. The voice was calling his name. Ben? He was Ben Jemez, right? Oh, God, the pain….

No, the voice was real.

"Ben Jemez."

It came louder this time, cutting through the swirling clouds of agony.

"Is your name Ben Jemez?"

He cracked his eyes open. No one there. Just the empty dungeon. Knives. Whips. The scientific equipment. He knew it. His mind was falling apart.

"Keep your focus, Ben. He does this at first, but after a few days he'll stop using the collar and just use … well, other things. You'll like it. You'll see."

Aw, shit. Ben usually never swore, even in his mind, but for the scantest of seconds he'd hoped that the voice was someone to rescue him. That it was Jake. Or Po. But the voice was far too hesitant, too simpering, to be one of them. It was only the wreck of a man that called his captor *Master.* Six.

"How did you know my name?" he said through gritted teeth. Somehow, talking seemed to make the pain worse and he clamped his mouth shut.

"Easy. You chanted it for hours. My name is Ben Jemez. My name is Ben Jemez. My name is Ben Jemez. Over and over again. I thought you'd already lost your mind."

"Like you lost yours?" he managed to force out.

The simpering voice laughed. "Me? I didn't lose mine, I told you. The Master saved me."

Not that nonsense again. He had to change the subject, or else endure more preening talk of his master. He wasn't sure if he could endure that.

"Tell me about your ship. The *Fury*. Tell me about Pritchard. What was it like serving under him?" Speaking was agony, but it focused him. He decided to keep talking— anything to keep his mind off the unimaginable pain still coursing through every digit, every limb, every vessel, every strand of muscle and tendon, every hair, every—

"That monster left me here. He was humbled, you know, after that battle over Earth. He thought he was invincible, the bastard. Thought he had the whole thing planned out. He was a meticulous planner. Every detail, even the small stuff didn't escape his notice. He thought he was brilliant. Well, he was a fool. An arrogant fool. Nothing more."

"You keep saying *was*."

Six laughed again. "Of course I am. That bastard has been dead for over a year."

"How could you know that?"

"Because," sneered Six. "Because when he left me here, we had been planning on going to November space and beg help from those pirates. Can you imagine that? The pirates. After all that time battling the Empire and tyranny and saving puppies, that bastard was going to go hat in hand to the November family. You've heard of them, right? Worse than the old Italian mafia. No one enters their space without permission. No one trades on their worlds without their say-so. After restocking at Destiny, that was his plan. Go to the November family.

Thought he could convince them to join his cause or some shit like that. And now he's dead, the arrogant bastard."

"How do you know?"

"My Master told me."

Ben managed a gruff laugh. Somehow, even a forced laughter masked the pain. "Right. And you believe what your master tells you?"

"I never told him the *Fury* was headed off to November space, and yet he came to me one day and told me Pritchard was dead, at the hands of November pirates."

Whatever. Ben rolled his eyes, then held his breath against another wave of pain. Panting, he forced out another question.

"What's your name?"

"I told you. Six."

"Bullshit. What's your name? Before you came here."

Six's voice rose in intensity. "I told you. I was born here. There is no before."

"But you just talked to me about your ship and Pritchard for five minutes. What was your name there?"

Ben could tell that the cognitive dissonance confused the man, since he hesitated for several seconds before repeating, "I was born here. On that table. You could see the blood on the floor for—"

"Yeah, yeah, you told me that. Come on, man. Don't do this. Don't be what he wants you to be. Don't be a slobbering, cowering prick."

Six's voice trembled. "But he makes me so. I can't be anything else."

What in the world was he talking about?

But he didn't get the chance to ask. The door behind him

burst open and the quick, erratic clomp of heavy boots on the floor told him Doctor Stone had arrived, and the pace of his steps told Ben that he was excited.

"Seven! You're still alive! And awake. G—g—good. That tells me something, Seven. It tells me you're strong. Not like that filth in the corner. Here, let me adjust this for you...."

And just like that, the pain stopped. At least, the absence of all feeling qualified as being pain-free. He knew, intellectually, that his wrists and shoulders should be on fire from hanging for so long, but the collar-induced pain seemed to have numbed him to all the smaller, lesser feelings.

"There. I bet you feel like a billion credits now." Stone walked around to face him. Ben couldn't remember if he'd even looked in the man's eyes yet. He knew he had, but the past few days were just a hazy fog. Or was it weeks? He opened his eyes. The man stood before him, one hand on his hips. The stubble growing on his shaved head looked like it would be orange if allowed to grow. A white lab coat was still draped over his shoulders, though he now removed it and hung it on a nail sticking out of the wall. To be honest he looked like a scientist. Some nameless engineer who should be hard at work at some lab bench somewhere, but instead was leering at him, an electronic controller in one hand.

"I can tell you're going to be my favorite. You're going to be my masterpiece. My magnum opus." He smiled at him maniacally.

"What the hell do you want?"

"I told you, Seven, I want you to want me. That's all. Want me. Need me. Submit to me willingly. Want me as your Master. That's all. It doesn't have to hurt anymore. Just call me Master and kneel before me."

"A little hard to kneel hanging up like this," Ben said, with a forced sigh, hoping the delusional fool would take the bait.

"Patience, Seven. You haven't even called me Master yet." Again, the stuttering seemed to melt away as the man got into the swing of things. He apparently thrived off of dominating others, though he probably had to repress it in his professional work. *That would explain the stutter,* Ben thought.

"Nor will I."

The man reached up and patted Ben on the cheek. "We'll see." He walked over to the table and retrieved a knife that had lain there, unwashed from when he'd used it previously on Ben's chest. "Tell me, Seven," he turned back to look at him, "I trust you've talked a little to that rag of filth in the corner?"

"What have you done to him?"

"As he's no doubt told you, I've liberated him. But here's my problem, Seven, and tell me if you can help me out with it." He walked back over to Ben and came up close, leaning in to his ear and dropping his voice almost to a whisper. "I want someone to serve me willingly. Not like that pile of shit over there."

"You mean to tell me he wasn't willing?" Ben asked, not even trying to keep the sarcasm out of his voice.

"No. I injected him with picobots. I invented them, you know. I'm fucking brilliant. I've even clocked my own synapses —they run at 146 percent the normal firing rate of a n—n— normal human." He thumbed back at Six. "And he does everything I tell him to, believes everything I tell him to, without question. He can't *not* obey. But after I injected him and programmed him, I knew what I had done was folly.

What's the thrill of having a robot serve you? A fucking machine. No, Seven, I want a willing servant." He lowered his voice to a whisper. "I want you. Seven: perfection among the numbers, and now the most perfect of my servants."

Ben snorted. "Look, if all you want is a blow job, just cut me down and I'll see what I can—"

The man drew a hand back sharply and hit Ben across the face. A gleam came into his eye, which made Ben shudder inside. "You'll beg me for it. But no. Not yet. I need to break you first. Then, when I buy some more sluts from Velar, I'll let you join in."

He held up the knife, poised to carve something else into his torso. Ben held his breath and clenched his jaw in anticipation. The man paused. "Seven, just know that you have no escape, and no choice. You either do this, or you die, because if you don't I'll inject you like I injected him. I'd rather have a fucking robot than a dead body. At least they can pleasure me. And really, you don't want that shit in you. The picobots are good, but I've still got to pass six sigmas of reliability before I make my final delivery to the Empire." He paused, and shook his head with a leering smile. "And I've only got two. Who knows what that'll do to you? It seemed to be enough for that Admiral, though. He made a surprise visit. Just delivered a box of the stuff to him yesterday."

Stone leered at him, and brought the knife to bear. Ben closed his eyes and waited for the cold blade.

The pain wouldn't hurt if he welcomed it, would it?

CHAPTER FIFTY-FOUR

Gavin couldn't take his eyes off the deck crew, which scurried about on the flight deck, loading armaments, refueling, re-oiling, and frantically preparing every fighter in the vast, long bay for takeoff. He leaned over to Jet, who sat next to him on one of the benches lining the bulkhead.

"You ready for this, Floppychop?"

She didn't respond, and he glanced over at her. The short, black tousled hair spilled over onto her forehead like an angry mop, and he was surprised to see her eyes watery and red.

"You good, Jet?"

She nodded, then snorted a laugh as she wiped her nose. "Yeah. Just fine. The whole situation just reminded me of my parents, that's all."

Gavin held his tongue, knowing she'd talk if she needed to.

She did. "It was just like this. Three years ago. They were both flight engineers. Worked down in Fort Walton. At the base."

"One of the ones that was attacked?"

"Yeah. I was seventeen. Rules were lax in the Resistance force, and I begged them to let me come to the base with them. You know, watch the whole thing first-hand. We were gonna win, ya know? It was exciting."

She fell silent. A nearby tech swore loudly as he spilled his tool cart and his supervisor yelled at him to clear the mess away before the nearby fighter lifted out.

"Yeah. Too exciting. That was D-day. They bombed the place. The whole fucking place. Even the civilian buildings where my parents worked. The flight engineering building? Just gone. Vaporized. You know why I lived?"

"Why?" he said, numbly.

"Because I left to go to the cafeteria building to get a candy bar out of the vending machine. The bombs started, and a few minutes later, I looked out, and the building they were in was gone."

Silence. Then she snorted a forced laughter. "So food saved me. Funny, huh? I guess that's why I joined up with the fleet as a galley cook. Stupid. Totally stupid. Clichéd."

He murmured, "It's not stupid." Out of the corner of his eye he saw Lieutenant Grace march their way, stopping to bark out orders to various deck crew techs. "In fact, I think you're pretty damn brave. To sign up after shit like that. My family's all nice and safe in the St. Louis suburbs. I just got out to see adventure."

Jet nodded. "Yeah, well you're about to get it, Newbie." She turned towards him and smiled—the first genuine, non-smirky smile she'd shown since they'd met.

Friends at last, he supposed.

CHAPTER FIFTY-FIVE

"Move, people, move! Get your asses out there! Quadri, what the hell are you doing?" Anya Grace marched over to the fighter pilot who'd stooped to help a tech pick up a large box.

He grunted with effort—the box looked dreadfully heavy, containing several thousand rounds of ordnance for one of the fighters. "Just helping the techs, sir. The faster the ship gets loaded the faster I get out of here."

Anya jabbed her finger at the waiting fighter. "The faster you get your ass in your fighter the faster you get out of here. Move!"

Quadri glared at her as she shoved him aside and took his place with the box, but turned to run to his fighter. The box was far heavier than she thought, and she strained to keep her face from contorting.

"Careful, sir, if we drop this, the whole deck blows," said the tech. Su, his name was, if she remembered right. She chided herself for not knowing her people's names yet.

A real commander would know his name. A real commander would protect her people and get them some extra hands—Su looked like he was about to pass out.

"How long have you been on duty, Su?"

He glanced at an antique-looking timepiece on his wrist. "Eighteen hours, sir. Busy day."

Anya puffed as she pulled on the box's handle and looked up to see how far they had left. Just ten more meters to the fighter's undercarriage.

"Who the hell signed off on your duty hours?"

"You did, sir."

"Well dammit, Su, I don't read those things. Next shift, only ten hours, ok?"

"Uh, sir, don't we have an Imperial battle cruiser bearing down on us?"

Anya flashed a wry grin. "Sure, but I don't want Occupational Safety to come down on me. Those bastards are worse than any battle cruiser."

Su laughed. Good. Keep the people in good spirits. Keep them engaged. Distract them from wondering why the hell some washed out space jock was ordering them around.

After several more minutes of harried shouts, yelling, pointing, lugging, and swearing at her pilots, she saw that nearly every fighter was filled.

Except one. She regarded the empty bird, and tried to remember the name of its former pilot. Washburn? Wallingford? Washington? She'd only met him a few times, before the battle at Liberty Station. He'd died in the collision with the *Caligula*—thrown from his bunk and asphyxiated by the decompression.

Fuck you, Jake.

She didn't envy his position, his responsibility, but she'd be damned if she was going to let him get away with poor decisions that killed her people.

But the *Caligula* was bearing down on them once again, and they needed every fighter available out there.

She noticed a young pair sitting in the corner, talking in low tones, watching the commotion all around them.

"Ashdown. Xing. You're up."

They jumped to their feet. "Uh, sir?"

She strode over to them. "You heard me. We're all dead unless you two can stop the Imperial bastards. Come on. Newbie, you're pilot. Floppychop, you're the gunner. Get moving."

"But, sir," began Ashdown, "We've hardly begun our training. Even you said how shitty we've been flying."

She picked up their helmets from the bench and thrust them into their chests. "Well your shittiness will have to suffice."

"But are we ready to fly in a real battle?"

Anya met his eyes. They looked scared. Terrified, even, but at least the boy was controlling himself well. Admirably, in fact. "Look kid, here's the secret. None of us are ready. When you get out there and you've got five bogeys firing at you from ten different directions, your training goes out the window and you just fight to survive. I've seen you. You're a scrapper. You're a fighter. In fact, don't ever tell any of the other jocks this, but you're a natural. Now get the fuck out there and bring me back some Imperial heads." She pointed at the last remaining fighter.

They both pulled themselves up straight. Ashdown more than his friend, Xing. She was ok—better than most of the other recruits—but nothing like the fresh-faced boy next to him.

The girl would learn fast, though. Just like Anya had. Without another word she marched off to go deal with another minor crisis as the two rushed to their bird.

And she had the sneaking suspicion it would be the last time she'd see them. The feeling nearly killed her. She almost shouted out for them to stop, that she was kidding—really, how could they even think that they were ready to fight—but she stopped herself. She didn't just suspect she wouldn't see those two again, but all of them—every last fighter. Every last jock.

This could very well be their last stand, and so they might as well throw everything they had at the Imperials.

Those two would either die out there fighting, or in here watching the fight, like Anya. She swore again to herself and wiped her brow as she marched over to tell off another tech for spilling oil all over the deck.

CHAPTER FIFTY-SIX

Gavin Ashdown was born with a videogame virtual controller in his hands. He loved the thrill of the overwhelming odds that the game console would throw at him. The strategy, the tactics that went into a successful fighter campaign. And when you mess up, you get a redo. The game starts over, and you live to fight another day.

But as the swarm of fighters approached from the *Caligula* he wondered where his reset button was. *Does this game have cheat mode?* he asked himself. And even as he thought it he shook his head, wondering why he was even thinking things like that when the enemy was seconds away.

"You ready for this, Newbie?" asked Jet, who snorted.

"I told you, that's not my callsign." His friend had been trying to tag him with that for days now. Gavin eyed the closest wave of fighters nervously.

"You don't get to pick your own callsign, Newbie. Lieutenant Grace called you that, fair and square."

"Look sharp, Floppychop, we've got our first bogeys coming in. Ready?"

"Ready."

"I'm doing the Grace maneuver. Be ready for it."

Jet snickered before Gavin whacked her shoulder and clarified, "Not *that* Grace maneuver. Come on, she's your commanding officer."

"Hey, she's the one that told us about it," Jet said with a smirk. "Ok, fine. All ready on this end. Let's show 'em what we got."

Gavin accelerated full bore towards another fighter, as if engaging them in a game of chicken. Red bolts blazed all around them as he wove the fighter to and fro, but Jet threw back fire of their own. With a flick of a finger, Gavin shifted the ship out of existence, reappearing just fifty meters behind the other fighter, and with its ass now in view, Jet blasted it. *To hell,* Gavin thought.

Man, maybe this is just a videogame.

"Ready for another one?"

Jet snorted. "Bring it." Her breathing picked up and a slow smile grew on her face.

Gavin swerved the fighter around to another enemy. Their comm blared to life. "Holy shit! Did you see that?" It was Quadri's voice, and he didn't sound pleased.

"What?" came another voice over the open comm. Gavin thought it sounded like Lee's.

"One of these bastards just shifted, and blasted the hell out of Brooks! He's gone, man. They're learning their micro-gravitics!"

Gavin pressed on the accelerator, aiming for their next target, which wove back and forth and through wide loops, trying to shake them. But in the blink of an eye, it was gone.

Swearing, Gavin pounded the gravitic shift switch, shifting them blindly a few hundred meters towards the planet below. And just in time, as, from their new perspective, they watched as their former quarry pelted the space they'd just occupied with a rain of fire.

"Shit. He's right," said Jet. "What the hell do we do now?"

Gavin grit his teeth, trying to ignore the wreck of Brooks's fighter plummet down through the atmosphere below. "We beat the hell out of them. Come on, let's go."

CHAPTER FIFTY-SEVEN

Sergeant Jayce eyed the small gray patch amid the sprawling brown terrain far below. It stood apart from the main town, just like Volaski had said, and their sensors had picked up the telltale readings of an ion-beam cannon. From what the man had said, there were probably two lasers trained on the shuttles as well. Velar was distrustful by nature, and would surely have all available surface-to-air weapons locked on them just as a precaution.

"Making our final approach," said the pilot.

Jayce thumbed another wad of snuff into his cheek. "Good. My finger's getting itchy."

Sergeant Tomaga peered at him over the shaft of his rifle. "You know our orders. No killing of innocents."

"What the hell would you know about that?" Jayce glowered at the former Imperial. Daring him.

Tomaga didn't answer, but looked down at his rifle and rubbed his sleeve against a stubborn smudge on the barrel. Jayce grinned—he'd hoped to provoke the man. Make him a little angry. Get his blood going before they landed—heavens knew that they needed it.

The pilot pulled up on the accelerator, bringing the speed of the craft down to something more amenable to landing.

And then all hell broke loose.

CHAPTER FIFTY-EIGHT

It was daytime, which surprised Jake. He'd thought it was the middle of the night, but soon he realized that down below, down in the mines, it was whatever time the boss said it was.

But not anymore. He cringed to think about what was happening to the boss right now. After all, the man was a slave too. But their fellow captives thought of the man as worse than their captors, precisely because he was one of them—he was a slave, and yet he held the whip. He colluded with the enemy and therefore he was worse than the enemy. Maybe Jake shouldn't have handed him over to the others after all.

But there was no time to second-guess himself. He had to find that railgun, and he had to find his best friend.

If Ben was even still alive.

There were two guards sprawled out on chairs watching a porno vid in the control room near the shaft's exit, but Avery cold-cocked one of them with the butt of a short shovel he'd found in the hallway and Jake punched the other as hard as he could in the nose when the man snapped around to see them. Blood in his eyes, he didn't see the business end of Avery's shovel as it connected bluntly with the back of his skull.

Jake wiped the blood off his hand, and shook the pain away. "Where from here?"

Tovra pointed down the corridor. "Out this building and into the next. Storage building. Very top."

Jake took Jeremiah's hand and led him down the corridor, with Tovra, Alessandro, and Avery following close behind. Luckily, the rest of the building seemed to be deserted, and when they peered out the door towards the storage building next door, they saw commotion some distance off near one of the main buildings they'd first entered. But there was no one nearby, so they ran for it.

Once inside the storage building, Jake saw that they wouldn't have it so easy. Dozens of slaves trudged back and forth between several large bins, apparently sorting chunks of ore into a variety of different grades. A handful of men with sidearms and handheld devices similar to the Boss's Domitian control device sat around the outer walls, looking for trouble.

Jake whispered back to Bernoulli, "You got your omni-scanner ready? I think now's the time."

"Ready, friend," said Alessandro.

Avery pointed towards a pair of guards with their back to the group, and Jake nodded his approval. With the shovel still in his hands, and shielded from the rest of the warehouse by a stack of plastic barrels, Avery and Jake crept behind the two men. Simultaneously, Avery pounded one man's head with the shovel as Jake grabbed the other from behind in a chokehold.

The man bucked backwards, throwing Jake off-balance and making his sprain throb in pain. He wrestled the man to the ground, and, looking up, dodged away just in time for Avery's shovel to connect with the man's head with a sickening crunch.

"Hey!" A guard several dozen yards away spotted them and drew his sidearm, diving behind a concrete column before popping off a few rounds. Avery wrenched the sidearm out of the holster of the guard they'd just felled and took cover behind another column, as Jake fished the gun from the other guard sprawled out on the floor, pushing Jeremiah to the ground with his other hand.

"Stay down," he whispered in his ear, scrambling around the barrels to try and catch the guard in the crossfire. He nodded once to Avery, who laid down suppressing fire as Jake dove through an open space to another column—this one with a better angle on the guard. Out of the corner of his eye he saw two more guards advance on Avery, but they hadn't seen Jake yet.

He watched, waiting for just the right moment. Too soon and he'd blow his cover. Too late, and it'd all be over….

There—the guard peered out from behind the column, and Jake pulled the trigger, smearing the man's brains all over the column next to him. The body slumped against the concrete and fell to the floor.

The other two remaining guards dove for cover as they saw Jake, but as they did, Avery advanced and flanked them as Jake collided with another slave bolting for the exit. The slaves who hadn't dropped to the ground cowering in fear ran for their lives, and Jake tried to blend in as he ran for the next column.

He peered around the corner and made eye contact with Avery again, who signaled him to lay down suppressing fire. Checking the clip of his gun, he nodded and popped around the corner with a barrage of bullets aimed at the two columns obscuring the remaining guards. With a flash of motion, it was all over. Avery sprinted towards the columns from the other direction, reached around the corner, and fired twice without looking. Two bloody bodies slumped to the ground.

His stomach still in his mouth, Jake forced himself to breathe. Adrenaline was nice, but not the kind that accompanied bullets. "No-look shots. Nice," he called out to Avery.

"Meh. Sloppy. But I'll take it." Avery wiped the sweat off his forehead as he scanned the rest of the warehouse for more guards.

"Jake. There's the stairs," Alessandro said, pointing to a darkened stairwell on one wall. Jake turned to the prisoners still cowering on the ground.

"We're about to see a whole lot more action. If you can fight, find a weapon. If you can't, then hide. We have some business upstairs, and I'd be quite obliged if some of you could see that we're not disturbed."

A heavy-set man on the ground near Jake stirred. He looked new—the extra folds of fat suggested he'd only recently arrived and had not yet been subjected to very many months of a slave's ration. "Is this it? Are you setting us free?"

Jake nodded. "I sure as hell hope so, sir."

Without waiting for more chitchat, Jake grabbed his people and dashed up the stairs. The upper level of the warehouse was more of a storage room than anything else. A thick layer of dust coated dozens of old, cobwebbed pieces of equipment. After some searching, Alessandro hollered.

"Ha! This is it." He yanked a dusty blanket off the long

barrel of the railgun and ran a hand over it. "Nice. It's brand new, friend, looks like it's never used."

Jake ran over to the gun. The barrel was pointed at one of the walls, but he saw the housing that would elevate it upwards, towards the ceiling, which had several tiles missing as if it had been built in a hurry.

"Here's the controls," said Avery. He pressed a button and the screen flared to life. "Still has power too. Must be powered inductively—I don't see a line anywhere."

Alessandro fiddled with one of the panels on the large gun, and tested the latch on the loading chamber. It opened.

"Well, this just might work," he said as he examined the tiny chamber. He turned to the stack of crates nearby and lifted the lid off one of them. "Ah. The ammunition. Good," he said, as he inspected a shell, "I think we're in business, friends. My vial will fit. But just barely."

Alessandro fished in his pocket for the vial of anti-matter, and, screwing off the top of the shell, inserted it deep inside.

"Ready," he said, as he screwed the top of the shell back on and placed it in the firing chamber.

Avery furrowed his brow at the controls. "I can't seem to raise the barrel. The controls aren't responding."

"That's because I've remotely disabled it," said a voice behind them all, with a tone of mockery.

Jake turned.

Velar. Her arms were raised, holding a gun, and a Domitian control device, both pointed straight at Jake's head.

CHAPTER FIFTY-NINE

Captain Titus steadied himself on the command console as the *Caligula* rocked under the barrage of the *Phoenix*'s railguns. "Status?" he barked at the tactical station.

"Moderate damage on the starboard hull, but no breaches. We've lost two railguns and a laser turret."

Titus studied his console—starboard was their weaker side, having been hit hardest during the battle of Geneseo Station over Earth, and he swore softly to himself as he realized the ship might never recover fully without a complete overhaul at the Praesidium Shipyards.

"Bank to starboard. Show them our left flank."

"Yes, sir."

Trajan monitored the situation from the captain's chair, softly humming some nameless tune to himself. He appeared completely unconcerned with the situation, as if he knew its end from the beginning.

The humming stopped. "Wing Commander? Has our fighter squadron deployed yet?"

A voice answered over Trajan's comm on the chair.

"Yes, sir. Engaging the Rebel fighters now."

Indeed, Titus glanced up at the viewscreen as the battle commenced, and he winced as one of their own flared up and exploded.

Trajan continued, "You have authority to engage in the tactics we discussed, Commander. Use the new fighters to their full capability."

"But sir, we haven't tested them in combat. Regulations dictate that—"

"Those are my orders, Commander. *Execute* them faithfully. Trajan out."

Titus could imagine Commander Burris wince on the other end of the comm as the Admiral emphasized the word *execute*. The meaning was clear.

Titus turned back to the front of the bridge. Within moments, the effect of Trajan's words played out on the screen as their fighters began using the micro-gravitics, turning the new technology back on the Rebels themselves. He smirked as one of the enemy fighters exploded as one of their own appeared suddenly behind it out of nowhere.

Trajan thumbed open his comm again. "Chief of security, prepare the cargo holds to receive a large number of prisoners."

Titus glanced back at him. "Is that not a bit premature, sir?"

An icy cold stare met his own gaze. "It is not. I've studied this commander at the helm of the *Phoenix*, and she stands no chance against us. She is driven by a sense of revenge, and nothing more. I can see it in her tactics thus far. I can read it in her music, Captain. It speaks to me, and tells me she is found wanting."

Titus nodded once, and turned back to his console. He grimaced as another one of their fighters flared into a brief fireball. It was too early to assume victory on this one—the *Phoenix* was in far better shape than they'd supposed, and even with the micro-gravitics, their fighters were struggling against the enemy. The Rebels had had several weeks to train with the new micro-gravitic drives. Theirs had only trained with them for a few days.

"Communications. Send the gravitic pod you have prepared."

"Aye, sir," came Ensign Evan's voice behind Titus. Titus glanced at the Ensign inquisitively.

Trajan answered for the young man. "To signal the *Sphinx*, Captain. I believe they have a grudge against the *Phoenix*."

Titus smiled. So, that was the source of Trajan's confidence. He felt somewhat miffed that the Admiral had not told him about the other ship waiting in the star system adjacent to the Destiny system, but the now sure knowledge of their victory made up for it. Still, he thought it was time to have another word with Evans about keeping information like that secret from the captain of the ship.

"Good thinking, sir."

Trajan's previous sneer gave way to a dry smile. "I know, Captain. No need to ingratiate yourself. Now sit back and relax. Enjoy the concert."

CHAPTER SIXTY

Jake eyed Velar nervously and took a step so that he blocked her view of Alessandro.

Velar jerked her arm. "Stop! One more step and I'll have you on your knees begging for mercy. Or, better yet, I'll detonate the device in your head, like your friend several days ago. That was great fun, wasn't it?"

Jake wanted to swear at her. To rip her arms from her sockets and beat her with them to a bloody, quivering pulp. The way she talked so callously of Suarez's demise made him quiver with rage, but he kept it under control. Gritting his teeth, he forced himself to think.

"Velar. Such a pleasure to see you here. I was worrying I'd have to hunt you down. How considerate of you to save me the effort."

"Save it. Step away from the railgun. Now!" She motioned with the Domitian controller.

Jake took a few steps away. He heard the others follow suit.

"Tell me, Velar. Where is my friend? Where is Ben?"

She laughed. Her long earrings dangled against her neck as she regained her composure. "Mr. Jemez? He fetched quite a price. The most I've ever sold a slave for. Double, in fact. I have a certain client who likes a little extra fun that his wife refuses to give him. He's an artist, you know. At least, that's what he tells me. You should see some of the designs he's carved on some of the other slaves I've sold him. Truly remarkable. He chains them up, and uses them as his canvas with his blade as a brush. Distracts him from his day job, you see."

Jake's lips trembled. "You monster."

She held her hands up. "Hey, I can't control what my clients do with their property. He's a little odd, sure. Maybe cruel, even. But in time, your friend will love every second in that dungeon. All the others did. Eventually. They call him their master. Something about those bots he injects them with. Kinda cute, I think."

Jake boiled. He had half a mind to race towards her and break her face, Domitian Collar be damned.

But he stood his ground. Would Ben make it? He was made of some strong stuff, but this sounded pretty bad. And it killed Jake that he was responsible. It was his fault. He was in command. All those dead crew members, and now this.

Jake heard a whisper in his ear. "Ready. Go now!"

Without waiting an extra second, Jake sprang forward and charged Velar, who, unflinching, pressed down on the controller.

And made Jake's head reel in a shock of fiery pain. Pure pain. Worse than the previous shocks. Worse than the bone regrowth injections Doc Nichols had given him a few weeks back. He fell to his knees and held his head between his hands.

"No!" Avery took a step forward, but stopped when he saw Velar point the controller at him.

Jake screamed. A primal, agonized scream—at least, that's how it sounded to his own ears. It was a pain that he couldn't comprehend. Like nothing he could even imagine feeling. He tried to speak, to beg Velar to stop, but no words could pass his lips. Only incoherent moaning.

And just as suddenly as it came, it was gone.

He opened an eye, and to his surprise, Velar was scrambling up from the floor where Jeremiah had knocked her down, reaching for the controller. He swung a foot out and kicked it away before lunging at her, but came up short and she bolted away.

Jeremiah started running after, but Jake called after him.

"Jeremiah! No, she could have more guards down there."

The boy paused, and turned back.

He mumbled, barely audible. "Did she hurt you? I just didn't want her to hurt you. She couldn't hurt you. I wouldn't let her."

Jake cocked an eyebrow at him, wondering what had inspired the kid's sudden change of ferocious loyalty, but then winced as he stood up. "No, she didn't hurt me. Not permanently. Good work, kid." He spun around to Alessandro. "What the hell, Bernoulli, why didn't it work?"

The scientist looked flummoxed. "I don't know, friend. Maybe her model of controller can cut to the front of the queue of commands in the buffer. Who knows?"

Jake hobbled over to the gun, trying to avoid using his sprained ankle. "Fine. So can we get this working, or not? She's bound to be back any minute with her thugs."

Alessandro and Tovra bent over the panel of lights and indicators, and within a minute, the railgun pointed towards the drop-panel ceiling.

"You sure that casing will survive impact with the ceiling?" Jake eyed the thing suspiciously.

"Relax, friend. Look. The ceiling is cheap plastic. Nothing to worry about."

Jake rolled his eyes. "Yeah, that's what I said about this whole mission, and look where that got us."

Tovra glanced up at him. "Well count me as one that is very happy that you came. And Jeremiah."

Jeremiah had come up close behind Jake, looking all around the room, as if searching for a threat, or preparing himself to defend Jake again. How odd…. Just twenty minutes earlier the boy had tried to rip his throat out, and now it seemed as if he felt compelled to defend Jake like he had defended the boss earlier. He put a hand on the boy's shoulder.

"All right there, Jeremiah?"

"Uh huh."

Jake searched the boy's darting eyes. Not much for words, apparently. Except when going into that trance like he did before. Trance, program … hell, whatever it was. Maybe the kid was just transferring his loyalty from one authority figure to the next. Surely he was watching how Avery and Bernoulli were obeying his every command, and perhaps that triggered his sudden switch. Whatever it was, there was no time to figure it out.

"Just stick by me, kid, and I'll get you through this. Don't worry."

Jeremiah looked up at him, as if undecided. "Ok," he said, finally.

Tovra hacked and coughed for a moment, and cleared his throat. "Well, I suppose our cover is blown. Is this even necessary? The railgun, I mean?"

Jake opened and closed his mouth. Actually, he wasn't sure. They had only planned on shooting the vial of antimatter out the railgun to create a distraction, and make it easier to escape to a freighter or a shuttle in the ensuing confusion. But Velar already knew they'd escaped. She'd be ready for them next time.

Bernoulli nodded. "Yes. We continue."

"Why?" said Jake.

"Because, friend. The massive electromagnetic pulse that this will generate will knock out most of the electronic systems here and for miles around. If we want to have any hope of making it past whatever orbital defense system Velar has in place, we need to knock it out before we fly."

He turned to Tovra. "Does she have orbital defense?"

Tovra held up his hands. "Well I don't know that. But she's got this railgun. Sure, it's mothballed, but I think we can safely assume she's replaced it with something else. Something with more punch. She does seem like the paranoid type."

"Ok. Let's do it. Al?" Jake turned back to the scientist. "We good to go?"

Bernoulli looked up from the control panel. "Yes. Everyone ready? I recommend we take cover downstairs when this thing fires." He finished typing in the parameters for the launch of the projectile with the anti-matter vial inside. The long shaft of the gun began to rise up towards the ceiling with an ominous whirr.

Jake nodded. "Let's go. Everyone downstairs." He waved Tovra and Avery towards the stairs, and pointed Jeremiah after them. "You coming, Alessandro?"

"One moment…." A few more buttons tapped, and the scientist looked up. "Ok. Run."

CHAPTER SIXTY_ONE

Sergeant Logan Jayce shielded his eyes from the piercing white explosion that rocked the shuttle with a giant shock wave. The shuttle bucked and threw Jayce against his restraints. Out of the corner of his eye, he saw one of Tomaga's men thrown violently against the ceiling, catching his head on the angled edge of a metal compartment. Blood gushed from the man's face as he dropped back into his seat, unconscious.

"What the hell was that?!" Jayce peered out the window. Behind the shuttle and to the right were the other two crafts, each streaming smoke from their hulls and losing altitude.

"We're going DOWN!" the pilot roared, punching his console with a fist as he desperately tried to regain control of the engines.

"What?" Jayce leaned forward and looked at the controls. Power was out. Main engines offline. "Can you restart?"

"The reactor is completely gone. Just knocked out dead, sir."

"Glide it." Volaski said, serenely. Jayce rolled his eyes at the bravado.

The pilot's fingers danced over the controls. "This is a shuttle. Not an airship, or even a fighter."

"I've glided half a dozen freighters down after getting in a tight spot. Just extend the foils and bank to—"

"Look, *pirate*," began the pilot, "I don't give a damn what you—"

Jayce noticed the ground approaching faster. "Private, just give him the damn controls. Now!"

The pilot glowered at him, but unstrapped his restraint and got himself out of the seat. Volaski slid in behind him and his hands danced over the console.

"We're coming in pretty fast. This is going to get rough. ..." Volaski concentrated on his readings and lifted up the bow of the shuttle as Jayce peered over at Tomaga, who nodded grimly.

"Bet you wish you'd stayed behind now."

Tomaga didn't answer, but stared out at the rapidly approaching ground. Jayce peered out the viewport at the two other shuttles. Both appeared to have lost power as well and were gliding in, apparently under a little more control than they were. Jayce wondered if the other pilots were more experienced than theirs, or if their shuttle was more damaged than the others. He glanced at the short, brown-haired young man now sitting in Volaski's old seat. Barely a young man— couldn't be a day over twenty. Shit, the Academy was sending the little bitches out way too young. Jayce strapped his assault rifle a little tighter to his torso and gripped his armrest a little more firmly.

"Five seconds to impact," Volaski said. "Coming in at only one hundred kph. We just might make it...."

CHAPTER SIXTY-TWO

Senator Galba rushed down the hallway on deck fifteen again, as if reliving his path from the other night. Only this time, the ship rocked from the pounding thuds of railgun fire and secondary explosions. Someone was giving the *Phoenix* a run for her money. Possibly two someones, from the sound of things.

He had to succeed this time. The *Phoenix* must be stopped in her tracks. The Plan depended on it. The Emperor and his inner circle had wagered everything, and Old Earth was the lynchpin. The capstone in the arch. For The Plan was like a great arch. Sweeping across history—their future history—and the survival of the Empire depended on its successful completion.

And for that, the *Phoenix* must be neutralized. Captured, preferably. But destroyed, if necessary. He'd love to see The Plan come to fruition, and possibly gain a seat in the Emperor's inner circle. But that was a secondary prize. His first prize was the knowledge that he saved humanity. That he saved the Empire. For the Empire was all that was left of humanity.

And so he began to jog. Gods, he hadn't jogged in years. His knees cried out in pain and his breath escaped his lips in short, painful bursts. But he soon entered the small utility room he'd found before, and locked the door behind him.

Private Ling—nor anyone else—would interrupt his work this time.

The ship rocked, and the deckplates rumbled. The sounds of battle raged distantly in the background as slug after slug pounded the weary hull.

It only took moments. He'd studied the ship's schematics for what seemed like an eternity ever since Willow gave him a uniform and the bandages that helped him disguise his face. Overloading the power conduits to the ion beam cannons was a relatively simple task. He knew exactly which circuits to trip, which subsystems to order into diagnostic mode, and in a flash, it was over, and he stood up and unlocked the door.

Deck fifteen, in spite of the continuing explosions, was strangely quiet. All the regular crew was gone, of course, it being the recreation deck, leaving only the Fifty-First Brigade. But from the angry klaxons sounding, he supposed they had all been ordered to quarters for their own safety.

Except one man, apparently. Or at least, he was flagrantly ignoring the general quarters alarm.

"Private Ling?"

The bruised face looked up at him. He was sitting at one of the tables, kicked back with an old porno magazine. A paper one, like the ones that only exist in the back alleys of forgotten frontier worlds.

"Senator?" The man flashed a toothy grin. He'd apparently lost a tooth in whatever fight he'd been in.

Galba smiled and sat down next to him.

"I'll no longer deny it. But there is something you should know."

The smile disappeared. The magazine lowered to the table. "And what is that?"

"I'm a prisoner here. Like you. And just between you and me, I hate the Resistance. Hate it. Despise it."

Ling's eyebrows shot up. "Really? Aren't you the head of the Truth and Reconciliation Committee?"

"You follow politics, soldier?" Galba reached for the magazine. Ling drew it away before he could touch it.

"Some. Enough to know you've got quite the reputation as an Old Earth lover. The defender of the Terrans, is what they call you, you know."

Galba winced. "Embarrassing, yes. But there's something you should know, soldier." He leaned forward, and dropped his voice, as if betraying a state secret. In actuality, he was.

Ling whispered back. "What?"

"I'm on a special mission from the Emperor himself. My work with the Commission was but a ploy. A plan to reintegrate Old Earth into the Empire, but on our terms. We fully intended to punish the Resistance. They're all violent criminals. All of them. Terrorists. Disruptors of the peace the Empire has established." He lowered his voice to a whisper. "But there's a way you can help get us back on track. I've studied your background—don't look so shocked, soldier— after we first talked, I went and looked you up. Every soldier has a private file that only people like me can access, you know. And you know what?"

He waited for a reply that never came. Only baited breath.

Expectant, blackening eyes.

"I liked what I saw. You've got balls, soldier. Fucking big balls. And integrity up the ass. I want you on my team. And I've got a job for you right now, if you're interested. If we're successful, I'll take you back to the Emperor, and you can be his personal bodyguard." He cocked his head at the marine, as if in hesitation. "Only if you're interested, of course."

A slow grin spread over Ling's face. "I'm in. Anything to send these fuckers to hell. What do I do?"

Galba stood up and put out a hand. Ling grasped it, and stood himself. "Come with me." He turned to the hallway that led to the stairwell, before pointing back to the table. "And bring the magazine."

CHAPTER SIXTY-THREE

Fifteen minutes later, they were in the empty quarters. A vacant room three doors down from Ayala's. No sheets on the bunks; boxes of equipment lined the walls as if it were an annex of the storage closet nearby. Most of the quarters were empty in that hallway, but this one was special in that it now contained an auxiliary computer terminal that he'd smuggled in from one of the electronics storage rooms.

He pointed to it, and collapsed on the bed as the deck rocked from another blast, beckoning Private Ling to sit at the terminal.

"We need to hack in. I presume your training included basic tech? You are urban combat, after all."

Ling scowled at him. "Of course. In fact, I'm our squadron's combat engineer."

Galba smiled. A dry, cold smile. "How convenient. Let's get started."

CHAPTER SIXTY-FOUR

Ben figured he'd been hanging for years. In fact, he started to have trouble remembering what came before. Had his arms always hurt? Had the tendons always felt so stretched? Had his shoulders always been out of their sockets, or was this a recent occurrence?

He shook his head. There was no use in going crazy. Not like Six. Not like that poor shell of a man. He tried to focus on what Six had told him before. About Pritchard and the *Fury*.

"Six? You still there?" Every word was agony. But it woke him up. "You awake?"

A stirring nearby told him yes. "I'm here, Seven. We're not to talk. Don't you respect our Master? He'll punish us again. Don't you remember what he did to me? You got the knife, sure, but I got the whip. The whip is glo—"

"Six, listen. I can get us out of here. I can—"

"Ha! You? Look at you! You've been carved up like a roasted chicken. There's a pool of blood on the floor under you. What do you think you'll do to the Master? You're nothing. I'm nothing. He's everything."

Ben's head swam. Six was right—he must have lost a lot of blood. He tried to lick his lips, but his tongue was as dry as felt, and it scratched against his cracked lips like burlap.

"Tell me about the *Fury*, then. You were left here? How long ago?"

A pause. "I was born h—"

"No! Stop it! Stop your fucking crazy shit and tell me how long you've been here!" The yelling made Ben's head sear with pain, but it was almost intoxicating. It cleared his head against the haze of dehydration and blood loss.

Another pause. "I don't know. Years, I think. Many years."

Ben forced his hoarse voice out of his dry throat. "The D-day celebration was only a week or so ago. The day we remember Dallas." *And my parents,* he thought.

"Dallas? Oh, yes. I remember that. Right before the coward shifted us away."

"It was three years ago," Ben said. "How long after were you taken?"

Six took a long time to answer, as if sifting through a lifetime of memory. "Months. Maybe four or five."

"So, you've been here for two and a half years." Ben tried to push his shoulders down and lift his torso up against the sagging weight of his body, but his strength had long since left. "I'm sorry. That's a long time to live like this."

"Oh, no. I didn't come here at first. I went to the mines. Four months. 116 days. I counted. Every one, I counted. They worked me until I'd lost fifty pounds, then the Master saw me, and desired me, and bought me. But before he bought me, I met another prisoner. Another crew member from the *Fury*."

"Another one?" Ben was having trouble keeping the man's

story straight. Had Six come down alone? He couldn't remember.

"Yes, another. He was new. He told me Pritchard was dead, and the *Fury* destroyed. That's when I lost hope. That's when I felt privileged when the Master came for me. He rescued me. He saved me from that pit of rock and hunger. Now I have another hunger. A better one. A hunger for *him*."

The man's meaning was clear, and it sickened Ben. How could another man descend to such a state? Even if it was probably induced by those bots the man had been injected with. How could he give up, and hand over his mind to the Master?

He caught himself. No, not *master*. But what other name did he have? None, as far as he knew. But calling him master, even in his head, would never do. Something else. A name that would give him something to hold onto in defiance, even if only in his own mind.

Dickwad.

Yeah, that'll do. He smirked, in spite of himself.

But what had Six said? Pritchard dead? The *Fury* destroyed? Impossible. It was not true. He decided it was not true.

"Six. Can you come over here? Just for a moment?"

"I'm not to move. If I do, he'll know. I must not disobey."

"Just for a moment. You can go right back. I promise. Just real quick."

Six hesitated, and Ben opened his eyes and craned his neck around to look at him, in spite of his protesting joints and muscles. The man sat in a cage, whose door sat slightly ajar. No shackle or restraint bound Six's arms or feet, unlike Ben, who hung by shackles at the wrists and whose legs were spread wide by shackles holding his ankles down taut.

"Please. Just for a moment."

Six stirred, and crawled out of the cage. "Ok, but just for a few seconds. What do you want?" He stood up and crept over to Ben, tentatively avoiding the clotted blood on the floor.

"Can you reach up and release my arms? I think you can do it without a key, if you just—"

"No!" Six looked up at him wide-eyed. "We can't! He'll kill us. He will. He'll kill us if we behave like that."

"But I can get us out of here. I just need my arms, and I promise, I'll get you out of here."

The man backed away, and started to crouch back down towards his cage.

"No, wait!" Ben closed his eyes. "Just ... fine. Don't release my arms. Fine. I won't ask you that. Just come back. Please."

He opened his eyes, and saw Six looking at him with his head cocked. "Then what? What do you want? Don't ask me to let you go. I won't do that. It's madness."

Ben shook his head. "Don't release me. Just, if you could, the chains holding my legs down are stretching my shoulders and arms. It really hurts. Bad. I think it's damaging my shoulders. Could you, maybe, just loosen them? A little? I can't escape with them loose."

Six thought about it for a moment. "Fine. But just the legs. Don't ask me about your arms. I won't do it."

"Fine." Ben sighed. Just the legs. Look, just flip those latches. That'll relieve the pressure on my arms. And I'll thank you kindly."

Six moved towards the restraints holding his ankles pointing taut towards the floor. Ben licked his lips again, in spite of their dryness, hoping against hope that the man would actually do it. With those latches flipped, he'd be able to lift his legs. The chain would slip right through the restraint on the ground without the latches.

Six stooped, and fingered the latch on his right ankle.

He shook his head, and flipped it. He reached for the other and flipped it too.

"Better?" Six looked up.

"Yeah, Six. Much better. Much better. Go back to your place now. The master might come back any second. Thank you."

As he watched Six crawl back into the cage he lifted up one leg, letting the chain slip through the floor restraint. He raised his foot all the way up to waist-height. Then the other, before lowering them back down. The strain was murder on his shoulders, but it was worth it.

He could move his legs. And that was all he needed.

CHAPTER SIXTY-FIVE

Megan Po sucked in her breath as the *Phoenix* rocked under the bombardment from the *Caligula*. Another blast announced the impact of a torpedo, and the shock rattled yet another light fixture loose from the ceiling—still damaged from the battle at Liberty Station.

She gripped the edge of the command console to maintain her balance. "Ayala, status of railguns. How much is left?"

"Down to ten percent, sir. After that, all we've got are the ion beam cannons and gigawatt lasers. And the quantum field torpedoes, of course."

The torpedoes. If only they could get one through. One would be enough to take out the entire ship, but the *Caligula* would be sure to shoot it down before it got anywhere near close enough to cause any damage. It was far more likely to damage their own fighters than their adversary.

"Engineering! I want my gravitic thrusters back," she said into her comm.

"Sorry, sir," a voice answered. She couldn't tell if it was Chief Simmons, or one of the other engineers. "It's still out.

That blast underwater just killed us. We won't have it back up for a day at least. And that's *without* any more damage, sir."

"Right," she said, wincing as another blast rocked the ship. Looking up at the viewscreen, she watched as the fighter battle unfolded as a flurry of red and blue streaks, punctuated every now and then by an explosion marking the passing of one of the ships—hopefully Imperial, she thought. They'd lost far too many pilots to afford losing any more in this needless battle.

"Commander," said Ensign Falstaff, "I'm getting reports that the strike force has engaged the slavers on the surface."

"Keep me apprised of their progress, Ensign." Finally, a bit of good news. The sooner their team was back on board, the sooner they could get out of there.

But how? That question was still unanswered. Perhaps the only way out of there was crashing into the *Caligula* again. But something told her Trajan wouldn't allow that to happen this time. They'd be ready.

Po scowled. There was no way out of this one. They had to get one of those torpedoes through. Somehow.

A flicker on the screen announced the end of her hopes.

Another ship. Just as large as the *Caligula*.

"Ayala?" she turned questioningly towards the tactical octagon.

Ensign Ayala shook her head. "It's the *Sphinx*, sir. They're bearing down on our position."

Po sank back into her chair, and sighed.

"Well, shit."

Ayala continued. "One minute until intercept." She glanced up at Po, a questioning look in her eye. "Commander? Orders?"

"Redirect all available power to the ion beam cannons. Hit 'em with all we've got," said Po.

And a moment later, as if in defiant answer to her order, a blast sent half the bridge crew to the floor and the other half clutching onto whatever they could reach. Po gripped her armrest. "What the hell was that?"

Ayala pulled herself up from the floor, shaking her head, and studied her board. "Power overload, sir. All forward and starboard ion beam cannons are out!"

Great. Po grit her teeth. Don't give up. There's plenty left to do. Don't give up.

"Conventional thrusters. Keep the *Caligula* between us and the *Sphinx*." She pointed wildly at Ensign Roshenko at the helm, and indicated the Admiral's ship looming on the viewscreen, just a klick away. "Take us in nice and close, Ensign. Tactical? When we get up close and personal, blast them with all the juice we got in the gigawatt laser turrets."

"Sir," began an Ensign at the tactical octagon, "the *Caligula*'s refractive shielding is still up."

"Yes, but at that proximity, we just might hit them. And if we don't, we might get lucky and the beams will refract towards the *Sphinx*." She hit the comm button to sound a general alert. "All hands, prepare for conventional thrusters. Hold on to something folks." She turned back to Roshenko. "Now, Ensign."

Po grabbed onto her armrests, and her back pressed back into her chair as the ship began to move forward under the conventional thrusters. She far preferred the gravitic thrusters, as they produced no sensation of moving.

"Distance?"

Ayala called back from tactical. "600 meters."

"Take us to one hundred meters."

The rumbling grew louder as more and more railgun slugs from the *Caligula* made it through the defensive screen that flared out from their hull, crisscrossing the space between the two ships, intersecting with the vectors of the railgun fire, with explosive results. With less distance, more of the slugs managed to impact the hull, and it showed in the faces of the bridge crew, as Po looked around and saw that their looks of concentration had turned to fright.

"Easy, people. We'll get through this. Just give them all we got." She looked back at the tactical octagon, with a grim, half-hearted smile, "and if we lose, let's make them pay dearly for it."

"Sir," began Ayala, "the *Sphinx* is here, but we're shielded by the *Caligula*. They're moving to flank us."

"Match their vector. Keep the *Caligula* between us. Fire all lasers."

How much longer could they keep this up? Minutes, perhaps. Eventually, the *Sphinx* would wise up, and outflank them simply by positioning herself orthogonal to the *Phoenix*'s axis of rotation around the *Caligula*.

An idea struck her.

"Science? How far away do we have to safely be from a target to detonate a quantum field torpedo?"

"At least three klicks, sir. And even that is cutting it close. I recommend five."

5000 meters. And they were at one hundred meters from the *Caligula*. Under conventional thrusters they'd only be able to accelerate at about one g, which means by the time they fired the torpedo at point-blank range at the *Caligula*, they'd only have a second or two to get away. And they couldn't just shift a torpedo over with gravitics—the *Sphinx* had demonstrated that much during their first encounter a few days ago.

Unless....

She slapped the comm. "Torpedo control, this is the bridge. I want two quantum field torpedoes carried down to the flight deck, stat." Stat? What the hell was she, a doctor? She shook her head and focused. "Copy?"

A harried voice answered. "This is Ensign Peak, sir. Commander? These things emit lots of radiation. We're not suited up, and it'll take time to—"

"I'm sorry, Ensign Peak, we don't have time for that. It's either this, or we're dead. You decide."

A moment's silence answered her. "Yes, sir. We're on our way."

God help her. She put her head in her hand. Those torpedoes emitted so much radiation, each worker would likely receive several lifetimes worth the highest recommended limit in just a few minutes.

"Godspeed, Ensign. Bridge out."

Ayala barked out from across the bridge. "Sir, the *Sphinx* is flanking. They're moving towards—"

"Yes, I see it Ensign." She watched the front viewscreen as the third ship moved to a point that gave them a clear shot. The *Caligula* still pounded their undercarriage—at least that part of the hull was the most heavily shielded. "Move us in closer, Roshenko. Make them kiss our ass."

As the thrusters fired, she felt lighter in her seat, indicating the acceleration vector had shifted downward. She gulped. Flying with gravitics always thrilled her. Flying with conventional thrusters? Not so much.

Jake, where the hell are you?

CHAPTER SIXTY-SIX

Dammit, where the hell am I?

Jake hadn't expected the explosion to be quite so violent, but it threw him and everyone else to the ground as the shock wave hit. For several moments he couldn't hear, or think, as if his head was stuffed under a giant pillow and squeezed by someone sitting on top—like his older sister used to do to him. Back in their house on Whidbey Island. Strange that that memory came back to him then. He'd run across their property, hiding in the trees from the calls of his mother. He wondered what she was doing right then, on Earth. Was she safe? Was Earth safe?

But when he stood up he gathered his senses. "Run!" he said, pointing across the compound towards a building that looked like a hangar, where, he supposed, Velar would keep whatever shuttle or other craft she owned. The sprawling compound was a confused mess of people—guards, slaves, traders, all pulling themselves off the ground and shaking the dust off their clothes. Many people had sustained mild injuries, which, Jake realized, was his fault, but he had no time to think about it. No time to care.

He pulled Jeremiah along towards the hangar when he noticed some people pointing upward before starting to run themselves, scattering to dash behind buildings or piles of rock.

Jake glanced upward, then yanked Jeremiah to the ground just in time. A shuttle—one of their own—came careening through the air and slammed into the ground before sliding several hundred meters into a section of the compound's brick wall. On the other side of the courtyard, two other shuttles— smoke streaming from their hulls—similarly streaked through the air and slammed into the ground, skidding a ways before coming to rest.

And to Jake's relief, out jumped several of his marines, accompanied by a few of Tomaga's men from the Fifty-First Brigade. He wondered at Po's judgment in sending them down on such a sensitive mission, but had no time to think about it as the entire courtyard erupted in gunfire.

Pulling Jeremiah along behind him, and making sure his other companions still followed, he dashed to the cover of a small shed, and peered up at one of the nearby buildings. Sure enough, several of Velar's guards crouched behind cover at the windows and doors, firing on the newcomers. Numerous other buildings around them housed more guards, all firing on his men. He could see no way through, no path to reach their rescuers. Every open space was filled with a storm of bullets, as the marines from the *Phoenix* battled the defending guards— more sprang up in each window and doorway of the compound every second.

"Avery! We've got to get to the landing party. Can we clear

a path?"

Avery studied the situation. Nearby was a smallish building that appeared to be some sort of barracks. Only a few guards fired from the windows. "There," he said, pointing. "You kick the door in and I'll clear the first room."

Crouching, they scurried as fast as they could to the rear of the small brick and mud structure. Jake paused to let Avery ready himself, and when the soldier motioned, Jake kicked, using his good foot, even as the sprained one protested at bearing all his weight.

Avery sprang through the door as it flew inward and fired a single shot from his sidearm through the head of the room's occupant, who slumped to the floor underneath a window.

Jake looked down at the man's face—a look of shock seemed permanently painted there, and Jake realized he recognized the man as one of Velar's guards. One of the men who'd accompanied her when they first entered the compound a few days ago. Or was it a week?

Avery burst into the next room and picked off the man at the other window of the building. "Stairs?" asked Jake. Alessandro and Tovra looked around, and shook their heads. Good. The building was secure. They picked up the assault rifles dropped by their previous owners.

"All right, let's see if we can't relieve some of the pressure on our people," said Jake, as he peered out the window, holding his assault rifle close to his chest. He took aim at a few snipers on the top of an adjacent building who held down a group of the Fifty-First Brigade, and with a few trigger-pulls, dropped both of them.

"Nice shooting. Infantry?" Avery said, nodding in

approval.

"Paintball. Grew up with it. Played every Wednesday," Jake quipped.

Avery raised his eyebrows in surprise, and possibly skepticism, but turned back to his window and scanned the other buildings for guards. Jake searched the groups of rescuers, and to his surprise, saw a face he hadn't expected. A face that made his stomach drop.

Volaski.

The pirate captain huddled behind the burning shuttle with Logan Jayce—a soldier he recognized from the *Phoenix*—firing at a group of guards who'd taken cover behind a large metal bin full of ore just twenty yards away from them.

Volaski. The one who'd helped sell them into slavery, and whom Velar had sent back up to the *Phoenix* to lure the others down to Destiny's surface. It appeared he had succeeded. Was this now a show he was putting on?

But it didn't add up. Velar had sent him to bring more *Phoenix* crew members down, and he had, but now he was shooting and killing Velar's guards.

What the hell was going on?

CHAPTER SIXTY-SEVEN

"Have you bypassed that firewall yet?" Senator Galba looked on expectantly, over Private Ling's shoulder. The soldier stared at the screen, as if unhearing. "Private?"

"Huh? Oh, almost, Senator." The young man didn't take his eyes off the terminal, and tapped at a few more keys. "It's a standard Imperial encryption, and luckily they taught us all the backdoors back at the Imperial Academy. Shouldn't be long now."

Galba paced the room, all four meters of it, before returning to the lone window that peeked out into space just above the bunk. Bright flashes streamed out from the ships, indicating the railgun slugs that impacted the *Caligula* some three kilometers away, and the Imperial vessel pounded back with fire of her own. A swarm of fighters doggedly fought in the space between the two ships.

And then a third swung into view. Another Imperial capital ship, which unleashed its own salvo at the *Phoenix*.

Won't be long now, he thought. Still, best to plan for contingencies.

"Senator, we're through."

Galba strode back over to Ling and pointed at the screen. "First, enable my diplomatic code as a level one shadowed bypass. That way I can access critical ship functions without anyone knowing."

A few clicks of the buttons later, and Ling said, "Code?"

"Alpha one-one-thirteen alpha omega."

Ling entered in the code, but cocked his head. "The first alpha is for Senators?"

The young marine knew far too much for his own good. "Correct. And I am the 1113th Senator of the Imperial Republic."

Ling nodded in understanding, but paused again. "And the alpha omega at the end? What does that mean?"

Galba smiled. "You'll soon find out."

CHAPTER SIXTY-EIGHT

Less than ten minutes later, the deed was done. Private Ling had momentarily commandeered the external ship communication system, which let Galba send his message. Trajan would be *relieved*, of course, to know the Senator was still alive. He smirked. Relieved might be too strong a word. Resigned, more like it. The other man never seemed to trust Galba. He could never rid his voice of the loathing he so clearly felt for elected officials—even around Galba, one of the Emperor's most trusted associates.

"And now, Private, we wait."

Ling glanced up at him. His puffed up eyelid had started to deflate, revealing a bloodied, capillary-strewn eye. The Resistance marine must have clocked the Private pretty hard. "Wait, Senator? Wait for what?"

He patted the soldier's shoulder. "It's far too dangerous to make the trek back to deck fifteen. You saw the situation on the way here. Repair crews running everywhere, secondary explosions in the corridors near the power conduits. We'd be liable to be either killed or caught. No. Best to wait until the night watch."

"Fine." Ling stood up, and walked towards the bed, grabbing the porno magazine Galba had tossed there when they had entered.

And now, bereft of any entertainment, the Senator paced the short room again before stopping. He walked straight towards the doors, which slid open at his approach.

"Stay here. I'll be back in awhile for you."

Before the Private could protest, the door slid shut, and Galba bent over to examine the keypad. Quickly, he entered the lock function, then entered his diplomatic code to set an override on the interior unlock function.

Straightening up, he whistled as he ambled back to Willow's room, three doors down, and slipped through the sliding doors to wait for his love.

CHAPTER SIXTY-NINE

Anya watched the unfolding battle from the relative comfort of her command station at the rear of the conference room next to the fighter deck.

And it rankled her.

She needed action. She needed to be at the center of things, in control of her own destiny.

She was in control of the whole fighter squad all right, but others were doing the fighting for her, and she hated it.

"P-two, watch your right flank! Shift your asses out of there! P-nine, cover them! That bogey's ripe for the taking!" She yelled a constant stream of bellowed instructions into the comm, as two assistants at a nearby station kept tabs on fuel and ammunition levels, enemy fighter strengths, and the overall tactical situation to feed to the Wing Commander.

"DAMMIT!" She pounded the board, cracking the edge of the dark plastic casing. Another P-town fighter exploded in a brief fireball. Jenkins. And his gunner, Tonks. Shit.

"P-five, cover P-fifteen, they've got three bogeys on their ass. Come on people, work with me. Pay attention to what your team is doing—gunners, do your jobs!" She hit the board again in frustration. She hated losing her pilots. It only made her want to be out there even more. For a half second, she entertained the notion of hopping in the last remaining fighter still out on the flight deck. What would Po say? Likely blow a gasket. If it were Mercer up on the bridge she'd do it just to hear his shrieky, blustery voice cry at her for insubordination. And then later that night she'd pull him into her cabin for a good fuck. It'd been too long.

"Lieutenant Grace, this is Commander Po," said an agitated voice from the comm. Anya had hardly noticed the explosions that rocked the *Phoenix*, having been too focused on the raging fighter battle outside to pay them any heed. But the tone of Po's voice brought her back to the shuddering deckplates and rumbling percussive blasts that hit the hull.

"Grace here."

"Lieutenant, the *Sphinx* just shifted into orbit and is bearing down on our position. Gravitics are still out. We need to end this, now."

"Simple enough. What you got?" If only they'd thought to just end the battle earlier, Grace thought sarcastically.

"The quantum field torpedoes. We need to get one over to the other ships. We can't just fire them—they'll get shot down. We could shift them over, but the problem is their new gravitic field exclusion zones that you discovered around the—"

"Yeah, I remember." She thought back to the close call she had engaging the *Sphinx* the week before. "Are you suggesting what I think you're suggesting?"

"I need a few of your pilots, Grace. Equip two fighters with a quantum field torpedo each, and send one to the

Caligula, and one to the *Sphinx.*"

"That's going to be some pretty fancy flying, Commander. Pretty risky."

"Then send your best. This had to work, or we're dead."

Grace knew it. They had to succeed, they had to win this battle, or they'd never even get a chance to lose any future battles. This was it.

"Then I choose me. And I'll call Quadri in from—"

"No! We can't afford to lose our Wing Commander. Someone el—"

"Commander, if you want the best, I'm it. Sorry, but I'm going. You're right, we have to end this, now."

And before Po could respond, she punched the comm off.

Grace turned to the deck officer who hovered in the background, waiting for instruction. "You heard the Commander. Get those torpedoes loaded up on my and Quadri's fighters."

Another tap at the comm. "Quadri? You still alive?"

His voice scratched over the speaker. "For the moment, Lieutenant. What's up?"

"Get back to P-town. I've got a job for you."

CHAPTER SEVENTY

Ben had no sooner relaxed his legs, letting them hang back down as if fastened tight by the floor restraints, than Doctor Stone returned. Slamming the door open, he stomped across the stone floor, either very happy, or angry—Ben couldn't tell. But the pace seemed to suggest something out of the ordinary.

"So, Seven, seems you've got some determined friends. Looks like they managed to land a strike team at Velar's place. Quite a hard landing, from what I heard," he snorted irreverently, "I'd be s-s-surprised if any of them survived the missiles that Velar's folks sent up.

He finally paced around to face Ben, just six feet away or so. Just a few feet closer. Just two steps....

"But don't get your hopes up, slave. There's no way your friends will come calling here. We're too isolated." He took a step forward, leering at him with hungry eyes. Just one more step. One more....

"Remember that, Seven. You're here forever. They'll never find you. Hell, I don't even exist. Not on the records, at least. Trajan and the Emperor don't want it publicly known that they deal with me. You're mine, and you can never escape. And if you try," he licked his lips, almost as if he hoped Ben would put up resistance, "I'll bleed you. I'll carve you. I'll sign you, with my knife as my pen. You'll never get out of here, so don't even try...." He looked as if he were about to take another step forward.

But he turned, and strode over to a cabinet. Pulling out a small syringe, he circled around to stand behind Ben, and shoved his head forward roughly.

"But just in case, I've changed my mind. I think you'll need these after all. But don't worry, I won't use them to program you like I did the pile of shit over there. Not yet, anyway. But I want you controllable should you choose to rebel." He moved in close, and pressed his body up against Ben's back. "I expect you'll rebel. It's who you are. It's why I chose you, my perfect slave."

The picobots.

No. He tried to think of something to say. Something to stall, or to dissuade him from injecting them.

But the needle came too quickly. It plunged deep into his neck, and Ben cried out as the cold liquid shot into his muscle, accompanied by searing pain.

As if on reflex, he wrapped his legs around the man's knees and thrashed his thighs forward as hard as he could. The man shouted out, but a sickening thud broke the cry as his body flipped backwards and his head collided with one of the empty metal restraints sticking up out of the floor.

His sagging shoulders screaming from the strain of holding the weight of two, Ben strained his head to look down. The man lay prone on the floor, a trickle of blood pooling under his shaved head.

But he breathed. He was alive.

"Six. Come over here. Now!" Ben shouted, rolling his head back and forth.

"No! The Master sai—"

"The master is dead! I killed him! Now get me down from here before I kill you too, dammit!"

Hesitation. "But, but you're hanging. You can't hurt me. You're hanging."

Ben strained his neck around to stare at the man peering out from behind the bars of the cramped cage on the floor. "You see me? I see you. I just killed your master with my feet alone, and it only took me half a second. Imagine what I could do to you if I put my mind to it." He paused, to let his words sink in. He was bluffing, of course, but perhaps the other man's mental state would mask it. "Now get over here!"

Whimpering, the man crawled out and stood, apprehensively approaching Ben. Slowing, he reached up to one of the restraints holding Ben's wrists, grabbed it with two hands....

And nearly ripped the metal in two.

Ben fell, and screamed in pain as his free arm fell and he remained suspended by one hand.

"The other! Get the other!" Ben tried to reach it, but couldn't lift his free arm more than a foot.

Six latched onto the other one, and like a machine just yanked the metal apart, twisting the hardened iron as if it were plastic, and darted away back to his cage as Ben's arm fell down to his side.

Was he seeing things? Did Six just twist wrought iron with

his bare hands? He shook his head—definitely a hallucination.

The unconscious captor on the floor groaned.

"You lied," said Six, regarding the prone, bloodied man with a mixture of awe and fear. "You said you killed him, but he moves. You lied to me."

"It was just a little lie," Ben began, as he knelt next to the moaning figure. "A temporary lie." He reached down, his shoulders still searing with the pain of three days hanging, and pulled the man's arm up with two hands. He took it into the crook of his arm, and yanked as hard as he could as he reached up to the chain, in an attempt to lock the man down.

But he'd overestimated his own strength. In fact, he had very little. Not a chance he'd be able to lift the arm, much less the whole body.

His former captor moaned louder, but only breathed more rapidly as he tried to struggle, now waking up.

If Ben didn't incapacitate the man, he'd lose his chance. Dammit. What to do? He glanced at the knife on the table across the room, but thought it too risky to run for it. The man could get up by then and Ben didn't know if his arms would cooperate in a fight.

Dammit, what would Jake do? Why did he even follow the brash bastard around, anyway?

But he knew exactly why. Jake was everything he was not, and Ben was everything Jake was not. Jake let him get in situations he'd never dream of getting into himself. Let him do things he'd never consider doing in the presence of anyone else. He gave Ben the swagger he'd always lacked. How many bar fights had Jake dragged him into?

The bar. The Liberty Station bar. How Jake had kicked

that man over and over, until he was a bloody pulp. Until he'd never get up again. He pounded the man so mercilessly hard not just to win that battle, but to make sure that particular group would never give him trouble again.

Swearing, Ben stood up with a grunt, and grabbing the man's arm, held it up taut, and recalling his jujitsu training, he twisted it, stepped on the man's face and leveraged the arm against his own leg as he snapped the elbow with a cupped fist.

The captor screamed.

"How does it feel, *master?*" said Ben, sneering the title. He kicked the man over onto his other side and wrenched his other arm free from under him, and repeated the vicious break. The man screamed even louder, howling and wailing.

"Please! P—p—please don't kill me!"

Ben circled around the crippled man, limping as he walked —he must have landed funny when he fell. "You want mercy? After all this time? All these years of sadism? How many have you killed? No. I think it's time you took your leave of the world." He strode over to the table and picked up the still bloody knife. He seemed to get off at the sight of other people's blood. Ben wondered if the man would get off at the sight of his own.

The man eyed the knife with wide eyes. "No. Please. No. Stop. I—I—I don't want to, I mean, please, no—"

Ben stooped down and grabbed the man's shirt, wrenching his head up a foot off the ground.

"No!" But this voice came from behind. From the cage. Six scurried over to Ben and pawed at him. "No! Please! Please no!" The fawning man wrapped his arms around Stone's head, shielding him.

"Six. Move. You're free now. We can go. My people are here to rescue us—all we need to do is find them and get the hell out of this hole. Just move away."

"Just promise you won't kill him."

"I can't do that, Six."

Six fixed his crazed eyes on Ben. "Then I can't move." Apparently the picobots were having their effect on the man.

Ben roared. "Get the fuck away from him you little pile of shit!" he clamped his mouth shut, shocked at his words. He rarely swore. He'd never spoken to anyone like that. But he regarded the broken man beneath him with contempt. How could anyone allow themselves to stoop so low? Even if coerced and tortured?

Is this how he would have ended up?

Six cried, joining his voice to the moans of the bloody captor beneath him. Ben softened his voice. "Six. Move. I promise I won't hurt him. Not yet. We can both decide what to do with him. Please."

Six looked up at him. Confusion spread across his face, and he searched for words.

"My name is Rhys. Before. Before, my name was Rhys. Before I was born there, on that table." He glanced up at the blood-stained table nearby. "You promise you won't kill him? I can't kill my own father. He's like my father. My Master."

Ben felt like vomiting, but kept a straight face. "I promise. Really, Rhys."

Slowly, Rhys released his grip on the man's head and stood up. Ben stood with him. "Ok. Let's just get the hell out of here. He's not going anywhere, for now."

Doctor Stone whimpered, and tried to move his arms. But

he cried out each time he moved. "Wait! Don't just leave me here! Don't just leave me here! You can't leave me here!"

"Won't your lab crew come help you?" Ben sneered, as the two men neared the door.

"I never let them come here! No one will find me for weeks!"

"Well then," said Ben, searching for words. He found none. "Good luck!"

He shepherded Rhys out the door and followed him behind. "Oh, wait, stay there, I need to tell him one more thing," he said to his new friend.

Ben slipped back into the room—the dungeon—his prison—and pulled the door closed to a crack behind him before bringing the knife up.

"What are you doing?" groaned the man.

Ben held the knife up. "Ending your miserable life. Consider it a favor."

Blood trickled from the man's mouth onto the floor as he laughed. He laughed. The son of a bitch was crazy. The master leered his ghoulishly bloody face at him. "You will hurt those closest to you."

Ben cocked his head, staring down at the bitter face.

"What did you say?"

"I told you, you'll hurt those closest to you. Those dearest to you. I command it."

Ben rolled his eyes. "What, still deluding yourself with the *master* act? You must be crazier than I thought."

Stone continued, ignoring Ben. "You know what the picobots do?"

Ben's fingers twitched around the knife, ready to throw.

But curiosity overcame him. He paused.

The man went on. "Over the next few weeks, they would have let me own you. Control you. You would have wanted me. They would have taught you to want me. I could have programmed you like I programmed Six. But," he coughed up more blood. "The picobots make you susceptible to suggestion, and the first command is always the most potent. It will stay with you the rest of your life. You'll never forget it. Never."

Ben raised the knife.

With a swift motion tempered by years of practice under the most renowned combat masters in North America, he flung the knife at the master, and it plunged deep into his forehead.

"You can't leave me here," Stone said, but he spoke slurred, as if on autopilot. The man slumped without another groan.

Ben slipped out the door and shut it behind him, firmly. "There. I just had to tell him that before we left."

Rhys cocked his head as they walked up the stairs. "What did you say?"

He pulled Rhys along the hallway. "To go to hell."

CHAPTER SEVENTY_ONE

As the deckplates rumbled with the explosions from the *Phoenix*'s laser turrets, Captain Titus steadied himself on the command console. "Tactical, redirect the defensive screen to sector eight—there's a few Rebel fighters breaking away towards us."

"Aye, sir," came the reply.

Admiral Trajan nodded in approval. Titus found that the man tended to micromanage all the events leading up to military engagements, but would leave the actual operations during battle up to Titus and the other commanders on the bridge.

A particularly strong blast nearly knocked Titus off his feet. An Ensign at the operations center fell out of his chair, apparently having forgotten to fasten his restraint. Titus made a note to chide the man later.

"Damage report," he said.

"Crews are reporting minimal casualties, sir, but there is decompression on decks nine and ten, forward. Eighty percent of all offensive weaponry undamaged. Gravitics are online, but engineering reports some of the field generators have taken hits."

"Very well. Commander Burris? Status of the fighters?"

The Wing Commander's voice sounded over the comm. "Not good. We've lost half our squadron. We just haven't had the time to practice with those new drives—"

"A poor excuse, Commander," said Admiral Trajan, interrupting. His voice took on a dangerous tone. "I specifically instructed you to make sure our pilots had plenty of time to practice, even if that meant double shifts. I expect to see you in my ready room when this is over, is that clear?"

Commander Burris hesitated. "Yes, Admiral. I'll inform the squad leader to—"

"Sir!" Ensign Evans at communications waved a hand. "The *Sphinx* has just shifted into orbit and is hailing us!"

"Open the channel." Admiral Trajan stood up from the captain's chair. The Captain's voice crackled through the comm.

"*NPQR Sphinx* reporting as requested. What are your instructions, Admiral?"

Trajan scratched the rim of his eye socket. "Captain Thracius. A pleasure to hear your voice. If you would be so kind as to direct your fire on the *Phoenix* and encourage her to surrender. Our goal is to maim and capture, Captain, not to destroy. Mercer is on the planet, and the odds are high that we can take the ship intact."

"Very well, sir. On our way to your position."

The tactical chief called out, "Sir. The *Phoenix* has parked herself just meters off our port bow."

Trajan raised his eyebrows and turned to Captain Titus: "Prepare the boarding parties. They are to shoot anyone who even remotely resists. If they so much as scowl at our men, they die. We have been far too lenient with these people. Is that clear?"

"Absolutely, sir," said Titus. He relayed the order down to the marines, finally sensing the end was near.

They could soon resume their normal routine, at last.

CHAPTER SEVENTY-TWO

The gun battle raged outside the small brick shack, and an occasional bullet grazed the window frame next to Jake, which sent him ducking for cover, showering him with brick debris.

"Alessandro, buddy, you watching that door? I don't want any guards sneaking up on us!"

The scientist called back. "Yes, friend!" The gangly man had grabbed a rifle from one of the fallen guards and held it up awkwardly to his chest. Unfortunately, it was clear he had never handled a weapon in his life. Luckily, Tovra stood on the other side of the doorway, grasping his assault rifle in a far more competent position. Jeremiah sat in a corner with his hands covering his ears, squinting against the bright daylight streaming through the window.

Jake turned back to the scene in the compound. Their team of marines was pinned down behind the crashed shuttles. Dozens of guards raked the craft with fire from the relative safety of their windows and doorways, immobilizing the defenders.

"They're not going to make it. They've got no way to

advance," said Avery.

Out of the corner of his eye, Jake saw movement—near the main building of the compound where they had been taken the first day.

He pointed. "That's Velar over there, with her entourage. She's directing a bunch of them towards the other side of the compound."

"I did hear an explosion or crash over there the same time our boys came down," said Avery. "I wonder if it was another shuttle."

"Could be. But I think we might have a chance to behead their whole operation. Come on. I think we can thread our way over there. There's a series of metal bins, a few vehicles, and some brick out-buildings between us and them. Should be enough cover, especially since our boys got them all kinds of distracted."

Avery nodded and stood up, following Jake to the door.

"Stay here," he told the three others. Jeremiah looked at him with wild eyes. "Don't worry, son, I'll be right back. Tovra and Alessandro here will keep you safe." He paused at the doorway before turning back to the boy. "But if any guards do get in, feel free to go bat-shit crazy on them, ok?"

To Jake's delight, the boy nodded vigorously. But he didn't have time to say another word as Avery had already taken off. He chased the old soldier across the short space between them and the line of metal bins, dusty and full of ore. Sprinting past them, staying as low to the ground as possible, they wove around the vehicles and sidled up to one of the low brick out-buildings near the main structure of the compound.

"Look. She's still sending a group off to the other side of

the compound. She's only got two men with her now, both heavily armed. It's either now, or never. You ready?" Jake glanced to his companion.

Avery sniffed and wiped his brow. "Let's do this."

"I'll take the one on the left, you've got the one on the right. And if Velar raises her Domitian control device…."

"I'll take care of it," replied Avery, with a grim nod.

"Alright … now!" They both sprang out and raced the remaining distance between them and the last out-building that blocked their view of the main compound. Taking positions at opposite sides of the structure, Jake fingered a quick three-second countdown, and they popped around their corners.

Jake aimed as swiftly as he could, getting the man on the left in his sights. He fired off three quick shots: the bullets pierced the man's chest, spraying the wall behind him with blood. He saw the other man drop as the back of his skull exploded as he jumped out from the building and ran towards Velar.

She looked surprised, and reached into her pocket for the Domitian device. As she withdrew it, a round of gunfire sounded out, and pierced her wrist. She cried out, and dropped the device just as Jake reached her and kicked her legs out from under her.

"It's over, Velar."

Avery ran over to them, and punted the Domitian device away from Velar as she began to lean towards it. The sounds of gunfire still raged around them, but to Jake's ears, it sounded lessened, as if tapering off. Looking to his right he watched as Sergeant Jayce, Sergeant Tomaga, and the pirate Captain Volaski sprinted towards them from one of the nearby buildings.

Jake held up his rifle at Volaski. "Stop. Not another step, Captain."

Sergeant Jayce waved him off. "He's with us, sir. Risked his neck to get us here."

Volaski slowed, and approached. With just steps remaining between them, he lowered his rifle and removed the handgun strapped to his leg.

Velar managed to struggle onto her knees. "I knew it," she spat. "I knew you—"

But before Jake could say anything, Volaski raised the handgun, pointed it at her head, and fired at point-blank range.

She slumped to the dust at their feet.

Jake pointed the assault rifle at Volaski. "What the hell are you doing? She was unarmed."

Volaski smiled. A grim, heartless smile. "And she's still unarmed. What's your point?"

Several of Volaski's men approached from the direction of one of the fallen shuttles, which Jake recognized as the shuttle he'd arrived in several days ago.

Jake stooped to examine her. A single bullet hole, in the middle of her forehead. Out of the corner of his eye he saw Volaski stoop to retrieve something on the ground.

"And to think we've all been held here by this one little box," the pirate murmured, fingering the Domitian controller in his hand.

Somehow, it just felt wrong to Jake. The woman had tortured him, enslaved him and his crew—Ben was still missing —but for her second-hand man to just mow her down without so much as a word, either of greeting or taunt, struck him as odd. He stood up and faced Volaski.

"So what now? Are all the people here just from the city? We can help evacuate them if needed—"

"No, Captain," said a sweating, bleeding Sergeant Jayce as he came running up. "You're needed on the *Phoenix*. The *Caligula* is here and there's a battle and shit going on."

Jake swore. Volaski tucked the Domitian controller into a pocket on his vest. "I assure you, Captain, I can handle things from here. Really, I could never have done this without your help." He extended a hand to Jake with a cold smile, who took it reluctantly.

"I'll need a shuttle, or something to get us back to our ship."

Volaski nodded. "Of course. There's one in the hangar. Take it. It's yours. We'll keep these damaged shuttles of yours as payment."

Jake shook his head. "Unacceptable. Those ships are property of the Resistance and—"

"Captain," said Volaski, waving a hand, "I don't think you have any alternative. Just go, take the shuttle, take your people, and be gone." He glanced over at Alessandro, and Jeremiah, who'd finally come out of hiding in their brick shack. "Except him," he continued, pointing at Jeremiah. "He stays here."

"Where's Tovra?" he asked Alessandro.

The other man shook his head, his face grim. Jeremiah pointed at one of the guards nearby. "Men came for us. Ran at us. Shot at us." He fell silent.

Alessandro walked over to Jake. "They pinned us down, and Tovra was hit in the chest. The kid went ape-shit crazy again, grabbed the assault rifle, and stormed the bastards. Took them all out. Every last one. Nearly bashed the last one's head off with the butt of the rifle. By the time he came back, Tovra was gone. Bled out."

Jake balled his fists, and snapped his head back to Volaski. "What in the hell do you think you're talking about? The kid is not staying here. None of them are."

"You heard me. My property stays here. Those are good workers you're fixing to take. We'll need every hand we can get to even survive in the coming months."

Jake could hardly believe his ears, yet the more he thought about it, the man's behavior didn't surprise him. He was, after all, a pirate. "Eat shit," he said, swinging his assault rifle to bear on Volaski, whose men trained their own guns on Jake. Avery, Jayce, and Tomaga followed suit, forming a tangle of guns each aimed at a different person.

Volaski laughed. "Fine, Mercer. Take him. But only him. Just get the hell off my planet. There's money to be made here."

Jake maintained the grip on his gun, seeing that Volaski's men hadn't lowered theirs. "So, you're just going to keep your slaving operation going? We're exchanging one tyrant for another?"

Volaski held up a hand to his chest as if to say "me?"

"Tyrant? Give me some credit, Mercer. I don't intend to hardly ever use these blasted collars," he said, fingering the Domitian Collar around his neck. "Me and some of my boys here have been fixing to do this for months. All we needed was an impetus, if you will. Your boys gave me just the firepower I needed to pull it off, and for that I thank you kindly." He nodded to Sergeant Jayce and Tomaga, who glared at him now that it became clear what Volaski's intentions had been all along. "Now, if you'll excuse me, I have a mining operation to run. Leave your shuttles, they can't be—"

An engine roar cut him off, and Jake looked about to see the source. Not finding any, he looked up. A large freighter swung around the compound and throttled its engines as it settled into position overhead. They heard the distinctive whine of the gravitics as it lowered itself to the ground, not thirty meters away, in a dusty clearing near the overloaded ore bins.

As the hatch opened, Jake couldn't believe his eyes. Dirty, bloody, and stooping, Ben Jemez hobbled out the exit, a sidearm in each hand. He glanced at the raised guns. "Is this a bad time?"

More of the *Phoenix* strike squad, as well as Volaski's men had congregated around the group with raised guns, all clustered around the fallen body of Velar and her two guards. They looked from one to another, wondering what to do. Jake knew there could be another bloodbath if he didn't say something. Slowly, he lowered his weapon.

"On second thought, Volaski, we won't be needing your shuttle after all." He took a step forward, eliciting nervous motions from one of Volaski's guards. Jake extended his free hand. "Regards, Captain Volaski."

Volaski waved a hand at his men, who lowered their weapons. "Until next time, Captain Mercer." He eyed Ben, who held onto the door of the freighter for support.

Jake turned to go, but glanced back at the old pirate. "Actually, there is one more thing. What we came here for." He pointed to the freight containers lining the grounds of the compound. "I want that ore. Those are the reject bins anyway, right?"

Volaski shook his head. "I've already got buyers. Just get the hell out."

Jake smiled dangerously. "I'm not asking." He lowered his voice, and with an even bigger smile continued, "We're returning to our ship now, and we're going to kick some Imperial ass. When it's all over, I expect a freighter filled with all that ore in my shuttle bay. If it's not there by tomorrow morning at the latest...." He trailed off, hoping the other man would catch his meaning. Surely Volaski knew at least some of the capabilities of the *Phoenix*, having seen her in action against the *Sphinx*.

Volaski grit his teeth, but then mirrored Jake's broad smile. "Godspeed, Captain. And if you manage to survive your encounter with the Imperials, you're welcome to our ore. I understand your engines could use a tune up." He shook Jake's hand, trying hard to stifle a sneer, and then retreated, waving his men to follow.

Jake breathed a silent sigh of relief as he turned to run over to Ben. At least *that* mission was accomplished. They had their neodymium—assuming they could defeat the *Caligula*. But at what cost? His mind wandered to Sergeant Suarez's crossed, bloody eyes as he approached his friend.

"You've looked better," he said, stepping up the extended ramp.

"So've you." Ben's voice sounded raw. As if he hadn't had a drink in days. Jake eyed the deep, bloody wounds on his chest and abdomen.

"We need to get you up there. That's bound to get

infected, if it already isn't." He turned to the *Phoenix* crew members, including Jeremiah, and waved them aboard.

"Might be a tight fit," observed Ben. He hobbled into the ship after Jake, who also limped, still smarting from his sprained ankle.

"Just for a few minutes. We've got to get up there, Ben. The *Caligula* is here, and if I know Trajan, there's at least a few more ships on the way."

"What do you intend to do?" Ben asked as he followed Jake into the pilot's compartment.

Jake turned, and brandished his assault rifle with a lopsided grin. "Do you have to ask?"

"Yes."

He put on a reckless smile. "We're going to blow that shit up."

CHAPTER SEVENTY-THREE

"What have we got left, Ensign Ayala?" Po steadied herself on her armrests as another blast rocked the ship. The lights flickered ominously. The air recirculation had ceased over ten minutes ago. She knew their time was short—that whatever brilliant idea she was going to have needed to come quickly, or else not at all.

"Life support is out. Gravitics are out. Power down to twenty percent," Ayala answered, working furiously at her console. "We've lost about half our offensive capabilities. Starboard railgun crews report they're completely out of slugs." The white-haired young woman looked up. "If this doesn't let up soon sir, we're finished."

Po clicked open her comm. "Grace. Are those fighters equipped yet?"

Anya Grace's voice cursed, yelling at someone in the background. "We're ready. I've got Quadri flying one, and I'm taking the other. Just don't look out your window—I've heard these bastards get pretty bright."

Po nodded. "Very well, Grace. Launch on my—"

"Sir!" Ensign Falstaff's face had turned an even more ashen white. "The *Caligula* just messaged us that they'll fire nuclear warheads if we don't surrender in the next five minutes."

Po snapped to the tactical octagon. "Sensors? Can you confirm?"

The short man next to Ayala scanned his board, and nodded. "Confirmed, sir. Radiological signature detected. I'm reading at least three warheads armed and locked on us. All from the *Sphinx*."

Po sunk back into her chair. "On our starboard side," she muttered, realizing that with the railguns on that side of the ship out, they were unlikely to be able to intercept them with any defensive screen. And Trajan most likely knew it. "Grace? You still there?"

"Where the hell do you think I am?" came the terse reply.

"You're clear to go. Godspeed." Po breathed a silent prayer of hope. She'd never been religious. Not like her father, who prayed with the intense passion of an evangelical minister. It had never been for her. But she did now—not so much for actual divine intervention, but because it reminded her of the old man, how he'd grab her shoulders before the start of every school year and plead with his god to send her good grades. And somehow, whether from her fear of letting down her father or letting down his faith, she made it happen. She smiled at the memory, in spite of their dire situation.

"Commander, I'm detecting a freighter approaching us from the surface. It's coming in really fast," said Ayala.

Ensign Falstaff added, "And they're hailing us."

"Pipe it through," said Po.

The entire bridge fell silent, waiting on the transmission with baited breath, not daring to hope that it could be their Captain. Rumbling explosions rang out through the expectant silence.

"Megan, good to see the ship still in one piece. Mind sending us an escort? There's an Imperial fighter closing on us." As Captain Mercer's voice sounded throughout the bridge, the crew breathed a collective sigh of relief. Po was tempted to roll her eyes—what did they think he was going to do that she hadn't? If the situation were any less dire, she'd be offended.

But wasn't the bridge crew right to be relieved? Hadn't Mercer somehow managed to get them out of the sticky situation at Liberty Station during the commemoration? It wasn't all blind luck, was it?

"Acknowledged, sir. Lieutenant Grace, stand down and send another one of your boys out to escort that freighter on their approach vector."

"Fine," Grace said, and Po could make out another expletive as the impatient Wing Commander yelled at one of her aides to make the call.

Moments later, Po watched as a lone fighter peeled off from the continuing battle, which had now intensified thanks to the arrival of the *Sphinx*'s squadron. But even so, their own fighters, with their superior gravitic drives, seemed to be holding their own—the one bright spot in the increasingly hopeless situation.

"Commander, the *Sphinx* is arming the missiles," said Ayala, her voice almost at a whisper.

Po glanced at the clock. Two minutes left. They weren't going to make it.

CHAPTER SEVENTY-FOUR

Jake gripped the controls of the freighter, occasionally glancing over at his co-pilot to check on the man's progress. "You hang in there, ok? Don't go bleedin' all over the carpet," he said, pointing down to the stark metal deckplate.

Ben grunted a gruff laugh. "I'll be fine. Just get us to the ship—looks like we need you to blow some smoke in the Admiral's face again while we regroup," he replied, glancing out at the two Imperial heavy cruisers still pounding away at the *Phoenix*. Jake wondered exactly how many blasts from railguns the ship could take—it had certainly seen its fair share over the past few weeks. More than its fair share. He wondered if the CERN boys had managed to come up with some special hardened hull plating.

"Captain, this is Gavin Ashdown. I'm here as your escort sir—We've got your back."

Jake glanced at Ben. "Gavin who? I don't remember any pilot—" he trailed off as he saw Ben mouth the words *new recruit*.

"Lieutenant Grace sent us out, sir, said we were ready.

Floppychop and I are at your service."

Jake nodded. "Sure thing, son. We can use all the help we can get. Just get us safely home's all I ask." Still looking at Ben, he added in a lower tone, "What the hell is Anya doing, trying to kill us?"

Ben tapped a few buttons on the console to adjust their attitude. "Anya? Try to kill you? Nah. Just trying to screw you. But, what's new?"

Jake gunned the drive to weave around an Imperial fighter, which their escort blasted through with a stream of red gunfire. "Touché."

CHAPTER SEVENTY-FIVE

A few minutes later the freighter, barely fitting through the bay doors of the *Phoenix*, landed jarringly on the deck, and Jake dashed out the descending ramp before it finished moving. Catching sight of Anya in her flight suit he yelled. "Where the hell do you think you're going, Lieutenant?"

She was halfway up the steps of a fighter. "Out."

Jake shook his head and thumbed towards the conference room. "Bullshit. No mission is so important that we can afford to lose our Wing Commander."

She rolled her eyes. "How convenient. Just like the mission to get the neodymium was so important that we could afford to lose our Captain, Chief of Security, and Chief Engineer all in one go? Time to practice what you preach, Mercer."

"I've learned the error of my ways," he replied, with a tight-lipped nod. She was absolutely right, of course. He realized how stupid he'd been to go down to the planet himself. He should have sent some ensign from engineering. Someone—as much as he loathed even thinking it—expendable. At least, when it came to protecting the rest of his ship and crew, he realized he had to start thinking in such draconian, heartless terms. Otherwise, they'd all die, and quickly. He had to exchange his soul for their lives. "What has Po got you doing, anyway," he added, as he eyed an oddly-shaped torpedo attached to the undercarriage of her fighter.

"That's a quantum field torpedo," she said. "Any questions?"

Of course. Jake made a point to commend Po on her brilliance. "Got it. But you're not going, and neither is Quadri," he said, glancing at the other fighter similarly equipped, and its pilot standing nearby.

Anya fumed, looking like she was about to explode. With hands on her hips, she said, "And who the hell do you suggest I send, *sir*?" The emphasis on "sir" was cold.

Jake glanced back at a young Gavin Ashdown, and his younger-looking long-haired copilot, who were just now jumping out of their fighter. He didn't even know her name. Floppychop? That was her callsign, he assumed. "Send them. One per fighter. They fly ok, right?"

She puffed out some air in exasperation. "Ok, sure, but only ok. Dammit, Jake, they've only been flying for less than a week—"

"Seems like they fly good enough to me. They were holding their own out there in the fighter battle, right?"

"Yeah."

"Then do it. All they've got to do is shift over, launch the torpedoes, and shift back. Piece of cake." He stared into her eyes and lowered his voice so that no one around them could hear. "We can't afford to lose any more senior people, Anya. I know you don't like it, but I don't give a shit. Now move."

And before she could reply, he turned back to Jeremiah, who was walking towards him with Ben. "Get to sickbay," he said, pointing at his friend. "Jeremiah, stay with me," he added, thinking it wiser to keep the unpredictable youth in his sight, at least until he could assign him some quarters. But that could wait.

For now, his job was to save the ship.

Again.

CHAPTER SEVENTY-SIX

Gavin could hardly believe his ears when Lieutenant Grace barked their new orders at them, and as she marched away to tend to the fighter battle still raging outside, he leaned over to Jet. "She's kidding, right?"

"Didn't sound like it," she said. They walked over to the waiting fighters, Gavin still in a daze. Lieutenant Grace had ordered them each to pilot a fighter solo, get in close to one of the Imperial ships, fire the quantum field torpedoes at close range, and then fly like a banshee out of there before the quantum-field induced blast took them out as well.

"You up for this?" Gavin asked. He knew his friend was an excellent gunner, but she hadn't excelled as much at the flying—not as much as Gavin had, at least.

She wrenched her headset back on around her ears, and combed her fingers briskly through a tangled knot of hair. "Yeah. I'm fine. Let's do this—everyone's counting on us."

Gavin nodded. Jet was right. If they could pull this off, the ship would be saved and they'd be heroes. He almost grinned inside at the thought of it, how just a few weeks earlier he was scrubbing the galley floors and now he was on the verge of being not just a regular space jock, but a celebrity. He slapped his friend on the shoulder before climbing inside his waiting fighter and slid into the pilot's seat.

Running as quickly as he could through his preflight checklist, he glanced out at the fighter deck and counted the fighter maintenance bays lining the wall. Sixteen. How many times had he done that now, he wondered. And would he do it again? Was this the last time he'd fly out of that bay? For a moment, he had the terrifying sensation of impending death, like he was about to fly straight into a solid steel wall, but he shook the thought aside and finished his checklist.

"You ready, girl?" he said into his comm.

"Ready. Let's blow the fuckers up," Jet replied.

He chuckled. "They'll never know what hit them."

CHAPTER SEVENTY-SEVEN

Jake had no sooner walked onto the bridge than Anya announced through the comm, "It's showtime, Mercer. They're out, and awaiting your word."

"Thank you, Lieutenant," he said, trying to keep his voice formal. He wondered if she'd ever forgive him. If she'd ever let him rip her shirt off and press up against him like that one blissful morning in Florida.

Po shot him an angry look, which surprised him. "Did I just hear Anya say that they're out? I ordered her on that fighter. And Quadri on the other one."

Jake shook his head. "Sorry, Commander. I need Grace on the flight deck running the show. And Quadri is too—" He glanced around the bridge, and leaned in close to her. "We can't lose any more experienced pilots. The recruits will have to do this one."

She shot him icicles out of her eyes, pursed her lips, and looked as if she were about to argue, but just shook her head. "Jake, our time is almost up—Trajan threatened nukes if we didn't surrender in five minutes," Po stood up from the chair.

His chair.

"When was that?"

"Five minutes ago."

He approached the center of the bridge with Jeremiah in tow, who looked warily around at the officers staring at them with questioning faces. "You sure like to cut things close, Grizzly," he said, using her old callsign. "Get me the Admiral," he said to Ensign Falstaff.

"Channel open, sir."

Jake sat down in the chair vacated by Po and cleared his throat. "Admiral Trajan, this is Captain Mercer of the *USS Phoenix*. It's so good of you to drop in—it really saved me the hassle of hunting your ass down myself." He smirked a lop-sided smile.

Admiral Trajan's icy voice sounded over the comm. "Please, Captain, spare me the bravado. I take it you will not surrender? We're detecting your railguns are not operational. Do you really think you can stop these nuclear warheads aimed at your ship?"

"Well, Admiral, this is progress. At least you're now referring to the *Phoenix* as ours." He paused, letting the moment settle. "No, Admiral, we won't be surrendering today. Not while I have a Vesuvius mine floating under your ass. Funny, seems like you can find just about anything down on Destiny."

Silence. Jake wondered if the channel had been cut.

"You're bluffing, Captain, there's no way you could have launched any such mines without us knowing. Vesuvius mines have anti-matter, and as such they emit the tell-tale gamma-ray signature of matter-antimatter recombination."

Jake leaned forward in his seat. "Are you absolutely sure about that, Admiral? Are you willing to stake your life on that bet?"

"I tire of this, Captain. Surrender now, or face the consequences."

With a flick of his finger, he switched the channel over to Jet Xing. "Floppychop, you're good to go. Target the *Sphinx*. Mercer out."

He flipped the comm back over to the *Caligula*. "Admiral, I told you, I'm just not in the surrendering mood today. So you're just going to have to come over here and suck my fat cock if you want me to give up my ship. And since you're not going to do that, well I guess a little demonstration of the mines is in order."

And, as if on cue, the *NPQR Sphinx* exploded in a dazzlingly white blast. When the glare had faded, they watched in awe as the angry red embers—remnants of vast sections of the huge ship—disintegrated before their eyes. Soon, only a hazy, debris-ridden cloud remained.

Jake had automatically shielded his face from the bright flash on the viewscreen before he remembered that the screen would not damage his eyes by looking at it. When the embers of the explosion faded away, he scanned the screen, looking for any sign of the former Imperial cruiser. But there was none. It was utterly destroyed.

"Po? The fighter?"

Po studied her board at the XO's station, then glanced over at the tactical octagon to shoot a questioning look at Ensign Ayala. But the crackle of the internal comm answered Jake's question. "Captain, this is Lieutenant Grace. Xing did not make it out."

A cold silence pervaded the bridge. No one dared speak. Jake looked up at Po, who closed her eyes tight.

"Ashdown is standing by," she continued, letting the sneer saturate her voice as she continued, "should I send him, too, sir?"

Jake closed his eyes too. This is the price, he told himself. This is the price of freedom. Of safety for his ship and his people. The burden of command. This is the price of freedom.

And he repeated it over and over to himself, until Po broke the silence. "Captain, the *Caligula* has shifted away. They're gone."

But all Jake could see, in his mind's eye, was the flip of tangled short black hair as Jet Xing ambled off to her fighter.

This is necessary. This is the price of freedom. This is the price of freedom.

He tried repeating it over in his mind.

Eventually, it might make him feel better.

It had to.

CHAPTER SEVENTY-EIGHT

Admiral Trajan rose from the Captain's chair and approached the command console. Titus was absolutely sure that Mercer was bluffing, but it appeared that Trajan had started to think otherwise.

"Helmsman, is our emergency gravitic shift course entered in?" Admiral Trajan asked.

"Yes, sir, emergency coordinates are for Vega—the nearest anchor star, sir."

Titus could hear Mercer's profanity-laden voice in the background squawk on. The bravado of these Rebels was starting to really annoy him.

"Sir! The *Sphinx*!" yelled the sensor officer. On the viewscreen, half out of view and behind the *Phoenix*, he saw the blue-white cloud enveloping the *Sphinx,* over-saturating the sensitivity of the camera.

Titus couldn't believe his eyes. They were this close to crushing the Rebels forever. This close. He snapped his head towards tactical, preparing to give the order to launch the nuclear missiles, and end it once and for all.

Admiral Trajan remained remarkably calm. He paused only a brief moment before turning to the helm. "Helmsman, shift us away."

Titus turned to the Admiral. "But, sir! The fighters! We've still got nearly twenty men out there, counting the men from the—"

"And would you have me sacrifice our lives to possibly save theirs, Captain?" the Admiral replied without even looking up from the command console. His voice sounded distant, almost lazy, as if he'd already mentally withdrawn from the situation and was busy planning the next moves.

Cold, calculating bastard.

And yet Titus knew that the Admiral was absolutely right. There was nothing they could do. Another one of those mines could be right under their hull. Still, it didn't make the course of action any more palatable.

"Engaging gravitic drive, sir," the helmsman said, and moments later the view of the flicking and wheeling fighters engaged in their dance of death, set against the backdrop of the massively damaged *Phoenix*, was replaced by the shimmering red orb of some out-of-the-way giant star.

"Not to worry, Captain," the Admiral continued, as if reading his thoughts, "I finally have these Rebels figured out. We've made a mistake, but it is a mistake that will soon be rectified. It is clear that Mercer imagines himself some kind of guerrilla fighter who intends to build some sort of ragtag fleet to retake Earth. And now that I know his true intentions, we can lay our trap. And this time, there is no escaping it."

Titus wondered where he'd heard that before. But all he could do was sigh, and say, "Yes, sir."

CHAPTER SEVENTY-NINE

Jake and Po watched as Doctor Nichols continued the surgery. Ben's wounds were extensive, but not life-threatening, and Nichols insisted that he'd make a full recovery with minimal scarring, despite the deep, jagged cuts all over his back, chest, face, and arms.

Jake murmured to his friend standing next to him. "He's not going to like those scars one bit. Nichols thought he could fool him, but Ben's been around long enough to know what those cuts will look like in a year."

Po shrugged. "And his mental wounds? Jake, you described to me the pain that just a few moments of that Domitian Collar were like. He went through hours and hours of it, hanging there like that. It broke that other man—the one that came back with Ben. The *Fury* crew member."

Jake nodded. "That guy had been here for nearly three years. Ben only had a few days. And besides," he turned to Po, "Ben's made of some pretty strong stuff. He'll pull through."

He turned back to look at the ongoing surgery. Nichols seemed to be wrapping things up, mopping up the stitches with some swabs. "What do you think we should do about all those slaves down there? Volaski doesn't seem too keen on giving up his little fiefdom, the bastard."

She nodded. "Let's just make sure he gives us the neodymium we need, and then we can decide. But really, we've no business here."

He knew she was right, but it sounded cold. "Liberating slaves is not our business? I thought that was the reason we're out here. To liberate."

She turned to him. "To liberate Earth, yes. And whatever other world that wants to join us. But I think it's clear that we're not welcome here. No sense in getting ourselves involved in trying to break up the slave-trade on Destiny, as commendable as that would be."

It felt unfair. It felt like a raw deal, and Jake felt dirty for nodding in agreement, but he did, and he tried to forget about the pale, sallow faces staring back at him in the darkness of the mine. No future. No hope. Only a lifetime of dusty, back-breaking work, far from the light of Destiny's sun.

Liberate. The word reminded him of Jeremiah's words. Back in the dark of the cave, when he'd muttered that strange bit about liberating captives. And death. Jeremiah said he'd die. He told Po.

"Well of course you're going to die, Jake," she said, catching him off guard.

"What?"

"You're going to die. So am I. So is everyone. What's so peculiar about that? Jeremiah the prophet, huh?" She chuckled. "Sounds like he needs to brush up on his prophesying." She lowered her voice in mock-holiness, "This just in: today will end in you filling your stomach with floppy pork chops."

Jake grinned, but the smile was short-lived. Floppy pork chops. Sounded a lot like Floppychop. Po's smile fell too, as she read his face and knew his thoughts.

The door sliding open behind them cut off his thoughts. "Friend! I thought I'd find you here." Alessandro Bernoulli, freshly shaven—except for his trademark half-mustache—ambled into the observation ward. "Good news. The shipment of neodymium from the surface isn't as contaminated as we thought. I only need to do a few purification runs on it, and then we can start infusing it into the matrix. We'll be out of here faster than a premature ejaculation—"

Jake, horrified, held up a hand to hush the man, but Po just laughed, the previous moment forgotten. "You don't need to protect my virgin ears, Jake." She patted him once on the shoulder before walking away. "I've got to go meet with Tomaga and his men. They performed brilliantly down on the surface, and I should congratulate them. And thank them."

"They really did. Thanks, Po," Jake replied, and watched as she slipped out the door, which slid mostly shut behind her, getting stuck with several inches to spare. The strain and trauma of two orbital battles, and the crushing ordeal of sitting under the polar water for a few days had had their effect on the ship, and it seemed like everything was only half-working or not at all.

Bernoulli nodded in the direction of the ongoing surgery. "Your friend, the Commander. Is he all right? He looked like shit when he rescued us." Alessandro indicated the prone figure in the next room. Nichols had stepped away momentarily to retrieve another tube of surgical glue.

"He's fine. And when he's done in there, I want you in there next to get that damn implant out," said Jake, fingering his own Domitian Collar that still surrounded his neck. The image of Suarez's cross-eyed, blank stare as he collapsed to the ground would forever haunt his dreams. Hell, this job was turning nightmarish, with all the grim blue faces of the dead staring back at him when he closed his eyes at night. The men and women that died as a result of his decisions. Suarez. That young, new fighter pilot—what was her name? Xang? He couldn't even remember, and it disgusted him.

Bernoulli wiped some grease on his uniform, which looked almost as dirty as the frontier clothing he'd worn previously. "Not to worry. That's why I'm here. I don't know how this thing will respond to the fluctuating fields when I outfit the gravitic matrix, so I need it out before I go back down there."

Jake nodded his approval, but only stared at his friend lying on the table, in a small pool of blood from the surgery. The one who should be the Captain.

CHAPTER EIGHTY

Ensign Ayala hurried down the hallway, eager to make it back to her quarters after spending the previous fourteen hours on the bridge. Po had gone to tour the damage from the battle, and Captain Mercer was getting some much needed sleep, leaving her in charge of the bridge again. Surely it was time to promote her to Commander. Or at least Lieutenant, for all the command-related duties she had been doing.

Command. It was not why she entered the Imperial fleet and maneuvered her way into a position aboard a ship staffed by the Resistance. She entered it to, somehow, be a thorn in the Empire's side. Not just a thorn. A dagger. A poison-tipped dagger.

Nodding at the repair crews that marched past, she turned the corner that led to the crew quarters for the junior-ranked commissioned officers. Ensign Alley, it had come to be called. Out of the eighty or so ensigns assigned to the *Phoenix*, only fifty-five remained alive, and the quarters of the dead were each marked with a little penciled in 'V' at head-height on the doors. So many dead. And here she was. Betraying them.

No. Not betrayal. Love was not betrayal. To deny her feelings would be the true betrayal.

But did he return the feelings?

Of course he did. He was the one that pulled the strings to get her assigned to the *Phoenix*, after all. Why would he put his neck out for her if he didn't love her?

She strode into her quarters, and froze.

He was standing there, just on the other side of the door, his finger to his lips, as if shushing her. He beckoned her to enter.

When the door slid shut, she whispered, "What the hell are you doing?"

Galba's face contorted into a broad grin, with sly eyes. "I've found him."

"Who?"

"Your saboteur."

Could it be?

She circled around him, debating whether to disrobe and distract them both—the battle had been harrowing, after all, and she needed to blow off some steam, or to cut to the chase.

"Where? She decided on the latter. Hot sex could wait.

Galba's smile broadened even further. He held up a finger and pointed at the wall. "Three doors down. One of the Fifty-First Brigade. I caught him in there, digging into the computer system. When I checked on the terminal down in the utility room, I could see him navigate through the various critical ship's systems. He even blew a few power routing stations halfway through that battle. Didn't you guys feel that up there? Surely it disrupted something."

Willow nodded, hesitantly. He was right, of course. The

explosion had crippled the port ion-beam control system at a critical moment in the showdown with the *Caligula* and the *Sphinx*. They'd nearly lost because of it. But what if it was Galba who'd caused the blast? "Yes. Yes, we felt it. How do you know it was the Imperial marine?"

Galba's brows rose. "Don't believe me? Just go check for yourself. He's in there right now, no doubt hard at work disrupting some other critical system. Which one do you think it will be next? The CO_2 scrubbers? The internal gravitics? Hell, he seemed pretty suicidal last time we talked on deck fifteen, maybe he'll just overload the antimatter tanks and be done with it." He made an explosive motion with his hands. "But personally, I'd prefer he didn't. I have many good years ahead of me."

She turned towards the door. "Fine. I'll take care of it."

Galba reached for her arm. "Willow, be careful. He's dangerous. Got in a fistfight with one of our burly marines a few days back. I don't want to see anything happen to you. Shall I come too? Maybe we can both convince him to surrender."

She pulled away from his grasp. Clearly, he had no idea who he was dealing with. She wondered why her acrobatic moves during their marathon tantric sessions hadn't suggested a more powerful constitution than he gave her credit for. "I'll be fine, Harrison. Trust me." She forced a thin smile before heading out into the hallway and let the doors slide closed before she reached down under her shirt and extracted a small pen. At least, it looked like a pen. Five centimeters long, and full of Trimethylacetylbenzine. T-MAB, her people called it. Not the Belenites, but *The Red*. Her secret brothers.

At the third door, she stopped, and took a deep breath.

She must be swift.

The door did not move, so she entered her override code into the keypad.

The doors slid open, and, just as Galba had said, there sat a man at a computer terminal set up just next to the bunk. She stepped inside, the doors closed, and the man stood up.

"You're out of your authorized area," she said, in as neutral a voice as she could muster. In reality, she seethed. Here was the man responsible for possibly dozens of deaths. He nearly cost them the battle not half an hour before.

"You Rebel scum. I'll go wherever I please. This is still an Imperial ship and I am an Imperial—"

She had closed her eyes and held out her arms in the traditional calming stance of the warriors of her people. Back when her people had warriors. The stance that calmed the nerves, but prepared them.

Prepared them for action.

"Hey, what the fuck do you think you're doing, you Rebel bitch? Trying to work some of your Belenite voodoo shit on me?" He took a menacing step forward, which, due to the cramped space of the room, nearly brought him nose to nose with her.

Like lightning, she sprung, dropped to a crouch and lashing out with her foot, catching him on the ankles and sending his back arcing to the floor. But before he landed, she'd already spun around and met his fall with a quick stab with the T-MAB pen, which thrust a small needle into his back and ejected enough of the drug to fell an elephant.

He roared in anger and sprung back onto his feet. He

swung at her, but missed as she dodged away faster than anything he'd likely seen, and she smashed an open palm into his nose, which spurted blood all over his face and shirt.

She counted. Five, six…. He was already wavering on his feet, and he punched again, this time as if moving through molasses. Like the molasses her grandmother used to put in her cookies when she was young, scampering about on their family's refugee starship, orbiting some god-forsaken red giant star.

His knees buckled, and he fell, but she caught him, and lowered him gently to the floor. His eyes darted back and forth, but he didn't move a muscle. Nor could he.

She whispered in his ear. "Now you've made me sin. Belenites must not draw blood with their hands."

His mouth moved, and he forced out some breath.

"Fuck you."

She smiled. "You've made me sin, and now a penalty must be paid. An expiation. You are familiar with T-MAB? The drug I injected you with? Long ago, hundreds of years ago, when my people first settled Belen, we found a lush world, full of native greenery, animals, birds, fish. Never before had a world been found with more than simple cyanobacteria. Never. It was like our own Eden, unsullied by man. Our first fathers decided it was a gift from the Celestial Enlightened One, and as such, sacrifices of thanks had to be made. And just like in the Old Testament," she stroked his face, "we chose goats."

She drifted forward to his ear, and whispered. "But they were gentle. They injected the goats with T-MAB before the sacrifice, to make the process as easy as possible for the poor animals giving their lives, answering for the sins of the people."

The man's lips quivered, and he struggled to speak again. "But … but … no blood. Belenites can't draw blood…."

She smiled, and stood. "You're quite right. But just as when our first parents fled the Garden, and the Enlightened One spoke to them, telling them that the serpent should have power to bite their heels, he also told them they'd have power to crush his head." She lifted up a boot. "And so it is."

Before he could speak again she smashed it as hard as she could down on his throat.

And again.

And again.

And again.

A snap indicated a severed spine and a crushed windpipe.

She smiled. The expiation was made. Her hands were clean. The Enlightened One smiled upon her, she knew. And her brothers and sisters, *The Red,* would be proud.

The ship was safe.

And soon, so would her people.

CHAPTER EIGHTY-ONE

The *Caligula* orbited the nameless red giant star slowly, since they had found it necessary to put some distance in between them and the vast, flaming orb. The gravitic thrusters had been damaged in the battle with the *Phoenix*, and they could not safely maintain the usual close orbit. So instead of the red fire filling their viewscreen, it shimmered distantly, looming about as large as Corsica's sun—a red giant itself.

Titus scanned the damage reports. Two days until the gravitic drive would be repaired. Power generation at forty percent. Half their railgun turrets and ion beam cannons nonoperational. Refractive shielding down. Deckplate gravitics operating at less than fifty percent below deck eleven—he imagined that must make repairs harder, or easier, he wasn't sure.

Ah yes. The casualty report. He winced. Forty-two dead. Sixteen missing behind collapsed bulkheads.

He chided himself for checking the casualty report last. That's what *he* would do. Only someone coldly pragmatic and utilitarian like the Admiral would be interested in the damage report before the casualty report. He swore to never become like him. Never.

"Captain? Are the capacitor banks charged enough for a shift yet?" Trajan's voice came calling like a deadly songbird. The voice was so oddly resonant and melodious at times that Titus wondered if the man hadn't in fact been a singer at some point. The madman seemed to have mastered just about every other instrument, so why not voice?

"No, sir. Are we planning on leaving soon?"

Trajan looked up from his console at the captain's chair. "Why, yes. Yes, we are. We've just received a gravitic communications pod, and we have urgent business elsewhere."

Urgent?

"Sir, we're hardly in a position to attend to urgent business. Especially if it requires a fully functioning warship."

Trajan held up a hand. "Not to worry, Captain Titus." Titus snapped his head towards the Admiral. That was the first time in his memory that the man had addressed him with both his title *and* his name. A wide, sly smile covered the Admiral's face. "The situation will not require any offensive force."

"Sir?"

Trajan stood up, and paced to the center of the bridge, staring up at the glimmering red giant star on the viewscreen.

"I've just received word, Captain. Several months ago, I dispatched a warship to the Titanis Sector, containing the Empire's most highly trained and effective special operations teams. And they've finally reported back."

The Admiral paused, as if drawing out whatever tidbit of information he had for maximum suspense. And frankly, Titus was tired of it.

"Yes?" The Captain nodded, tiredly. And yet he couldn't help the tingling on his neck hairs as he regarded the Admiral's posture. Clearly the man was excited—as excited as Trajan ever got. The news must be huge indeed.

Trajan turned to face him. "They've succeeded in their mission, Captain." The Admiral closed his eye, and turned back to the screen, looking down, as if in quiet triumph. "This was the final piece, Captain. Now, The Plan can commence in earnest."

"But sir, what about Mercer? What about the *Phoenix?* And the *Heron?* We haven't even found that—"

Trajan held up a hand. "Patience, Captain. Those two ships are not my concern at the moment. The *Phoenix* is now a heap of spare parts, and the *Heron* was in just as bad shape when it disappeared. All that matters now is The Plan. And survival for the Empire."

CHAPTER EIGHTY-TWO

It was late, and Jake needed sleep. Doc Nichols had insisted—after the required scolding, of course. The doctor had reiterated, once again, his diminishing trust in the Captain, especially now that he'd reported back with one less man than he'd left with.

He looked up from his command console. Good. Po had finally left. Presumably to sleep as well. He supposed that would be the first time she'd slept in days.

Standing, and making for the rear of the bridge, he called out to tactical. "Ayala, you have the bridge."

The white-haired young woman nodded curtly at him. "Yes, Captain. And blessings as you sleep." She flashed a knowing smile.

"Thank you, Ensign. If you see any Imperial cruisers while I'm out, just blow the shit out of them, ok?"

She winked. "Got it."

The hallway was deserted. Debris still littered the floor, but at least it had been pushed to the wall. He limped. His sprained ankle, the one he'd injured in his ill-advised stunt jumping over that ravine in San Bernardino just weeks ago, still had not fully healed. He shook his head at the unreality of the situation. That was less than a month ago, and yet it felt like a lifetime.

"Captain Mercer? This is Ensign Falstaff on the bridge, sir."

He approached a wall panel and touched the comm button. "Go ahead, Ensign."

"Sir, we've just received a gravitic pod. Origin unknown. But it's marked for your eyes only."

He raised his eyebrows. Who in the world would be contacting them? How on Earth did anyone even know they were there?

"Thank you, Ensign. I'll take it in my ready room."

He paced down the hall and entered the room—he'd hardly used it since taking command. Po had used it more.

And it was meant for Ben.

He shook his head of the thought, and sat down in the chair. A section of the screen flashed red.

Priority One Message.

He tapped the screen, and entered his command authorization code. Shortly, the flashing notification disappeared, replaced by the message itself. He shook his head and blinked, at first thinking he was misunderstanding. Or dreaming.

It couldn't be.

It was true.

This changed everything.

He checked the sender information, and just as Ensign Falstaff had said, it was blank. Every source metadata field was meticulously erased. He checked the gravitic signature recording—perhaps they could triangulate its source. But that, too, had been scrambled. The sender had overlapped a noise filter on the gravitic wave that carried the pod, removing all information about its origin.

Damn peculiar.

He read the message one more time, just to be sure he'd not misunderstood, and then bolted out the door. He repeated it over and over again in his mind as he raced for the bridge:

Admiral Pritchard found.

Titanis Sector.

Imperial custody.

Thank you for reading Chains of Destiny!

To be notified when the next Pax Humana Saga book releases, please sign up for my mailing list: smarturl.it/endimailinglist
If you enjoyed Chains of Destiny, will you please leave a review? That is the best way to support my work and keep the stories flowing!

Other books by Nick Webb

THE PAX HUMANA SAGA

Episode 1: The Terran Gambit
Episode 2: Chains of Destiny
Episode 3: Into The Void

THE LEGACY FLEET TRILOGY
Constitution

Warrior

Victory

Independence

Defiance

Liberty

The Earth Dawning Series

Mercury's Bane
Jupiter's Sword
Neptune's War

Come talk to me on:

My Website: www.nickwebbwrites.com
Facebook: facebook.com/endiwebb
Twitter: twitter.com/endiwebb

Email me at authornickwebb@gmail.com

Made in the USA
Middletown, DE
18 August 2020